NANCY SWIMMER

BIBLIOGRAPHY

Fiction:

Nancy Swimmer: A Story of the Cherokee Nation (1999)
The Lost Sunshine (1994)
And Now I See (1989)
Ivy (1986)
Water Oaks (1980)

Non Fiction:

Talladega Superspeedway (1994)
The Alabama Gang (1994)
Remembering Davey (1993)
Silver Britches (1982)
They Wore Crimson (1979)
The Basketball Tide (1977)
Bolton's Best Stories of Auto Racing (1975)
Unforgettable Days in Southern Football (1974)
War Eagle (1973)
The Crimson Tide (1972)

NANCY SWIMMER

A STORY OF THE CHEROKEE NATION

by Clyde Bolton

Book design: Bob Weathers
Jacket illustration: Ernie Eldredge
Author photo: Joe Songer
Editors: Michael Herring, Jonathan Holbrook, James Lawrence, Xolti Morgan and Michal Shar

First Trade Edition
A leatherbound, signed and numbered limited edition has been previously published by Southern Treasures

Library of Congress Cataloging-in-Publication Data

Bolton, Clyde.
   Nancy Swimmer : a story of the Cherokee nation / by Clyde Bolton.
      p · c m .
   ISBN 0-9630273-3-6 (alk. paper).
     I. Cherokee Indians Fiction.   2.   Trail of Tears, 1838 Fiction.
   I. Title.
   PS3552.05877N36   1999
   813'.54--dc21   99-37204
                                         CIP

Published by Highland Press
Printed in U.S.A.

10   9   8   7   6   5   4   3   2   1

To Jake Reiss

A friend to writers

A friend of mine

PROLOGUE

A BIRTHDAY PARTY BEGINS

Poppy is kicking the door and yelling that her arms are full, and when some-one finally opens it, the cold wind that is ripping across Oklahoma precedes her into the house, and everyone stampedes for a spot before the fireplace.

"Shut that door!" a half-dozen chorus, but Poppy pays them no attention. She is looking for me, and when she spots me she winks and makes that funny little wrinkled-nose face that she reserves for just us two.

"Surprise!" Poppy shouts, and I pretend it is, though I don't know why anyone would be surprised by a birthday cake on a birthday. But it's Poppy, and I pretend to be so surprised that I drop the newspaper I am reading.

A neighbor has baked a pretty white cake. It is huge, for there are many people at the party. It is decorated with sugary rosebuds and script that wishes a happy birthday and many more to Amaw, which little Poppy called me when she couldn't say Grandmaw, and which she still calls me.

Poppy places it on my lap and hugs my neck and laughs when I tell her how surprised and grateful I am. She shoos everyone away from the fireplace and makes them inspect the cake. "Did you see it?" she yells at an old neighbor who is coming in the back door from a visit to the outhouse, still trying to get his pants buttoned. "No, you didn't see it. Come here and look at this cake."

The only reason I put up with these parties is Poppy. She is my great-great-grandchild, fifteen years old, and she doesn't look on me as a relic, as my other relatives do. She loves me, and she enjoys being with me. She doesn't merely pay an obligatory ten-minute visit and fiddle with her hands while she tries to think of something to say, the way the others do. She spends the day, and sometimes the night. She realizes I am a person, not just something the family is obliged to feed and water and shelter until it dies, like the cow and the chickens.

But, damn, she won't let me just sit. "Up, up!" she commands, and she grabs my arm and leads me to the table, and when I try to take the nearest chair she scolds, "No, no! The head of the table for the birthday girl!"

So I sit at the head of the table, and five people take the other seats, and every-one else stands while Poppy passes out saucers and plates and forks.

"Gather 'round," she says, and they draw even closer, and she squeals: "It's the 8th of January, 1913, and Amaw is ninety-eight years old today. We'll sing Happy Birthday, and then she will blow out the candle and cut the cake."

They do, and I do, making a joke that we would have been there until summer if there had been ninety-seven more candles, and I greedily lift off one of the sugary rosebuds for myself, which delights Poppy. "A flower for my fairest flower," she says.

I live with a grandson and his wife. They are good to me, but I realize they will be relieved when I die. They are in their fifties and have raised their children. He is a tired old farmer, his wife is sickly, and there isn't anything extra. I know they are afraid of what would happen if I became bedridden. Once I overheard my daughter-in-law tell a neighbor, "People just aren't supposed to live that long." I didn't get angry. They're not.

Poppy, who lives just down the road with her parents and two brothers, assures me I will move in with her and her husband when she is married, and she will give me great-great-great-grandchildren to play with. I remind her that what little money I have accumulated is earmarked for her college, and I'll never live to see her married, much less a mother, but she always interrupts, assuring me that I will live to be a hundred and ten. After all, she says, I never expected to see ninety-eight, did I? I tell her there were times in my life when I didn't expect to see the next day.

Everyone knows Poppy will get all my money, and that has created jealousy and criticism. I don't care. Poppy loves me. She has always been my girl. Before she could walk, she would ignore her parents and crawl to me. Besides, if I divided it among my herd of descendants they'd have about a dime apiece.

Poppy commands the guests to bring their presents. They cover the table with their tribute. There are so many people that the house will barely hold them. Many I don't even know, including the newspaperman who arrived early and almost wore me out with his questions and who now stands in a corner making notes.

Poppy hands me the presents one by one, announcing the name of a giver. I unwrap them and say thanks while Poppy oohs and aahs. "What a beautiful scarf!" she says. "It will go with the blouse you got for Christmas."

Poppy's boyfriend stands in the kitchen door, silent, motionless. He hasn't spoken all day except to say hello. He is a pretty little fellow, but he is overwhelmed by her, and while she is proclaiming a lace handkerchief the nicest she has ever seen, I am thinking, "You'd better get some lightning in you, boy, if you're going to marry that woman some day."

I am weary, and I apologize that I must rest before opening the other presents. Poppy doesn't object this time, and she announces that it is now time to play games. She has, of course, arranged several in advance. She politely asks if I want to play, but already she is helping me to the couch. "You all play, and I'll just watch," I say.

I take a seat and pretend to be watching the players, but I am really thinking about the accumulation of ninety-eight years. When Poppy gets everyone into action, she joins me on the couch and snuggles her head on my shoulder and says, "I hope you have a happy birthday, Amaw Nancy."

She is fifteen. Can anyone really be just fifteen?

CHAPTER 1

My name is Nancy Swimmer.

My grandmother, one of the four midwives to attend my mother at my birth, named me The Swimmer as I was coming out, before the cord was cut, before I was washed. I was kicking, and my arms were flailing, and she shouted, "She swims! She swims against the Oostanaula in its springtime haste! She is The Swimmer!"

My mother, Rain, was delighted. She had boasted of how I'd kicked during her pregnancy. Now she simply changed the story to say, "She swam inside me. I wondered if she was a fish. She woke me at night swimming."

When I was 5 my grandmother told me of Nancy Ward, the Beloved Woman of the Cherokees, and I named myself Nancy. I have been Nancy Swimmer ever since.

"They called her Wild Rose, because when she was young her skin was as smooth as rose petals, but Nancy Ward could shoot like a man," my mother's mother, Plum, told the story over and over. Always she glanced around her as if expecting a spy and added in a low voice, "And she was smarter than most men."

Grandmother told of Nancy standing beside her husband Kingfisher during the Battle of Taliwa in 1755, chewing on each of his musket balls to increase its deadliness before handing it to him. When he was killed she snatched up his weapon and continued to fire against the Creeks. The Cherokees said she was instrumental in the victory, and they gave her the title Beloved Woman. She thus had a voice in tribal councils, and she could pardon condemned captives.

I tried to imagine myself fighting on as my slain husband lay at my feet, but each time I would start to cry, so I had to change the game. Instead, I would be the merciful, magnanimous Wild Rose as she spared a doomed Creek. The undeserving warrior, who had reconciled himself to a torturous death by fire, would gasp with surprise then kiss my bare feet, his tears streaking the dust that powdered them, and pronounce me the wisest, most wonderful of persons. He would shout my name as he ran into the forest to freedom.

My father, Staring Otter, waited outside the little birthing shelter he had built of brush, and when grandmother brought me into the morning light, wrapped in soft rabbit skins, he asked whether I was a boy or a girl. "A girl," she said. "I named her The Swimmer. It pleases Rain. Does it please you?"

He gazed at me, touched his forefinger to my cheek. "If it pleases you and Rain it pleases me," he said. "I will stoke the fire to welcome the baby." He lifted a stick of firewood and preceded my grandmother and me into our log house, tossing the fuel into the fireplace and stirring the rejuvenated blaze with a long, blackened stick. "You have made a good child," he told my mother as the midwives helped her into bed under the dancing lights the flames cast upon the wall.

That four-room cabin would be home for my first fourteen years, and I would spend them with a father who was as bitter and dismayed as an animal that had been trapped and held so long that it no longer believed it could escape.

Staring Otter's life had begun to unravel when he consented to fight by the side of Andrew Jackson. Once he had called Jackson Sharp Knife, but the day came when he would spit out that name and forevermore refer to him as Chicken Snake.

Major Ridge himself recruited Staring Otter. He was a commanding presence as, on an autumn day in 1813, he rode into our village upon a huge horse. The men recognized the chief—celebrated as one of the assassins of Doublehead, the traitor who was bribed to cede the best Cherokee hunting lands to the whites—and they stopped what they were doing and gathered around him, wishing they owned a pair of white man's black boots like the ones on his feet. They were not as certain about the stiff, uncomfortable looking white man's black coat on his back. Incongruously, he wore two feathers in a headband with a deer's tail in back.

That was to distinguish the Cherokees from the enemy, the Creek Red Sticks, he told the men. The Creeks' civil war had spilled over into the white man's world when the frenzied Red Sticks had invaded Fort Mims to take some mixed bloods and had indiscriminately massacred nearly four hundred whites. Now the Cherokees must join the whites against the Red Sticks, he said.

Staring Otter spoke up. "Why?"

Because, Major Ridge replied, the Red Sticks had placed the Cherokees in jeopardy. The Americans would see only Indians against whites, without regard to tribal affiliations. The Cherokees must establish themselves on the side of the whites.

There was another reason. Major Ridge was an advocate of the Americans' policy of urging the Cherokees to become civilized. He agreed that it was time for the men to replace the weapons of the increasingly unproductive hunt with the plow and hoe, for the women to learn spinning and weaving, for families to leave the villages and begin individual farms. Why, a man could go on a hunting trip for months and return to find the cloth his wife had made during his absence was worth more than his entire bag. The Red Sticks, though, said the Great Spirit was angry because the Indians had mills and feather beds and tables and looms, and if the Red Sticks could establish power then barbarism would rule. They must be stopped before the canker spread.

Now, Staring Otter suspected that Congress' wish to civilize the Indian wasn't based on a concern for the Indian's well-being so much as the realization that if he became a farmer instead of a hunter he wouldn't need as much land, and more would be available for cession to the Americans. But my father was a young man in

1813, the promise of adventure was appealing, and he supposed it was necessary to fight. He raised his hand and became a member of Major Ridge's band.

What a mixed force it was that would battle the Red Sticks. Mountain Cherokees looked like warriors from the past. Mixed-blood Cherokees couldn't be told from white men. General Jackson's Tennessee volunteers were recognized by their coonskin caps and homespuns dyed in butternut juice.

Instructed that the United States did not make war on women and children, the aged and the helpless, the Cherokees moved on the village of Tallasahatchee. But Americans under General John Coffee already had struck. My father and the others were greeted by the sight of more than two hundred corpses of men, women and children lying about the town. The Cherokees gleefully danced about the dead, shooing off the protesting buzzards and seeking scalps overlooked by the whites. My father refused to participate, and when an Indian dangled a child's scalp in his face he hit the man with a rock.

A dazed Creek woman found hiding in the woods told Staring Otter the white men burned a house with many warriors inside then ate potatoes basted in drippings of oil from the roasted Creeks.

The whites and Cherokees routed the Creeks at Talladega, and the dispirited Creeks appealed for peace. Jackson granted it—but before the word could be spread there were attacks at other Creek villages. Staring Otter wondered why the Creeks at first put up no resistance as he and the other Cherokees slaughtered sixty-one of the enemy in one of the Hillabee towns.

My father had killed his first man. The victim was a boy of perhaps sixteen who had dropped the deer skin he was tanning to run for his lance. Staring Otter's .69-caliber musket ball had knocked his head from his shoulders.

The Cherokees learned they had attacked a people who thought there was peace. But most didn't care. They had defeated the enemy, and that was all that mattered. My father, though, buried his head in his blanket without sleep that night.

In January of 1814 the Cherokees' enlistment ended, and Staring Otter returned home to his wife of three years, Rain. There were no children to greet him, for their marriage had produced none. My grandmother, Plum, who lived in the log house, poured him a cup of whiskey, but before he would drink it, he said he wanted to tell them of his experiences as a soldier. He would recount them in detail, he said, and neither he nor the women would ever mention them again. He did, then he wiped the tears from his eyes and drank five cups of whiskey and went to bed before sunset. After the fourth cup he told my mother he didn't care about the warrior tradition of the Cherokees, for there was nothing glorious about killing another person, not even a Creek.

But a few weeks later, when Major Ridge came around raising a new troop of cavalry, he re-enlisted. The fight was not over. The job was not completed.

It was on the march to the Horseshoe that Staring Otter glimpsed Sharp Knife Jackson for the first time. My father was perched upon his horse when he noticed the general leaning against a tree, breathing heavily. Jackson was thin, sickly look-ing. His skin was red and rough, his hair disheveled. He grasped his belly with his right hand, trying to contain the pain. His left arm dangled, nearly useless from a wound he had suffered in a recent duel. But if his intestines and arm were ravaged, his blue eyes were as piercing as bullets. When he turned them on Staring Otter, my father looked ahead and urged his horse on.

The residents of six Creek towns had gathered at the Horseshoe for a last stand. A horseshoe-shaped bend in the Tallapoosa River in Alabama formed a peninsula of about one hundred acres. A zig-zag breastwork of logs sealed off the neck of the peninsula, and the river provided protection on three sides.

At 10:30, on the morning of March 27, 1814, Jackson's men began an artillery bombardment of the log barricade. After two hours it had produced no results. The Cherokees who waited outside the bend of the river grew impatient. They eyed Creek canoes that were tied up along the peninsula's banks.

Finally, the Cherokees could stand it no longer. They leaped into the river, stole the canoes, and began ferrying their warriors to the peninsula, where the Creeks were assaulted from the rear.

Now Jackson ordered a frontal charge, and his men poured over the barricade. Fighting raged throughout the afternoon, and the Red Sticks were wiped out, nine hundred of them dying to fifty-five of the combined forces of Americans, Cherokees, and friendly Creeks. Menawa, a Red Stick chief, was wounded, but he escaped by donning a slain woman's clothes and prostrating himself upon a pile of dead women until he could flee in the darkness.

The noses of the Red Stick corpses were cut off, to be sure none was counted twice. The winning Indians scalped the dead, but the whites were more imagina-tive. They flayed corpses to make souvenir belts, and they even knew a method to secure enough hide for bridle reins.

With a knife, they began near the heel and made two cuts, three inches apart. These cuts were continued up the leg and back, across the shoulders and down the other leg to the heel. The resulting strip was skinned out and treated, and the sol-dier had a bridle rein of human skin. Years later, when Staring Otter recognized one of the reins on a horse tied outside a tavern, he cut it into pieces and scattered it upon the ground.

My father killed three men in what Jackson called the Battle of Horseshoe Bend. As a Red Stick advanced on a fallen Tennesseean, Staring Otter leaped between them and took the thrust of a lance in his left leg. It cut the big bone in two, almost severing his leg. One of Jackson's doctors treated him, and for most of the march to their fort my father was out of his head, bumping along on a travois. The wound grew angrier, more fiery, and the doctor urged amputation, but a Cherokee shaman chanted over Staring Otter, forced his own medicine into the cut and down his throat, and the leg healed. The shaman said its full usefulness would return, but it didn't. He was never able to do more than barely lift it. He reconciled himself to hobbling with a crutch.

When my father reached his home on the banks of the Oostanaula, he found the cabin's oak-shingle roof burned, the corncrib destroyed, the fence leveled, the corn, maple sugar and clothing stolen, the swine and cattle shot dead and rotting. My mother and grandmother huddled in the house, wet and naked except for blankets the intruders had missed.

Five white men had raped my mother and my grandmother. Then, as their cackling laughter rang through the forest, they had forced the women to run, firing shots over their heads.

The Tennessee militiamen, returning home, had cut a swath of plunder and destruction through the country of the dismayed Cherokees—the people who had fought shoulder to shoulder with them at the Horseshoe.

Lies, a pack of lies, Jackson replied when the outrage was made public. After all, he had issued orders against any such behavior. It simply didn't happen.

My father repaired the damage to the property as best he could, but the damage to his soul was permanent. When he would become drunk on the homemade whiskey he obtained from a white trader, he would ask his neighbors if they could describe the frontiersmen who had committed this betrayal, for he was haunted by the improbable notion that one of them might have been the man whose life he had saved, for whom he gave up the use of his leg. No, they were just white men, the neighbors always said.

The marriage of Staring Otter and Rain had produced no child, but now my mother was pregnant. When I was born, it was evident one of the five frontiersmen was my father.

Rain and Staring Otter never mentioned to each other the circumstances of her pregnancy, not while her womb was full of the little girl who swam or afterward. My mother hoped, even dreamed, that I would have her husband's features, that what she suspected wasn't true. But I didn't. I resembled a man my mother had seen only once and whom she would never see again. The man who made her pregnant was one of the five, and they were five among thousands.

Throughout her marriage my mother had wanted a child. She hated the man who gave her one, but not the child herself. She gave birth to a half-white, half-Indian daughter, and so be it. She loved me as much as a mother can love an offspring. When I was old enough she told me all that I have told you. I must know about myself, she said. I must know about her. I must know about Staring Otter. She would keep no secrets from me.

I never thought of Staring Otter as other than my father. He never treated me as other than his daughter. The cyclone of events that disrupted his existence of hunting, fishing and farming stole the zest, the hope from his life. He brooded. He was silent, intractable. But if I had been a full-blood and his true daughter he would have been no different. The killing and the loss of the use of his leg and the whites' turning on their former Cherokee allies left him with a sense of emptiness and foreboding that only worsened as the relationship between the Cherokees and Americans deteriorated.

Before the war he had been interested in the civilizing process that the U.S. so zealously promoted among the Indians. But after his return to the banks of the Oostanaula he wanted nothing that smacked of the white man's ways. No, he wouldn't become a planter, though the land was there for his use. Let those Cherokees who wanted money and two-story mansions and boots from London and dresses from Augusta have them. He would plant just enough and fish just enough and trap just enough to feed and clothe himself and his family, and that was all. The Cherokees had endured before the interlopers came with their broken treaties and fancy clothes and smallpox, and they would continue to endure.

He didn't need their whiskey, either, he told my mother, and after months of frequent drunkenness he traded no more pelts for their poison. He sweated and quivered and vomited only air for two days, but he never drank whiskey again.

My father never learned to read and write, in either the English or Cherokee language, but one evening as he sat on the stone steps of our cabin and listened to the chorus of tree frogs, he motioned for me to take my place on his knee, and he spoke from memory a prophecy made long ago by conjurors. I was a small child and didn't understand, but over the years I would hear him recite the prophecy word for word many times—and I would comprehend. It told how our "elder brother," the white man, would take our country:

"Your elder brother will settle around you. He will encroach upon your lands and then ask you to sell them to him. When you give him a part of your country, he will not be satisfied, but ask for more. In process of time he will ask you to become like him. He will tell you that your mode of life is not as good as his, whereupon you will be induced to make great roads through the nation, by which he can have free access to you. He will learn you to cultivate the earth. He will even teach you his language and learn you to read and write. But these are but means to destroy you and to eject you from your habitation. He will point you to the west, but you will find no resting place there, for your elder brother will drive you from one place to another until you get to the western waters. These things will certainly happen, but it will be when we are dead and gone. We shall not live to see and feel the misery which will come upon you."

Always Staring Otter would conclude that it was happening, just as the conjurors knew it would.

As for Andrew Jackson, the man with the aching guts whose bullet eyes had met my father's for a brief moment, his victory at the Horseshoe broke the Red Sticks' power and was the first step toward national fame. He took a bigger one less than ten months later, on January 8, 1815—the day I was born—when he defeated the British at New Orleans. In 1829 the Tennesseean who had spat the word "liars" at his ravaged Cherokee allies became president of the United States. A year later he signed the Indian Removal Bill which told all the tribes east of the Mississippi River to surrender their land to the whites and move west.

CHAPTER 2

The Oostanaula isn't wide and it isn't long. It isn't a Tennessee, certainly not a Mississippi. It is no Chatooga, roaring a challenge to the young and foolish to test their manhood among its foam-dashed rocks. Except when the spring rains choke the branches and send them rushing to its body, it plods so slowly that one may study the reflections of the overhanging trees on its surface and name the birds on their limbs. If he can but swim, a small child can play safely in the Oostanaula.

It provided my family water for drinking and washing. It lured the deer that Staring Otter hunted, the beaver and otter that he trapped, provided the fish that he plucked from the surface after he had stunned them with powdered buckeye that he churned into the flow. It caused the bottomland to produce succulent corn and fat beans.

Water, sun and fire are the three holy gifts of the Great Spirit, and on the evening before a hunt Staring Otter would go to water and plead: "Give me the wind. Give me the breeze, Yu! O Great Earth Hunter, I come to the edge of your spittle where you repose. Let your stomach cover itself; let it cover itself at a single bend, and may you never be satisfied." To the fire he would say, "And you, O Ancient Red, may you hover about my breast while I sleep. Now let good dreams develop."

Always he spoke those olden words, ignoring the less traditional Cherokees who laughed at him. He even performed the immemorial rituals of asking an animal's permission before killing it, sacrificing the deer's tongue by giving it to the fire, passing his moccasins over flames to protect his feet from snakes.

When he was ill he turned to the old panacea of a plunge into cold water. I can remember my mother fretting on the bank of the Oostanaula in January, squeezing my tiny hand, pleading with him. She knew that many years before, smallpox had been brought to Carolina by slave ships and that within a year it had wiped out nearly half of the Cherokees, many of them hastened to their deaths by cold plunges, the worst "treatment" of all. Staring Otter knew the story, too, but an old shaman who lived nearby protested that the disease was a penalty for violation of ancient ordinances and that was the only reason the plunge wasn't effective. So Staring Otter plunged.

Staring Otter accepted the pension that President Madison granted to those Cherokees who were wounded by the Creeks, and he took the thirty-eight dollars the U.S. decreed as just compensation for the damage done by the Tennessee frontiersmen to his home, his animals, his wife and his mother-in-law, but he disdained anything else that, as he said, was "stained white."

Washington was president when the U.S. first set itself to civilizing the Cherokees. Over the years the whites sent us plows, spinning wheels, looms, cotton cards, tools, seeds. Instructors taught the women domestic arts and urged them to plant cotton. Forget the ancient occupations of war and hunting, the men were advised, and become farmers. Leave the village and plant many acres.

Before his expedition to the Horseshoe, Staring Otter had been intrigued by the prospect of such a transformation of the people, but now he scoffed and ground the tip of his crutch into the soil and told anyone who would listen: if you want to know how the whites really feel about you—how they will feel about you when their wave, choked with covetous settlers, is crested and poised to wash over your land—remember the proposal Jackson made in 1817 when he was a treaty commissioner. Move beyond the Mississippi, the Chicken Snake urged the stunned Cherokees, his allies. Exchange your ancient homeland for unknown ground, and as you depart we will magnanimously give you a rifle, ammunition, a blanket and a brass kettle. Or, if you prefer, a beaver trap instead of a kettle.

Staring Otter repeated the words of Tecumseh, the majestic Shawnee chief, who had sought to unify the Indians against the whites—who, indeed, had inspired the Creek Red Sticks: "The Great Spirit gave this land to his red children; he placed the whites on the other side of the water; they were not contented with their own, but came to take ours from us."

But Staring Otter was a warrior without a heart, a brave propped upon a crutch, not a lance. When Rain, my mother, said some of the methods of the whites obviously were superior to the old Cherokee ways, he retired to the yard to work on his bows. When she planted a patch of cotton and then spun and wove the fluff into dresses for me, he hobbled to the river to watch the turtles sunning on a log.

Like other Cherokee women, Mother worked in the fields, planting and gathering the corn, beans, melons, squash, and pumpkins that we ate. Staring Otter hunted and trapped as best he could, but mostly he made bows and traded them for food.

They weren't ordinary bows, but prize examples of the art of bow-making. Many Cherokees had guns and didn't have to rely on the bow and arrow for hunting, but Staring Otter's creations were so beautiful, so perfect, that most men wanted one—and since they could duplicate neither his knowledge nor his skill, they traded venison, bear, furs, honey, even livestock for genuine Staring Otter bows. A two-day ride for the sole purpose of acquiring one was not considered an unreasonable sacrifice.

My father made his bows only from the finest specimens of honey locust or black locust. When I was a little girl, he paid me scant attention, but it did please him to take me into the forest where he would declare that he could not find the required trees. Always one would be in my path, and I would shriek with delight, proud of my uncanny ability to discover locust.

Only bear gut would do for the strings of Staring Otter's bows. A strong layer of tissue surrounds the intestines and liver and stomach of a bear, and hunters would bring it to my father, who would roll it and stretch it into a long string.

He made his arrows from cane gathered only in the late fall, heating the shaft over the fire and straightening it on his knee, attaching the feathers with glue made from boiling deer hooves. Always he told the purchaser of a bow that he was giving him without charge six arrows and a pot of bear grease to protect the bow and string from dampness. "Remember, never leave the bow strung," Staring Otter would shout to the pleased buyer as he departed, forever the merchant concerned for his customers.

I wouldn't have dared say it, but even as a child I discerned that my father, who was so determined to shut whites and their ways out of his life, resembled in his salesmanship William McDonald, the Georgian who regularly stopped his trading wagon at our settlement and, while he showed the cloth and kettles, told Rain and the other mothers how pretty their children were.

Sometimes it was necessary for Staring Otter to hunt deer to feed his family. I was amused but also frightened when he donned the deerskin he kept folded on a shelf above the door. It was the hide of a huge buck, and it covered my father. He placed the hollowed deer's head over his own and peered through the eye holes. I squealed and ran to Rain when he lowered his head and threatened me with the antlers.

When a deer came to drink from the Oostanaula, Staring Otter crept to within easy shooting distance of the trusting animal before bringing it down with an arrow.

Rain encouraged him to hunt deer, to exercise his mind and body, but she was terrified when he went on a bear hunt, as he occasionally did. One of her older brothers had been killed by a bear when he was fourteen, and she still dreamed about the mangled, shredded body that was returned to camp on a litter.

Staring Otter and his friends hunted bears when the beasts had gorged themselves on fruits and become fat. A lazy bear would find a tree that was rotted out but still standing and make that its home. The Cherokees would wander through the woods, looking for such trees. If they spotted claw marks on a trunk, they knew a bear was probably inside.

A man would rap on the tree, then everyone would hide. If a bear lived there it would climb to the opening, survey the surroundings and, finding nothing, slide back inside, merely annoyed.

With the bear now located for certain, the men would collect canes into a bundle, and one of their number would climb a tree, carrying the canes and some fire. He would light a cane and toss it into the opening of the bear's den. He would throw the torches until the bear exited the burning tree. Then the other hunters would fire their arrows at the animal, sometimes bringing it down even before it was free of its home.

"It's all right," Staring Otter would tell Rain. "I'm always the one who climbs the tree and throws the canes." But she knew he was lying. With his dangling leg, he couldn't climb a tree.

Our settlement was small. It consisted of perhaps a dozen log houses, many occupied by relatives—uncles and aunts and cousins and those who had married into the family. We lived beside the Oostanaula, and the morning sun woke us as it peeked through the open doorway. "The Great Spirit has fired his torch and says arise!" Rain, always the first up, would shout playfully—but forcefully—every morning. At dusk the whipporwills would begin their chorus, and she would light a lamp in the window so the birds would come close and sing us to sleep.

Each household had its own patch of cultivated land, separated from the others by an untended strip, but we all cared for each other's plots. The men broke the cornfields in the spring, and then the females took over, planting the crop. A woman dug a hole, a girl tossed four kernels of corn into it, an older girl poured water into the hole and, using a hoe made from a flat stone, covered the seeds. We planted beans, squash and other foods between the rows of corn. We never hurried, for we enjoyed each other's company, and we were pleased to gossip.

I delighted in operating the spinning wheel that my mother brought onto the porch of our house on warm, sunny mornings. I giggled when the settlement's communal loom, under my direction, produced cloth that would be dyed with bark of the black walnut.

Staring Otter carped against Rain's fondness for the ways of the whites, but she paid him no attention. Cherokee women as a rule don't knuckle under to the men as white women do. It was her family, for we traced our lineage through the mother, not through the father as the whites did.

I loved the woods, the river, the animals. I cherished the notion that if blue jays played around our house we would have fun and laughter, that the wren who chose our cabin for her home brought good luck. But I wanted more. I wanted a magnificent two-story brick mansion such as the one Cherokee planter James Vann built, clothes from Philadelphia like those that belonged to a white politician's wife who passed near our settlement on her way to Nashville.

But mostly I wanted to read, to learn.

The handsome lady had bade her carriage driver stop so that she could meet the three Cherokee children who had wandered from their village to catch tadpoles in a marsh left by rains. Her husband sighed and grumbled and remained inside the coach, but she stood in the mud that soiled her shiny black boots and patted me on the head and spoke to us in English, which I didn't understand. I replied in Cherokee, which she didn't understand. She had her driver untie her trunk, and she allowed me to run my fingers through dresses of velvet and silk and to put on her purple-plumed hat and bejeweled gold necklace. On pieces of paper she wrote a story of our meeting, noting at the end that she hoped some day we would be able to read it, and gave them to the three of us. She presented the two little boys with bone-handled pocketknives that were inscribed with the name of her husband the politician, and she gave me a book.

On its pages were drawings of peoples of many countries. I marveled at houses built on the side of immense, jagged, snow-covered mountains, at smiling children who wore shoes made of wood, at robed men who rode strange, humped animals across what appeared to be a land that consisted entirely of sand. There were no Indians in the book, and I wondered if we were really the Principal People, if the Cherokee Nation was really the center of the earth, as Staring Otter always had stressed.

Rain couldn't read them, but she told me each group of markings on the pages represented a word, and that the whites knew the meaning of the markings and thus had only to open the book to learn about distant lands. It was possible for a white who lived in, say, Augusta to convey his thoughts to a white who lived in Washington City without actually speaking to him face to face.

I wished that I could write my emotions and hand them to Strong Hickory, my sweetheart, and run and hide behind our cabin. I wished I could write about a bear hunt and send the story to the children who wore wooden shoes, because I doubted there were bears in such a well-ordered, flowered country. I wished I could write my name.

And then the Reverend Charley Marley rode into our settlement on the handsomest red horse I had ever seen.

He was a young man, in his early twenties (though, of course, that isn't young to a ten-year-old), and perched atop his head was a beaver hat that was a dilapidated as it was tall and round. The hat, he said, had belonged to an important person in London, and Charley had acquired it from a trader. He wore buckskin leggings and moccasins, but around his neck was a blue silk scarf and upon his back was a yellow cotton shirt and a red uniform coat that had made a vivid target of a British soldier at the Battle of New Orleans. The trader who had swapped him the coat for furs swore the hole on the left front was made by the bullet that took the luckless Englishman's life.

Charley Marley was three-quarters Cherokee. His paternal grandfather was a Highland Scot trader who married an Indian. Their union produced Charley's father, who took as his wife the daughter of a prominent Cherokee. Charley liked to say that he inherited his height from the whites, his beauty from the Indians.

I thought Charley was beautiful, the most beautiful man I'd ever seen. He stood six feet, three inches, taller than anyone else my young eyes had beheld. High cheekbones and blue eyes highlighted a laughing face. I thought his clothes, though outlandish, were gorgeous. His horse was a friendly monster that sniffed my hair and seemed, like its rider, to smile at me.

All the children of our settlement gathered around him, and he bellowed, "What have we here? Are these the Little People I've heard so much about?"

No, no, we chorused. The Little People are a foot tall, and they live behind the waterfall, in the flowers, in tiny caves. They sing and dance and play pranks. The men have beards to the ground, and the women are the prettiest of creatures. We had never seen one of the Little People, but we almost had. No, no, we aren't the Little People.

"Then you must be the chief of this village," Charley Marley proposed to Strong Hickory.

No, no, we shrieked. Strong Hickory is just a boy, not a chief.

Charley Marley got off his horse and removed the blue silk scarf from his neck. With his left forefinger, he stuffed it into the fist he made with his right hand. He opened the hand, and the scarf had disappeared. Then he took some apples from the saddlebag and began to juggle them. He juggled three. Then four. Then five. Then he fed one to his horse and tossed the other four to the children, handing Strong Hickory a handsome hunting knife and telling him to divide them equally.

A half dozen men and women had gathered, and Staring Otter demanded, "Who are you?"

"I am Charley Marley, Cherokee, minister of the gospel, educator," he answered. "I have come to bring The Word and the words. If you will have me, I will settle in your midst and teach your children about Jesus and verbs and Paris, France. I will teach the adults, too, if you wish."

"You're a fool," Staring Otter answered. "Take your silly hat and coat and tricks and go to Augusta where the white people will appreciate you."

"But I believe I am appreciated here," Charley Marley said calmly. "The children obviously are pleased that my apples and I aren't in Augusta."

"You aren't a minister," Staring Otter said. "Ministers have passed this way before. They don't dress like rainbows and perform shamans' tricks. They shake their Book in our faces and tell us to stay away from the Ball Play."

"I have a Book," Charley Marley answered, reaching into the saddlebag for his Bible. "But I won't shake it in your face. As for the Ball Play, I play myself. I am quite good at it. Despite all that, I am as much a minister as they are. All ministers aren't exactly alike, any more than all birds or all fishes or all hunters are alike."

"We don't need you and your white man's ways here," Staring Otter said. "Now, get on your horse and..."

"You say you play ball?" one of our neighbors, The Bull, asked, clamping his hand firmly on Staring Otter's shoulder to shut him up.

"Better than any man in this community," Charley Marley answered, seizing what he considered an opportunity.

"We have a team, but always we lose," The Bull said. "We are small men, and slow."

"I am a big man, and I am fast," Charley Marley said. "I haven't played on many losing teams."

Our community's twelve-man team was an object of ridicule in all the neighboring towns. Even the children knew it, for the wives joshed their husbands because the team never won. Two of the players were in their fifties and much too told for the strenuous, violent, running game, but they played in order that the team might have enough men. Their pride wouldn't permit them to do otherwise. I knew that The Bull saw in Charley Marley an opportunity to retire one of the old men, to replace him with an awesome-looking player who perhaps could lead our team to a victory.

Staring Otter was trapped by his own words. He had told Charley to leave and take his white man's ways with him, but the Ball Play was a traditional part of Cherokee life. Staring Otter had lost heart for the games as he had lost heart for everything else, but he couldn't argue that they weren't as Cherokee as buckskin.

"Maybe we could win back our swine," The Bull said, and the other bystanders nodded. Our men had been goaded into wagering ten pigs on the outcome of a game with a team from Oothcaloga. They had lost, of course, and the women had been furious.

"You would let this man live here simply because he looks like a ball player?" Staring Otter protested weakly. "Only if he promises to leave his Book in his saddlebag and to teach our children nothing. Paris, France. Huh!"

"I am a minister first, a teacher second," Charley Marley said evenly. "I am a ball player third. If you wish me to stay and fulfill the third role you must accept the first two, also."

"I call for a vote," The Bull said.

Only Staring Otter's hand was raised against Charley Marley. For a moment I felt inexplicably sorry for my father, but the feeling was replaced by aching disappointment when he exclaimed, "Very well, let him stay—but he will not teach my child. She is Cherokee, and Cherokee she will remain."

Charley Marley grinned, reached into his saddlebag and produced a Ball Play stick that was webbed with strips of raccoon hide. He waved it above his head, and the men laughed. Staring Otter turned and walked away, cursing and dragging his damaged left leg behind him. Charley tossed the stick to Strong Hickory. "You can have it," he said. "I'll make another."

Then from his saddlebag he withdrew several sheets of paper. They were printed identically with columns of symbols that meant nothing to me or the other bystanders. He passed them out to the children and adults, and I brushed my fingers over the figures, but they would not rub off.

The papers Charley Marley distributed to the bewildered Indians would alter my life forever. They were the talking leaves of Sequoyah.

CHAPTER 3

Charley Marley had met Sequoyah by chance on a ferry as they both crossed the Coosa River in Alabama. The middle-aged half-breed had a shrunken leg. He wore a turban and smoked a long clay pipe. He had barely spoken, but when Charley began reading his Bible, Sequoyah became talkative.

He told Charley he had invented a syllabary, and if the Cherokees would memorize it and use it they would become the only tribe in America with a written language. More than any other single thing, he believed, his syllabary would enable his people to compete with the whites. Charley instantly recognized the importance of Sequoyah's invention, and he agreed with him that it could be the instrument of a monumental leap for the Indians.

When they had crossed the river, Charley offered to share his jerky and water with the man, so they tied their horses and sat under an oak tree, and Sequoyah captivated the preacher-teacher with the story of his invention.

He was a silversmith, he said, a maker of earrings, bracelets and ornaments, and he kept his records by drawing a picture of the person who ordered a bauble and beside the picture entering a mark that represented the price agreed upon. It was not an efficient method, and he envied the white man his ability to communicate by writing.

Sequoyah—who could not read or write any language—considered the problem. On a stone he began to scratch marks with a pin, each representing a sentence, such as "My wife is well." But there were many possible sentences, and soon there were more signs than anyone could have remembered.

So he made marks that represented words, but again there were simply too many.

Surely there were fewer sounds made by the Cherokee tongue, sounds that in combination formed words. Sequoyah determined there were eighty-six distinct sounds. On bark, with pokeberry juice, he made a sign for each.

It would come to be called the Cherokee alphabet, but it differed from the English alphabet in that it was a syllabary, a listing of marks that represented syllables rather than letters, and Sequoyah worked on it for many years, often in the face of ridicule and discouragement.

He had become obsessed with his mission. He built a small house near the one in which he and his family lived, and there in solitude he perfected his syllabary. His crops were overtaken by weeds. His distraught wife thought he had gone insane. Perhaps she was correct, he said, but he would continue. His friends told him that he was making a fool of himself. He replied that if it were so, he was not making fools of them. They had not caused him to begin his work, and they would not cause him to stop.

Once his syllabary was in place, he taught it to his six-year-old daughter. Now he was ready to prove its validity to those who came to his house to fret or scoff.

His method was simple. He would station his daughter at the wood pile. A visitor would accompany her. The other visitors would go into the house with Sequoyah, and one of them would speak a sentence. Sequoyah would make marks on a slate or a piece of paper. Then his daughter would join them in the house, Sequoyah would show her the transcription, and she would immediately speak the sentence.

The work of a witch, some said, fleeing from this turbaned cripple. Some simply denounced it as a trick. Others realized Sequoyah's syllabary was as genuine a method of communication as the white man's mysterious Talking Leaves.

Chiefs who had been skeptical finally endorsed the syllabary, and it was sweeping the Cherokee Nation like a windblown fire. Children and adults easily learned it. Communication not only was utilitarian but fun. Directional signs written in the syllabary were attached to trees along roadsides. Sequoyah visited Cherokees in Arkansas, taking along letters from their relatives in the East and returning with notes from the Western Indians.

We had heard of Sequoyah's invention, but no one in our settlement had seen it until Charley Marley passed out copies. He hesitated when I held out my hand, but he decided that, despite Staring Otter's belligerence, I should have one, too. Except for the note and the book the politician's wife had given me, it was the only paper I had ever seen. Keep these markings, he told the children and adults, and from them I will teach you to write the Cherokee language. Then I will teach you to speak and write English, and you will know as much—more—than the white man.

Charley asked The Bull if he might pitch his tent on the bank of the river under a towering poplar, for the time being, and The Bull told him the men would help him build a log house, that he could consider himself a neighbor as if he had lived in our settlement all his life. Charley winked at me and climbed upon his huge red horse.

I rushed home, wondering as my bare feet stirred the dust of the village's worn paths what I should do with the piece of paper. Staring Otter wouldn't be pleased. Should I hide it and try to attend Charley Marley's classes in secret? That would be impossible and, besides, I wasn't comfortable lying to my father, even if he was obstinate. I decided to appeal to him through my mother and grandmother. Mother could overcome his opposition, for Cherokee women usually had the last word where their children were concerned.

They were preparing supper in iron pots that hung over a lazy fire in the fireplace. Staring Otter was outside, working with a string of bear gut for a bow. I showed Rain and Plum the paper Charley Marley had given me, careful to jerk it back when Plum attempted to touch it with hands stained by venison blood. I told them about the magic man and his huge horse and about Sequoyah and how Charley would teach me and the other children and anyone else who was ambitious how to read the Cherokee language and even the white man's language. Then I could read the book the politician's wife had given me and understand the ways of the chubby-faced children who stood under windmills.

Didn't it sound wonderful? Yes, Rain said, but that didn't mean it was wonderful. A man didn't simply ride into a community and commandeer all the children. She would ask Staring Otter to investigate, and …

"He doesn't like Charley Marley," I blurted.

"Then maybe I shouldn't like him either," Rain said.

"Charley's wonderful," I cried. "He has this beautiful red coat, and he can play ball better than anyone. The Bull likes him very much. He said…"

Mother wiped her hands on a piece of soft buckskin and asked Plum to finish supper. "I'll visit Sweet Melon," she said.

"I'll go, too," I said.

"You'll stay here and help your grandmother cook. Wash your hands."

I felt I was winning. She and Sweet Melon were friends, and Sweet Melon's husband, The Bull, no doubt even now was filling his wife's ear with an admiring account of the arrival of Charley Marley.

I fidgeted at the fireplace, hoping my mother would return promptly with the good news that I could study at the feet of Charley Marley. "I make the best cornbread of anyone," Plum interrupted my thoughts. "Learn to cook well, and you will catch a man. Even ugly old Stream over Rocks has a man, because she cooks the next best cornbread of anyone."

"If I learn to read, I won't need a man," I said, ignoring the fact I was in love with my playmate Strong Hickory. "I will know more than most men."

"You will always need a man," Plum said. "Believe me, I know. My man Silent Turkey has been dead for many years, but I still need him."

"Why don't you get another man?" I asked.

"I don't love another man. The man I need is dead, and no other can take his place, so I don't have a man."

"Did my grandfather love you because you cooked tasty cornbread?" I asked, my attention slipping away from Mother's inquiry at Sweet Melon's cabin.

"Among other things," Plum said. "Cooking isn't the only way a woman pleases a man."

I didn't know what she meant, and I knew I wasn't supposed to. Often when a grownup seemed to be speaking to a ten-year-old, she was really speaking to herself, sharing with herself a secret that the child could only guess. I couldn't guess at this one, so I didn't pursue it. "Tell me again how Silent Turkey got killed," I asked.

"Oh, Nancy," my grandmother sighed. "I've told you more times than there are leaves on the trees. All right. He and a friend were hunting. They came upon a white trader who sold them whiskey. They drank it beside their campfire at dusk, and it made them bold. They decided to slip through the forest to a Creek village and steal some horses. This would prove that they were very brave.

"They smothered their fire and began a walk of many hours, continuing to drink the whiskey from their two jugs, stumbling through the woods. It was almost sunrise when they arrived at the Creek village, by now braver than rattlesnakes.

"The guard slept, and they silently removed the rails from the horse pen and pushed the horses to their freedom. They got on the last two horses, and they would have escaped without the man even awakening, except they couldn't resist the urge to scream a notice of their success. They were past the watchman, but the other men at the edge of the village were awakened by their whoops, and before they could reach safety their horses were brought down with arrows. The two drunken men were surrounded and bound and brought before the village chief.

"They would run the gantlet, he said. The men and women of the tribe, bearing clubs, would form two long lines, and the prisoners would sprint between them. It was the custom that if anyone survived and reached the chief's house he would win his life. But that almost never happened.

"Silent Turkey had barely begun his stumbling run before a lick to the head knocked him to the ground. The Creeks swarmed over him, quickly killing him with their blows. His friend, Dark Path, tried to clear his mind by taking a deep breath. He covered his head with his arms, yelled a challenge to his tormentors, and charged into the deadly lines. The clubs rained upon him, breaking his hands and arms and ribs and even his skull and legs, but somehow he completed the run and threw himself into the chief's open doorway.

"The Creeks were amazed that a man could survive such an assault, and when a shaman declared that he was protected by the Great Spirit, the villagers began petting him like he was a baby."

Plum smiled, and I marveled that the passing of the years would allow her to smile when relating the story of the death of her husband. "I always thought Dark Path was protected by the whiskey, not the Great Spirit," she said.

She saw that I didn't smile, that the story elicited the same delicious horror it always did when she told it, and she petted me understandingly on the head. "The Creeks cared for Dark Path until he could ride, then they put him on a horse and escorted him to within sight of his village. He never had total use of his arms and legs again, and sometimes he didn't make sense when he talked. But he told me what happened to Silent Turkey, my young husband, the father of my baby Rain, and I have just told it to you for at least the hundredth time. Now go and get your father because the meal is ready."

In my most pleasant, lilting voice I told Staring Otter his food was prepared. He nodded but never looked up. I stood like a pine, not speaking or moving, for a few minutes until he reached a convenient stopping point in the construction of a bow. Then I took his hand as we walked to the cabin.

He seated himself and said, "Where is Rain?"

"She is visiting Sweet Melon," I said. "She will be home soon. Let me fix your plate."

"You hold my hand? You fix my plate?" he said. "What have you been up to?"

I froze. "Nothing," I said.

Staring Otter ate without commenting on the food. "More," he said, handing me his plate, and I bounced over to the pots at the edge of the fireplace, too accommodating, too eager to please. He stared at me, and I thought I saw recognition in his eyes. "Why is your mother visiting The Bull's cabin at mealtime?" he asked.

"She is visiting Sweet Melon."

"I heard you when you said that. Why?"

"I don't know," I said. I wasn't a good liar. My eyes lowered from his to my plate.

"You know about the preacher who came?" Staring Otter asked my grandmother.

"I know," Plum answered.

"He brings the ways of the white man," Staring Otter said. "He is hung with them, like a peddler's wagon is hung with pots and pans and traps and shovels."

"Rain will be here soon," Plum said dismissively. "I'll fix her plate." She ladled peas and corn and cut a piece of venison from the roast.

"He brings Sequoyah's nonsense to our community, and now everyone must learn to read and write the Cherokee language," Staring Otter said. "Then they will learn to read and write the Georgians' language. Then they will adopt the white man's religion and forgive him for stealing our land and killing our livestock and burning our homes and … all the other terrible things he does."

He was almost yelling now, and Plum walked outside the cabin. Staring Otter ferociously cut the venison on his plate and said no more.

He didn't even look up when Mother arrived. She glanced at me imploringly, sighed, and took her seat. "Sweet Melon and The Bull believe Sequoyah's method of writing is a great thing," she said, as if we were alone. "They will learn it, and so will their son Strong Hickory. So will you and I, Nancy."

"No!" Staring Otter slammed his fist onto his metal plate, and the remnants of food were catapulted all the way against the wall. Mother and I jumped, as we had the night a lion screamed outside our door.

Traditionally, the final decision regarding Cherokee children was the mother's, but it was evident Staring Otter wasn't making a mere token objection. Rain breathed rapidly, but she didn't respond.

"Because I listened to the whites, my leg is destroyed, and I sit here and make bows rather than be a full man," he said, his voice as hard as flint. "White men who call me brother overrun my home and ravage my wife and her mother and kill my livestock and price at thirty-eight dollars that which is priceless. They are stealing our lands through ridiculous treaties and thievery, and Cherokee country is shrinking like wet rawhide in the hot sun. In one breath their government tells us to become civilized like them, and in the other it calls us savages who could never become civilized—whichever view suits their purposes on that particular day. They ask us to migrate to the West so that they might have our beautiful hills and valleys—but one day they will stop asking and force us from our homeland. Well, this family is Cherokee, not white, and its members will go to their graves Cherokee."

Always I had read in Mother's face a look that told me be patient, I can handle your father, but this time I saw only hurt and bewilderment. I had never heard Staring Otter speak so adamantly. Usually he recited a plaintive, half-hearted catalogue of his indictments of the whites, and Mother went on with her work at the loom or her purchase of an Augusta dress from the peddler. But not this time.

"Just because whites read and write their language, it doesn't mean that Cherokees who read and write the Cherokee language are adopting the ways of the whites," Rain said, but there was no assertiveness in her voice. She spoke as if she were asking a question. "Whites eat and drink," she said lamely, "but no one suggests we are imitating them because we eat and drink, too."

"You aren't going to do it," Staring Otter declared. "Nancy isn't going to waste her time learning silly games, and neither are you. If you wish someone in Oothcaloga to know what's on your mind, go and tell her, don't send a slate to tell her. The man who rode into our midst today is a trickster who gazes into a pond and sees only the one-quarter white in his face, not the three-quarters Cherokee. To invite him into the fellowship of our community, as The Bull and the others did, is to welcome a rattlesnake—but one who has the guile to remove his rattles."

Hearing such passion from the lips of her husband overwhelmed Mother. She always had understood the wellsprings of his hatred of the whites, but she hadn't been intimidated by him. Perhaps at this instant she saw across the table from her a man who, after all, had been forbearing in accepting as his own, without complaint, the daughter of an unknown white rapist. For whatever reason, she said, "All right, my husband."

"You have a paper?" Staring Otter asked me.

"No."

"Give it to him, Nancy," Mother said.

I went to my bed and reached under the mattress. The corn shucks rustled, and I produced the copy of Sequoyah's syllabary that Charley Marley had given me.

Staring Otter took it and gazed at the strange symbols. His appearance softened, and for a moment I thought he was going to hand it back to me.

But he didn't. He walked across the room to the fireplace and carefully placed the paper on the coals. He and my mother and my grandmother and I watched as the magic preacher's gift flared and then just as quickly turned to ash.

I was determined I wasn't going to cry, not then, not when he could see me. I wished that the Red Stick warrior's lance had found Staring Otter's heart instead of his leg. I wished that I were Sequoyah's daughter, standing beside the woodpile and reading his messages and mystifying the unbelievers. I called Staring Otter the most hateful name I could think of. I knew it was hateful because Staring Otter always spat the words when he applied them to Andrew Jackson. "You're a chicken snake," I said, and then I walked through the moonlight into the dark woods and wept until there were no more tears.

CHAPTER 4

Spring painted our valley green and spangled it with white and red and pink and yellow and purple. A sun that proudly ruled cloudless blue skies drove away the winter's chill and caused even Staring Otter to be expansive. "It is good to be Cherokee," he said, a rare smile on his lips. "The Principal People at the center of the earth. To want more is to accuse the Great Spirit of not being bountiful."

I wanted more. I was a child, but I knew there was more, for I had seen it, and to me that was evidence of just how beautiful the Great Spirit was. Why would he create these advantages if we were not to want them? I loved things Cherokee—the feel of soft buckskin, the Green Corn Dance, the legend of the great dog who stole an old couple's corn meal and flew through the sky, the meal dropping from his mouth and forming the Milky Way—but I wanted to read and write and learn about the other sides of the earth.

The Bull and the other men had helped Reverend Charley Marley build a log cabin, and the women of our settlement—giggly at his good looks when their husbands were absent—usually prepared his supper. In exchange, he taught Sequoyah's syllabary three days of every seven and on Sunday mornings proselytized for the Christian religion.

His classes were much better attended than his preaching services. All the children except me went to his school, and so did most of the adults. Word spread, and youngsters from the forest came to our settlement, too. Most of the people, though, ignored his ministry.

I stood on our porch at dusk and listened to the children squeal as they played games with the syllabary. Charley made learning fun, Strong Hickory told me, and he wished that I could come. But Staring Otter was adamant that I wouldn't study the ways of the whites, and in this Rain supported him, against her wishes.

Charley Marley chose his opportunity carefully, and once when Staring Otter was ill he tried to visit him. Charley brought a succulent turtle stew that he said was prepared from his mother's special recipe. He stood on the porch and talked to me as Rain went inside to ask if Staring Otter would see him. She returned and, embarrassed, told him he'd better go. When he offered to leave the stew she said no.

I wasn't permitted to attend Charley Marley's classes or his church services, but I made a point of talking to him when I saw him out of doors. Once I followed him to the river bank where he sat on the ground and propped his back against a cottonwood tree and read his Bible.

"Will your father object to us talking?" he asked.

"How did you learn all the things you know?" I said.

He looked into my eyes for what seemed a long time, decided chatting with me was a risk worth taking, smiled, and said, "My grandfather was a white trader, an adventurer, a man of action. His brother was just the opposite, quiet, thoughtful, a Presbyterian minister in Scotland.

"My grandfather married a Cherokee woman, and they had a son, my father. My grandfather returned to Scotland, supposedly just for a visit, but he got involved in some business venture and never came back to his wife and baby. His brother denounced him for deserting them, and my grandfather said if he was such a high and mighty soldier of the faith, why didn't he cross the ocean and win the Cherokee country for Christianity? All right, he said, he would. Their mother, my great-grandmother, couldn't live with the knowledge her older son was casually abandoning a wife and child and her younger son with the soft hands and soft voice was going to an untamed land. She took to her bed and never got up again."

"What is untamed?" I asked.

Charley laughed. "I'll compare the two lands," he said. "Scotland is a meadow, and Cherokee country is a blackberry thicket; Scotland is a cow, and your country is a bear."

I told him I thought I understood, and he continued.

"My grandfather's brother became an itinerant missionary to the Cherokees, preaching the gospel and teaching subjects one would find in a school in Scotland. He eventually located my grandfather's wife and child and, as best he could, cared for them. He never married, but he was happy among the Cherokees, and they liked him. I can still remember the joy and excitement in our village when he would return from one of his pilgrimages.

"I looked upon him as a grandfather rather than a granduncle, and I wanted to be like him. My father became an important chief, the owner of a ferry, an inn and a store. He and my mother, a chief's daughter, sent me to Brainerd, a missionary school in Tennessee, and then to the Foreign Mission School in Cornwall, Connecticut."

"Connecticut? That's a funny word," I said.

"It's far away," Charley Marley said. "Very far away."

"Farther than Washington City?" I asked. I had once spoken to a Cherokee, an acquaintance of The Bull, who had been to Washington City to meet the White Father. He had told me Washington City was halfway around the world.

"Much farther than Washington City," Charley said.

He held my rapt attention as he told me about going to school with Choctaws, Chinese, Hindus, Hawaiians, Marquesans, Bengalese, Malays, and Abnakis in

Cornwall. Except for the Choctaws, I didn't know what they were, but I wanted to meet all of them. I laughed when he pulled the corners of his eyes back in imitation of a Chinese.

When he finished Cornwall he didn't affiliate with any denomination or any missionary organization. He simply declared himself a freelance minister and returned to Cherokee country to teach the people and to introduce them to Christianity.

"And that's my life story," he concluded.

"Teach me," I said.

Charley sifted the sand of the river bank between his fingers. "I can't defy your father," he said. "He would catch on quickly. Even the neighbors would be angry if I did that, and they might ask me to leave. I don't want to leave because there's a great work to be done here. I'm sorry."

I heard footsteps in the dead leaves left by winter and turned to see Rain approaching. She nodded at Charley Marley and said, "Nancy, your father would not be happy to find you here. Let's go home."

"No!" I yelled.

"Nancy, we're going home."

I grabbed Charley Marley's arm, but it became rigid under my touch, and he avoided my pleading eyes, staring at the stream where it larruped a log.

"He isn't my father!" I screamed. "He is an ignorant Indian. My father is a white man. He's probably in his fine home in Tennessee right now, reading a book to his other children, and I wish I was with him."

Unlike whites, Cherokees don't hit their children. But in this instance my mother slapped me in the face, and I melted to the ground, startled and sobbing. It was the only time in my life either parent ever struck me.

Until I was 6 years old I had accepted without question my lighter complexion. Why not? All Cherokees weren't the same height or weight. They didn't have the same-sized noses or speak in the same tone of voice. And I had seen Indians who were as light as me. But an older playmate, repeating what she had overheard her parents say, told me my father was a white man.

"You're blind," I told her. "Staring Otter isn't white."

"Staring Otter isn't your real father," she said. "Your real father was a white man from Tennessee. He made your mother do it."

"Do what?"

Then she explained sex to me. Or filled in the blanks, rather, for I had seen livestock mate and give birth, and I had picked up enough to know that for some reason the awkward performance by male and female was a necessary forerunner of the lamb's appearance from the grunting ewe's body. But it had never occurred to me that humans did the same thing.

I told Mother what my friend had said, and she asked me to accompany her on a walk beside the river. She recounted being raped by the Tennessee volunteers and explained that I was half white, half Indian. But she loved me nonetheless, and so did Staring Otter. I cried, not because I was half white, but because she had been mistreated and because she and her husband loved me. "Never feel that any of it was your fault," she said perceptively.

For a day or two I suffered under the weight of the revelation, but then it passed, and I rarely thought about it. Now here I was using it against my mother, piercing her heart with a lance of cruel words. I knew I was being hateful, corrupt, evil, but the guilt vied with my yearning to be like Charley Marley and the politician's wife and read books and learn about a world the Great Spirit would never have made if we were supposed to despise it as Staring Otter did.

"Go with your mother," Charley said softly as he lifted me to my feet. Crushed, I snuggled my head against Rain's breast, she put her arms around my shoulders, and we walked to our house. We both wept. I suppose each waited for the other to say she was sorry. Neither said it.

I was defeated, but only momentarily. In my bed that night I gazed through the open doorway at the ebbing and flowing luminescence of the fireflies and wondered how I could secretly learn the syllabary of Sequoyah.

Of course, I finally reasoned—and the notion hit me with such force that I was afraid I had spoken the words aloud—I would get Strong Hickory to relay Charley Marley's lessons to me. No one would know but Strong Hickory and me, not even Charley.

The idea so excited me that it was only with the greatest difficulty that I finally slept. It was as if the thought itself woke me the next morning, and I rolled out of bed immediately and danced to Strong Hickory's cabin. I peeped inside the door and saw that he and The Bull and Sweet Melon were still asleep, for daylight wasn't yet fullfledged, and when I rapped on the log beside his head, I woke up the family.

Sweet Melon appeared at the door, wiping her eyes, and asked, "What do you want, Nancy?"

"I'm sorry," I said. "Is Strong Hickory up?"

The drowsy faces of The Bull and Strong Hickory popped out of the doorway. "Son, if you marry this one, be prepared to get up before the sun does," The Bull said. He was always joking with us, but I was embarrassed.

Strong Hickory carelessly wrapped a breechcloth around his waist and joined me in the yard. He yawned and stretched, and his arms and chest and legs were as smooth and hairless as a baby's.

"Do you want to fish?" he asked sleepily.

"No, no," I said impatiently. "I want you to teach me."

"Teach you? You know how to fish as well as I do."

"Come with me," I said, and we walked to a huge rock outside the village. He followed as I scrambled to the top. It afforded a view for miles, but the morning mist obscured the river valley below us.

"Not fish," I said. "Teach me to read and write."

Strong Hickory squirmed visibly on the rock. "I don't know," he said. "I'm not a teacher. I'm getting bored with the Reverend Marley's classes. I can't see much use in knowing how to read and write."

"Oh, Strong Hickory," I said. "It would be the most wonderful thing in the world."

"Not so wonderful," he said. "It's interesting at first, but then it's like sliding down a hill on the greased pine poles. When you've done it a few times it becomes tiresome."

He tossed a sycamore ball into the air and threw another one at it, missing. "And he keeps insisting that I come to what he calls church on Sunday. I went one time, and he told us there was a man named Jesus who was murdered and was buried and came back to life and flew away. He said this was true. So I told him about the Great Buzzard, how the father of all buzzards had flown when the earth was wet and flat, and how he had grown weary, and how every time his wings dropped they scooped out a valley, and how when he lifted them they pushed up a mountain. But he just laughed and said my story was a good one but it wasn't true. I know it's true, because my great-grandmother said it is."

I didn't believe it was true, but I dared not say that to Strong Hickory. I wasn't interested in murdered men flying away any more than I was interested in a buzzard creating the Smokies, but I was interested in the syllabary, and Strong Hickory was my last hope.

"You're so smart," I cooed. "You're the smartest boy I know. You could teach me." I picked up his hand and kissed the back of it—a seductress at age ten.

Strong Hickory gulped. "Let's get married," he sputtered. "Do you promise?"

Now it was my turn to stammer. "Married? We're children. We can't get married."

"I mean some day. Do you promise?" He was agitated; he touched the wet spot on the back of his hand to his lips.

It seemed like a solemn promise, not something you should say simply to get your way. When I had thought about getting married I had always thought about Strong Hickory as my husband—but to promise?

"You could teach me to read and write," I said.

"Do you promise to marry me when we're big?" Strong Hickory insisted.

I looked away. The sun was melting the mist and playing on the surface of the Oostanaula. "I promise," I whispered.

"I wish we could get married today," Strong Hickory said in that jittery voice. He hesitated. "I'll show you something if you'll show me something," he gasped, as if speaking the words required a great deal of courage.

"What?"

"You know."

"What?"

"You know."

Suddenly I did know. I leaped to my feet. "I do have something I want to show you," I said innocently, already heading back to the village, "and there's something I want you to show me. I want to show you the bow Staring Otter made as a gift for Chief Pathkiller. He says it's his finest one yet. I want you to show me the wren's nest that keeps Sweet Melon from closing the door of your cabin."

"Wait," Strong Hickory yelped, but I didn't wait, and he scrambled up and was at my side. I let him hold my hand as we followed the path back home.

Smitten, Strong Hickory agreed to try to teach me the syllabary. Yes, he would tell Charley Marley he had lost his copy and get another one and give it to me to replace the one Starting Otter had burned. No, he wouldn't let Charley suspect I was disobeying my parents. Yes, he would meet me every afternoon in the forest, at the ruins of a cabin that had been knocked down by a windstorm many years ago. Yes, I would honor my promise to marry him someday. No, I wouldn't show him something if he would show me something.

We would begin that afternoon, as soon as we finished our morning's chores. I hurried through my work, scrubbing clothes against the rocks in the Oostanaula, pulling weeds from the vegetable plot, feeding and watering the sheep and swine, skinning a rabbit a neighbor had brought us. The more I could find to do, the more quickly the time would pass.

I was burying the rabbit's guts when I saw Strong Hickory leave his house and walk toward Charley Marley's. A few minutes later he returned, a copy of the syllabary in his hand. He nodded at me, glanced toward the forest, and my shoulders tingled. "I've finished my chores," I yelled to Mother. "I'm going for a walk."

I felt deliciously conspiratorial, and even the woods seemed darker and more enveloping than usual as I disappeared into them. Under the force of the angry wind that struck it years ago, the logs of the abandoned cabin had remained dovetailed at only one of the four corners. They were rotted and scattered upon the ground and covered with pine straw. A harmless black snake slithered away as I vaulted over a wall and into what remained of the roofless enclosure.

Strong Hickory made a noise like an owl—our secret call since we were five— and I was so pleased that I laughed out loud. "I've got it," he yelped, waving the paper as he joined me. We pushed up pine straw and sat upon it, and I reverently touched my copy of the Cherokee alphabet.

"All right," I said.

"All right?"

"Teach me."

Strong Hickory gulped. "I don't know how to teach," he said.

"Try to remember what Charley Marley said that first day you all were at his house."

Strong Hickory licked his lips and cracked his knuckles and scratched in the dirt with his bare toes. Finally, he blurted. "He said it wouldn't be difficult."

"What else?"

"I can't remember."

I could hardly breathe. "Let me look at this and see if I can get any clues," I said.

But I might as well have been trying to learn the secret of the universe by studying a speck of sand. I had no idea what any of the marks on the paper meant.

"What is this?" I asked, pointing to a symbol.

Strong Hickory leaned over the paper and squinted, like an old man. "I think it's... I don't know," he said.

"This one?"

"I don't know."

"This one?"

"I'm not sure."

I was furious with Strong Hickory. He had been given an opportunity I coveted with all my being, and he couldn't even identify the first two symbols. But I knew I couldn't show my anger. After all, he didn't owe me this.

We proceeded, tediously. I tried to pick it out of him, but I might as well have been trying to pluck hummingbirds from the air. He was impatient, and he sighed every other breath. Every noise in the woods brought him to his feet. "A turkey!" he shouted at the sound of a distant gobble. "I want to see it," and he bounded onto the slanting wall of the ruined cabin.

I gave up for the moment. "I've got to go home," I said. "Please, Strong Hickory, when you go to Charley Marley's today listen carefully. And ask him about these parts you've missed."

"I will," he said, happy to be unleashed. "I will."

But he didn't. He was little help the next day. And the next. And the next. I strained to learn, to find clues in his voice that might reveal to me what even my so-called teacher didn't know. I made some progress, but it was so slight that I was discouraged.

There was nothing to do but keep trying, continue prying from the stony soil of Strong Hickory's unreceptive mind whatever random seeds of knowledge might have taken root, however tenuous. But he was weary of our sessions and at the brink of revolt, and I knew I must say something to keep him coming to the ruined cabin.

"How would you like to have one of Staring Otter's bows for your very own?" I blurted.

Strong Hickory's eyes widened. "That would be wonderful," he said, "but I could never buy one of his bows."

"It would be a gift, from me to you, for teaching me."

"But how could you get one?"

"After all, he's my father," I said, trying to sound flippant.

"But he doesn't want you to learn. He wouldn't give you a bow to give to me to teach you."

"I'll get the bow," I assured him.

And I did. Staring Otter had eight of them stored above the ceiling in our cabin, ready merchandise for any customer. I stole one of them while he and Rain and Plum visited neighbors. Guilt washed over me like the gagging wave from a decaying deer carcass.

I took it to our next session at the cabin and gave it to Strong Hickory. He rubbed the handsome locust as if it were an icon. "It's really mine?" he said.

"Staring Otter is giving it to you because you are my best friend," I said. "But he doesn't want anyone to know it, not even your parents. You must hide it and use it only when you're alone."

"But why?"

"Because he commands fancy prices for his bows. If word got out that he gave one away it might make them seem less valuable. He did it for me, and now he wants to forget it. He doesn't even want you to mention it to him. He knows you appreciate it, so don't even thank him."

I think he searched my eyes for signs of a lie. I never blinked, and he must not have seen any, for he said, "Thank you, Nancy Swimmer. I love you." He even vowed to become serious about learning Sequoyah's syllabary and teaching it to me. "I'll confess to Reverend Marley I've missed a lot of the lessons by playing and not paying attention and ask him to go back over them," he said.

And he did. Strong Hickory worked harder for me, though it was obvious he would never really be interested in reading and writing. Our sessions were more productive, and if we weren't running we had at least advanced from the pace of a crawl to that of a slow walk.

But I received scant pleasure from our progress. I could scarcely look my parents in the eye. I was a thief, and I experienced no feeling of justification in my crime. Whatever else could be said about Staring Otter, he had provided sustenance and security and been a father to one who wasn't really his daughter. I had no right to steal from him.

I had hoped he wouldn't miss the bow, but only a few days passed before he did. The sun was setting purple behind the forest, and my family and Strong Hickory's were taking their places at an outdoor meal, about to eat fish caught and baked that afternoon by The Bull, who prided himself on his cooking, when Staring Otter said, "A strange thing has happened."

I knew his next words before he spoke them. "Someone stole one of my bows. I had eight, and this morning there were seven. If someone was going to the trouble, why wouldn't he take them all?"

"A Chickasaw was passing through the day before yesterday," The Bull said. "He asked to camp for the night beside the river. I didn't like his looks. He ..."

Sweet Melon rose to her feet and passed her hand in front of her husband, stopping him in mid-sentence. "I think my family owes your family an apology," she said to Staring Otter. "This morning I found a bow under Strong Hickory's bed. It didn't occur to me that it might be one of yours. I wouldn't have thought anything about it, but it was a handsome bow, so I intended to mention it to him later." She gazed at her son and waited.

His startled eyes passed from his mother's to his father's to Staring Otter's to mine. He took a deep breath and said, "I stole the bow."

The cleansing power of confession vied with the knowledge that I'd never read and write as I whispered, "No, he didn't. He's just saying that to protect me. Strong Hickory has been teaching me the lessons of Charley Marley, and to keep him interested I gave him one of my father's bows. I told him it was a gift to him from Staring Otter. He didn't even know until now that it was stolen."

No one spoke for what seemed an eternity until Staring Otter muttered, "Even when they are not here, the whites bore into our families like corn worms."

CHAPTER 5

The theft of the bow triggered a renewal of Staring Otter's demand that Charley Marley leave our village.

I peeped from around the corner of our house as our neighbors—including Charley—gathered before my father and heard him denounce the minister as an interloper who was disrupting our way of life. I expected Staring Otter to be overwhelmingly rebuffed, but I was surprised when several nodded in agreement.

I should have suspected. In the eyes of some, the exciting, intelligent magician who had ridden into our settlement a few months before had served his purpose and become a nuisance.

The were pleased that he taught their children, and in some cases them, the Cherokee syllabary, but his preaching of the gospel left them unsettled. They believed in a Great Spirit but had little or no personal relationship to this creator. They revered the unity of nature. They simply had no niche for Jesus, the man who had been murdered and then had flown away.

Strong Hickory told me that Charley's confident good nature cracked when he was conducting Bible classes. The more he insisted, the more the Cherokees resisted. His pupils, children and adults, argued with him, and Charley lost his composure. When they asked him to prove the story of the murdered man who flew away, he couldn't, and they silently crossed their arms in justification. The fact was that Charley had not converted a single one of his neighbors to Christianity, and they began to view him as an outsider. Now that they had taken all they wanted from Charley Marley, they decided that maybe Staring Otter was correct, maybe he was a bad influence on the village.

The Bull remained his staunchest advocate. "By simply teaching your children to read and write, he has prepared them to compete with the whites in the world that is changing," he told the gathering. "The Reverend Marley is our friend, one of us, not a panther who has stolen into our village in the darkness to kill our precious little sheep."

Staring Otter smirked and said, "But mainly he's a good ballplayer. Is that not correct, my neighbor?" Some of the others laughed.

My father insisted upon a vote, and the people decided Charley Marley could stay—but this time the tally was frightfully close.

Charley asked to speak, and he took his place in front of the group, beside Staring Otter. My father started to limp away, but Charley asked him to stay.

"Are you a wagering man?" he asked.

Staring Otter shrugged.

"If you are, I will give you a wagering man's chance to be rid of me."

"What?"

Charley gazed into Staring Otter's eyes with such intensity that his challenge caused my father to take a step backward. "I am told that for years the ballplayers from the village of Oothcaloga have easily defeated those from our settlement," he said. "Our players have never defeated their players. Well, they have challenged us once more—adding the laughs and insults of those accustomed to finding easy prey. We have accepted, and the teams will meet on the neutral ground of New Town. For the sake of argument, Staring Otter, let's say that you are a wagering man. Which team would you prefer?"

"This is a waste of time," my father said, but when he tried to leave, Charley put his hand upon his shoulder.

"It's a simple question. Which team do you believe will be the winner?"

"Oothcaloga, of course," Staring Otter said in a bored tone.

"I believe we will win," Charley Marley said, "and I am willing to back my belief with a wager."

Staring Otter was uneasy, but he said, "I'm listening."

"It's simple," Charley said. "If we lose, you will get what you want: I will leave this village that very night and never return. You will never see me or hear from me again. If we win, you will allow me to teach the Cherokee syllabary to Nancy Swimmer for six days."

Staring Otter spat in the dust, almost on Charley's moccasins. "You'll never teach my daughter, not even for six breaths," he said.

But a married woman whose romantic advances had been rebuffed by Charley Marley and who had voted for him to be banished from our village shouted, "It's a fair wager, Staring Otter. Accept it. You wanted us to stand with you in sending him away, and we did; now we want you to stand with us when we have a real chance to get rid of him."

"Yes," demanded a man who had voted against Charley. "That's right."

My father was caught in a trap of his making, but he thought fast. "I want the terms of the wager adjusted," he said. "If our village wins in the Ball Play, you get Nancy Swimmer for six days—but at the end of the six days you leave, forever."

"That isn't fair," The Bull roared. "Reverend Marley made you a fair wager, now accept it."

"No," Staring Otter said in the confident tone of one who knows he has the advantage.

Charley raised his hand to silence The Bull and said, "Done."

I could stand it no longer. I ran from behind our house to Charley's side and grabbed his arm. "I don't want you to leave because of me," I cried.

"Get away from him," Staring Otter said, but my mother stepped from the audience and stood between us, glaring at her husband. When he opened his mouth, she cursed him, but no one laughed.

Charley put his arm around my shoulder and led me away from the people. "It's all right," he said softly. "Perhaps it's better that I leave here. I have accomplished much in the way of teaching, if little in the way of preaching. Perhaps I need to sow on more fertile soil—if there is any in the Cherokee Nation."

"But why would you do this for me?" I asked. "And six days isn't much. Strong Hickory has been studying for months, and he has learned very little."

Charley chuckled and said, "Strong Hickory doesn't know the meaning of the word study. You and Strong Hickory are as different as a bear and a bird. I have never seen anyone else as consumed with the need to learn as you are. If we both work hard you can acquire at least a grounding in Sequoyah's syllabary in six days. I'm convinced that once that seed is planted they can't kill it, and some day, perhaps when you're grown, you can nourish it, and it will grow. I told your father six days because I thought that was the most he might agree to. In fact, I doubted he would agree to anything, but I'm glad he did. Now let's go back—I've got to prepare myself for a Ball Play."

And he did prepare himself. Charley ran—loped—for miles each day, increasing his endurance. At first the villagers laughed—Staring Otter more shrilly than anyone else—but, one by one, the other players began to fall in with Charley. No one in our settlement had ever trained seriously for Ball Play before, but now they were covering great distances at a steady pace, interspersing their daily excursions with short dashes at top speed. They stretched and lifted boulders, and their appearances changed as their muscles hardened and their bellies disappeared.

I wouldn't have thought it possible, but Charley became even more beautiful. It was as if a woodcarver had whittled away excesses that you hadn't realized were there to produce a perfect talisman. He was wonderful, and at times I wished old Hidden Snake, our village shaman, could speak an incantation that would add five more years to my ten, and the little girl would become a woman before Charley's astonished eyes. But at other times I simply wished that I were Charley's daughter, with all this brilliant, caring man had to offer a child.

The Bull was our village chief, which did not mean he was a ruler but that he was a respected man whose counsel frequently was considered sound. He met with the chief of Oothcaloga at New Town, and they decided on the rules of the Ball Play.

In some Ball Plays there were fifty, even more, to a side, but our village was small and it was decided there would be twelve men to a team, playing to twelve scores, over a field about two hundred yards long. The goals would be stakes set into the ground eight feet apart. The opposing chief knew of Charley Marley's great prowess and questioned whether he was a true resident of our village, but The Bull convinced him he was.

I had attended Ball Plays since I was in my cradleboard, and though I had never seen our team win one, I was thrilled by the speed and brutality and accompanying pageantry.

The game was simple. A player held a hickory stick in each hand. The stick was about two feet long, and the curve at the end was webbed with strips of raccoon or squirrel hide. A small, round ball stuffed with hair or deerskin and covered with deerskin and sewn with deer sinew was propelled by means of the sticks through the goal posts. As far as roughness, almost anything—except striking an opponent with a stick—was permissible. Broken bones were commonplace, and men had been killed during Ball Play.

Strong Hickory said his father told him that after the Choctaw men completed their game, the women played. I wished I were a Choctaw.

For seven days no player touched a woman. Rock Climber's wife was pregnant, and therefore he could not play, for some of his strength was being transferred to the child. No one ate rabbit, for the rabbit panics in a desperate situation. No one ate frog, for its bones are brittle. No one ate the flesh of any weak or sluggish animal. No one ate greens with stalks that are easily broken. They ate the flesh of animals renowned for speed and courage. The raccoon was a favorite, for though small it was ferocious and smart.

"Do you believe all this helps?" I asked Charley Marley one day.

He laughed. "If the others saw me eating frog legs it would certainly hurt," he said.

It was the day before the game, and he was carving grooves into the handle of a Ball Play stick to improve his grip. He looked around him, saw no one else was watching and offered the stick. "Here," he said. "You can look at it."

I stepped back. No Cherokee would allow a female to touch and thereby weaken his stick on the day before a game. But he laughed and extended it, and I took it and used it to toss an imaginary ball. When I handed it back to Charley he whacked it across his palm and said, "See, it's as strong as ever. I'll probably even play better when I think of my friend having touched it."

Oh I loved him. That night when I knew the Ball Play dance was being performed in a nearby field, I lay in my bed and pictured Charley swaying, for the ballplayers themselves were the male dancers in this ritual. They circled a fire, chanting to the rattle of a gourd filled with pebbles. There were replacements for the female dancers during the performance, but the players danced all night long, except for a few times when old Hidden Snake, the shaman, led them to the river where he offered his prayers for their success. I imagined I could hear the sounds made by the single stick of the drummer as it struck the drumhead of stretched groundhog skin, but I don't believe I really could.

I was up before daylight, engulfed in excitement, barely able to swallow the corn mush that my grandmother prepared. I twisted my shirt impatiently until

Staring Otter slung himself onto his horse, signifying that the trip of a few miles to New Town was about to begin. Mother and I walked, though in actuality I frequently was dashing ahead of the procession that included several other families.

Staring Otter had stopped attending Ball Plays, but he was excited about this one because he believed that when it was over he would be rid of Charley Marley. He explained to me that old Hidden Snake was at this moment probably leading the players to water, advising them to sit and rest but not to lean against a tree or a person. He was pleading with them to play well, assuring them that all his magic powers would be directed against the opponents. The players were replying gratefully by yelping like dogs.

"Soon he will be scratching them," Staring Otter said, and he laughed when I folded my arms across my chest in terror.

Using an instrument that featured seven sharpened splinters of turkey quills, Hidden Snake would rake their arms and legs and chests and backs, making almost three hundred bloody scratches on each player. No one flinched or made a sound. Some, to increase the flow of blood, would scrape their wounds with stones.

Then they would plunge into the river and emerge dripping with cold water and impatience. They marked their bodies with paint and with charcoal from a tree that had been struck by lightning but not killed. Their skins were rubbed with chewed bark of a slippery elm so their opponents could get no grasp.

Once again Hidden Snake took the players to the water, and there he prayed to the river—the Long Man—that his team might be as strong as the rushing waters. He prayed to the Red Bat and the Red Deer and the Red Hawk and the Red Rattlesnake to impart their nimbleness, speed, sight and fearsomeness to the players of our village. He prayed for each man individually by name, and he cursed the opponents, calling the names of their better players.

We were among the first spectators to arrive, and we staked out places near the center of the field. Soon hundreds of men, women and children joined us. Wagering became rampant. A man beside me offered the Negro slave who accompanied him against a quantity of swine. Another recognized Staring Otter and said he would bet a horse against one of his fine bows, but my father declined, explaining that he, too, was for the team from Oothcaloga. I was embarrassed by his traitorous pronouncement, and I left his side to stand between Mother and Sweet Melon.

But my attention was diverted to shouts in the forest, and then our players popped out from among the trees, yelling and waving their sticks. They wore only breechcloths. I easily picked out Charley, for he was the tallest, the most handsome. I grimaced at the thought of the scratches, and I knew that Charley, the Christian minister, wasn't comfortable with our shaman praying to the river and the Red Rattlesnake or even praying for victory, for he had told me so. But I could see the excitement in his eyes, and though he seemed to be looking directly at me when I waved and yelled, he did not see me.

An old man moved to the center of the field where he was surrounded by the players. He delivered a brief harangue and tossed the ball into the air so that it fell into their midst. There were yells and grunts and the clack of sticks hitting sticks, and the game was under way.

An Oothcaloga player snatched up the ball with his stick and dashed toward the goal on our end of the field. Charley ran him down, lowered his shoulder and planted it in the small of the man's back. The Oothcalogan crumpled and dropped his stick and the ball. The Bull recovered it and sped toward the other end of the field, but he, too, was rebuffed.

Hidden Snake and the Oothcalogan medicine man moved among the players, willing the ball toward the appropriate goals, our spectators cheering when our old shaman deftly dodged an oncoming pack. He carried a hand mirror he had acquired from a white trader, and he used it to direct the rays of the sun, the source of life and power, onto our players' naked backs.

I felt hands on my shoulders and turned to see a young man standing on his tiptoes, straining to see past the spectators who leaned this way and that with every move of the ball. He was an Indian, but he wore the dress pants and coat of a white man. I had never seen him before, and I knew he wasn't from our village, but he cheered for Charley Marley, shouting his name.

This Cherokee who was attired as stiffly as a Puritan minister and yelling lustily at Ball Play was a curious sight, and I couldn't take my eyes off him. I began to laugh, and he grinned and scrubbed my head with his knuckles. Immediately we began trying to outshout each other in praise of Charley Marley.

Finally, when our throats became too weak to respond, he asked, "Who might you be, little big lungs?"

"I'm Nancy Swimmer," I said. "I'm a friend of Reverend Marley. Who are you?"

Mother scolded me for being impertinent, but the man said, "It's all right. My name is Elias Boudinot. I've known Charley for years. We were at the Foreign Mission School in Cornwall, Connecticut, together. You've heard of it?"

"Yes, Reverend Marley told me about it. I wish I could go to school."

His easy laughter contrasted with wistful, serious eyes. "Well, there's no reason you couldn't go to...," he began, but a voice that came from behind us interrupted:

"What in the hell are you supposed to be? Goddamn if you Cherokees ain't a piece of work."

We turned, and I recognized Lorenzo Cadwallader.

"Are you speaking to me, sir?" Elias Boudinot asked, but the man waved his hand dismissively and turned his eyes on me.

"You a pretty thing," he said. "What's your name?"

I swallowed hard. "Nancy Swimmer."

He surveyed me from headband to bare toes and grinned. "I'm Cadwallader," he said.

"I know," I blurted in a breaking voice, and he laughed like a yelping coyote.

"Yeah, I guess everybody knows me, don't they? See y'all later." And he walked away, making a point of glancing back at my skinny legs and grinning.

Lorenzo Cadwallader was a white Georgian of about fifty. Everybody did know him, or, rather, recognize him. He wore filthy homespun clothes and a shapeless leather hat, and a rifle was slung across his shoulder. His eyes and nose existed in a long, heavy, graying beard that concealed his mouth. He smelled like a rotting carcass.

He called himself a blacksmith, but mostly he was a troublemaker, a dispenser of homemade whiskey, a brawler, a thief who would steal anything from a bead to a horse. Some said he was a rapist and a murderer. He had been scalped by the Creeks and survived the ordeal, and when he was drunk he would remove his hat and yelp with laughter as everyone recoiled at the sight of the purple scar that covered the top of his hairless head.

With permission of the Indians or of the Indian agent, a white man could live in the Cherokee Nation. The Cherokees would never have allowed Lorenzo Cadwallader to live among them, but he had influence with the agent for some unknown reason, and so here he was, like a smallpox sore.

I couldn't have known that day that within a space of minutes I would meet two men who would change the path of my life, the brilliant Elias Boudinot and the repulsive Lorenzo Cadwallader.

I was watching Cadwallader walk away when those on the other side of the field mounted a cheer. I turned to see an Oothcalogan, ball in stick, breaking away from his pursuers, speeding toward the goal and, finally, all alone, casually tossing the ball through the posts. The scorekeeper drove the first peg into the ground.

Staring Otter, who had been watching with some friends, joined Mother and me. He glanced disapprovingly at Elias Boudinot, the Indian dressed as a white man, and put his arm around my shoulder, almost imperceptibly drawing me from the stranger.

Oothcaloga scored again. And again. "Three to none," Staring Otter said. "Another defeat for our players." He suppressed the smile that our neighbors knew was in his heart, but Sweet Melon glared at him.

But when an Oothcalogan had an opportunity to pop out of the herd and score, the player's legs buckled, and the ball fell from his stick. "They're getting tired," Elias Boudinot whispered to me. "Your team is stronger in this heat."

He was right. The Oothcalogans were superior ball players, but our men were in superior condition, thanks to Charley's regimen. Charley made three goals, and the score was tied.

At that point I think Staring Otter knew his favorites, the Oothcalogans, were beaten. "This crutch is breaking my arm," he said, and he hobbled to the shade of a nearby oak, sat in the dust and rested his back against the tree, his eyes closed.

The score had reached eleven to five, our favor, when Charley, stalwart and fresh, trotted without pursuit to the goal and scored the winning twelfth point.

The supporters of the teams strode onto the field. Congratulations were exchanged. Bets were settled. A Cherokee master told a Negro slave that he now belonged to one of my neighbors, who in turn blurted out that he really had no need of a slave, and he'd just take a pig or two instead. The Bull won a handsome bay horse. Fights erupted and just as quickly ended. Old Hidden Snake grinned toothlessly as he was acclaimed a shaman of powerful medicine. Our people slapped Charley Marley on his naked back, for he had scored nine of our twelve goals.

I raced to Charley's side, and he kissed me atop my head and whispered, "We'll begin our studying tomorrow."

He and Elias Boudinot clasped hands and called each other old friend. Charley told him I was his smartest pupil. "We've met," Elias Boudinot said. "I can see that she would be."

Charley was covered with sweat and dirt and blood. Bruises were turning his arms and legs and back black, and there was a deep cut across his cheek that surely would leave a scar. But he was flushed with victory, and he waited to accept the plaudits of the last person before he plunged into the cold waters of the creek that gurgled past New Town.

A neighbor helped Staring Otter onto his horse, and we began the trek home, Mother and I walking at his side. We chattered about the game, but Staring Otter was silent until she produced a necklace she had won on a bet with a cousin from Oothcaloga.

"You won a trinket, and the magician won a Ball Play," he said, "but he lost the right to live in our village. He has Nancy Swimmer for six days, but I doubt he can do much damage in that time. And then we'll be rid of him forever. So I think I was the real winner. I would have been the winner no matter how the game turned out."

I was tired and hot and gritty with the dust that blew up from the road, and for a moment I felt pity for this miserable, intractable man. But I knew pity was a luxury I couldn't afford at the moment, and I vowed it was I who would be the winner.

CHAPTER 6

I went to bed early, determined to be fresh the next morning, but the sounds and sights of the Ball Play and the anticipation of studying at the feet of Charley Marley chased through my mind like spooked rabbits. I grew frantic and tried to will sleep, but it wouldn't come.

Finally, after midnight, I got out of bed and went outside and walked in the light of a moon that was nearly full. There was silence except for the sounds of the creatures in the forest and the roar of The Bull's snoring, and I became relaxed. When I returned to our cabin I slept without dreams.

I had asked Mother to wake me at the first daylight, and she did. She whispered, but Staring Otter grunted and turned toward the wall. In the next room, my grandmother, who always said a miserable night was one of the prices you pay to grow old, stared at the ceiling, wide awake.

I was tired, almost aching, from missing sleep, but I bolted to the door and gazed at Charley Marley's cabin. I saw shadows moving in the lanternlight, and the thrill washed away my weariness.

Plum got up, mumbling to herself, and made corn mush. I ran to the river, dived into a deep hole the men had created with a half-dam, and felt my past wash away. I knew that, in a sense, my life was beginning that day.

I put on my best outfit, a yellow calico dress Mother had gotten from a white trader, barely ate, and said goodbye. Staring Otter was awake, but he didn't turn from the wall. Mother—caught in the middle between daughter and husband—whispered well wishes and shooed me out the door.

I ran through the dust and the dew to Charley Marley's house. I rapped on the door, it swung open, and he smiled as I presented myself as a candidate for an education. "What a beautiful dress," he said. "What a beautiful student."

Even through the bruises and scratches and cuts and a black eye, Charley was gorgeous. He was as tall as a tree. His face reflected authority but also gentleness. His teeth were white and straight. Thank goodness he hadn't lost any teeth in the Ball Play, as so many did.

We would begin the day with prayer, he said. We got on our knees, closed our eyes, and raised our faces to the ceiling. The Reverend Marley asked his God to bless this undertaking of trying to cram so much knowledge into a little Cherokee girl's head in so short a time. He thanked his God for the bounty of his life. He asked God to guide me through my life, to give me prosperity and make me a worthy servant.

I waited for a reply from the sky, a ghostly hand on my shoulder, a sack of gold to appear on the floor. But nothing happened, and I opened my eyes. Charley said, "Amen and amen, and now let's get started on our lessons." I hoped so abrupt a dismissal wouldn't offend his God, but Charley didn't seem worried.

We sat facing each other in handsome, curvy chairs that Charley had made from willow limbs. Crisp morning light from a window fell across the copies of Sequoyah's syllabary on our laps. Charley pointed to the first of the eighty-six symbols, and my great learning experience began.

Hours passed as if they were minutes, and we reached early afternoon. By then my head began to hurt, my shoulders ache, and my concentration waned. Right at that time, Charley said, "That's enough for today." I was disappointed, but he added, "The mind is like a cloth used to wipe up a spill. It can absorb only so much at a time. It has to dry out."

Charley spoke another prayer and dismissed me. With a copy of the syllabary in hand, I stepped into the blinding sunlight, and I knew what he meant. I was weary, my brain fogged. I couldn't remember the last syllable we had studied.

Staring Otter didn't speak or even look at me that evening, and Mother was reluctant to discuss my lessons in his presence. I didn't care. I'd learn the syllabary, or as much as humanly possible, without their help or support. I had Charley Marley.

Fatigued from staying awake the night before and from intense study, I went to sleep early. But in the night my mind reeled with images of ball players killing other ball players with lances as a huge bear lumbered down the field with ball in stick—of the Oostanaula surging over our village and drowning us all—of Elias Boudinot appearing in the sky and introducing himself as Charley's God. Nausea seized me, and I didn't know whether it was a dream or real, but at once I knew, and I was on my feet, bolting for the door. I didn't make it; I vomited on the floor with a great yelling eruption that instantly raised my father and mother and grandmother to their feet and sent Rain reaching for the lamp.

I told myself I was merely excited from working with Charley, and that I had upset my stomach, but I knew better. I had suffered the same symptoms a couple of years before—nausea, stomach cramps, muscles that ached as if they had been pounded. It had passed in a few days.

The nausea subsided, and I breathed heavily. "I'm all right," I told Mother, but I didn't get back to my bed before I felt the wave returning. This time I reached the yard before I vomited. The sound brought several curious neighbors from their houses.

I returned to bed, but sleep came and went, came and went, like the wind on a roiling summer afternoon. I vomited twice more, and the second time there was nothing left to come up. Finally, worn out, I slept peacefully.

I awoke to find Charley Marley standing over my bed beside Mother. Staring Otter sat on a chair in the corner. "She's a sick little girl," I heard Mother say. "Last time, several people in the village were ill. I hope that won't happen this time."

I smiled wanly, and Charley touched the back of his hand to my forehead. "She's very hot," he said.

"Am I going to die?" I asked. I remembered the story of smallpox killing half the Cherokees. "Do I have smallpox?"

Mother sat on the bed beside me and hugged me. "No, you aren't going to die. You don't have smallpox. You will be running and playing before you know it."

"We'll have to postpone our lessons for a few days," Charley told me. "Then we'll take up where we left off."

Staring Otter forced himself to his feet. "No!" he said. "We agreed that you had six days. This is the second one. Tomorrow will be the third one."

"But she's too sick to continue," Charley protested.

"Then don't continue," Staring Otter said.

Charley was speechless. He glanced from Staring Otter to Mother to me, found no answer in our faces, and stormed from our house.

I felt thoroughly defeated. No spunky perseverance formed in my thoughts or on my lips. I knew that Staring Otter finally had won. Charley Marley would not teach me to read and write.

Staring Otter said he wouldn't be surprised to learn that old Hidden Snake, the medicine man, had made me ill to prevent my studying. Hidden Snake knew best in all matters. I had seen his power at work at the Ball Play, hadn't I? After all, he could fly like a bird and burrow under the ground like a mole, so he surely could make a little girl sick, especially if it were in her best interest.

I was too exhausted to hate my father or to pity him, to ask him why Hidden Snake's tremendous powers had never worked at the Ball Play before Charley joined the team, why no one had ever actually seen him fly like a bird or burrow like a mole. I was an empty vessel.

For three days I lay in my bed, as lifeless as a cornhusk doll. I didn't eat. I wouldn't speak to Staring Otter or even look at him. "How are you, Nancy?" he would ask, but I would gaze at the ceiling.

I awoke on the fifth day feeling much better. I ate a bowl of light turtle stew and kept it down. Only that day remained of our six, Charley's and mine. Perhaps I could study that afternoon, I thought, simply as one last affront to my father, but I knew I really didn't feel that well.

I walked outside and stood in the morning light, shaky, propped in the V formed by the meeting of the logs of two walls of our cabin. There was no sign of life in the village.

"Where is everyone?" I asked Mother.

"They went fishing in a pool upriver. They are going to play games and cook fish. The entire village is having an outing. Your grandmother went."

"I'm sorry you couldn't go," I said.

"I don't mind," she answered. "Some day you'll have children, and you'll understand. Besides, your father probably wouldn't have gone. And even if he had, he would have made everyone else miserable."

Staring Otter heard our voices and hobbled from behind the house where he had been making a bow. "You are better?" he asked brightly. I couldn't bring myself to answer him. I nodded.

We heard the approaching shuffle of two mules. Into the clearing appeared tired, plodding animals, and riding bareback were Lorenzo Cadwallader and a black slave.

They stopped, and Cadwallader smiled at us and sang in a raspy voice a ditty that was making the rounds among Georgians: "All I want in this creation is a pretty little wife and a big plantation, way up yonder in the Cherokee Nation."

Thonged to his mule's neck was a rifle, and strapped to the rider's leg was a sheath that contained a huge knife. I felt as helpless as a fish in a barrel.

Cadwallader looked about him and saw the village was unoccupied. "Where is everybody?" he asked.

"Just there in the forest," Staring Otter said.

"Odd, I don't hear no sounds coming from the forest," Cadwallader said. "Uh uh. Looks like y'all the only ones here."

A half-dozen iron pots, connected with thongs, hung on either side of his mule's flanks. "I came to do some trading," he said. "But don't look like there's nobody to trade with except just one family."

He grinned at me, each of his front teeth either missing or rotten. "I'll still trade, though. I'll trade you a nice pot for that little girl."

Mother put her arm around my shoulders and drew me to her.

"How about it?" Cadwallader said.

"Come back another day," Staring Otter said. "The Bull was saying yesterday he has furs to trade."

Cadwallader glanced toward The Bull's cabin. "That's his'n, ain't it? I reckon the furs are in there. And The Bull ain't. Ain't nobody in this whole village but a little girl and her maw and a old crippled Indian who obviously ain't really her paw. Seems to me it would be mighty easy to leave here with a little girl and a bunch of furs and God knows what else and keep my pots, too."

The crooked smile vanished from his face, and he snatched up his rifle and pointed it at us. "Ain't no need for nobody to get hurt," he said. "But it don't really make a damn with me if they do. Any way y'all want it. Let's take a peek inside that lean-to behind The Bull's cabin. You lead the way, little girl—Nancy, ain't it? Hell, you'd make me a good little wife. Like the song says, a pretty little wife and a big plantation, when the timid government finally gets around to running the savages out of Georgia. I'll make them let me keep you."

I don't know where I got the courage to say it, but I did. "This isn't Georgia. This is the Cherokee Nation. And we aren't savages." Mother gripped my shoulder and whispered for me to shut up.

Cadwallader responded with that same yelping laugh I had heard at the Ball Play. "Damn, I like that," he said. "I like my women with some fire."

He prodded Mother with his rifle, and we walked to the lean-to at the back of The Bull's cabin, my legs weak and shaky, Staring Otter hobbling on his crutch, Mother trembling with fear. Cadwallader dismounted and motioned for Mother to open the door. Inside, stacked neatly, were many beaver and otter pelts.

Cadwallader pulled the knife from the sheath on his leg. "I'll trade The Bull a couple of scalps for all this," he said. "Hide for hide, you might say. Y'all know I can't really let you live to send a bunch of Indians after me and my little bride-to-be. You come here, Maw."

Mother recoiled, but he pointed the rifle at Staring Otter. "Come here or I'll blast his brains into Alabama."

The concussion struck my ears like fists, and I waited for my father to fall—but it was Cadwalader who dropped his rifle, grabbed his temples with both hands, took two steps forward and crumpled at our feet. He spun on his back, and I saw that the creature whose jerking hand reached toward me had only half a face. His last breath escaped, and he didn't move again.

Charley stepped from beside The Bull's cabin, smoking rifle in hand. He had shot Lorenzo Cadwallader through the back of the head.

The minister stared at the body that lay at his feet, blood seeping into the dirt. "Please forgive me, Lord, for killing one of your children," he whispered, "but I had no choice." With the back of his hand he wiped tears from his cheeks.

I ran to Charley's side. "He wasn't a child," I said. "And you didn't have a choice."

Mother was breathing with difficulty, and she sat in the dust, her back turned to Cadwallader's body, until she could regain some composure. Then she went to Charley and took his hand and said, "You did what you had to do. He would have killed us and done no telling what to Nancy. I thank you."

Cadwallader's mule had bolted at the sound of the shot, but now it was sniffing at the corpse of its rider. The black slave had held his mule steady. Obviously he had decided his chances were more favorable if he kept his place rather than try to escape and perhaps be shot, too. From the animal's back, he stared at Charley, silent, unmoving.

Charley tied the reins of Cadwallader's mule to a bush and told the slave to remain where he was, that he wouldn't hurt him. "I'll have to bury the body," he said. "There would be big trouble if the Georgians knew about this." He dragged the remains of Lorenzo Cadwallader into his cabin, got a shovel and disappeared into the woods, the slave following him.

Staring Otter hadn't spoken. Finally, with his crutch he pushed himself toward home.

Two hours later Charley and the slave returned. They draped Cadwallader's stiffening body over his mule and led the animal into the forest. I heard another shot, and I knew that some friend of Cadwallader had shot Charley, and I bolted into the woods, screaming Charley's name, Rain running behind me, yelling for me to stop.

Charley called, and I followed the sound of his voice, and I saw him standing in a clearing, beside a huge pile of dirt and a wide grave in which Cadwallader's mule groaned and jerked its legs. Charley was drenched with sweat, muddy, breathing hard.

"Are you all right?" I screamed.

Charley managed the faintest of smiles. "Yes, I'm all right," he said. "I shot his mule, too. I'm going to bury mule, pots, rifle, and man. I don't want to leave any evidence."

Charley's lips quivered, and he gazed over the treetops. "God forgive me, I thought about shooting the slave, too. But I told him to go and forget he was here. He said he hated Cadwallader, that he was glad he was dead."

Mother begged me to return with her, but I took my seat on the ground against a tall pine and said I was going to stay with Charley.

"You should go home," he said. "This is no sight for a child."

But I insisted on staying—and I did.

Charley had led the mule to the graveside and shot it. It toppled into the hole, which was about five feet deep, but he had to tug at it and even break two of its legs to make it fit. I would have simply rolled Cadwallader's body into the grave, but Charley placed it carefully beside the mule, crossed its hands on its chest, covered it with a blanket, and said a prayer. Then he shoveled the dirt and spread pine straw over the scarred earth, and there was little evidence of the ill-fated visitation of Lorenzo Cadwallader.

The excitement was over, and when I got up my wobbly legs reminded me I had been sick. I wished Charley would carry me back to the village, but he was worn out. So I walked at his side, having to stop and rest only once.

The village was still deserted. Charley said he was going to bathe in the river, and he would talk to me when he got back.

Behind my house, Staring Otter trimmed a piece of locust for a bow. I stood before him, close enough to touch him, but he wouldn't look up. Finally, when I turned to leave, he said, "I'm happy you weren't harmed. I'm happy you are feeling better." That was all. I didn't answer.

Inside the cabin, Mother sat on the side of my bed and wept, rubbing her hand across the indentation left by my body in the cornhusk mattress. "The whites hate us so," she said. "You are my most precious possession, but even your birth was the result of a white man's hate."

We embraced, and our tears mixed on our cheeks. Mother wet a cloth from a bowl of rainwater and wiped my face and my brow as I lay on the bed. She then stroked my long black hair. The familiar touch and the familiar smell of my mother and the familiar sound of the husks comforted me, and I slept. So did Rain, lying on her side, holding me on her lap as if I were a baby.

We leaped simultaneously when we heard a cough, and there in the doorway stood Charley. He was bathed and fresh and wearing white homespun pants and shirt he had acquired from a trader. "I came to be sure everyone is all right," he said.

"Everyone is," Mother said, "because you rescued us. I wondered, did your God appear to you and tell you to kill that man?"

Charley looked down at his moccasins. "He didn't appear," he said. "He didn't tell me in words that I heard with my ears. But perhaps he did tell me. I don't know. I would like to think that he did, for I had never killed anyone, and I hope I never do again. I know I did the right thing, but it would be a comfort to think God directed my hand."

Mother nodded. "We do not hear everything with our ears, do we? Once when Nancy was a baby she was playing in the clearing in front of our house, and I was cooking. Suddenly, I knew there was danger. I rushed outside and snatched her up and brought her inside. I had barely closed the door when a panther ran through the village, chasing a fawn. Could that have been the Great Spirit warning me?"

"Perhaps," Charley answered. "We are told God works in mysterious ways. That was mysterious. Why couldn't it have been?"

"Are your God and the Great Spirit the same?" Mother asked.

"There is one God," Charley said. "He is our God, and he is a Great Spirit."

Mother nodded, pleased. "The Cherokees don't think of the Great Spirit as a personal God," she said, "but Sweet Melon has attended your services, and she says you speak to him as if he were a helpmeet in this very room with you. That must be comforting."

Charley took my hand and gazed into my eyes. "I'm sorry, Rain, that I can't stay and tell you and Nancy about my God—our God, the Great Spirit. I'm sorry I can't stay and teach her to read and write. Education is the best hope of the Cherokees—the only hope, I believe. But I'll be leaving the village. I want to say goodbye."

I couldn't say goodbye. I threw myself onto my bed, buried my face in the bedclothes, and sobbed.

I heard the clop of Staring Otter's crutch on the board floor as he entered the cabin. "I was telling your family goodbye," Charley said. "Goodbye to you, too. Good luck."

"Sit," Staring Otter said, and I raised my head to see him tap a chair leg with his crutch. Charley obeyed, and they faced each other across the table where we ate our meals.

Staring Otter looked at Charley's homespun garb, smiled sardonically, and said, "White man's clothes."

Charley shook his head at the impossibility of the man and started getting up, but Staring Otter swept his crutch over the table and nudged him back into his seat.

"You saved my life," he said. "You saved the life of my wife and of my daughter. I will give you anything I have—my livestock, my bows, my house. It is only right. Name it."

"Anything?" Charley asked.

"It is only right," Staring Otter repeated.

"You know what I will ask," Charley said.

"I do. And it kills me. But ask it."

"I want to remain in the village and teach Nancy. I want to teach her to read and write in Cherokee and in English and to teach her about the world and about the Christian faith."

"Then stay, you chicken snake," my father said.

>>>→ • ←《《

CHAPTER 7

~~~~~~~~~~~~~~~~

Harriet Gold Boudinot could tell you about persecution—indeed, persecution from within one's own family.

Her brother burned her in effigy. Her father, a deacon, forbade her marriage. A brother-in-law, a minister, told her she was opening afresh the wounds of Jesus and compared her to Cain and Judas. Another brother-in-law accused her of having "animal feelings."

Members of the church choir in which she sang tied bands of black crepe around their arms to show their disapproval. A Christian school denounced her as "criminal."

Her crime? She was a white woman who wanted to marry an Indian and become a missionary to the Cherokees.

And—in the face of opposition distinguished by numbers as well as intensity—she did. On March 28, 1826, she was wed to Elias Boudinot, the spectator I had met at the Ball Play less than a year before the wedding, the Cherokee in white man's clothes, the Indian whom Lorenzo Cadwallader had insulted.

Now it was February of 1828, and Harriet and I sat in straight chairs on the porch of their two-storied frame house at New Echota and gazed at the purple and gold of the sunset reflected in the pool of the community spring and talked, woman to woman—or woman to girl; Harriet was twenty-two, and I was thirteen.

I worshiped her. She was a Puritan mystic. She believed that God and the saving power of Christ were as real as the trees on the slope that faced us to the south. To her, this world was but a waystation on the road to her true destination.

In my nobler moments I wanted to be like her, and there were times when I felt transformed, almost ethereal. But then Strong Hickory would make me angry and I'd scream at him, or I'd boil with impatience because I couldn't understand the wording in the Bible, or I'd hate my father, or I'd think sexual thoughts, or I'd just plain question whether there even was a God.

Then she would pat me on the knee and smile her understanding smile, as if I were a younger sister, and reassure me by reciting an apt passage from the Bible and—at least while I was in her presence—I would be calm again.

She was sweeping her front porch the first time I laid eyes on her. She saw me staring and smiled and crooked her finger. I joined her, and she was delighted I could speak English. We drank sassafras tea, and I bombarded her with questions about Connecticut, her former home, and we became fast friends.

With the grudging permission of Staring Otter, I had learned the Cherokee syllabary and the English language. I read everything Charley Marley could procure—newspapers from Philadelphia and Augusta, the Bible, English novels, broadsides. Tears came to my eyes when I gazed upon the pages of the translation of the New Testament into Cherokee by David Brown, a Cherokee preacher and former classmate of Charley and Elias at the Foreign Mission School in Cornwall, Connecticut. But what I longed most to read was still a few days from print. It was *The Cherokee Phoenix*, the first Indian newspaper, and Elias was the editor.

New Echota was a few miles from our village, and I visited the town almost daily, caught up in the excitement of what was going on there. It was the Cherokee capital, the center of the civilizing process the whites had been urging upon us since 1791, when George Washington was president.

Over the years the Cherokees had discarded the traditional clan system of ruling a tribe and created a republican government patterned after the Americans'. The Cherokee Nation was divided into eight judicial districts with a judge, marshal, and local council applying the law in each. A legislature was created, and like that of the U.S., it was made up of an upper and lower house. We formed a supreme court—twenty years before Georgia did, incidentally. We adopted a constitution.

In 1825 the legislature provided for establishment of a capital that centered around the council house site in New Town. The village would be called New Echota in honor of Chota, a beloved old Cherokee town.

In 1826 surveyors divided the new capital into a series of streets and one hundred one-acre lots. The main street was New Town Road, a principal north-south passage through the Cherokee Nation. There was a two-acre town square.

Once Major Ridge, the speaker of the council and the man who had recruited Staring Otter to fight Creeks, rode by the Boudinots' place where Harriet and I were working in the garden and said New Echota reminded him of Baltimore.

We smiled and noncommittally said he and the other leaders had planned the town well, but when he left we clasped each other's shoulders and snickered, for New Echota was certainly no Baltimore. A new council house and supreme court building were the largest structures. There were four stores, three of which weren't open except during sessions of the council. There were a few houses. New Echota was a mere village of perhaps fifty permanent residents, with the population swelling to about three hundred during court and legislative activities.

Yet, for me New Echota was exciting and alive. It wasn't so much what it was as what it represented. Charley Marley had told his pupils the Cherokees' best chance of survival against the land-hungry Americans was in imitating their civilization. It was one thing to take the land of near-naked men who believed the mountains were created by a buzzard, something else to evict men who dressed like the whites, talked like the whites, did business like the whites, worshiped like the whites. In other words, civilized men.

And if New Echota wasn't civilization, I thought, what was? It was the capital of an Indian nation that was advancing into civilization with incredible rapidity, a nation that had turned from the hunt to agriculture, a nation that butchered hogs and beef cattle instead of singing the scalp-dance song, a nation that hummed to the sound of the loom and the spinning wheel, a nation that composed its own alphabet, a nation that was about to print its own newspaper.

But a sword hung over the Cherokees, a dangling blade that was written into a document called the Compact of 1802.

That year Georgia ceded its western claims—which became Alabama and Mississippi—to the United States. Part of the payment was a U.S. guarantee to extinguish, in Georgia's favor, Indian title to all land within the state's boundaries. The land would be "peaceably obtained, upon reasonable terms."

The Cherokee Nation included parts of Georgia, Alabama, Tennessee and North Carolina, but half of the Eastern Cherokees—including us—lived within the borders of Georgia. Most of the rich Cherokee plantations were there.

Georgia's impatience increased over the years. If the U.S. wasn't going to remove the Indians, the state growled, it would have to do the job itself. Georgia seethed when, in 1822, the Cherokee Nation told the U.S. it would never cede another foot of land. Maybe the doom of the Cherokees was already sealed, I don't know, but if it wasn't, that sealed it.

Damned impertinent Indians. Forming their own legislature and courts and even drafting a constitution. Declaring national sovereignty within the borders of Georgia. Acting like they're by-God white folks. And vowing they weren't going to cede any more land.

Why, the Cherokees had always ceded land. They had ceded land because the whites had moved in and the federal government said there were too many whites to evict, and the Indians decided they might as well get paid for the ground and hope the encroachment ended there; they had ceded land for money; they had ceded land because certain chiefs had been bribed. The Cherokee Nation had shrunk like a cheap shirt. And now they were saying they would cede no more land.

But I was young, and I could easily dismiss politics from my mind—even the politics of the destruction of the Cherokee Nation. I could forget Georgy, as most of the whites called it, and dream of myself dressed in Harriet Boudinot's pretty clothes and married to an Indian who not only could write, but who always dressed as a white man and who was the editor of a newspaper. I begged Harriet to tell again and again the dramatic story of their romance, a story that made me cry and my shoulders tingle, and usually when her protests and sighs had ended, she would tell it.

The story began with the love of a Cherokee man and a white woman—but they weren't Elias and Harriet.

John Ridge, the son of Major Ridge, the progressive Cherokee planter and statesman, was a student at the Foreign Mission School in Cornwall, Connecticut. Among his schoolmates were Charley Marley and John's cousin Elias Boudinot.

Cornwall was an agricultural village. It was traditional in New England that the houses were built around a green, and so it was at Cornwall. Harriet would close her eyes and picture the green when she would tell me about Cornwall. I would watch her swallow against the twinge of homesickness that the image called up.

Beside the common was an unimposing building that housed the school, which had opened in 1817, the year before John, Charley and Elias were enrolled. Foreigners, Indians of various tribes and American boys studied and lived together at the school, which was a visible testimony to the Puritans' missionary zeal and, supposedly, the brotherhood of man. They got up at 6 a.m. and embarked on a day that included Bible reading, devotions, prayer, physical labor and the study of such subjects as geography, rhetoric, history and the classics.

While he was at Cornwall, John Ridge fell in love with Sarah Northrup, daughter of the steward of the school, and their love didn't wane when John returned home. In January of 1824 they were married, and John took his bride to Cherokee country.

But there was an uproar at Cornwall. A newspaper attacked the mixed marriage and the school and stirred the embers of racial hatred. The embattled managers of the school timidly fell in line and said their Christian brethren should be concerned only with the souls of the heathen and forbade further mixed marriages.

Near the green in Cornwall stood the home of Benjamin Gold, a prominent man, a deacon, an agent of the Foreign Mission School. In the autumn of 1824, his daughter Harriet stunned her parents by asking their permission to marry Elias Boudinot.

She had maintained a correspondence with him after he had left Cornwall two years before. They remembered Elias, for he had visited in their home. They knew that he had joined the First Congregational Church, but the notion of their daughter—the granddaughter of a Congregationalist minister, the niece of two Yale men, the sister-in-law of two clergymen and a general—marrying an Indian and going to live with him in the Cherokee Nation was too much. No. Absolutely not. It was unthinkable.

She wanted to be a missionary to the Cherokees, she explained, and there could be no better opportunity than marrying a Christian Cherokee who also wanted to bring the true faith to his people.

They refused permission and Harriet became ill, so ill that a doctor feared she would die. Her parents realized she had lost the will to live, and they were overcome with the terrifying notion they were fighting against God. Finally, they said she could marry Elias Boudinot.

They knew there would be repercussions and they fretted. They waited until Harriet had recovered to announce the impending marriage.

And there were repercussions—nasty ones. The agents of the school published their disapproval—calling anyone who condoned the arrangement a criminal.

Harriet hid in a neighbor's home and from a window watched a mob burn her in effigy—her brother Stephen setting the fire, Stephen who had raged that he would kill Boudinot. A church bell tolled, as if her soul were departing.

But Harriet was staunch. She took her solace from the words in her testament: "Blessed are ye, when men shall revile you, and persecute you, and say all manner of evil against you falsely, for my sake. Rejoice and be exceeding glad: for great is your reward in heaven: for so persecuted they the prophets which were before you."

Even a heathen wouldn't burn his sister in effigy, she thought.

Other family members pleaded with Harriet, but to no avail. Harriet Gold and Elias Boudinot were married at the home of Benjamin Gold. Stephen, whose threats had been reduced to bitter grousing, worked at a sawmill during the ceremony.

Those who warned that the Foreign Mission School couldn't survive another mixed marriage were correct. In the autumn of 1826 it did, indeed, close its doors.

The twenty-one-year-old woman told her parents goodbye and left with her husband for the Cherokee Nation. She was strong-hearted, pure-hearted. "I cannot but rejoice in the prospect of spending my days among those despised people and, as the time draws near, I long to begin my work," she said. "I think I may reasonably expect many trials, hardships, and privations. May I never be disposed to seek my own ease any farther than is consistent with the greatest usefulness."

On December 1, 1826, after they had stayed a few months with his people, Elias Boudinot and Harriet Gold Boudinot arrived at a dilapidated missionary station called High Tower. Four years before, the station had been established by the American Board of Commissioners for Foreign Missions. The founder had been called to other duty, and the place had suffered.

But the Etowah River streamed past the mission's cabin, symbolizing to Harriet the flow of life, and from her window she could see the rich Conasauga Valley, which she knew would be green in the spring. She was happy. She was serving the people and the Lord.

Elias was happy, too. His family lived at nearby Oothcaloga, as did his childhood friends. In 1818 he had departed for Cornwall bearing the name The Buck, but in Burlington, New Jersey he had stopped at the home of the president of the American Bible Society, who also had been president of the Continental Congress. The old man offered financial assistance to the aspiring student, and in gratitude The Buck took the name of the celebrated philanthropist for his own. He thus enrolled at Cornwall as Elias Boudinot, and it was as Elias Boudinot that he returned to Cherokee country to serve his people.

Now he was one of the better educated men in the Cherokee Nation, a leader, a link between the Indians and whites. The missionaries who had been distressed by his fondness for Ball Play had even forgiven him that.

The autumn council of 1825 had allocated $1,500 to establish a newspaper that would be printed in both Cherokee and English. That wasn't enough to purchase a press and two fonts of types, one of which would have to be specially cast, so Elias was named to solicit additional funds from the whites—and to be editor of the newspaper once it became a reality.

Evangelical Protestantism was on the march, and Elias spoke at churches in Charleston, New York, Salem, Boston, Philadelphia.

"You behold an Indian," he would say. "My kindred are Indians, and my fathers are sleeping in the wilderness grave—they too were Indians. But I am not as my fathers were—broader means and nobler influences have fallen upon me. Yet I was not born as thousands are, in stately dome and amid the congratulations of the great, for on a little hill, in a lonely cabin, overspread by the forest oak I first drew my breath; and in a language unknown to learned and polished nations, I learned to lisp my fond mother's name. In later days, I have had greater advantages than most of my race; and I now stand before you delegated by my native country to seek her interest, to labour for her respectability, and by my public efforts to assist in raising her to an equal standing with other nations on the earth."

Civilizing the Cherokees obviously was practical, he would continue. The world should know what the Cherokees had accomplished in that regard and what they could accomplish with the help of their white brethren.

In the Cherokee Nation, he would say, were eighteen schools, sixty-two black-smith shops, seven hundred and sixty-two looms, thirty-one gristmills and 2,488 spinning wheels—hardly the trappings of a savage existence.

Now the Cherokees needed a printing press.

After he spoke in Philadelphia, his remarks were printed in a sixteen-page pamphlet that left white readers startled by an Indian's power of expression and eager to contribute money. Harriet gave me a copy.

But for the meantime, while the Boudinots waited for the press, they served at the High Tower missionary station, Elias receiving twenty dollars a month to act as missionary and schoolmaster. By January the station was restored and a dozen or so scholars were on hand.

Harriet kept house, mother-henned the boarding students, entertained guests and, via the mail, assured her relatives that her in-laws were amiable, affectionate people who loved her and whose table included such familiar fare as sugar, tea, milk, corn, beef, pork, pudding, pies, and cakes.

One of the guests at High Tower was Samuel Austin Worcester, a twenty-eight-year-old minister and missionary from New England. Elias tutored him in the Cherokee tongue. One of the things I always think about when I recall Samuel Worcester is that he was preceded by seven generations of clergymen. I didn't believe it when he first told me, but over the years I saw so many queer things that I came to think anything was possible.

Worcester stayed at High Tower nearly two weeks, and he and Elias were so impressed by each other, they formed a friendship that lasted as long as Elias lived. Their friendship was based on love and respect for each other's intellect. When I'd see them together the thought would strike me that there might not be two brighter men in the same room at the same moment anywhere on earth.

As a boy Worcester had been a printer, so it was natural he would go to Boston to supervise the casting of the type for *The Cherokee Phoenix*. Finally, in January of 1828 the type and press arrived in New Echota. A ten week voyage from Boston had brought it to Savannah from whence it was transported in the hold of a paddle-wheel steamer upriver to Augusta and then hauled by wagon to the capital of the Cherokee Nation.

After teaching at High Tower during the winter of 1826-27, Elias had moved to New Echota. He and Harriet settled into a comfortable, two-storied, white-washed house with four rooms downstairs, three upstairs and five closets. "You must be planning on having a lot of children," I teased, and she laughed and told me to mind my own business. More than anything else, I admired the glass windows. I promised myself I would have a house with glass windows some day. Worcester moved to New Echota, too, and I thought it symbolic of their compatibility that Samuel and Elias lived in identical weatherboarded homes.

I liked Worcester's wife Ann. She marveled at my inclination to walk the several miles from our village to New Echota every day just to admire the capital and be with Harriet and other interesting people. "Where do you get all that energy?" she would demand, and I would beam at her attention. She was beautiful, spirited, in love with her husband, pleased to be his helpmeet.

Ann and Harriet were like sisters. They were foreigners in a foreign land, and they comforted each other. I know I must have pestered them, that there must have been times when two white adults from New England wanted to be alone without a thirteen-year-old Cherokee girl nosing in their conversation, but they never let on to me. They treated me like a beloved younger sibling.

Incidentally, I was not wrong when I teased Harriet about having many children. Her first was born in 1827, and before Eleanor was three years old she had a sister, Mary, and a brother, William Penn. In less than nine years Harriet would bear three sons and three daughters.

A small printing shop, twenty feet by thirty feet, was erected, and two white printers were hired. One was John Foster Wheeler, who quickly learned the Cherokee syllabary and who got along with Elias so well that he eventually married his sister. The other was Isaac Harris, who never learned the syllabary and who enjoyed irritating Elias and everyone else by spouting profanities. He tried to arrange some words in the Cherokee type, declared with a torrent of oaths that he could not, and left that part of the work to Wheeler.

I think it was Samuel Worcester who suggested the weekly newspaper be called *The Cherokee Phoenix,* indicative of the rise of our nation, but I never really knew.

Let that be part of the mystery. As far as I was concerned, it should have been named by God. As publication date approached, I was beside myself with excitement.

For $300 a year, Elias was editor, writer, proofreader and business manager. He was spread so thin, working so many hours a day. I felt sorry for him when, the press in place, Elias decided to run a test with Wheeler and Harris in attendance. I was awestruck. I gazed through the window, my elbows locked over the sill, my feet dangling. Then, with a smirk on his face, Harris demanded from Elias: "Where is the damn paper?"

"Where is the paper?" Elias repeated lamely.

"The paper," Harris said. "Newspapers are printed on paper. Where is the paper to print this one?"

In all the excitement, Elias had forgotten to buy paper. So he had to send the snarling Harris to Knoxville for it, a trip that took two weeks.

I haunted the newspaper office, careful to stay out of Harris's way. "Isaac, for goodness sake, she's just a girl," Wheeler would scold, but Harris didn't curb his cursing because I was there. "I'm sorry," he would say with mock apology. "Hand me that goddamn block, please, Justagirl."

I gazed at the thousand-pound press and thought of its power to send words and thoughts into the Cherokee Nation, the U.S., even the world. It was almost a holy object, and I felt the urge to bow to it. I wondered if that were idolatry. I wouldn't mention it to Charley. I didn't bow, by the way.

Elias had invited newspapers and journals to exchange their publications for subscriptions to *The Cherokee Phoenix*. On a table in the corner of the print shop were copies of *The Boston Statesman*, *The National Intelligencer*, *The Patent & State Gazette* of New Hampshire, *Niles' Weekly* and many others. I bored through them, from front page to back, reading everything, soaking up information.

I was disappointed when Elias told me *The Cherokee Phoenix* would reprint articles from the exchanges. I thought that somehow everything in the *Phoenix* would sprout from the fertile brain of its editor. "I could never write the entire paper," he said, amused. "Besides, it will be much more interesting this way."

The first edition of the first American Indian newspaper was dated February 21, 1828. I got up early the morning it was to be printed and headed for New Echota, walking so rapidly that Strong Hickory begged me to slow down.

On the day before publication, I solemnly explained to him what was going to happen and asked if he wanted to accompany me for the historic moment. He laughed and said it didn't seem very historic to him, that there couldn't be much in a Cherokee newspaper printed in the wilds that anyone would want to read but, yes, he'd go.

We were sweethearts, and I sometimes let him kiss me, but I was frequently angry with Strong Hickory. Maybe exasperated is a better word. He had retained little of what he had learned from Charley Marley, and he laughed at my constant reading and daydreaming. "You'd do better to master that hoe instead of a book," he'd say, "because that's what you'll be using when we get married." He had accompanied me to New Echota once before and said it was just another Cherokee village, nothing to get excited about. He grunted that the way I raved about the place, he'd expected Washington City.

I told him he sounded like my father—and when I said that, he knew I was serious and that he'd better shut up.

Staring Otter continued to cling to the old ways and berate anything that hinted of civilization. But he conceded that he had lost the battle with his daughter when he permitted me to go to Charley Marley and learn the Cherokee syllabary and English. To him, New Echota was the most despicable place on earth because it was the focal point of the civilizing process, but he did not deny me permission to visit there and associate with Harriet Boudinot and the other captivating people. He simply refused to discuss what I found so exciting. When I tried to tell him something that Harriet had said he got up and shuffled outside or interrupted with an unrelated subject.

I taunted Staring Otter. Maybe it was cruel, but I did it. "The first edition of *The Cherokee Phoenix* will be printed today," I said at breakfast. "I'll be there when it is. I'll bring you a copy. It will make a nice keepsake."

"Swan Woman asked me to make a bow for her nephew," he said to Mother, as if I weren't present. "I'm going to start on it now."

Strong Hickory and I arrived at the Boudinots' house before they had finished breakfast. I wore my best calico dress, a light blue frock from Augusta, but Strong Hickory was clad only in buckskin breeches, and when Harriet came to the door with a napkin in her hand she wouldn't look directly at him. She blushed and said, "I'm happy to meet you Strong Hickory," but her gaze was over his shoulder and focused on a distant hill.

I had begged him to dress appropriately, but he wouldn't. Sometimes I loved him, and at other times he could make me furious. Harriet asked us in, but I said we had eaten and would wait on the porch, and when she went inside I pinched Strong Hickory in the fleshy part of his back, at the waist, as hard as I could and left a black bruise.

I took a chair on the porch and waited, but Strong Hickory was too impatient for that, so he ambled to the communal spring in front of the Boudinots' and immersed his head and face.

On a small table beside my chair was a prospectus that promised the sole motive in establishing the newspaper was to benefit the Cherokees. The columns would be filled partly with Cherokee print and partly with English print, but matters of common interest would be printed in both languages and would appear in parallel columns.

The paper would carry the law and public documents of the Cherokee Nation, accounts of progress in education, religion and the arts of civilized life, the news of the day, and articles calculated to promote literature, civilization and religion among the Cherokees.

I was overcome by the high-mindedness of the pamphlet, and my shoulders tingled and tears ran down my cheeks. For a moment I despised Strong Hickory. How could he concern himself with catching spring lizards when *The Cherokee Phoenix* was mere minutes from birth?

I heard the sound of an approaching horse and knew without looking that it was the huge animal Charley Marley rode. He tied it to a tree and exclaimed, "Nancy! You're beautiful! I've never seen such a gorgeous dress."

He bounded onto the porch, and I stood and we hugged. He hugged me differently now that I was 13 than he did when I was 10, when we'd first met. I couldn't explain it. His hugs just felt different. Or maybe the difference was in me. Maybe I regarded them differently.

Charley still lived in our village, still taught his school—though he had practically exhausted the number of potential students from the surrounding countryside. He still preached—though he had converted few Cherokees to Christ. As I had grown older, I had come to realize that Charley simply wasn't a very good preacher. He was dedicated, sincere, but he was impatient. He was more accomplished on the ball field—where action produced immediate results and his speed and strength bent the other person to his will.

He was comfortable in our settlement, and there he stayed, though he told me he knew he should move on to new missionary fields.

Staring Otter had to give his neighbors a reason for suddenly permitting Charley to stay and for allowing me to study with him—he couldn't tell anyone of the shooting of Lorenzo Cadwallader—and so he simply declared he had decided that the encroachment of civilization was inevitable and that the young should be literate in Cherokee and English and thus equipped to deal with it. He wouldn't capitulate personally, but I could change.

It hurt him to have to say it, and it hurt him to smile and speak cordially to Charley when anyone else was present, but he did.

The tide that had been turning against Charley Marley among our villagers was thus reversed because its instigator, Staring Otter, appeared to have a change of heart. No one else really cared enough to carry the battle flag, so Charley again became a benign influence.

I still thought he was the handsomest man I'd ever seen. The sight of him—tall and lean, dressed in red breeches, a striped blue and yellow jacket and matching turban and riding that elephant of a horse—caused my breath to quicken. Strong Hickory paled into insignificance, a child playing with a frog.

"Elias invited me to be here when the first number of *The Cherokee Phoenix* is printed," Charley said.

"Harriet invited me," I told him. "They're eating, so I said we'd wait out here."

"I'll wait, too," Charley said in the tone he had recently adopted toward me.

For the last month or so he had spoken, if not quite as man to woman, certainly not as man to child. It was a little disquieting, but I was flattered.

We sat on the porch, in rigid chairs, and I looked straight ahead, an embarrassed half-smile fixed on my face. I felt Charley staring at me—his eyes as steady as twin shafts of sunlight. A person can take only so much of that, and finally I turned my gaze on him, unwavering. It was as if I were looking into a mirror, for his face was frozen in a little smile that I knew must be identical to mine. When I started laughing, he did, too. He reached over and took my hand from the arm of the chair and held it. I was delighted. He held it until we heard Harriet approaching the front door, and then he carefully placed my hand back on the chair, patted it, and got up and stepped to the edge of the porch and pretended to be interested in Strong Hickory's antics with a green snake he had caught at the spring.

"It's almost time," Harriet said. "Elias will be here in a moment."

Her dark hair was parted just to the right of center. It swept across her ears and was secured in the back with a silver bar. It descended to her shoulders. Her face was long and thin, her eyes large, her mouth tight, as if she listened more than she spoke. It wasn't an everyday face, but the perfect face for a Puritan mystic. How I loved that sweet woman!

Elias joined us on the porch, still buttoning his heavy black white man's coat, adjusting the stiff points of his white shirt under his black silk scarf. He could have passed for a senator in Washington City or a judge in Philadelphia.

Except that Elias definitely was an Indian. He called himself a full-blooded Cherokee, but Harriet told me there was a drop of white blood somewhere in his ancestry. His complexion was copper, his eyes grave, his hair black but cut in the style of the whites. He worried a lot.

Elias merely smiled a greeting at me, but he shook his friend Charley Marley's hand vigorously, as if they were about to participate in an historic event, as, indeed, they were.

"Are the printers at the shop yet?" Elias asked Harriet.

"Mr. Wheeler is," she said. "Mr. Harris isn't."

Elias rolled his eyes in exasperation. "Let's go anyway," he said.

We began the short stroll to the printing office, Elias and Harriet and Charley and I, and we saw Samuel and Ann Worcester approaching from their house, in the other direction. "Strong Hickory!" I yelled, motioning toward the building, but he waved me off and continued to search the edge of the spring for living creatures.

John Wheeler greeted us, and he and Elias talked shop, finally lapsing into silence while we waited for Isaac Harris.

Eventually Harris arrived on his unhurried horse, humming softly, "Morning," he said.

"You're late, Mr. Harris," Elias said.

"Well, I'll be goddamned," he answered. "I guess I am."

"As I've told you a hundred times, we don't appreciate that kind of language," Elias said, "certainly not around women and children."

I didn't appreciate being called a child, either, especially after Charley had held my hand, but I nodded in support of Elias.

"Well, let's don't spend all day talking," Harris said, unruffled, bounding into the small shop while we followed. "Let's get this goddamned press going." He knelt and began oiling the machine at various points.

The monstrous castiron press occupied nearly a fourth of the building's space. "Hellfire," Harris groused when the eight of us wedged ourselves into the shop.

I gazed at the metal type, locked into the chase and forming backward letters and words, and I couldn't envision a readable page springing from it.

Harris pushed me aside, not too vigorously but not too gently, either, leaving an inky smudge on my dress. "Back in civilization printers would have inking rollers," he told his audience, "but out here we're obliged to use these things." He inked the type with cotton balls and spread a sheet of paper over it.

Harris moved the lever, and the top part of the press descended upon the paper, mashing it onto the type. He spun the wheel the other way, lifted the sheet, and *The Cherokee Phoenix* was born. We cheered and applauded, and Reverend Worcester said a prayer of thanks.

The newspaper consisted of four pages, five columns to the page. It contained an editorial by Elias, the Lord's Prayer in both Cherokee and English, an article on Sequoyah's syllabary by Samuel Worcester and a portion of the Cherokee constitution. It was the first newspaper ever published for Indians or by Indians.

Five hundred copies were printed that day. Elias gave me one as a keepsake, and I asked for two more. "All right," he said, reaching onto the stack.

One was for Strong Hickory, but he merely glanced at it and asked if I'd carry it back to our village for him, since he had a more important prize, a terrapin he had captured at the spring. One was for Staring Otter, and I smirked when he ignored it—as I knew he would—and remarked to Mother that he was out of bear gut for bow strings.

I kept all three of them. I still have them.

CHAPTER 8

Harriet Boudinot was in the vegetable garden behind her house, her chin propped upon the back of her hand, which rested on the handle of a hoe. She gazed at the broken soil, as if she were examining each particle of dirt.

"Hello," I said.

He eyes remained fixed on the earth. She didn't answer. "Harriet, are you all right?" I asked.

"Am I all right?" she repeated the question in a voice that was barely audible. "I'm tired. So very tired. I wonder how it is today in the Litchfield Hills, at home. It's quiet—I know that. It's calm."

"Harriet!" a woman's voice came from the front porch. "Harriet! Where are you? I can't find the sugar."

Harriet didn't reply, or not so the woman could hear. "Keep looking," she whispered. "It's the white stuff in the cabinet, right in front of your eyes."

"I'll come back," I said, and I turned to leave, but in the same weak voice she said:

"Don't go. I just had to find a few moments alone, away from all the people. Don't worry about me. Stay." She laughed. "One more won't matter, Nancy. Stay."

She was a member of a large family herself, but she wasn't prepared for Indian family life. Cherokee custom dictated that she hadn't merely married Elias, she had married his entire family. When Elias's brothers and sisters called her sister, they meant it. An aunt wasn't someone who could choose to be distant or not. Sometimes she found herself hosting and cooking for twenty or more of his relatives. It was expected of her.

People came and stayed. And stayed. I was excited when I was among the guests. When they were all talking and flitting about, I would lightly touch my fingertips to the walls and feel them vibrate, just as Harriet's piano vibrated when she struck the keys.

"But…," Harriet said, suddenly straightening herself and chopping at the ground with the hoe. "I chose this life, and I'm glad I did. These are my people, Nancy Swimmer, and I want to live with them and die with them. This is my country. I only wish I had more time to serve God."

The times were bad, and they weighed on Harriet. Having a houseful of relatives wasn't the problem. Being homesick wasn't the problem. Those conditions were aggravations piled upon the problem. The problem was the growing animosity of Georgia toward the Cherokees, the hunger of Georgia for Cherokee land.

None of my friends who were my age knew or cared anything about politics—if, indeed, such a mild word can be applied to what was happening around us. Little Peach lived only to flirt with Tree Climber. A crisis to Strong Hickory was losing a game of chunky.

But I couldn't be in the company of Elias and Harriet Boudinot and Samuel and Ann Worcester—and Charley Marley—and not be aware something was wrong. I asked Elias to explain the situation to me, and he did.

We were embracing civilization and, because we were, the white people were supposed to look upon us with favor. It was working in the North, even in England, where the whites were effusive in their celebration of the Cherokees—but it wasn't working in Georgia, where it mattered.

If we became truly civilized, Georgians thought, we could never be kicked off our lands, and the state would be stuck with a permanent tribe of Indians. Our adopting a constitution hadn't elicited the Georgians' admiration; it had increased their alarm.

The constitution began with these words: "We, the Cherokee people, constituting one of the sovereign and independent nations of the earth, and having complete jurisdiction over its territory to the exclusion of the authority of every other state, do obtain this constitution."

An independent nation sitting smack-dab in Georgia? Georgians screamed that the state had better do something—in a hurry.

In December of 1827 the Georgia legislature mounted an official challenge to the survival of the Cherokee Nation. It declared that Cherokee lands within the Georgia limits would be under Georgia's jurisdiction. Such an act was necessary to protect Georgians living in the Cherokee Nation, the legislature said.

But that was just the first step. The same legislature, that same month, passed a resolution calling the Cherokees tenants at the will of Georgia, declaring that the state had the right to take their lands and extend Georgia's authority and laws over them. It accused the U.S. of bad faith toward Georgia in its dealings with the Cherokees. It closed with a restrained warning that Georgia would not use force to get its way unless it was compelled to do so.

If the Indians had not begun removal to the West by the end of 1828, Governor John Forsyth told the U.S., Georgia would begin action to extend its laws over the Cherokee Nation.

The United States sent a representative to make a removal treaty with the Cherokees. He failed.

The Cherokees, of course, didn't consider themselves bound by the Compact of 1802, through which Georgia gave up western lands to the United States in return for the vow of the U.S. to obtain the Cherokees' land for the state "peaceably" and "upon reasonable terms." But Georgia considered it a statement of something that must happen, that was by-damn going to happen—though Georgia tended to ignore "peaceably" and "reasonable" in its fulminations.

Even without Cherokee land, Georgia was the largest state of the twenty-seven. But it wasn't satisfied; it wanted more. So Northerners and Englishmen thought it cruel that half a million white Georgians were threatening eight-thousand Cherokees? So what?

It was an election year, 1828, in the Cherokee Nation and in the United States. The Cherokees were to select a principal chief to replace Pathkiller, who had died in office. The Americans were to choose a president—the incumbent, John Quincy Adams, who had never really been eager to champion Georgia's claims against the Cherokees, or the old Indian fighter, Andrew Jackson.

I wanted Major Ridge to become principal chief. He was a handsome old man, the speaker of the National Council, a warrior, an orator, rich, authoritative. And he was Elias's uncle, the father of John Ridge, the former schoolmate of Elias and Charley at Concord. Everything stopped when he rode by or entered a room.

I was helping Harriet clean house one day when he stopped for a drink of water and to talk *Phoenix* business with Elias. "You should be the principal chief," I blurted. "I hope you are elected."

He laughed roundly. "To be elected I would have to first be a candidate," he said. "I am not. Situations change, Nancy. There was a time when, I agree, I would have been a good principal chief, but not now. The principal chief must be an educated man, someone who can read and write English. That's not me."

Wistfully, he repeated: "No, that's not me."

By a huge majority, John Ross defeated William Hicks for principal chief in the first elections to be held under the new constitution. Major Ridge would be his main advisor.

John Ross. What a strange Indian chief he was. He was only five feet, six inches tall. Little John, we called him. But his lack of height wasn't really the unusual thing about him. The unusual thing was that the principal chief of the Cherokees was only one-eighth Indian.

He was a Scotchman. His father and his maternal grandfather spent nearly their entire adult lives as traders among the Cherokees. His father married a quarter-part Cherokee, and John was raised among Indian children.

Elias said John once told him of a time, before a Green Corn Dance, when his mother dressed him in a little white boy's suit, and his playmates made riotous sport of him. The next day he was back in his Indian garb.

John's father wasn't content to see him grow up as an uneducated Indian, though. He imported a schoolmaster and opened the first school in the Cherokee Nation. Later John attended an academy in Kingston, Tennessee.

John was thirty-eight years old when he was elected principal chief. He had a florid complexion, brown eyes, brown hair. He spoke English like any white but wasn't fluent in Cherokee. But the Cherokees recognized him as a devoted Indian leader, and he had enhanced his standing with them by marrying a woman who was a near fullblood. They lived in a big house near the head of the Coosa River where he was a merchant, planter and slaveowner.

The Americans elected Andrew Jackson to be their seventh president. The popular vote was 648,000 to 508,000—but Jackson more than doubled Adams's electoral votes. Adams won in New England, but with his frontier image, Jackson claimed every electoral vote south of the Potomac and west of the Alleghenies.

Jackson was a man of meager education who, during his colorful life, had been a duelist, cockfighter, breeder of racehorces and survivor of a Cherokee ambush. He also was the popular hero of New Orleans and Horseshoe Bend—where John Ross had fought beside him against the Creeks.

"The enemy has ascended the throne of the king," Charley said when Jackson was elected. That about summed it up.

I must have thought that summed it up, for I was walking beside the Oostanaula with Strong Hickory when I said, "Did you know that Jackson's election means the enemy has ascended the throne of the king?"

"Give me a kiss," he said.

"Be serious," I said. "The enemy has ascended the throne of the king."

"When we are married we will build our cabin on that hill," Strong Hickory said, pointing to an oak-shaded rise on the opposite bank of the river. "I selected that place years ago. Give me a kiss."

I suppose I thought that was romantic, for I gave him a kiss. It lasted a long time. I had to push him away to get my breath. Then we kissed again. For a long time.

"Let's go deeper into the woods," Strong Hickory said, his voice breaking, his hands trembling.

"Let's don't," I said. "I'm going home."

"No," he said. "Let's go to our cave. We haven't been there in a long time."

It wasn't really a cave. It was an overhang of rock, and we had played under it since we were old enough to enter the woods by ourselves. "No," I said.

He turned loose of my wrists and took a step backward, more desperate than angry. "I love you, Nancy Swimmer," he blurted, "but I might as well love the cold rocks of the cave." Then he bounded off into the woods, his arms held high, shaking his clenched fists.

I watched him disappear, and then I picked up a stone and threw it into the river with all my might.

"There's a cold rock for you," I shouted, envisioning it hitting Strong Hickory between the eyes.

"The enemy has ascended the throne of the king," I heard a voice say, and I was horrified when I realized it was Charley Marley's. He had been sitting on the ground, his back against a tree, scant feet away from where Strong Hickory had kissed me. It was his favorite place to read his Bible.

"You heard," I said, feeling betrayed. "You saw."

"I heard," he said, pushing himself to his feet. "I didn't see. I imagined. What was I supposed to do? I was here first. You were about to walk past me on your way home. You would have seen me even if I hadn't spoken. I didn't want to appear to be hiding."

I knew he was right, of course. He was always right. He was perfect. He was beautiful.

He also was a preacher, a man who told us what God liked and didn't like. "Was what I did with Strong Hickory wrong?" I asked.

Charley smiled. "No, it wasn't wrong," he said. "But you were right in not visiting the cave with him."

I nodded. "I'm heading home now."

"Nancy, wait," Charley Marley said.

"Yes?"

"I know how strange this is going to sound to you. But, Nancy Swimmer, I would like for us to be married."

Strange? Strange wasn't the word for it. Astounding was. Not astounding because I was thirteen years old—for a Cherokee girl marrying at thirteen wasn't unusual. But astounding because this was Charley. Wonderful, flawless, consummate Charley, my teacher, my preacher, my ideal. God himself might as well have asked me to marry him.

I started crying, like an infant. Charley stood there, perplexed. He tried to speak but couldn't.

I wiped my eyes on the back of my hand. My nose was running. He removed the yellow turban from his head and handed it to me, and I blew.

"When I'm fourteen," I said.

"Fourteen?" he said. "Why not now? Immediately?"

"When I'm fourteen."

Charley laughed. "All right. Fourteen."

He placed his hands on my shoulders and leaned forward to kiss me, but I moved my face. I loved him, I worshiped him, but I couldn't kiss my future husband when I'd been kissing Strong Hickory not five minutes before.

"I'll say something to Staring Otter and Rain," Charley said.

"Yes," I whispered. "I've got to go."

I ran, my bare feet spraying the dust of the riverside path. I ran towards New Echota, and I didn't slow to a walk until I could no longer get my breath. My side hurt, and I pressed it with the heel of my hand and kept walking.

I reached the little Cherokee capital, removed my hand from my aching side, threw back my shoulders and held my head high as I walked gracefully along the street that led to Harriet Boudinot's house—as gracefully as a young, white bride-to-be spinning a parasol on a boulevard in Baltimore, the city that Major Ridge envisioned in New Echota.

But I felt weak and panicky when Harriet came to the front door. "Nancy, you're trembling," she said. "Come in. I just made some hot tea." She steadied my elbow as I took a seat on the hide-covered couch that seemed as long and deep as a canoe.

"Charley asked me to marry him," I blurted before she could leave the room to fetch the tea.

"Charley who?" she asked, honestly, not at all coyly.

"Charley Marley."

Harriet gasped. "Charley Marley? Charley Marley asked you to marry him?"

I nodded. "I told him I would. When I'm fourteen."

Harriet laughed, but her face wasn't mirthful. It was contorted in disbelief. She took a seat on the couch and stared at me as if I might have been some never-before-seen specimen of little animal that sauntered in from the forest.

"I know Cherokee girls frequently marry very young," she said in a measured voice. "I know Indian girls are considered ready for marriage after their first menstruation. But, try as I might, I cannot get used to it. You are a child, Nancy. Charley's twenty-six years old and you're thirteen."

"That's why I told him I wouldn't marry him until I was fourteen," I said. "I thought about you, Harriet. I knew you would be stunned. I didn't want you to think of him as twice my age. At least when I'm fourteen and he's twenty-seven he won't be."

⠀⠀⠀⠀⠀⠀⠀⠀⠀⠀»»→ • ←««

CHAPTER 9

There was no supplication in Charley's voice when he asked Staring Otter for his daughter's hand. "Nancy and I wish to be married," he said. "We would like your approval."

He told me that my father gazed into his eyes for the longest, his face blank. Then he said, "Grant me one wish. I suppose you will have a Christian wedding?"

"Yes, of course," Charley said.

"Please have a traditional Cherokee wedding, too."

"All right," Charley said. "We'll have two weddings."

My mother hugged him, and so did my grandmother. "Care for my child," Rain said, "my only child."

Charley told them we wouldn't be moving into their cabin, as Cherokee custom dictated. We would live in his house. Staring Otter already knew as much. He nodded and left the room. The weary, embittered traditionalist had lost his daughter to an apostle of the white man's ways, and he knew there was no sense fighting.

I had to tell Strong Hickory. It wouldn't have been fair not to face him. I went to his cabin, and when he stepped outside he was grinning, recovered from being miffed because I wouldn't go to the cave with him.

I blurted it out: "Strong Hickory, I am going to be married to Reverend Charley Marley."

He grinned, certain there was a joke, trying to anticipate the next line. But I said no more, and his lips quivered, and he turned and went back into the house without a word.

Sunday I attended Charley's church service, which was held on the banks of the Oostanaula, a few yards from the spot where he had proposed. To his surprise, I accepted Jesus Christ as my savior and presented myself for baptism.

It wasn't that I was particularly moved by Charley's sermon, for, as I have said, Charley wasn't an inspiring preacher. He became frustrated because what was so evident to him wasn't evident to others, and his listeners had the feeling he was arguing with them. It wasn't that I was about to become a preacher's wife and therefore felt it imperative that I be baptized, either. It was simply an urge, a hunger that had been building in me for a year and had reached a point at which it must be satisfied.

Charley baptized me the next Sunday morning, in the Oostanaula. It was November, and when we waded into the water it was so cold I thought I would never recover my breath. The last thing I saw before I closed my eyes and he cradled me in his left arm and held my nose and lowered me backward under the surface was a merry, bright yellow leaf floating by.

Most of the villagers attended my baptism. My mother and grandmother did. So did Elias and Harriet Boudinot. Strong Hickory didn't. Staring Otter didn't. During the three months between my betrothal and my marriage, Staring Otter treated me no differently than usual. He never mentioned Charley, never mentioned the wedding. He kept his own counsel, rarely spoke to me. But, then, he rarely spoke to anyone. We co-existed.

Once I felt impelled to tell him I loved him, that I appreciated his having raised me, to try for the hundredth time to explain. But I didn't.

One morning Charley and I were sitting on his porch, discussing the book of John, when we saw a black man who was perhaps in his early thirties enter the village clearing. He spoke to a boy who pointed toward us. As the man approached, I noticed that he wore homespun pants and a shirt that appeared new. It was December, but the day was warm, and his sleeves were rolled up, and he carried no jacket, wore no hat. When Charley put down his Bible the man lowered his gaze and continued to walk toward us.

He stopped short of the porch and recited: "I am Moss. I am your wedding present, delivered early so that you might get the most use of me. Mr. Bartholomew Bramlett hopes you will be happy and live as long as the Oostanaula flows, Reverend Charley Marley and Miss Nancy Swimmer."

Then he handed Charley two pieces of paper, one that expressed the same sentiments and another that was a bill of sale for himself in exchange for one dollar.

Charley looked at me, and I looked at him. "Who is Bartholomew Bramlett?" I asked.

"I know him," Charley said. "He's a rich planter. He lives about ten miles from here in a huge house. He farms many acres and has many slaves. He's three-quarters Cherokee. One of his grandfathers was white. He's oh, thirty-five, I guess, never married."

"How do you know him so well?" I asked.

"Remember when I preached at Oothcaloga last month? He came to all three services. He said he is interested in Christianity. He said he could help me."

"Help you?" I asked. "How?"

"He said he might build me a church. A real church, like one in Augusta or Cornwall or Charleston. Though not as large, of course. He might help me with money and food so I could become a fulltime minister."

I was surprised that Charley had never mentioned Bartholomew Bramlett to me, but I didn't say anything.

The black man gazed off into the forest, awaiting our bidding. When he crossed his arms at his chest I noticed they were hideously disfigured with smooth burn scars. I couldn't take my eyes off them.

"Do you mean Bartholomew Bramlett has sent you to be our slave?" Charley asked Moss.

"Yes. You are now my master."

Charley shook his head. "Go back and tell him I don't mean to appear ungrateful, but I don't need a slave." he said.

A wave of sympathy mixed with disgust washed over me. "Tell him we think slavery is a great evil," I said.

"Now, Nancy…" Charley began, but I interrupted him and brazenly asked Moss why his arms were scarred.

"I used to belong to James Vann," he said. "He burned me with a torch when I was a boy because I was hungry and stole an apple."

James Vann. Everyone knew of James Vann. Cherokee mothers used to frighten their misbehaving children by telling them James Vann would get them if they weren't good.

Before he was shot to death, Vann had been the wealthiest Cherokee, the largest slaveholder. He was a halfbreed planter who lived in a magnificent two-storied brick manor at Spring Place.

No weirder Cherokee—no weirder person—ever lived. When he was sober he was a cordial, even-tempered man; when he pitched one of his frequent drunks he became a cruel, homicidal devil.

It was Vann who gave the Moravians land to establish a mission school at Spring Place and fields to plant their crops. It was Vann whose plantation was the site of the missionaries' first service for slaves. It was Vann who regularly whipped slaves for the slightest infraction. It was Vann who strung up a white woman by her thumbs until she confessed to having stolen from him. It was Vann who beat his wife until her brothers warned him direly to stop.

And it was Vann who accused a young black slave girl of stealing from him and tied her to a stake and stacked firewood around her and burned her to death.

One morning in 1809, over a whiskey breakfast, Vann told his wife: "I have already killed one man this morning, and when I finish this quart I am going to kill another." But he didn't. His brother-in-law called him to the door and shot him dead. No one was surprised that James Vann's life ended in violence.

The story goes that Vann's kin inscribed this epitaph on a wooden slab that marked his grave:

Here lies the body of James Vann
He killed many a white man
At last by a rifle ball he fell
And devils dragged him off to hell

"Tell me what happened, about your arms," I persisted, and Charley lifted his eyes skyward and shook his head, dumbfounded by my rude persistence.

"Old Vann always thinking somebody stealing from him," Moss said. "He beat my mother with a board because he say she steal his ring. But his wife find it on the floor where it came off his finger when he drunk and falling down. So he beat his wife.

"I mad 'cause he beat my mother, so I keep one of his apples when we picking. Somebody tell on me, and he tie my wrists to a tree in front of me and stick a torch between my arms, trying to make me confess. I did confess, and he lock me in the dark cellar for seven days without nothing to eat. My mother slip me some cat-tail poultice so my arms don't rot off."

The enslavement of blacks by Cherokees was a product of "civilization." Traditionally, the Indians had disregarded material wealth, but as they followed the example of the whites in becoming serious farmers and even wealthy planters, they recognized a ready source of labor. So they imitated their white neighbors in practicing black slavery. The same Cherokees who screamed that their rights as humans were being denied by the whites, in turn denied to the blacks their rights as humans.

"Tell me how much better today's ways are than yesterday's," Staring Otter would say to me when black slavery was mentioned. "Tell me how admirable it is for one man to possess another." I could not.

The Cherokee Phoenix and its sources of reprint material transported me into realms of thought that previously were as distant as the stars. Eventually, more than a hundred publications would exchange copies with Elias Boudinot's paper, and I consumed their articles like a starving girl who had discovered not just bread but a feast. The Phoenix was responsible for so much incoming and outgoing mail that it became necessary to open a post office at New Echota, with Samuel Worcester as postmaster. Slavery was one subject I had never thought much about until journals in opposition to it arrived at the tiny print shop and the *Phoenix* itself came out against the international slave trade.

I remember one article in the *Phoenix* that made me weep. It was entitled "A Scene in Africa" and reprinted from the American Colonization Society's *African Repository*. It described the cruelty of the capture of slaves in their homeland and their transportation to the so-called New World. I memorized part of it: "Here every day for centuries, has the human body been bound in chains, the ties of kind fellowship, of nature's strongest affection, ruthlessly sundered, and hope of which smiles in death, made to perish by living agony. My God! Who can describe the miseries of those crowded to death in the dungeons of a slave ship?"

If I could only write like that, I thought. Right now it would have to be enough that I could feel like that.

"Is Bartholomew Bramlett cruel to you?" I asked Moss.

"He not like old Vann," he said. "He don't whip nobody. Don't burn nobody or shoot nobody. One day a man swap one he hogs to a Choctaw traveling by for whiskey, and Master lock him up in a smokehouse for two days without nothing to eat, and I see Master cry later 'cause he had to do it. He not mean like old Vann."

"It isn't right for one person to own another person," I said, but Moss didn't respond. He obviously didn't know what to make of a thirteen-year-old girl doing all the talking while her twenty-six-year-old fiance served as part of the audience.

"Tell Mr. Bramlett we thank him, but we can't use a slave," Charley said. "Tell him he is invited to our wedding."

I was infuriated. "Tell him slavery is against the laws of God and man," I said, glaring at Charley, "and tell him he'd better not come to our…"

Charley grasped my arm and told me to calm down, and Moss welcomed the opportunity to march away from this remonstrative girl and return to the predictability of Bartholomew Bramlett's plantation.

"You invited that … that slavemaster to our wedding," I sputtered.

Charley took me in his arms, guided my face to his chest and stroked my long black hair. "He is a man in search of God," Charley said. "I want to help him."

"He is a man who might help you," I said, determined to get in the last word, though I continued to snuggle against the Reverend Charley Marley.

Full of my role as young bride-to-be, which Harriet celebrated with zestful attention, meticulous planning and big-sisterly advice, I braved the piercing rain of a December afternoon in 1828 to visit the Boudinots. I found Elias in a rage, which was so uncharacteristic of the thoughtful editor that I was afraid to enter his study, even to speak to him from the hallway.

"Come with me to the kitchen," Harriet said, an embarrassed, forced lightness in her voice. "We'll fix tea."

"No," Elias shouted from the lamplit room. "Let her come in here. Every Cherokee needs to know this. We might as well start with Nancy."

He tossed a copy of *The Georgia Journal* of Milledgeville, the capital, onto the library table that separated us. Hooded with ink from his pen was the headline of the story. "Read that," he said. "Although I'm sure the good white folks of Georgia wouldn't believe any Cherokee capable of reading."

The story said that Governor John Forsyth had signed a bill declaring that as of June 1, 1830, all Cherokee lands in the state would be partitioned among adjacent Georgia counties and would be subject to the laws of Georgia. "All laws, usages, and customs made, established, and in force in the said territory, are hereby declared null and void."

Just like that.

"Can they do it?" I asked.

"With Andrew Jackson in the White House?" Elias replied. "Do you know what he told Georgia's congressmen after he was elected president? 'Build a fire under them. When it gets hot enough they'll move.' That's what he said. Well, they've built the fire."

The Georgia legislature's resolution of 1827 that called the Indians tenants at her will had been disquieting, but it was more in the nature of a warning of the state's displeasure. "But this measure could mean the end of the Cherokee Nation if it is enforced," Elias explained, calm now, gazing out the window, his brilliant mind searching for answers.

There was nothing in his expression to indicate he found any.

The first of our two weddings should be the Christian service, Charley said, and I agreed. The Cherokee wedding should be the adjunct. The Christian service should be the one that binds us.

I turned fourteen on the eighth day of January, 1829, and two days later, on a chilly but cloudless Sunday afternoon, the Reverend Samuel Worcester married us in a ceremony on the front lawn of Elias and Harriet Boundinot's home in New Echota.

I wore a dress that was vividly white in the brilliant sunlight. Harriet had it brought from Augusta as a wedding gift. Charley was gorgeous in a grey white-man's suit, replete with claw-hammer coat, that he special-ordered from Savannah through a trader friend. Harriet even let out one of her dresses and gave it to Rain, and my mother was more beautiful than I had ever seen her before. Staring Otter went fishing.

Samuel Worcester asked if I would have Charley as my husband. "With all my heart," I answered, and I heard Harriet whisper amen.

When the ceremony was over, Harriet hosted a reception in her parlor. A mixed-breed in expensive black clothes sipped coffee and stood alone in a corner, watching as Charley and I accepted congratulations. He was the last to wish us well, patting Charley on the shoulder and clasping my right hand between his. He continued to hold my hand until Charley introduced us.

"A most beautiful bride," Bartholomew Bramlett said. "A most admirable husband, my good friend, Reverend Charley Marley. God must be pleased today."

His eyes never left mine. I removed my hand. "Thank you," I said lamely. Charley looked uneasy, but I wasn't going to let the man's presence spoil my wedding. "Excuse me," I said, and I joined a group of ladies.

Our traditional Cherokee wedding was held the following night in the seven-sided council house of our village.

The men feasted Charley at The Bull's house, the women feasted me with my favorite foods (though I was too nervous to take more than a couple of bites) at a house on the other side of the settlement. Charley endured the jokes any young groom is subjected to; the women at my party were models of decorum except for a few knowing smiles and uplifted eyebrows directed my way.

Our attendants led us into the small council house, and we stood on opposite sides. Sweet Melon, assuming the role Charley's late mother would have played, gave him a venison roast and a blanket. My mother presented me an ear of corn and a blanket.

Charley and I approached each other slowly until we were face to face. I took his blanket and folded it with my own, a sign that we would share a bed. I gave him the ear of corn, a promise I would prepare bread for our family. He handed me the venison, a pledge to provide meat. The Bull, our village chief, pronounced our blankets joined.

I glanced at Staring Otter, who sat with the men across the council house from the women, and he smiled and nodded. I was glad I could give him this small pleasure.

>>>→ • ←<<<

CHAPTER 10

Charley added two rooms to his one-room bachelor dwelling, and we had a comfortable house. The men of the village helped, felling, dragging and notching hickory trees for logs, chinking the cracks, cutting shingles with the iron froe and wooden mallet The Bull and Sweet Melon gave us for a wedding gift. The Bull himself took on that job, for he was proud of being able to slice white oak into perfect shingles.

Charley was solicitous, loving, proud of his young wife. At night he would brush my raven hair with careful, rhythmic strokes, a hundred or more of them. He had asked me not to cut it, and it was nearly to my waist.

The stores in New Echota prospered, especially during council and court, and huge wagons pulled by six horses brought great loads of goods from Augusta. Elias and Harriet arranged for a dealer to ship us a fine maple bed and two woolen blankets, their wedding gift to us.

Charley was in the habit of waking before daybreak, but I would coax him back into bed, under the blankets and an immense bearskin cover that had been my parents' present. We would talk, and finally he would go back to sleep, and I would nestle my head against his neck and consider how lucky I was and wish the morning light would somehow remain hidden over the horizon.

Staring Otter was civil with Charley, but he maintained a degree of coolness. However, it was an improvement, and all of us—Charley, Rain, Plum and I were thankful. At least we could sit in the same room with my father and carry on something resembling a conversation.

Eventually, Strong Hickory deigned to speak to Charley and me when he met us. That was all, though. It was as if he were merely being polite to strangers.

My husband loved the *Phoenix* as I did, and he was delighted when (after considerable hinting on Charley's part) Elias invited him to write an article on religion. Isaac Harris was angry when we showed up at the print shop on press day and asked for a copy. "Goddamned paper won't make a penny if we give them all away," he groused, as if it were his money. Charley bit his lip and said thanks when Harris handed us the sheet. He held it up in the sunlight that streamed through the window, and we read his byline, the ink still wet, and I gave him a big congratulatory kiss. "Shit," Isaac Harris said.

I stood in awe of the *Phoenix*. To me it was as magical as Staring Otter believed Hidden Snake to be—the old shaman who could fly through the sky, bore under the ground and energize the home team's ballplayers while disabling their opponents.

To gaze at the stack of fresh newspapers and know that they would soon be in homes in Philadelphia, in newspaper buildings in New York, in the governor's office in Milledgeville, in humble Cherokee cabins in Tennessee—well, I was overwhelmed. "He doesn't subscribe," Elias whispered as if telling a secret, "but I expect a copy is forwarded to Andrew Jackson." I wanted to touch them all so I could say my fingers had been on the president's paper. He might be a demon from hell, but he was the president.

Each of its four pages consisted of five columns of type in a ratio of about three columns in English to two in Cherokee. Each of Sequoyah's characters represented a syllable, so the same statements required less space in Cherokee.

Elias combed the exchange papers for material, and the *Phoenix* printed a miscellany of articles ranging from the benefits of laughter to cannibalism in New Zealand to poetry to healthful recipes to Worcester's translation of scripture to Cherokee news to Elias's editorials.

Many Cherokees had a taste for the white man's alcohol, frequently with disastrous results, and Elias railed against its use. After reading one of his editorials, I solemnly vowed to my husband that drink would never touch my lips.

"We need more stories about the doings of average Cherokees," Elias said one evening as he and Harriet and Charley and I sat on their front porch in the afterglow of a fine meal our hostess had prepared. "Could you write us some pieces like that, Charley?"

It just popped into my head and out of my mouth: "Perhaps a story about a Cherokee who makes the finest bows in the nation?"

Charley laughed and hit his thigh with his fist. "You mean Staring Otter? He'd shoot me with one of those bows if I even suggested it."

"I didn't mean you," I said, without a trace of a smile. "I meant me."

Charley laughed again and said, "You?" And then you could see by his expression that he knew he had made a mistake by speaking that one deprecating word.

I waited a moment before I answered, for I knew I must submerge my temper. "You wrote an article for the *Phoenix*," I said levelly. "It must not be too difficult."

My rejoinder and his befuddled look tickled her funnybone, and Harriet quietly turned her head to hide an expanding grin, but she couldn't suppress a laugh, and it sputtered past her tight lips, spittle spraying Elias's sleeve.

"I'm sorry, I'm sorry," she said, but her laughter was uncontrollable, like a stream gaining impetus as it tears down a dam, and Elias began to laugh, and then Charley, and finally me.

"Well, I didn't mean you were illiterate," Charley said lamely. "I just didn't know if you were serious."

But that just made it worse, and Harriet howled and bounded into the house, leaving guffawing apologies in her wake.

"That was good for her," Elias said, wiping the dampness from his eyes with his sleeve. "She needed something to relieve the pressure. It hasn't been easy on Harriet, leaving her family, moving here, living among strange people."

"I'll admit that Charley is strange," I said. Then I let him off the hook. "But I love him." He took my hand, and it disappeared in both of his.

"If I were going to build a cabinet, I'd study the work of a cabinetmaker," Elias said. "I've always believed the best way to learn to write is to read. Nancy reads the print off the exchange papers in the *Phoenix* office. Usually they are blank when I get around to them."

I beamed. I squeezed Charley's hand, and he squeezed mine.

"I believe Nancy is quite capable of writing a story about Staring Otter," Elias continued. "And she certainly knows her father far better than most journalists know their subjects. Therefore, Nancy Swimmer, I commission you to produce said article for *The Cherokee Phoenix*. The editor's budget dictates that your remuneration will be the grand sum of zero dollars."

I would have paid him to let me write it. I was choked up. "Thank you, Mr. Boudinot," I muttered.

"Mr. Boudinot?" Elias protested. "No more of that. We're all old married folks here. From now on, it's Elias."

Yes. Elias. For I was a writer, and writers called their editors by their first names.

But reality eventually intruded on euphoria, and in bed that night I asked Charley, "How am I going to get Staring Otter to agree to let me write a story?"

"Old reporters like you shouldn't have any trouble getting information," he said.

The confidence—the feeling of invincibility—that had attended me in the presence of the great Elias Boudinot and his wife had vanished, and now I felt like any fourteen-year-old girl who was about to face a disapproving parent. Staring Otter would say no, I would sputter something ineffectual, he would say no again, and that would be that.

"Perhaps you should write about the bows," I whispered to my husband, ashamed of my cowardice but desperate for escape. "After all, Charley, you wrote that wonderful article for the *Phoenix*, and you've written all those sermons."

It was dark, but I knew Charley threw back his head when he laughed. "Not me," he said. "Staring Otter would use my gut instead of a bear's for his bowstring."

"You don't love me," I said pitifully, in one last bid for sympathy.

But Charley was intractable. "Not enough to get an arrow between my eyes," he said, and when he tickled my ribs I couldn't help laughing.

"Go to sleep," I yelped.

"Good luck, and good night," Charley said, glad to end the conversation.

I lay awake for what must have been hours, but when morning came I told myself the only way to do it was to do it. I called on my parents, and Mother offered me a hot cup of coffee laced with rich cream. "I get it from a trader," she explained. "I've become a morning coffee drinker. Staring Otter is displeased, but he merely grumbles that I look like a white woman sipping at my foul drink."

"Where is he?" I asked.

"Out back. Working on a bow."

I was delighted. It gave me an opportunity to approach the subject.

"How are you, Nancy?" he asked, glancing up from his workbench.

"I am fine," I answered. "What a handsome bow. It must be for someone special."

"It isn't for anyone in particular," he said. "It's for whoever wants to buy it."

"Your bows are so magnificent that I guess it just seems they should be for someone special," I gushed.

Staring Otter laid his knife and strip of wood aside and looked at me suspiciously. "What do you want, Nancy?" he said impatiently.

I was disappointed at myself for being so transparent. Staring Otter didn't appreciate being played for a fool, and I didn't blame him. I decided to be honest.

"I want to write a story about you for *The Cherokee Phoenix*," I said. "I will need your cooperation."

"Me? Why me?"

"About your bow-making. How you select the wood. How you prepare it. The little extra touches that make your bows the best."

"No," he said. "I've never shared my secrets with any person. Why should I share them now with many?"

I thought quickly, and later I was proud of myself for it. "We could stay away from the details and write more about your life," I said.

"No," he answered.

"As you say, many would read about your bows, how fine they are, and they probably would come and ask you to make bows for them."

"No," he repeated, but this time less forcefully.

"It's called advertising," I said. "The *Phoenix* runs advertisements, and people pay to have them in the paper, to spread the word about their products and services. But you would be getting an advertisement for free."

"No," he said again, but he added: "What about my life? What would there be to write about my life?"

"How you fought at the Horseshoe," I said. "How you were wounded. Your recollections of the battle. How you saw Jackson."

"What makes you think you could write it?" he asked in a tone that told me he was interested and hoped for a reassuring answer. "You are just a girl."

"I am a married woman," I objected, but I immediately softened my voice. "I read all the exchange papers. I not only pay attention to the contents of the stories but to how they are written. I know I could do it."

"How would you go about making a story for a newspaper?" Staring Otter asked.

"I would come to you with pen and paper and ask you questions and write down your answers. It's called an interview. Then I would take your answers and make of them a story, writing it with a pen on paper. I could write it in English and in Cherokee, and I would present it to Mr. Boudinot, the editor, the head man of the newspaper, and he would change anything that should be changed, and then the printer would print it on the large pieces of paper that make up the newspaper, and newspapers would be mailed through the post office."

He couldn't have understood it all, but he nodded and said, "I have one condition."

I was ecstatic, but I tried not to let my excitement show. "Name it."

"When the story is completed, when it is in the form in which it will appear in the newspaper, you must read it to me, and I can change anything I want to change before it is printed."

I couldn't imagine a reporter for a newspaper in Philadelphia or Boston agreeing to such a stipulation, but I knew I had no choice. I should have told my father that I would ask the editor if his terms were agreeable, but I was eager to begin, so I said simply, "Done."

Staring Otter turned to his workbench, but I said breathlessly, "I can interview you now, if that's agreeable." I had brought paper and pen and ink in a carpetbag Harriet had given me.

"Tomorrow," Staring Otter said—postponing the interview, I suspected, for no other reason than to assert his control of the situation.

I leaned over and kissed him on the forehead, embarrassing him, and shot into the house and exclaimed to Mother that he had agreed to the story. Then I ran home and told Charley.

"I'm going to New Echota," I said. "I want Elias and Harriet to know."

"You spend your life on the path between here and New Echota," my husband said in mock complaint, but he added that he was happy for me, and he was smiling when I bounded out the door, embarking on foot for the capital.

The path paralleled the Oostanaula, and as the cold wind blew across the river and into my bones I had time to think, time to worry. Suppose Elias said I was ridiculous for believing he would permit the subject of a story to, in effect, censor it? Suppose he had decided that I was, after all, too young to write a newspaper story? Suppose he had, upon reflection, decided it simply wasn't an interesting subject for an article?

The pounding of my feet as I bounced onto Elias's porch betrayed my excitement, told the editor, who was at his desk and framed by a front window, that I was running. I couldn't hear the words, but I read his lips as they said, "Come in, Nancy."

"Staring Otter said he would cooperate," I blurted. "He said I could write the story." I held my breath, waiting for Elias to tell me there would be no story after all.

"That's wonderful," he said. I exhaled.

"There may be a problem," I said gravely. "He wants me to read the story to him before it's printed, so that he can change anything he doesn't like. I told him that was all right, but I probably shouldn't have. I should have asked you."

"That's fine," Elias said.

"Fine?"

"In this case, yes. Not in all cases, but this time it's all right. It's a harmless story about a man who makes bows."

As far as I was concerned, it would be the most important newspaper story ever written. And Elias Boudinot was the most important newspaper editor. I thanked God. And I thanked Sequoyah.

Staring Otter stuffed more wood than was necessary into the fireplace, and the resulting blaze fought the lingering cold of March, 1829, like an antic swordsman dueling an unseen enemy. He sat on a homemade bench, near the fire, and I spread my paper across the table on which Rain and Plum served their meals.

"I know that you always have considered a man's bow a very personal thing, almost like one of his arms," I began.

"It is as you say," Staring Otter answered formally, as if he were talking to a stranger. "The firearm will never replace the bow, for any fool can stand far away and point a rifle and pull the trigger, but skill is involved in drawing near to an animal—or a person—and shooting true with an arrow. It is best done with a perfect bow, and the perfect bow not only operates perfectly, it is perfect in appearance."

He had been rehearsing. Good. So had I, of course.

His prepared answers met my prepared questions, and the interview went smoothly. Once into it, Staring Otter demonstrated a feel for self-promotion. He discussed in broad terms how a bow was prepared, but at certain junctures he would smile and say, "And it is here that I apply one of my personal touches that I will not reveal."

Sycamore and hickory make inferior bows, he said. Honey locust and black locust were the only woods he would use. He chopped down a small tree, cut a section slightly longer than the intended bows, and with wooden wedges and mauls split the log. Then the wood was divided into quarters and then into eighths.

Careful carving rendered bow blanks that were half heart wood and half sap wood. The soft inner wood formed the belly of the bow. The blank was carved to the approximate size of the finished bow, the ends rounded and notched. Then it was strung backward and put aside to dry.

After the bow was dry, it was strung in the opposite, operative position and tested for strength. Then the final trimming was completed, the thickness of the bow, and thus its pull, determined by the strength of the archer.

"Some make the string from hemp, but I use only bear gut," Staring Otter said, affecting his best superior sneer. "Granted, it is easier to pull a plant than to kill a bear, but I have always been impressed that a bear once sacrificed himself so that other bears could use his gut to make a bowstring to shoot arrows at men."

He believed the old Cherokee myths, as surely as he believed there was burning wood in the fireplace beside him. Oh, well, it would spice up my story.

Staring Otter closed his dissertation by saying many bow-makers determined the length of the bow by measuring from the tip of the chin to the tip of the fingers of the outstretched right hand, but that his secret method was superior. "There are many secrets in the process of converting a tree that bends in the wind into a bow that produces meat for a meal that I have not told you about," he said, delight in his voice.

Discussing his life gave him no such pleasure. I had guessed it wouldn't, and I saved those questions for last. It pleased him to play the role of great artisan, but he saw the permanently crippled soldier only as a victim, not as a hero, and he spoke uncomfortably about the Horseshoe, leaving out the details.

Finally, I said, "We don't have to get into this. I have plenty of material to write about Staring Otter the bow-maker. There is no need to write about anything else."

My father took my hand, something he never did, and tears welled up in my eyes. "That would be good," he said.

I don't know why, but I was closer to Staring Otter that day than I had ever been before. Perhaps it was because trust was implicit in his permitting me to interview him and tell his story in a newspaper. Perhaps it was because for the first time he treated me as a woman instead of a little girl. Perhaps it was because this intractable man finally bent a little.

I worked on the story for three days, from sunup to sundown, neglecting my husband, taking walks along the river to clear my head. I tried to make every word fit. "Good writing travels on strong verbs and stumbles on useless adjectives and adverbs," I had read in an exchange paper, and I combed my story with that in mind.

Finally, it was completed. I presented it to Elias Boudinot and stood silently before the great man's desk in the study of his home, my hands folded at my waist.

"I'll read it in a week or two," Elias said, but he grinned at my horrified expression and assured me he was joking. "I'm eager to see this story," he said, and he motioned me toward a handsome mahogany chair covered in burgundy velvet.

Elias read my story twice without comment, and I thought I was going to smother when he shuffled the pages and began reading it again. Finally, he placed my work on his desk, carefully squaring the five pages.

"Nancy," he said, "this story is excellent. Frankly, I am amazed that it is so good. Except for one or two changes, it will run in the *Phoenix* just as you have written it. You have paid attention to the writing in the exchanges, recognized what was good and what wasn't, retained the wheat and discarded the chaff. This piece is worthy of a professional, and you are only fourteen years old."

I wanted to cry, and I wanted to shout. My emotions swirled like the pine cones that Strong Hickory and I used to toss into the whirlpool formed by the rocks in the Oostanaula.

I lifted my chin and straightened my shoulders. "I want to be paid for the story," I said.

Elias, startled, frowned. "I told you there's no money in the budget for your story," he said.

"I want to be paid one penny," I persisted. "You said the story was worthy of a professional. If you pay me, I will be a professional."

His frown disappeared, and he cocked his left eye, lifting his cheek into an ironic smile. "You are right," he said. "A professional should be paid." He reached into his pocket, held up a penny, and pressed it into my hand.

I vowed to always keep it, and I have. A blacksmith punched a perfect round hole in my penny, and it hangs on a gold chain around my neck.

>>>→ • ←‹‹‹

CHAPTER 11

Reading the exchange papers that came to Elias Boudinot's office quickened my sense of history and drama. They were passageways into a world in which conflict was the norm. I appreciated that right there in the Cherokee Nation, just an ink dot on the map, I was living in historic times, dramatic times.

I even sensed the drama in my own everyday existence. I was the fourteen-year-old wife of a minister who had saved my life by shooting to death another man. I was the friend of the editor of the first Indian newspaper and his wife, a couple whose love story could have been from the pages of a novel.

I wrote feature articles for the newspaper, knowing they would land on the desks of important men throughout the United States. I followed up the story on Staring Otter with other innocuous pieces on a woman said to be one hundred and eight years old, a child who, in the presence of a medicine man, had fallen from a high bluff and miraculously been uninjured, and a man who owned a five-legged calf. Perhaps Andrew Jackson himself would read my description of the mutant named Legs.

Furthermore, I lived a short walk from New Echota, the capital, a village in which legislators and judges who dressed as white men convened to govern the Cherokees, the most civilized of all the tribes. It didn't really resemble Baltimore, any more than a puppy resembled a stallion, but I understood how a proud Major Ridge could close his eyes and imagine that it did.

These were dangerous times for the Cherokees, a people vastly outnumbered by white Georgians who were determined to take their lands, but I found the danger exhilarating. If that be perversion, then I was perverted.

But I don't believe it was. Living with Charley Marley—a man who spoke to Jesus as offhandedly as he might speak to a neighbor—and being under the influence of Harriet Boudinot—a mystic who truly lived her life as if this world were merely an anteroom to God's stupendous banquet hall—gave me courage. If God be for us, who were Andrew Jackson and Georgia to be against us?

In the midst of adventure and uncertainty coexisted the routine of daily life. Charley hunted some and I gardened some, but mainly we got on because of the generosity of others.

"He is our spiritual leader, the man who brings the voice of the Great Spirit into our midst," The Bull, our town chief, would lecture the villagers. "He must have time to study, to prepare his messages, to teach the children and adults religion and the ways of civilization. You, Star Horse and Mary, send food to the reverend and Nancy for the next five days."

Our neighbors saw little need for a spiritual leader, but The Bull was persuasive, and so they provided for us, though I knew they complained behind our backs.

The Cherokees' approach to religion was lackadaisical when compared to that of Christians. They believed in a supreme being and an afterlife of rewards and punishments. They acknowledged the existence and influence of evil spirits. But they had little concern for a personal relationship with the Great Spirit. "They simply don't love him," Charley would say.

My husband's inability to pierce their attitude with his exhortations to accept the living Christ left him frustrated and angry.

His predicament was exacerbated by his freelance status. He represented no denomination, for he would not be bound by any rule in which he did not believe. (He never appreciated the irony of the Cherokees' taking the same stand against his preaching.)

So Charley had no denominational support—for his pocketbook or his morale. His truly was a voice crying in the wilderness. Moravians, Presbyterians, Baptists and Methodists sought to Christianize the Cherokees, but Charley was just Charley.

I think he was jealous of Samuel Austin Worcester, Elias Boudinot's friend, neighbor and collaborator in New Echota. In Charley's place, only a person of perfect spirit—a Harriet Boudinot, for instance—wouldn't have been.

A Congregationalist, Worcester was an able missionary of the American Board of Commissioners for Foreign Missions, a man who seemed capable of any good thing. He was a brilliant academic who had mastered Latin, Greek and Hebrew and was translating scripture and hymns into Cherokee. A leading contributor to the *Phoenix*, he was practical, too, proficient at printing, carpentry, blacksmithing and curing beef.

The Indians who sat stony-faced during Charley's sermons nicknamed Worcester "The Messenger," gave him their rapt attention, and under his influence were converted to Christianity.

He even looked like you'd imagine God's messenger would look. He was thin, fragile, angelic, and behind his face you knew there must be all knowledge.

Charley, on the other hand, looked like a ball player. He was handsome, robust—and I knew the thoughts many of the women had about him were decidedly unreligious.

If my husband's faith ever wavered, I never knew it. Sometimes in bed at night, when I couldn't sleep and troublesome thoughts were picking at my faith, I would ask him, "Charley, do you really believe all you say about Jesus? You've never seen him, never seen God the Father or the Holy Spirit. What if it's not really true? What if there is no God? What if it's just a myth, like the medicine lake in the mountains that the birds and animals keep invisible to humans?"

He would slip his arm around my shoulders and draw me to him and say, "It is true. It must be accepted on faith, for it cannot be proved in a courtroom. When you wonder whether you believe, simply ask God to give you faith and then conduct your life as if you did believe, and you will believe."

My faith was not impregnable, but it was strong, and I felt justified in my role of minister's wife and helper. I treated the ladies of the village to tea (a genteel practice I had read of in the exchange papers) and inexpertly taught a Bible class that was received for the most part with indifference.

Though some of them had been adults when I was born, they weren't uncomfortable with a fourteen-year-old hostess. It was simply the Indian way, and they thought nothing about it.

Harriet, on the other hand, never got used to Cherokee girls marrying so young, to my being Mrs. Charley Marley at an age at which white New Englanders were barely shed of their dolls. She had been twenty-one, half again my age, when she married Elias.

When her parents, Benjamin and Eleanor Gold, arrived in New Echota for a visit, forty-seven days after departing from Cornwall in a horse-drawn buggy, she introduced me merely as "my little friend Nancy, a girl who lives in a neighboring village." She was too embarrassed to tell them I was the fourteen-year-old wife of a minister of the gospel. I was hurt, but I knew that Harriet and her folks were from a different world, so I forgave her.

I usually dressed as a white woman, mostly in clothes handed down from Harriet and Ann Worcester. Some of the articles were threadbare, but not all. "There's plenty of wear left in this frock," Harriet would say, "but take it anyway, Nancy, because it will look good on you. Oh, some day Elias is going to have a fit about me giving away perfectly good dresses."

I knew some of the Cherokee women laughed at me, a woman, or girl, of the forest dressing as if I lived on a cobblestone street in Boston, but I didn't care. I was proud to look as nearly like Harriet Boudinot as I could.

I wondered what Harriet would think if she knew Charley Marley, the man of God, had killed another human to save me. If she knew that too-young Nancy Marley had witnessed a bullet blowing away half of Lorenzo Cadwallader's face. If she knew that just outside the village in which Mrs. Marley promenaded in her hand-me-downs, the worms fed on Cadwallader's guts.

"Does it ever bother you—shooting that man, I mean?" I asked my husband.

"I think about it," he said. "I'm sorry for the necessity, but I've never doubted that I did the only thing I could do. God has given me peace on that score. Does it ever bother you?"

"Sometimes I dream about it," I said. "And sometimes I become panicky at the thought of the Georgians finding out and..."

I began to cry. Charley enveloped me in his big arms and assured me no one would ever find out. "There's nothing to worry about," he said—but that didn't stop me from worrying.

One fragrant spring morning, while I washed clothes in a pot over an outside fire and Charley taught Sequoyah's symbols to three little boys who sat on the ground in our yard, legs crossed, minds wandering, Staring Otter paid us a visit.

"I have a gift for you, Charley Marley," he said. He extended both arms, and upon his hands rested a handsome bow.

"Oooh," the little boys gasped, scurrying to their feet, fingering its smooth wood, its taut bear gut string.

Was that a tear I saw in the corner of my husband's eye? "I am honored," he told my father. "A bow from the workbench of Staring Otter is truly a work of art and a prized possession."

"I am making pies from dried apples," I said. "They are almost ready."

Staring Otter nodded. "That would be good," he said.

Charley dismissed his pupils, and we sat on benches hewn from half-logs and enjoyed the warmth of the sun and the warmth of my father's gesture. It was one of those perfect moments that remains fresh in your mind though decades pass.

"I don't know much about shooting a bow," Charley said. "I probably couldn't hit the side of our cabin."

My father lifted his chin. "I would be pleased to teach you," he said. "Archery, too, is an art."

Staring Otter ate his pie and wished us a good day. I watched as he headed toward his cabin, his body twisting as his weight shifted between his good leg and his crutch and back again. I wanted to follow him, hug him, lay my head on his shoulder, but I knew to let well enough alone. The half-hour had been a good one.

In the distance I heard the clip-clop of a prancing horse pulling a buggy. I stopped stirring the boiling clothes and laid the wooden paddle across the edge of the iron pot. Several neighbors stepped outside. Rarely did a buggy even pass through our village.

But there was no surprise in Charley's eyes. He stood his bow against the house and awaited the arrival of Bartholomew Bramlett.

A regal bay horse pulled a well-kept black buggy, the red spokes of its wheels whirring against the background of the forest that springtime was infusing with green life. The liveried black driver kept his eyes just ahead of the horse, as if there were no room in his attention for anything except delivering the vehicle to its appointed destination.

Bartholomew Bramlett sat in the wide seat behind the driver, a red and green plaid blanket covering all but his face and head, which was topped by a wide black hat to which had been added a white feather that I judged to be from some tropical bird. The short man's face was blunt and broad, and his hat accented that unfortunate feature. Even when Bartholomew Bramlett smiled he appeared to be in discomfort, like a person with a sharp rock in his shoe.

Charley had told me he was about thirty-five and that he was three-quarters Cherokee, but he looked forty-five and neither like an Indian nor a white man, but more like the drawings of wild bushmen I had seen in an article on Australia. There was nothing attractive about him, and his sitting stark still and silent until his driver got down and removed the blanket somehow made him more repugnant.

"Reverend Marley," he said, accepting the driver's hand and stepping from the buggy. "Mrs. Marley."

"Mr. Bramlett," Charley gushed. "I am so pleased to see you."

"I told you I would arrive just before noon, and I have," Bramlett said, as if that were some praiseworthy accomplishment.

I nodded at the rich planter in the frock coat and stared blankly at Charley, miffed because he had known Bramlett was coming and hadn't mentioned it.

Bramlett handed Charley a package. "Coffee," he said. "From South America. Rich and rare."

"That sounds wonderful," Charley said. "Thank you. I'd like some now. Nancy, would you make us some coffee?"

"I don't know how to make coffee," I said. Charley's eyes narrowed at my lie.

"Come on, Bartholomew," Charley said. "May I call you Bartholomew? I'll make us some coffee."

I felt petty, but I turned my attention to the boiling clothes. I didn't even look when Charley stuck the loaded coffee kettle into the coals under my washpot.

The northern newspapers regularly carried articles exposing slavery. I read them and became furious; I read them and wept; I read them and despaired for mankind. Now here was my husband making coffee for a slavemaster.

"We can talk in the house," Charley said. "Or we can sit outside. It's not too cold."

Bramlett glanced at me. "Let's talk and ride," he said. I am enjoying the scenery."

He motioned for Charley to join him in the buggy. Charley, who wore a sleeveless cotton shirt, refused the driver's attempt to cover him with the blanket, but Bramlett pulled the woolen cover up under his chin.

"We'll return soon, Mrs. Marley," Bramlett said. "I won't get him lost."

I ignored the stupid remark and stirred the clothes in the gurgling water. I felt Charley's furious stare and gazed deeply into the bubbles.

When I heard the eager clip-clop of the horse's hooves, I threw the paddle onto the ground, kicked over the untouched coffee kettle, and hissed, "You...you...you Charley Marley!"

"Trouble between the great lovers?" a voice said, and Strong Hickory was grinning. It was the first time he had initiated a conversation with me since Charley and I were married. I was glad to see my old sweetheart from simpler days.

"Where did you come from?" I said, smiling to take the edge off the question.

"I was standing behind the corner of the house, looking and listening," he said. "I couldn't resist spying on that... that whatever it is."

I laughed, even slapped my hands together. "Right," I said. "Whatever it is."

Wearing only a breechcloth, shirtless and shoeless, Strong Hickory looked young, fresh, uncomplicated, unhindered. "Well," he asked, "who is he?"

I told him all I knew about Bartholomew Bramlett. "For some reason he wants to build Charley a church. He probably wants to buy his way into heaven because he owns slaves."

"Lots of people own slaves," Strong Hickory said. "What's wrong with that?"

"You mean you wouldn't mind being a slave?" I said, proudly, as if I had made some great conquest in logic.

"I wouldn't mind being your slave, Nancy Swimmer," he whispered.

I turned away, and Strong Hickory said, "Why did you marry that old man? Some day he'll be worn out and bedridden, and you'll still be a young woman and having to take care of him."

"Old?" I said—but not unkindly. "Charley's not old. He's twenty-seven."

"And you and I are fourteen," Strong Hickory said. "Sometimes at night I lie there and think about you and him in bed, no farther away than I can throw a stone, and I can't stand it. I can't sleep."

Minister's wife, friend of the Boudinots, seeker after education, wearer of New England clothes ... suddenly the fourteen-year-old girl in me overwhelmed it all, and tears were coursing through the light soot the washday fire had deposited on my cheeks. I wished Strong Hickory and I were frolicking in the woods, visiting our cave, wading in the Oostanaula, as we had ever since we were old enough to remember.

He reached to wipe my face with the back of his hand, and I said, "Not here. You know how people talk."

"Where, then?" he asked.

"Nowhere," I said. "I didn't mean somewhere else. I mean nowhere."

"You still love me," Strong Hickory said.

"I'm a married woman," I sputtered. "I don't love you."

Did I? At that moment I loved the memory of carefree days, of being my parents' little girl, of being a child of the forest—and Strong Hickory was a reminder of those sweet times. I loved my husband, but I needed a respite from the structured life I had sought so desperately. I thought about something Harriet had said: "You're a child-woman. Neither one, yet both. My goodness, what must go through your mind. How does it hold it all? My goodness."

"Let's take a walk beside the river," Strong Hickory said. "No harm in old friends taking a walk beside the river."

I knew I must say no, but I said yes. I told Strong Hickory to go ahead, and I would meet him as soon as I hung out the clothes.

"What am I doing?" I asked myself, but when the last piece of clothing was strung over the limbs of a bush I glanced about me to be certain no one was looking, and then I walked to the path that meandered by the Oostanaula and disappeared around a bend.

Strong Hickory sat on the burned corpse of a tree that had died and fallen after being struck by lightning. "You can't beat this," he said, jumping to his feet and flinging a flat rock across the surface of the river. It skipped three times and sank.

"I can beat that," I said, and looked until I found a worthy rock. I flung it with all my might, and it skipped four times and stuck into the opposite bank.

I almost cried again. We had skipped rocks together all our lives, always with the same words of challenge and acceptance, usually with the same result: me winning. Oh it felt good to do it again.

"Let's walk and enjoy the springtime," Strong Hickory said. He reached for my hand, but I withdrew it.

Then, when he reached again, I didn't resist. We strolled beside the river, holding hands, a boy and a girl who had been sweethearts for a decade.

Except that I was Mrs. Charles Lawrence Marley. I disengaged my fingers, hid my right hand under my left arm. "I should go home," I said frantically.

I stared straight ahead, excited, confused—but I didn't go home; I continued to walk with Strong Hickory.

"When we are married we will build our cabin on that hill," he said, nodding toward the rise across the river. I trembled, and I could barely breathe. We were standing where we had stood when we kissed that day—the day Charley proposed to me. Strong Hickory had remembered the exact words he had spoken that day.

I knew he would try to kiss me, and I was right. He put his left hand on the back of my head and leaned toward me—and I honestly can't say whether we kissed or not. If lips brushing make a kiss, I suppose we did. But that's all it was, for as soon as I felt his breath on my cheek I moved my face. My identity as Mrs. Marley won out over that of the young girl strolling with a sweetheart.

"What's wrong?" Strong Hickory asked.

"You know what's wrong," I answered. "What's wrong is that I am married to a wonderful man I love and who loves me. I want you and me to be friends always, Strong Hickory, but we can't go back to childhood."

"We were considerably more than children that day when you kissed me standing right here and then got a better offer from that old preacher and told him you'd marry him," Strong Hickory said.

There was no point in arguing with him. "I'm going back to the village," I said. "Please wait awhile before you come. I don't want people to see us return together."

He didn't answer. He kept walking along the river bank, away from the village. He tried to skip a flat rock on the surface of the water, but it sank.

I entered my house and closed the door. I brushed my face against Charley's shirt that hung on a peg and smelled the reassuring smell of my husband. I fell onto our bed and wept and thanked God for Charley and asked him to forgive me for the sin I had just committed. I thanked him for not letting me commit a bigger one, for when Strong Hickory tried to kiss me I felt as if the Lord were standing beside me, watching; I've always believed in divine intervention.

Now I saw my marriage from Harriet's viewpoint. It was one thing for a fourteen-year-old Cherokee who was caught up in a simple life of subsistence to be a wife, but I had crossed the line into a complicated, civilized society that required mature judgment, and fourteen was awfully young in that setting.

Well, I had no regrets. I was glad I had crossed that line. I wouldn't have it any other way. I just had to tell myself there could be no recess from the life I had chosen, no returning to childhood for even a few minutes. As Charley's Bible—our Bible—said, I should put away childish things.

I wondered if Strong Hickory would tell anyone what we had done. He might even tell Charley. I didn't think so. I had hurt him, but his dedication to me had never wavered. He loved me.

I was still lying on the bed when I heard the syncopated approach of Bartholomew Bramlett's horse. I was eager for the strange man to go away, for Charley to appear in our little house so I could prove my love to him—and to myself.

The buggy rolled to a stop outside the door, and I heard Charley say, "You'll never know how I appreciate this, Bartholomew. God bless you."

My husband bolted inside, excited. I ran across the room and hugged him, kissed him, whispered my devotion.

He misunderstood my attention. He thought I had changed my mind about Bartholomew Bramlett, thought I was approving the help the slaveowner was offering us. What else could he think in the midst of such a lavish display of affection?

"It's wonderful, Nancy," Charley blurted. "He's not only going to build us a church, he's going to build a separate schoolhouse with a dormitory. We can board students, give them a Christian education. Bartholomew will pay their way. We can do a great work for the Lord here. It's wonderful."

I wanted to love Charley, to make up for the guilt I felt for having walked with Strong Hickory, but I hated Bartholomew Bramlett. When I heard his name I envisioned miserable black slaves packed in a ship like the salt fish packed in barrels that rocked on the back of wagons traders drove through New Echota.

I couldn't fight with Charley, not at that moment, but I couldn't say it was all right for my husband to be in league with this awful man, either.

I whimpered, like a trapped animal, and then I ran from our house and into the forest, Charley calling after me. I could barely breathe, and I was leaning against an oak tree when Charley caught up to me. "What in the world?" he asked, fear in his voice. "Did ... did somebody bother you while I was gone?"

I was gasping, and I held Charley away until there was enough air in my lungs to speak. I almost told him I didn't deserve him, but that would have sounded too suspicious. "I hate Bartholomew Bramlett," I sputtered ineffectually. "I hate Bartholomew Bramlett."

"Is that what this fit is about?" Charley asked levelly.

I didn't answer.

"Frankly, Nancy, I think you're a hypocrite," he said. "You pick and choose a bit too much for my taste. Bartholomew Bramlett is a slaveholder, and you despise him. But Major Ridge is a slaveholder, and since you admire him you ignore that fact. John Ridge is brilliant, and you're attracted to brilliance, so it slips your mind that he's a slaveholder, too."

It was true. Major Ridge was a shining light in the Cherokee Nation, a father figure to me, and I chose to conveniently forget he worked slaves on his plantation. His son John—Elias Boudinot's cousin—was a lawyer and writer, and I rarely thought about his slaves.

"They never gave me another human being for a wedding present," I said lamely.

"They might have if they had thought about it," Charley said.

"That man's arms were burned. He was tortured because he stole an apple," I said, knowing that had nothing to do with Bramlett.

"James Vann was an evil man, a devil. However, it was Vann who burned that slave, not Bramlett," Charley said sternly. "Bramlett was no more responsible for that than the Ridges were, and you know it."

"You know slavery is wrong," I said, trying to take the offensive. "Why do you want to have business with a slavemaster? You are a minister, a man of God, a man of righteousness."

"That's correct," he said. "It is wrong. And if I stop having anything to do with anyone who does anything wrong, I not only will have an empty church, I'll have an empty life, because I will have to go off into the woods and live by myself and become a hermit."

Charley reached for my hand, but I jerked it away. Then I remembered letting Strong Hickory hold my hand, and I felt like the Whore of Babylon. I stuck my hand back under Charley's long fingers. He squeezed—but I didn't squeeze back.

Now we were walking into the village clearing, toward our house, and Charley didn't speak as loudly, but his voice was just as forceful. "Bartholomew Bramlett is a troubled man. He sits in the library of his mansion, surrounded by books, and he reads philosophy and religion and even history and science, hoping for a clue to the ultimate.

"He wants to believe the Christian religion. The notion of a glorious afterlife based on having accepted the kindly, humble Christ appeals to him. However, he simply hasn't found sufficient reason to do so, and he is too honest to say he believes when he doesn't.

"He knows that he is a sinner—that we all are—and that we can't conquer sin on our own. A Jesus who conquers sin for us is an attractive figure—but Bartholomew will not say that he knows Jesus exists if he doesn't know it.

"He isn't trying to buy his way into heaven, Nancy, as you have said. He understands that good works could never get a Christian into heaven, but he hopes that by doing good works, by becoming involved in a practical Christian endeavor here on earth, he will find the pathway that leads to faith.

"I think it's my place—and your place as my wife—to help him in that search, not to block him because he has faults, even a huge fault such as owning slaves."

"I hate him," I said peevishly.

Charley sighed and shook his head in disgust. "At this precise moment, Mrs. Reverend Marley," he said, "I suspect Bartholomew Bramlett is closer to God than you are."

$$\ggg\!\!\longrightarrow \bullet \longleftarrow\!\!\lll$$

CHAPTER 12

I knew a personable white trader named Lexington Brown who would whoa his horses in New Echota, climb off his creaking wagon, tip his hat to the Cherokee women, slap the men on the back, and inevitably get around to sympathizing with the Indians because of the pressure they felt from Andrew Jackson and Georgia. He was considered a true friend of the Cherokees, a man who would short himself in a trade before he would short an Indian.

But one day Lexington Brown and a Cherokee who had been his companion—almost a brother—for years, got into a knife fight beside a stream that snaked through a mountain cove. The Indian died instantly when Lexington Brown rammed a blade into his brain through his eye socket. Lexington Brown, his body shredded, lay on a sandbar in the stream for nearly an hour, his gold pan beside him, before he bled to death, no Cherokee willing to help him because of what he had done to one of their own.

What Lexington Brown died of was gold fever.

In the summer of 1829 gold was discovered in the Cherokee Nation. There were several versions of how the first find was made, but the one I preferred had a black slave picking up a nugget some thirty miles east of New Echota and asking his master what the pretty rock was.

Gold drives men crazy. It has destroyed many a good person such as Lexington Brown, the last fellow on earth you would have thought would have killed anyone or gotten himself killed.

If the Cherokees really believed they could control their land, they must have realized otherwise, at least in their hearts, when the cry of *Gold!* brought ten-thousand whites storming illegally into the Cherokee Nation. The intruders generally were the basest of men, cutthroats, brawlers, drunkards—wretches who didn't know what a bath was—thieves, rapists. They didn't care that the land and thus the gold belonged to the Indians. They cared only that they could become rich, and, well, if they couldn't, at least they'd always be able to come up with three and a half grains of gold to buy a pint of whiskey.

The whites entered the Cherokee Nation on foot, and they came on horseback, and they drove wagons. They threw up tent towns and shack towns, and they drank and gambled and whored and fought among themselves.

And if they didn't find gold, well, they'd just stay on anyway and farm Cherokee land or steal Cherokee livestock or rob Cherokee households or rape Cherokee women. There was plenty to do.

The Cherokee National Council appealed to the Indian agent, Hugh Montgomery, to remove the trespassers, and he in turn asked the federal government for troops.

A battalion of blue-coated regulars arrived in Dahlonega, but they might as well have been trying to put out a hundred fires with a sedge broom. As soon as one dispute was settled, another one flared.

Governor Gilmer told Andrew Jackson the presence of the federal troops was an affront to Georgia. The president was delighted to oblige Georgia by calling them home. Gilmer replaced them with the Georgia Guard, a group of callous, undisciplined vigilantes. The U.S. troops tended to side with the Indians because they knew they were the rightful owners of the land; the Georgia Guard stopped just short of the philosophy that the only good Indian is a dead Indian.

"Samuel said the discovery of gold will spell the doom of the Cherokee Nation," Ann Worcester said one sweltering day as she and Harriet and I mended clothes and rocked on her front porch. "I wonder what will become of us?" She spoke as if her husband were an Old Testament prophet who could not be mistaken.

"Charley said it's one more reason for Georgia to want to take our land—a compelling reason," I said, pleased to interject my husband's important opinion into the conversation.

"We must pray unceasingly," Harriet said.

In fact, I was silently praying as I returned from New Echota to our village. I was on foot, and I carried a carpetbag that contained our mended clothes. The heat was unrelenting, burdensome. Rain hadn't fallen for two weeks, and I saw a dust cloud half a mile away. I heard the approach of a furiously driven horse.

Fifty yards ahead of me, the rider began reining his mount, and even from that distance I could see the creature was frantic. The black horse was lathered white because it had been ridden to the point of exhaustion.

The rider was a young man of nineteen or twenty, dressed in filthy clothes. But he was clean-shaven, and he had the face and blond hair of a boy. I thought that he would be handsome if he had a bath and a change of clothes.

"Hello, Miss," he said cheerily. "Certainly is a hot day, isn't it? I wonder if you could point me the way to New Echota?"

He climbed down from his faltering horse and patted the animal on the nose. "Good boy," he said in a lilting voice. It was a strange scene. The horse had been abused by being ridden so hard, but the boy didn't appear to be in a hurry. And he was petting the animal as if he loved it.

"It's just a couple of miles to New Echota," I said, "but that horse might not make two more miles."

He smiled. "Who are you?" he asked.

"I'm Nancy Marley," I said. "My husband is a minister."

"A man of God," he said pleasantly. "I wish he were here. I would like to kneel in prayer with him. It would be refreshing, for I have come a long way and have a long way yet to go. I'm a religious man myself. I had a Bible in my saddlebag, but one of those white gold prospectors stole it. My mother gave it to me. My first thought was to rail against my ill fortune, but I remembered how Mother would have reacted if she had been alive, and I told myself that maybe that fellow would read something in my Bible that would change his life. I said a prayer for him instead."

"I would be pleased to kneel with you in prayer," I said, and I thought about people in the Bible having religious experiences on dust-choked roads in the Holy Land.

"Would you, Mrs. Marley?" he said. "That would be wonderful."

We got on our knees, the pink dust collecting on the purple dress Harriet had given me. We closed our eyes, and I folded my hands under my chin. "Dear Lord," I began, "bless this wayfarer as he ..."

The man shot to his feet and grabbed me behind the neck and pushed my face into the dust. "You goddamned Cherokee whore-lady," he said. "You copper-skinned harlot. You goddamn heathens get married when you're still children. Don't try to tell me how to treat a horse. I'll ride that goddamned horse to death if I want to, and I'll cut your goddamned throat so you'll be in hell with him."

He shoved my face deeper into the powdery dust, and I didn't dare even open my eyes. "You goddamned Cherokees think you're as good as white people. You steal all the goddamned gold from land that belongs to Georgians, and white folks like me can't find any. Now I've got to go back home to a drunk father and a whoring mother without a grain of gold to show for coming up here, and all I'll hear for six months is, 'We told you so; you should have stayed home on the farm and helped us.' It was my one chance, but you goddamned Cherokees got all the gold.

"Don't tell me your husband is a man of God. There's not a God. If there was a God, I wouldn't be going home empty-handed. Tell your husband I said he is a copper-skinned son of a bitch, and I dare him to do anything about it."

I flailed my arms at him, but I was helpless under his grip, and my arms went limp with the rest of my body. When I tried to breathe I inhaled the dust of the road. I waited for him to rape me and kill me.

But he didn't. He turned me loose. On my hands and knees, my dress and face and waist-length black hair covered in pink dust, I gasped for breath and looked up at him.

"I guess you're one goddamned Cherokee that knows who's boss, don't you?" he said.

I continued to stare at him. He's going to kick me in the face, I thought.

But he didn't. He just repeated: "I guess you're one goddamned Cherokee that knows who's boss, don't you?" Then, in a pleading tone, he said, "Say yes."

"Yes," I said.

That satisfied him. He had made me eat dirt, had insulted me, had insulted my husband, had forced me to acknowledge that he was in command. He climbed onto his horse and without even looking back furiously whipped the poor thing toward New Echota.

I watched him out of sight. "You bastard," I yelled. "You didn't even have guts enough to rape me and kill me."

The gold rush brought sick, and sickening men, indeed, into the Cherokee Nation.

Under the direction of a pudgy white man who munched on fruit and cakes and deer jerky, black slaves who belonged to Bartholomew Bramlett put in place the final white oak shingles on the roof of Charley's new church.

The pudgy man never raised his voice to the slaves. He spoke to them as calmly as he spoke to me. Like him, the three black men knew carpentry, and they didn't hesitate to make suggestions. "Good idea, Lemuel," he would say. Their relationship was more like that of boss and employees than slavemaster and bondsmen.

That irritated me. I wanted to hear the white man scream at the workers, curse them. I wanted him to beat them. I wanted to rush up to my husband and shout, "See! I told you Bartholomew Bramlett is so evil that he will even befoul hell."

Charley was excited about the church, but I blunted his joy by responding to his daily tidbits of news with a blank look and "oh" or "really?" Finally, he stopped talking to me about it.

"Big surprise coming tomorrow, Mrs. Marley," the pudgy man said as I passed the church.

"Really?" I kept on walking.

"That barrel of whitewash got a better disposition than that ole girl," one of the slaves who was partially deaf said in what he thought was a low voice.

I was furious. I turned and said, "Why you black ..."

I gasped at the sound of my voice. I was shocked, but it wasn't just that. When I was a toddler and would say something displeasing to my mother, I thought I could suck the words back into my mouth, and they would never have been spoken. I was trying to suck those words back into my mouth.

Suddenly, I could see clearly into my soul. Maybe I was an enlightened reader of newspapers from Philadelphia and Boston and a vocal hater of slavery, but I was still a Cherokee who had grown up surrounded by the practice, and lingering were the feeling of superiority over another race and indignation that one of its members would dare question anything I said or did.

"Sorry, ma'm," the black man blurted, terror in his eyes. "I didn't mean you to hear me. What I mean is ... I didn't mean ..."

"It's all right," I said. "You're quite right. I do have the personality of a barrel of whitewash where this church is concerned. I don't approve of your master, Bartholomew Bramlett. I don't approve of slavery, and he is a slaveholder. I don't approve of my husband, a minister, having business with him."

Again I turned and walked away—and again I heard a voice. It was the pudgy white man's, and this time I was meant to hear it: "Sanctimonious, too, ain't she?

Hates slavery but started calling Montgomery a black bastard before she caught herself."

I kept walking, I thought about the young white gold miner who hated me because my skin was darker than his. Copper-skinned harlot, he had called me. Black bastard, I had called the slave. Or I almost had. Were we any different?

I wanted to talk to Charley—not because he was my husband but because he was my minister. That night, after supper, I told him about the incident at the church. I told him I committed a terrible sin against a fellow human being.

"I heard about it," he said.

"You did? Who told you?"

"The white man, Rodham. He's a relative of Bartholomew Bramlett and the overseer of his plantation. He knew Bartholomew and I were friends, and he said he would resign the job of building the church and send another man if I wanted him to."

"What did you tell him?" I asked, not sure what answer I hoped for.

"I told him that was out of the question," Charley said. "I told him you did have a sanctimonious streak in you. But I told him you were a good woman, and some day when life polishes the rough edges and maturity improves your judgment, you'll be a great woman."

Was that a compliment? I didn't know. But I had come to Charley as sheep to shepherd, so I suppressed my temper. "I'm listening," I said.

"Don't be too hard on yourself," Charley said, "but be hard enough. You're fourteen years old, and you're going to make mistakes, say things you don't mean, hurt other people. You'll do it when you're twenty-eight, and you'll do it when you're one hundered and twenty-eight.

"All your young life you've seen the black people enslaved, treated like inferiors, so you spoke to one like an inferior, like you might speak to a balky horse. But the important thing is that you were immediately sorry. You'll never be rid of your old sinful nature, Nancy. You just have to battle it, try to control it. We're all in the same choppy waters, but Christ keeps some of us afloat."

"I'm just like the young white gold miner," I said, feeling better but not quite ready to be absolved. "He hates me because my skin is darker than his, and I hate the slave because his skin is darker than mine."

Charley smiled, more paternally than anything else. "He hates you, but you don't hate Montgomery. He's pleased that he treated you like he did, but you're distraught that you treated Montgomery like you did. There's a big, big difference."

I saw Charley's face light up. I knew an idea had hit him between the eyes.

"Nancy, I'll cite you a much better comparison than you and the gold miner," he said.

"What?"

"You and Bartholomew Bramlett."

I could have killed him. But you don't kill your minister. "There's nothing about me that's like anything about that man," I said in the calmest voice I could command.

"Sure there is," Charley said. "You both care passionately about doing the right thing. You both are seekers after truth, voracious readers. As strange as it sounds, I think you two basically agree on the slavery issue."

I couldn't have been more confused. "What are you talking about?" I asked. "He enslaves people. I wouldn't do that under any circumstances. We are as different as a bluejay and a turtle."

"I think Bartholomew is beginning to see that it is wrong for one person to own another person," Charley said. "But he is faced with a dilemma. He has a huge plantation, and it requires labor. In an ideal world he would simply call all his slaves together and tell them they are free, but in the real world it isn't that simple.

"But believe me, he is wrestling with himself. Going on inside him is a monumental struggle that reminds me of some inner battles you read about in the Bible. It will be interesting to watch the developments in the life of Mr. Bartholomew Bramlett."

My minister had made me feel I wasn't evil incarnate after all. If only he hadn't compared me to Bartholomew Bramlett. But I kept quiet, read a newspaper by lantern light, went to bed early, and assured myself I didn't resemble that awful man in any way. I wasn't going to give an inch where Bartholomew Bramlett was concerned.

The next morning, while I was sweeping the yard with a brush broom, Bramlett's buggy rolled into our village, its owner barely visible under his blanket, the driver wearing that same straight-ahead gaze. Behind it came a wagon driven by Mr. Rodham. Montgomery and two other Negroes were on the back, steadying a huge object.

"Charley," I called as the two vehicles stopped beside the church.

My husband stepped from our house, saw the men, and shouted, "Glory! It's the steeple. Bartholomew had it constructed in Augusta." He ran toward them like a little boy discovering a prize.

Rodham and the Negroes carefully slid a thin cone off the wagon. It was a copper steeple, a gorgeous orange piece that I reckoned to be fifteen feet long. It was topped by a three-foot white cross. The steeple caught the morning sun in orange brilliance, and I thought of the gold trappings of Jerusalem's temple where Christ taught.

I wanted to examine the steeple, to feel the heat of the sun in its metal, to hear the sound it would make if I thumped it. I almost relented and joined the men— but instead I dropped the broom and began walking away. If I were in New Echota I couldn't relent.

Harriet sat on the porch of her house. Pregnant with William Penn, she rocked Mary while on a quilt Eleanor played with a rag doll. Harriet looked haggard, even frail, but she smiled and held out her hand to me. "When this child is born I will have three under the age of 3," she said, her tone of voice as inevitable as that of someone remarking on night falling.

I took Mary and rocked her and smelled the familiar milky baby smell and wondered when I would become pregnant. It hadn't happened in nine months of marriage. Stoneseed, which Indian women swallowed to prevent pregnancy, appeared to work in my case. I was thankful it did, for I was in no hurry to have a child.

Elias spotted me through his study window and joined us. "Nancy, I'm glad you're here," he said. "I have a couple of stories I think you'll enjoy doing for the *Phoenix.*"

Good. I forgot about the sin of my tongue toward the black man, about Bartholomew Bramlett, about babies. I was in the element I loved.

"Charley's church and school are nearly finished," Elias said. "I'd like you to do a story about the project, what Charley hopes to accomplish, why this Mr. Bramlett gave of his resources to make it all possible. Interview your husband, interview Mr. Bramlett, give us plenty of background on each of them. You might even mention that Charley is married to a beautiful little Cherokee woman."

When I didn't smile, the grin left Elias's face. "What's wrong?" he asked.

"I can't write about Charley's church," I said. "I can't write about Bartholomew Bramlett."

Harriet stopped rocking. "Why?" Elias asked.

"The man is a slaveholder," I said. "You know how I feel about slavery. You and I have read stories in the exchange papers and discussed how awful slavery is. You have written editorials about it.

"My husband is a minister, a man of God. It isn't right for him to work hand-in-glove with a slaveholder, even if they are building a church and a school. That old Bramlett is just trying to buy a ticket to heaven, like you buy a ticket on a ship from New York to Charleston—if you've got enough money. I won't have any part of it."

"I see," Elias said.

"Do you? Really?" I asked.

"Oh, yes," he said. "I see, but I don't agree with your reasoning. All through the Bible the cause of Christ is pushed along by weak, sinful men, including the apostles. If Bramlett wants to build a church and a school, I say let him. Of course, I don't think Charley should pat him on the back and say he believes slavery is all right if he doesn't believe it. But I happen to know Charley hasn't done that. Bramlett knows Charley hates slavery.

"But the decision has to be yours. Well, I've got to get back to work."

Elias was stepping through the front door when I blurted, "But what about the other story? What is it?"

"Oh, I wanted you to interview Major Ridge the next time he's in town. I wanted a story on his life. No doubt it would have to be a series. But, of course, he's a slaveholder, too, so you wouldn't want to write that story, either."

One of my heroes—Elias Boudinot—was suggesting I write a story about another of my heroes—Major Ridge. "Wait," I said.

Major Ridge was a handsome old man, a force in Cherokee society whether we were at war or at peace. He was a legend. Somehow, his owning slaves didn't seem as offensive as the broad-faced, blanket-hidden, manipulative Bramlett's owning them.

"I want to do the story on Major Ridge," I blurted.

Elias gazed into my eyes for the longest time. Finally, I had to look away. "Nancy, if you think you're being high-minded, you're not," he said. "You're just being hypocritical. But if you want to do the story on Major Ridge, all right. I'll make the arrangements."

CHAPTER 13

W hen I got home the steeple was in place. It shone like a golden beacon, and a songbird was perched on the cross as if to proclaim the church belonged to every creature.

It didn't belong to me. I didn't mention the steeple to Charley. Usually he ignored my ignoring the church, refusing to give me the satisfaction of having my opinion considered. But this time, with his and Bartholomew Bramlett's church literally and figuratively finished in such dramatic fashion, my silence made him furious.

"What would you like for supper, Charley?" I asked.

"A little damned common sense out of you," he spat. It was the first time I ever heard him curse.

"I'll fix carnuchee," I said. The dish of corn mush and hickory nuts was one of his favorites.

"Don't fix it for me," he said. "I'm not hungry. You'd ruin anyone's appetite."

I didn't speak for an hour, and neither did Charley. Finally, I said, "Elias wants me to write a story about the life of Major Ridge."

"No," Charley said.

"No?"

"Major Ridge is a slaveholder," he said. "If you wrote a story about him that would imply that you approve of slavery. As a minister's wife, you must be above reproach."

His irony didn't register. "Charley, you don't mean it," I whined.

"Of course I don't mean it, Nancy," he yelled. "Write your damned story. I don't care if you write an article about Major Ridge, for goodness sake. I was just hoping it might ring a bell in your thick skull and you'd see how ridiculous you sound when you object to me letting Bartholomew Bramlett build me a church."

But still I didn't budge.

We barely spoke to each other the rest of that night, the next day, and the following morning. When Elias's messenger arrived to tell me Major Ridge would be at the editor's home for lunch and that I should be there and be prepared to interview him, I said simply, "I've got to go to New Echota," and I put on my most severe dress and left.

Major Ridge and Elias engaged in animated conversation as they rocked on the veranda of the house. They didn't see me, and I stopped at the corner of the whitewashed, two-storied home.

Major Ridge's face was stern, authoritative, the jowly hard-eyed face of a man who had seen the tragedy and joy that life had to offer and who was equal to whatever came next. His thick white hair was curly, piled atop his head like so much carded cotton, hiding his ears.

In the heat he wore a white linen shirt, open at the sleeves and neck, and mustard-colored pants that disappeared into gleaming black boots. The open shirt revealed ringlets of white hair on a broad chest.

He was the perfect picture of a great chief who had been a great warrior, a man who had donned war paint and taken scalps but who had been among the first of the Cherokees to adapt to the civilized ways of the whites. How many lives he had been able to cram into one!

I coughed, smiled and walked toward the two men. "Oh, hello, Nancy," Elias said. "Nancy Swimmer, this is Major Ridge. Major Ridge, this is …"

I was delighted when he said, "Oh, I remember Nancy. I met her at this very house. She was helping Mrs. Boudinot do the housework, and I recall thinking what a beautiful girl she was."

The old charmer! But I loved it.

"Nancy said she thought I would make a fine principal chief," he went on. "That was when I realized by what huge measure a woman's loveliness can surpass her political judgment."

We all laughed, and he insisted I take his chair, the only one with a cushion tied by ribbons to the frame.

"My nephew, Editor Boudinot, tells me you want to write an article about my life," Major Ridge said. "I can't imagine a more mundane subject, but if you and he are willing, so am I. I have been interviewed by renowned reporters in Washington City, but I must say never by one as comely as the reporter for the *Phoenix*."

So the old man was flirting a little? So what? One of the most famous persons in Cherokee history was paying attention to me, and I loved it.

"I'll leave you two alone," Elias said. He placed a bottle of ink on the porch rail and handed me a packet containing paper and pens. I felt as if a parent were deserting me in an unfamiliar city.

"I'll help you," Major Ridge said. "I know what you want to know without your having to ask it. Relax and write."

And I did. He spoke slowly, giving me plenty of time to scribble down the words and marks and abbreviations that would jar my memory later. For the most part, all I had to do was listen.

"I was born in 1771, in the village of Hiwassee on the Hiwassee River, in what the whites now call their state of Tennessee," he said, and I quickly calculated that would make him fifty-seven or fifty-eight. "My father was a renowned hunter, my mother a half-breed, the daughter of a Scots frontiersman and an Indian woman. I was one of seven children, a brood that included Editor Boudinot's father, Watie.

"When I was a child there was much fighting with the whites, so my father put his family into log canoes and floated us down the Hiwassee River to the peaceful Sequatchie Valley, a rich hunting ground of deer and bear and even an occasional wandering buffalo. As I grew up, he taught me to imitate the cry of a fawn to draw its mother near, to stun fish with the pounded pulp of buckeye—in short, to hunt and fish so that I might care for myself.

"As a child I had been called The Pathkiller, but when I was a young hunter my friends did me the honor of calling me The Ridge—for they said I walked upon mountain tops and thus could see far. I am embarrassed to speak thusly of myself, but that is what they said."

I realized I was grinning. He was wonderful. He could have been my grandfather, but I'll admit I was attracted to him as if he were twenty instead of nearly sixty.

There had been relative peace on the frontier for several years, and his family moved to Chestowee, near Hiwassee, he told me. There they were living when war broke out again.

The U.S. Congress ordered white squatters out of Cherokee territory, but they refused to leave. Under a flag of truce, a white man shot Old Tassel, the principal chief of the Upper Cherokees, and that made fighting inevitable. There was a call for men—and it reached Chestowee.

"I was seventeen years old," Major Ridge said, gazing across the public spring, as if the past were being played out on the stage of a hill in the distance. "My parents were ill, and they depended upon me. They begged me not to go, but I couldn't resist.

"The volunteers painted our faces vermilion, circling one eye with white and one with black. We danced the warrior dance, threatening the enemy with red and black ceremonial clubs—red for blood, black for fearlessness. We danced the dance repeatedly, each time more men joining in. Who could say no to such excitement, to the lure of the warpath?

"I shaved my head, leaving only a scalplock, to which I tied red feathers tipped with white. My face was painted, and I wore only a breechcloth and moccasins. I carried my weapons and some corn meal. I welcomed the danger, the hardship.

"We fasted the first day, and after that the only daily ration we had was a cup of meal. We Chestowee men met up with other Cherokees, and our force totaled two hundred.

"We set out to destroy a small settlement called Houston's Station, which was sixteen miles south of White's Fort, but we learned a force of soldiers were looking for us, and our leaders planned a clever ambush of the apple eaters."

Apple eaters?

Major Ridge laughed roundly at my question. He was playing me as if I were a new violin, and both of us were enjoying it.

"At Setico, a deserted town, there was an old orchard heavy with ripe apples," he said. "We hid and watched as the soldiers arrived. Like the Adam of your Bible, they couldn't resist the fruit. They dismounted, and some of them carelessly laid their rifles aside. That was when they learned the fruit was forbidden.

"Accompanied by the frightening music of war whoops and turkey gobbles, we charged from our hiding places. Our shots dropped soldiers like a strong wind blowing down withered cornstalks.

"Some escaped by riding their horses through the river and up a steep bank. One of our persistent warriors caught a soldier on the bank and engaged him in hand-to-hand combat. The white man threw him, and another Indian joined in. Now it was two against one.

"Then it became three against one, for I arrived on the scene and stuck my spear into him. Then I took my first scalp. In my first battle I had become a Mankiller."

Now he was silent, and he studied my face for my reaction. "Three against one," I remarked, for I thought that was what he wanted me to say.

"Three against one," he repeated. "It was war. Never mistake war for anything else. Never mistake it for anything in which being fair is admirable."

Sixteen—about half—of the white men escaped, Major Ridge said. The Cherokees wanted scalps, and even a skillful scalper required two minutes to complete his grisly work. While they were cutting, the enemy was getting away.

"Is this too much for you?" he said. "I shouldn't have spoken in such detail."

"I'm all right," I answered, but a chilling pain raced through my shoulders when I considered that I was sitting on a porch, rocking away, with a man who had been part of such a gory episode.

I was surprised to hear him chuckle, see him shake his head.

"Sometimes I wonder if the Great Spirit, or God, or whoever it is, enjoys playing little games on us," he said. "I learned later that the very man who killed Old Tassel was among the soldiers whom we ambushed. He was wounded, but he managed to crawl into a hollow log and hide. All around him, Indians were cavorting, but the soldier who caused it all kept quiet and escaped."

He chuckled again, shook his head at the ironies of the planet, and continued: "We proceeded to Houston's Station, but John Sevier, a seasoned Indian fighter, came to the settlement's rescue, and in the face of his huge numbers we withdrew. We delighted in the success of the ambush, though, and we returned to our villages in glory, singing the death song, bragging about our bravery, carrying green pine branches on which were displayed the scalps of the enemy."

Thus began his career as a warrior. Numerous excursions against the whites followed. He experienced victory and defeat. His parents died while he was on the warpath, leaving him responsible for two younger brothers and a sister, though he was but in his teen years himself. Still, he embarked on expeditions against the hated Americans.

"Ah, two incidents make me sick at my stomach when I recall them," Major Ridge said. "They are too awful. I shan't tell about them."

I was fascinated, and—just as he knew I would—I asked, "What happened?"

"Well, all right," the old chief said.

"Doublehead was truly an evil man, a merciless fighter, the kind of person whose cruelties caused Indians to be judged emotionally rather than judiciously.

"A group of Doublehead's men, including me, was hidden near a watering hole, assaulting passing whites. A Captain Overall, who was known to be an Indian fighter, and his friend Burnett came along. We killed them and took their nine packhorses.

"Doublehead got drunk on their whiskey and decided that we should eat Overall and Burnett. He said the settlers would hear about it and be terrified.

"Doublehead cut flesh from their corpses and broiled it. He also broiled their hearts and brains. Some of the men did eat a few bites. I refused. He said I was weak."

I felt nausea sweeping over me. I focused on a robin that drank from the public spring and forced the ghastly picture from my mind.

"Another time, a force of warriors attacked Cavett's Station near Knoxville," Major Ridge said. "The blockhouse was occupied by just one family, that of Alexander Cavett. There were thirteen of them, only three of whom were men.

"The Cavetts killed five Indians with their gunfire, but they were drastically outnumbered, and they surrendered with the understanding that our leader, John Watts, would exchange them for Indian prisoners held by whites.

"Our second in command was Doublehead. His brother Pumpkin Boy had been recently killed by the whites, and Doublehead was consumed with vengeance. When the gates of the blockhouse opened, I was startled by the war whoop that escaped from his throat, doubly startled to see him attack the women and children with his tomahawk.

"There was nothing I could do. I turned my head and looked the other way.

"Only one member of the family was saved. Watts rescued a boy, Alexander Cavett, Jr. Doublehead demanded his life, too, but Watts had some of his Creek friends in the force spirit him away. It did no good, for a few days later a Creek killed Alexander Cavett, Jr. and scalped him."

Major Ridge asked if I might get Harriet to brew us some tea. I was glad to stir about, to breathe deeply, to talk to her and her babies, to focus on life instead of death.

He joined Elias in his nephew's study for a few minutes, and I could hear them talking about *Phoenix* business. It was difficult to believe the well-spoken, well-dressed old farmer had cut scalps from the heads of enemies, had consorted with cannibals.

"Oh, Nancy," came Elias's voice, "I meant to tell you some news. Isaac Harris is gone."

I stepped into the study. "Gone?"

"No longer employed by the *Phoenix*. John Wheeler is our only printer. I put up with Harris's evil tongue too long as it was, and when he cursed me today I told him he was dismissed. The filth erupted from his mouth like lava from a volcano, and I didn't know what to do. We must have argued for five minutes. Major Ridge was standing outside the print shop, and he lost patience with Harris—and, no doubt, with me—and without a word came inside, twisted Harris's arm behind him and kicked him in the seat of the pants, sending him sprawling outside onto the ground. Harris brushed the dust from his clothes and glared at Major Ridge, but he didn't speak. He just walked away, and so we are rid of him."

"Good," I said, uncharitably. "I despised that man." I didn't believe that even a minister's wife was required to regret that an oaf such as Isaac Harris had lost his job.

I smiled at the Major. He smiled back. He may have dressed like an Augusta gentleman, but I knew he could still summon his identity as a warrior in breechcloth if the need arose. Perhaps it was overstating things to say Isaac Harris should be grateful he still had his scalp—or perhaps it wasn't.

After a recess of some fifteen minutes, Major Ridge and I returned to our rocking chairs on the veranda. "And now I will tell you about a new chapter in my life," he said.

"Finally, the fighting, like everything else in the world does, reached an end. The last big battle between the Cherokees and the Americans was at the village of Etowah. I hate to say it, but the Indians were defeated. George Washington offered peace to a Cherokee deputation in Philadelphia, presenting them a large silver pipe as a symbol of friendship. All those lives lost, red people and white people, men, women and children—and a pipe … oh, well …

"I settled in Pine Log, south of here, and began to live the peaceful life. I quickly got my first taste of what the whites call politics when I was chosen to represent Pine Log at the tribal council at Oostanaula.

"I was young, and about all I owned was an old white pony and some worn-out clothes. The Cherokees valued ceremony. A representative to the council should be well-dressed, mounted on a fine horse, displaying his trophies of war and hunting. I certainly didn't fit the picture.

"When I reached the council ground some of the younger members stared at me in disgust and tried to bar me from the council. Riper minds prevailed, though, and the older men asked me to sit with them.

"At that first council I kept quiet and listened. In my mind I sorted out the speeches, thought not only about the ones that made an impression on me but the ones that didn't. Why did some orators fire my emotions and others leave me unmoved? I peeled away the layers like peeling away the layers of an onion.

"The next year, in my second council, I did not keep quiet. In fact, I made a contribution to Cherokee society that I am quite proud of."

An extraordinary thing had happened as a result of Major Ridge's career as a warrior, he admitted. All the killing and wanton cruelty had increased his appreciation of the value of human life, heightened his compassion. He thus came to believe that some of the white man's laws and customs that protected the individual were superior to those of the Indian.

So the young Major Ridge attacked the Cherokees' traditional Blood Law and succeeded in getting it drastically modified. The young man who until recently had been shooting down whites shot down a cruel custom that dated from time immemorial.

The Blood Law decreed that blood must be paid for by blood. If a person killed another, he died at the hands of the dead person's relatives, even if the death was accidental. If the killer fled, the dead person's relatives had the right to take the life of the killer's nearest of kin. It was an eye for an eye in the strictest sense.

"It was an evil, nonsensical practice," Major Ridge said. "I know this sounds boastful, but I summoned all my oratorical skills and delivered a moving speech on behalf of repeal. The council voted to do away with the parts of the law that made accidental killing a crime and that substituted a kinsman for a fugitive. I am pleased that I accomplished this good thing."

The Americans encouraged Cherokee women to spin and weave and the men to give up the hunt—which was growing more and more unproductive—and become farmers. Forsake the villages and clear farms from the forests and raise grain and cotton and cattle and hogs, they advised.

"Many Cherokees refused just because the suggestion came from the whites," Major Ridge said, "but it made sense to me, and I was one of the first Cherokees to take their advice. I married a spirited, ambitious woman named Susanna Wickett. Quite frankly, she wanted to be rich, and so did I. Some couples pull in opposite directions, but not us. We are a matched pair."

Major Ridge left Pine Log and settled in the Oothcaloga Valley. He built a log house, complete with chimney, and he and Susanna set in to clearing the land, plowing and planting. Eventually, they would have orchards of apples and peaches and large fields of cotton and corn.

Several industrious families settled in the Oothcaloga Valley, and it became known as "the garden spot of the Cherokee country." Watie, Major Ridge's brother, Elias Boudinot's father, joined him in the valley.

"I bought Negro slaves to help," Major Ridge said offhandedly, and I sighed a sigh that caused him to glance at me. Why did he have to mention that?

It was in the Oothcaloga Valley that all of Major Ridge's and Susanna's children were born. Their first was a girl, Nancy, the second a boy, John—the cousin, fast friend and schoolmate of Elias Boudinot. The third was a baby who died, the fourth a feeble-minded boy named Walter and the last a girl called Sally.

The children learned no English until they attended white schools, for their father knew almost no English, and Cherokee was the speech of their household. It is difficult to comprehend, too, that the great Major Ridge was illiterate, signing with his mark.

"We worked hard, and our plantation prospered," Major Ridge said, "but I continued to serve on the council, and my influence grew. I became the one who announced and explained to the people the decisions of the council."

Major Ridge laughed nervously and got up and walked to the edge of the porch. He placed both hands on the banister and gazed into the distance.

"You must understand what I am going to say," he began. "I was a member of the political faction of James Vann. Yes, the same James Vann who some say was the embodiment of evil. And maybe he was. But James Vann was a Cherokee patriot. His faction favored civilization and fought exploitation of the Indians by the whites. When James Vann wasn't drunk, he was a wonderful man; when he was drunk—well, you've heard the stories."

I told him I understood, that I also had heard about the good side of James Vann. He was satisfied, and he returned to his chair.

"It's here that our friend Doublehead returns to our story," he said. "Little Turkey was principal chief and Doublehead was speaker of the Nation, but Little Turkey was overwhelmed by the aggressiveness of Doublehead—as many would have been—and Doublehead became a spokesman for the Cherokees in dealings with the Americans.

"Doublehead was susceptible to bribery, and the Americans didn't hesistate to use it to get whatever they wanted. Finally, he succeeded in arranging the cession to the U.S. of the best hunting grounds in the Cherokee Nation, a vast expanse north of the Tennessee River, stretching from Hiwassee to Muscle Shoals and including the Cumberland Plateau and parts of Kentucky. The grateful Americans reserved some of the land for the use of Doublehead and one of his kinsmen.

"Doublehead was branded a traitor by the Cherokees, but the chiefs as well as the people feared him. He applied the laws as he saw fit, and those who opposed him sometimes ended up dead.

"The Vann faction and other men decided Doublehead must die. James Vann, Alexander Saunders and myself were chosen to do the deed. I had hated him since the murders of the Cavett family; James Vann hated him because Doublehead had married the sister of Vann's favorite wife and beaten her to death when she was pregnant. Vann, in fact, had called Doublehead a traitor in Washington City and they had drawn knives, but nothing had happened.

"Vann became ill, and it fell to Saunders and me to execute Doublehead. We waited for him in a tavern. Doublehead came in after attending a Ball Play, tipsy and excited, his hand bandaged, and got in an argument with an old white man. I ran up, blew out the candle on his table, and shot Doublehead in the jaw. In the darkness, Saunders and I left the tavern, believing our mission was accomplished.

"We were shocked to learn later the Doublehead was alive. We also learned that earlier in the day, at the Ball Play, he had killed a man named Bone-Polisher who had called him a traitor. Bone-Polisher had chopped off Doublehead's thumb with a tomahawk, but that didn't keep the evil one from visiting the tavern and having a few more drinks.

"We learned that, with his jaw shattered and the ball lodged in his neck, Doublehead hid in the loft of a school teacher's house. Saunders and I and two men of Bone-Polisher's clan rushed into the room where Doublehead lay. He sprang to his feet, a knife in his hand, reaching for a pistol.

"Saunder's gun misfired and so did mine. Doublehead and I grappled, and I wondered if I might lose my life. Remember what I told you about forgetting fairness in a fight? Well, Saunders drove his tomahawk into Doublehead's brow, and another Indian grabbed a shovel and beat his head into mush. And that was the end of Doublehead."

Major Ridge placed his fingers together at his chest and flexed them, forming what children call a spider on a mirror. "I'm afraid I have led quite a bloody life," he said. "Perhaps you hadn't expected such gruesome tales."

"I'm all right," I said. "Go on."

Everyone thought justice had been served, and no one mourned Doublehead, unless it was the Americans, Major Ridge explained. None of his relatives attempted revenge and, in fact, his death led to the abolition of what remained of clan revenge, for no one believed his kin should be forced to seek vengeance. The application of punishment became a governmental function rather than a responsibility of relatives.

Increasingly, the Cherokees looked to Major Ridge as a leader. He was placed at the head of the Lighthorse Guard, a corps that rode the nation as judges, jurors and executioners of justice. He was appointed to a thirteen-member committee named to look after the Cherokees' national affairs. He became an ambassador to the Creek Nation. He was selected a member of delegations that met with Thomas Jefferson, James Madison and James Monroe during their presidencies.

"The Capitol was still under construction when we went to see Jefferson in Washington City in 1808," Major Ridge said, "but, oh, what a building. Its marble walls were as white as clouds. However when I returned to see Madison in 1816 those walls were black and defaced, for the British had torched Washington City in 1814. The whole town would have burned down if there hadn't been a sudden rainstorm. When I was there in '16 the Capitol still sat vacant on its hill, sheep were grazing below, and Congress was conducting its business elsewhere. That beautiful structure had been restored, though, when I met with Monroe in 1824.

"One thing is constant," he reflected. "Washington City is a big mudhole. Even Pennsylvania Avenue, where the President lives, is muddy. The streets are too wide, and it's a long distance from one place to another. Baltimore! Now there's a town. Washington City grew out of one man's dream, but Baltimore grew out of many people's needs. If you really want to see a sight, you should see the gas street lamps burning in the night in Baltimore."

And Jefferson and Madison and Monroe themselves? I could barely comprehend that I was chatting with a person who had stood with presidents.

"A tall man who looked tired—that's how I remember Jefferson," Major Ridge said. "His hair had been red, but it had turned grey—probably from dealing with all those Indians.

"Madison looked like a withered little apple. He was about five-foot-four, a hundred pounds, with a voice you could barely hear. You kept hoping a breeze wouldn't stir because he might blow away like a feather. He and his wife Dolley made a humorous looking couple. She was portly, a buxom woman. He was reserved, but she was friendly, gay. She called him 'my darling little husband.'

"Monroe. Hmmm. By glory, his looks were so commonplace that I can't summon his face to my memory. I remember thinking when I was there that he looked like a million other men—and a president ought to look different in some way, any way. Even if he's just a shriveled-up piece of jerky like Madison."

He laughed at his own joke, but his smile disappeared, and he said, "I returned from Washington City after the visit with Jefferson to find that James Vann had been slain. As your Bible says, he who lives by the sword ... Charles Hicks became the leader of our faction. A quiet man whose library contained the great works of English authors replaced an overbearing drunkard. I don't believe many people were sorry to see James go."

Major Ridge became a respected statesman—but his fighting days weren't over. A Creek civil war exploded into the white world when the Red Stick Creeks massacred nearly four hundred men, women and children at Fort Mims near Mobile. Major Ridge believed the Cherokees should declare themselves on the side of the whites before the mess became in the minds of the whites simply a whites-vs.-Indians thing.

The Cherokee council voted for non-intervention but, pushed by Major Ridge, they changed their vote to a declaration of war against the Red Stick rebels. Major Ridge recruited many braves to fight beside the Americans against the Red Sticks. "I rose to the grade of major during the Creek War," he said, "and I took that as my first name. Major Ridge sounds better than The Ridge, don't you think?"

I didn't tell him my father had fought with him against the Red Sticks, that, indeed, Major Ridge had recruited him. I didn't want Major Ridge to know I already had heard the stories. I wanted him to talk freely.

He did. About all the bloody fights. About the Battle of the Horseshoe, which had changed Staring Otter's life.

He told how the Creeks of six towns had gathered on a hundred-acre peninsula formed by a horseshoe bend in the Tallapoosa River, sealing off the other end with a zig-zag breastwork of logs.

He told how Jackson's men, on the other side of the breastwork, fired volleys for two hours with little success and how the Cherokees became impatient and stole the Creeks' canoes and inspired Jackson to prosecute the battle.

"Jackson's soldiers were on a rise about eighty yards from the barricade," he said. "Their cannons and rifles and muskets weren't doing much but making noise. We got tired of it, and three Cherokees—including Charles Reese, the brother-in-law of my brother Watie—dived into the river and swam across to the Creeks' canoes.

"One of them, The Whale, was wounded, but the other two brought canoes to us. We packed them with warriors, including me, and crossed to the other side, sending back more canoes to ferry more Cherokees.

"We advanced on the Creeks and drove them toward their barricade. But the incantations of their prophets rang in their ears, and they fought like madmen. Oh, the noise those prophets made! Their heads and shoulders were covered with feathers, and their faces were colored black, and they danced and screamed.

"Finally, Jackson decided to storm the breastworks. His soldiers poured over the logs and fought hand to hand with the enemy. The Creeks were caught between the whites and the Cherokees, and the fight continued for five hours. When more than half of the Creeks lay dead, the others plunged into the river, but sharpshooters on the other side opened fire, and they were trapped.

"I followed the Creeks into the Tallapoosa and killed six of them. I might have been killed myself if not for a friend. I was attempting to stick one man with my sword, but he closed with me, and it became a wrestling match. He tried to drown me, and I tried to drown him.

"I secured his knife and stabbed him, but he was strong and strong-willed, and he battled on. Finally, one of my friends killed him with a spear."

I thought of the difference in Staring Otter and Major Ridge. My father's life, his personality, was forever altered by the Battle of the Horseshoe; Major Ridge spoke of it as just another day's work.

Major Ridge and Susanna prospered, and their children were raised in a loving home. Tragedy struck when Nancy, who had married an Indian, died in childbirth, but Major Ridge envisioned John as a future leader of the Cherokees, perhaps even the principal chief. He realized that in this new day that was dawning, education would be all important, and he arranged for extensive schooling for his son.

"He attended the Foreign Mission School in Cornwall, Connecticut," Major Ridge said, "and two of his schoolmates were his cousin Elias and your husband Charley Marley."

He recalled the nasty incidents that arose from John's and Elias's marrying the white girls. "If Charley had done likewise, I suppose the world would have come to an end," Major Ridge said, bitterness in his laugh. He added, gallantly, "But I think all three made fine choices."

John became a gentleman of the green bag—a lawyer—one of the first in the Cherokee Nation. He was elected to the National Committee and later became its president and clerk of the National Council. His father was proud of him.

The Cherokees formed a republican government based on that of the U.S. The Cherokee General Council was composed of two houses, the National Committee and the National Council. Major Ridge became speaker of the National Council, or chairman of one of the houses. Later he was elevated to the newly created post of counselor, chief adviser to Principal Chief John Ross. He was a moving force in the adoption of the Cherokee constitution and the birth of New Echota as the legislative, executive and judicial headquarters of the Cherokee republic.

Major Ridge and Susanna maintained a second home near Head of Coosa, at a place that became known as Ridge's Ferry. The elegant, white, two-storied mansion "would look good in New England," John Ridge was fond of saying.

Major Ridge had the finest farm in the area—including those owned by whites. He also operated a trading post and a ferry.

And he had thirty slaves.

Six miles to the northeast, John Ridge built himself a fine two-storied home on a hill. At the foot of the hill was a spring from which a pretty stream poured, and John called the farm Running Waters.

"We live in a beautiful country, and there is great prosperity ahead for the Cherokees," Major Ridge said, patting my shoulder as he rose to signify the end of our interview. "No wonder the Georgians want to take it from us. There are Cherokees themselves, though, who might aid them, who might fall under the spell of the Georgians and Andrew Jackson.

"There is an old law specifying death to any Cherokee who, without permission from the authorities, enters into a treaty that disposes of the nation's land. It had never been written, though, and just last week, in council, I suggested it be put on paper. Now it is there in black and white for the Georgians, Jackson and the Cherokees to see."

Major Ridge proposed that the law be written, and John Ridge wrote it. It passed on October 24, 1829. Ah, the irony. How many times over the years have I thought about the irony.

CHAPTER 14

The slaves owned by Bartholomew Bramlett brought the pews that Bartholomew Bramlett assembled and aligned them inside the church that Bartholomew Bramlett built. Then they brought in Bartholomew Bramlett's pulpit, and there was nothing left to do but wait until Sunday when the first sermon would be delivered by Bartholomew Bramlett's minister, Charley Marley.

This was Wednesday, and I was sitting on a bench outside the house, reading a book that Harriet had given me about the Romans, when I saw a buggy approaching. It was Bramlett himself. I sighed and closed the book, laid it across my lap and held my place with my thumb. It was a clear, warmish October day, but Bramlett nevertheless was concealed under his blanket.

"Charley, you have a visitor," I yelled, being certain to convey to both my husband and Bramlett my annoyance at his arrival. I resumed reading my book.

"How are you today, Mrs. Marley?" Bramlett asked.

"Fine," I said, never looking up.

Charley stepped outside, buttoning his shirt, brushing back his hair with his hand. "What a pleasure, Bartholomew," he said. "The furnishings are in the church and school. Would you like to see?"

"Yes," he said, "but first I would like to chat with Mrs. Marley if I might."

I looked at him and at Charley. "What's this about?" I asked my husband, being as rude as possible.

"I'm sure I don't know, Nancy," Charley said in painful, clipped words that reflected his embarrassment at my behavior.

I wanted imperiously to tell Bramlett that we had nothing to talk about, but curiosity had the best of me. "All right," I said, looking at him and then at Charley.

"Let's take a ride," he said. "May I borrow your wife for a few minutes, Reverend Marley?" The artificial lightness in his voice made him even more repulsive.

I ignored the offer of his driver's hand and climbed onto the seat beside Bramlett. He nodded at the driver, who touched his whip lightly on the horse's flank, and we bounced along the bumpy road, over a hill and out of sight of the village.

"I'll dispense with the polite talk," Bramlett said abruptly. "I know you don't like me, and I'd like to know why."

"I suspect Charley has told you why," I answered. "Slavery is the most despicable thing I can think of. You're a slaveowner. My husband is a Christian minister,

and I don't think he should be involved with a slaveowner to the extent that Charley is involved with you."

Bramlett's broad face remained expressionless. "As I understand," he said calmly, "the Christian religion is for the imperfect."

I didn't answer. I didn't consider he had made a pertinent comment.

"I am considering becoming a Christian," he said. "At first I thought Christianity was quite absurd. But as I studied it I came to believe it possibly is true. I have my reservations, but I am still studying, still listening to the persuasions of your husband, and perhaps I will believe it in time. I hope so, for I know it can be of immense comfort. But I am not a person who can say I believe something unless I do believe it."

I didn't answer.

Bramlett sighed and pulled the blanket up until the tip of his chin was hidden. "I built the church and the school to assist a good man, your husband," he said. "I very much wanted to further his work. I hope they will be instrumental in bringing many Cherokees to Christ."

I turned and looked into black eyes. He gazed straight ahead. "You built the church and the school to buy your way into heaven," I said. "I've told Charley that all along. But it won't work, because the Bible says you reach heaven through faith in Christ."

Bramlett nodded. "Yes, Reverend Marley has told me it is your opinion that I am trying to save myself by works. I can assure you it is a quite mistaken one. I am well aware of the Christian view of how one achieves everlasting life."

"Why don't you free your slaves?" I asked.

"That's a simplistic solution to a complicated problem," he answered. "Perhaps some day I will. But to do so will require quite a bit of groundwork."

For the first time, Bramlett turned and looked at me. "I appreciate your concern for your fellow humans," he said. "I really do. I can assure you that I don't treat my slaves poorly. They are well housed, well fed, and they aren't overworked. I know that is not the case everywhere, but it is the case on my plantation. Most slaves would rather belong to Cherokees than to white men, and most slaves would rather belong to me than to other Cherokees."

"One man cannot own another man," I said. "He simply can't."

"I understand that you admire Major Ridge, that you are writing a story about him for *The Cherokee Phoenix*," he said. "Would you please tell me the difference between me and Major Ridge?"

"The difference is that you are involved with my husband, whose spiritual welfare I care about, and Major Ridge isn't," I said lamely.

"That answers your dislike for me," Bramlett said, "but it doesn't answer your regard for Major Ridge. I am a slaveowner and he is a slaveowner. If owning slaves is bad, it is just as bad for a national hero to own slaves as for an unattractive nobody like me to own slaves."

I knew he was right, and I knew I was being hypocritical—but my heart quickened when I saw Major Ridge, and I felt revulsion when I saw Bartholomew Bramlett, and that was just the way it was. "How I regard Major Ridge is none of your business," I said.

"That's not an answer," he replied.

"It's the only answer you'll get."

Bramlett leaned forward and said something to the driver, and he turned the wagon around in a field beside the road, and we headed back toward our village.

"I don't intend to come between a man and his wife," Bramlett said. "I had hoped to be a regular in Reverend Marley's congregation at the new church. I had hoped that his messages might lead me to Christ. But I don't want my presence in your lives to cause a divorce. So …"

Divorce? The notion of Charley and me getting a divorce had never crossed my mind. The word caused me to slide upright on the buggy seat.

"Charley would never divorce me," I said, as if I were talking to the dumbest person in the world.

Did he know something I didn't? Bramlett spoke in the reassuring tone of someone who has said more than he should have said: "Oh, of course not. I merely meant that I don't want to cause any diversion, any problem, between you and Reverend Marley—so I intend to vanish."

"Vanish?"

"The church and the school are yours—you and Reverend Marley's. You will use them to the glory of God without even so much as my presence or a word from me. I won't attend services, and I won't be in contact with your husband again. I will never lay eyes on the church and the school again. I recognize that I am a disturbing force, and I will exit your lives forever."

A better person might have felt sorry for Bartholomew Bramlett. I didn't. A perpetrator of what the exchange papers from the North called the greatest evil in America was withdrawing the influence he held over my husband. "Good," I said. "Thank you."

We didn't speak again on the ride back. The buggy pulled up in front of our house, the driver helped me down, and I went inside without a word. Charley was chatting with The Bull in front of the new church, and I saw him excuse himself and approach Bramlett.

Ten minutes later my husband came into our cabin, his lips trembling. He gazed at me as if I were a repulsive insect on his food, and finally he said, "Nancy, how could you?"

"Because I love you," I said.

"Well, I don't love you."

I began to cry, but when he yelled, "Shut up," I was so startled that I stopped.

"How could the wife of a Christian minister chase a lost soul away from the church?" he railed, in a voice as loud as the one he used in the pulpit to make a point.

"You've got your church, and we're rid of Bartholomew Bramlett," I whispered in a quivering voice. "What's so bad about that?"

"The church was always secondary," Charley said. "What I wanted was Bartholomew Bramlett."

"What?"

"Nancy, can't you see? My ministry has been a failure. The Cherokees aren't moved by anything I say. You know how few have given their hearts to Christ. Finally, I have a chance to make a difference, and you ruin it for me."

I'm sure my face reflected my puzzlement. I couldn't answer.

"Bartholomew Bramlett was a step away from becoming a Christian. He is a brilliant man, a rich man who commands so many resources. Do you honestly not realize what a force for Christianity he could be? He could build churches and schools all over the Cherokee Nation. He could buy books. He could fund the work of ministers. A Bartholomew Bramlett on fire for the Lord could be the difference in the Cherokee Nation becoming Christian or not."

The only rebuttal I could think of was the same argument against slavery that I had voiced so many times. I kept quiet.

"This wasn't about the church building, Nancy," he continued. "This was about Bartholomew Bramlett's soul. I believe there was a good chance that through me the Lord would have saved his soul. And perhaps I am being selfish. Perhaps I would be proud to be the minister whose words led Bartholomew Bramlett to the throne of grace.

"If he accepted Christ he might have eventually freed his slaves, Nancy. You might have gotten what you wanted. Now it probably never will happen. Are you that stupid, Nancy? Is something no more complicated than that too much for you, Nancy? You really are just a child, aren't you? You should be at home with your parents, playing with dolls."

His words pounded me into dust, like corn being reduced to meal. I wailed—like the child he said I was.

"Shut up," Charley said. "Don't cry now. If you're going to play games with my friend's life and my life, you're going to hear me out."

"Slavery is awful!" I screamed stupidly.

"A lot of things are awful," Charley said. "Walking along the river and kissing your childhood sweetheart when you're married to someone else is awful. You aren't perfect yourself, Nancy."

My arms and shoulders became immobile. Then my legs and body. I felt as if I had turned into a statue. I couldn't speak. My tears stopped, too. I just stared at Charley.

"Yes, I know about you and Strong Hickory that day," he said. "Someone saw you and gleefully told me. Perhaps you aren't properly the one to throw the first stone at Bartholomew Bramlett."

Charley took a deep breath. He said: "I want a divorce, Nancy."

My legs were moving, but they felt like the legs of a statue. I had to consciously will one in front of the other. But I realized I was, nevertheless, running, and I entered my parents' cabin, bolted the door behind me and reached into a deerskin bag under my old bed. My hands felt the familiar shape of Nancy Ward, my old carved wooden doll, and I fell onto the bed and hugged her to my breast.

Just as Charley suggested, I had gone home to my parents and my dolly.

Rain and Plum finally gave up asking what was wrong. I just shook my head furiously, and so they left me alone and sat beside the fireplace. I could hear the murmur of their voices and smell the tobacco smoke from my grandmother's clay pipe.

Finally, I heard the familiar shuffle of my father, accompanied by the thudding of his crutch on the puncheon floor. He spotted me lying on the bed, my face turned to the wall, and I heard him ask Mother what was wrong.

Staring Otter came into my room and sat on the bed. He patted the top of my head, tentatively. For him, that was a lavish display of affection. "What's wrong with my girl?" he said softly.

I could count on the fingers of both hands all the times in my life he had spoken so affectionately to me. I was overwhelmed, and I turned and wrapped my arms around his neck, dug my face into his shoulder, and cried all over again. I told him everything, even about Strong Hickory.

"This slavery stinks," he said. "It makes for much trouble.

"Indians were enslaving Indians long before my father's father was thought of, but usually it was nothing more than a case of ending up with a captive of war on your hands. Many times the enslaver didn't even know what to do with his slave once he had him. Then the whites began to urge the Indians to sell Indians to them for slaves, and there developed much warring among the tribes that could have been avoided but for the influence of the whites—who, of course, wanted Indians to be enemies, rather than allies, with each other.

"And now because the Indians see the whites enslave the blacks, they enslave them, too. The Indian who needed only a small cabin and a few acres now has a mansion and many acres, and he can operate his huge plantation only with the labor of the blacks. The ways of the whites are evil, Nancy. I have always tried to tell you, but you wouldn't listen."

For a moment, at least, I found comfort in the arms of my father, in thinking of the old Cherokee ways that he represented. My world of editors and newspapers and Christian ministers and white ladies from New England and wealthy plantation owners and Boston and Washington City and London was spinning too fast, and I was falling off. "Tell me why the possum's tail is bare," I was surprised to hear myself say.

There was great satisfaction in Staring Otter's chuckle as he recalled the Cherokee legend. "Yes," he said, "that vain old possum."

He slid his hands underneath his knee, hoisted his bad leg onto the bed, and leaned against the wall, his daughter's head on his chest. "The possum used to have a fine bushy tail," he began. "It was truly a thing of beauty.

"The other creatures admired it, but they tired of hearing possum boast about his tail. Always he bragged, bragged, bragged. Finally, the rabbit decided to do something about it."

"What did he do?" I heard myself in a little girl's voice.

"Well, you have to understand that the rabbit had only a stub of a tail because bear had pulled it off, so he was naturally jealous of any creature with a decent tail, especially a long, fluffy one like the possum's.

"There was going to be a great dance, and it was the rabbit's job to tell all the animals so they could attend. He stopped at the possum's house and asked him if he would be there—knowing he would be subjected to more of the possum's boasting of his tail.

'I will attend only if I can have a prominent seat so that all the animals may admire my wonderful tail,' the haughty old possum answered.

"The rabbit said he not only would arrange a special seat, he would send someone to dress and comb the possum's tail so that it would be displayed in all its glory.

"The rabbit left and went to the house of the cricket, the greatest of barbers among the animals, and gave him some instructions.

"The next morning the cricket showed up at the possum's house. 'I have come to prepare you for the dance,' he said.

"So the possum stretched out and closed his eyes and dozed off to sleep. The cricket combed out his tail and wrapped it in a red ribbon to keep it smooth until time for the dance.

"At least that's what the possum thought. As he wound the ribbon, the cricket clipped the hair off the possum's tail, right down to the bare skin."

I laughed gleefully at this story I had heard a hundred times, and that caused Staring Otter to laugh.

"That night the possum went to the dance, and the rabbit escorted him to his special seat, just as he had promised. When it came his turn to dance, he unwound the red ribbon and stepped onto the dance floor and sang, 'See my fine tail. See how beautiful it is.'

"The other animals shouted, and the drummers pounded their drums, and the possum sang even louder: 'Have you ever seen such a marvelous tail? I have the handsomest tail of any creature.'

"The animals shouted again, but the possum realized they were laughing at him. Then he looked down at his tail and saw that not a hair remained. His tail was as bare as a lizard's.

"He was so astonished that he couldn't speak. He fainted and rolled over on his back, his face frozen in a grin as he dreamed of his once-beautiful tail.

"And that's why the possum has a bare tail. And he still faints when he is startled, grinning as he dreams of the bushy tail he used to have."

The story was comforting, but I couldn't lie there on my old bed, in my father's arms, forever. "Charley wants a divorce," I said.

Charley and Staring Otter had been getting along, but I knew my father would have preferred he disappear, and I realized immediately I shouldn't have told him there was a possibility of our marriage ending, for he would have no sympathy.

"Divorce is no big thing," he said. "It requires only that you declare it. Cherokee marriages frequently don't last. Old Three Feet was married six times— four in one year."

"Yours and Mother's marriage has lasted," I said. "I want my marriage to Charley to last."

"Strong Hickory would be a better husband for you," Staring Otter said. "Even at his young age he is a great hunter. He dons his deerskin and deer head, and the deer let him walk right up to them. He knows their every mannerism, and when he moves he looks more like a deer than a deer does. I tease him that sometimes it's all I can do not to put an arrow in him."

I lifted my head from his chest and looked into the eyes of my father. I saw the hope, hope that his daughter might abandon all the ways of the whites that she had adopted, might after all marry a proper Cherokee boy and become a proper Cherokee wife.

And I will confess that for a moment the prospect was pleasing. After all, what had reading *The New York Observer* and *Niles' Weekly Register* gotten me but confusion and misery?

But the feeling didn't last. Reading the publications that arrived at the *Phoenix*, reading books, meeting the Boudinots and the Worcesters and Charley Marley had enriched my life, and I could never return.

I kissed my father on the forehead, got to my feet, and told Mother I would help her prepare the evening meal. "I have become quite good at making carnuchee," I said. "I've added a secret touch."

I expected Charley would cool down by evening and knock on the door, perhaps apologetic. He didn't. He didn't come the next day, either. Bartholomew Bramlett had said he didn't want to cause a divorce, and now I knew for sure Charley had mentioned the possibility to him. I knew now that our blow up was not a mere spat between a husband and wife who hadn't been married a year.

I stayed inside, peeping through a crack at the doorway, trying to see Charley. I spotted him at the church, hammer in hand, countersinking nailheads that protruded from the boards. He was proud of his church, and he wanted it to be perfect. Prouder than he was of his wife, I thought. He never glanced toward my parents' cabin.

Charley didn't come Friday, and he didn't come Saturday. He was to preach his first sermon in the new church Sunday morning, and I knew he was preparing for it, so he wasn't concerned with me. "He probably has forgotten I exist," I told Mother as we ate supper Saturday night.

"Nonsense," she said. "Married people have arguments, especially in the first few months when they're trying to get used to each other. A year from now you'll laugh about this."

"Forget about him," Staring Otter counseled. "While he's telling ridiculous stories about the man who was murdered and flew away, Strong Hickory will be stunning fish with powdered buckeye. Which one, I ask you, will be putting food on the table? Charley Marley is a fool."

"Don't call him a fool!" I snarled, and Staring Otter raised his hands in mock surrender and left the room.

I saw the flicker of a lantern in the church, and I knew Charley was there. I pictured him in the pulpit, rehearsing his sermon, practicing the gestures that, unfortunately, everyone recognized as practiced. I wanted to be on the front row of Bartholomew Bramlett's church. I hated Bramlett for trying to buy his way into heaven and for misusing my husband in the process.

I could stand it no longer. "I'm going for a walk," I told my parents and my grandmother.

The night was clear, and moving clouds blew across the lightpoints of the stars, but there was no moon to speak of, thank goodness. I reached the church, and I stood on an empty wooden whitewash bucket and looked through the glass window. There, indeed, was Charley, in buckskin breeches and hunting shirt, in the pulpit, preaching to the empty pews.

I watched for perhaps fifteen minutes. Charley would hoist his Bible, point it at the phantom congregation, jab his forefinger at a selected passage. Then he would stop in mid-sentence, shake his head in disgust, mutter something to himself, and repeat the process. I saw him close his eyes and lift his face to heaven and speak to the Lord, and I knew he was praying to be a better preacher.

I started crying, jumped off the whitewash bucket and ran to my parents' cabin. I blew past Staring Otter, Rain and Plum and got into bed and covered all of me, my head included, with a bearskin. Then I squeezed Nancy Ward until I tore the old doll's dress.

I tried to go to sleep, wanting to be unconscious for hours, days, but I was as wide awake as if it were mid-day. I heard the buzz of my parents and grandmother talking in the next room, until finally doors creaked and they groaned and sighed as they climbed into their beds.

Midnight came and went, and I gazed through the window at a naked tree limb that occasionally shook under the weight of a squirrel or the drift of a breeze.

I knew it must be at least one o'clock in the morning, and I could stand it no longer, so I got up and tiptoed out the front door. I hadn't pulled off my dress, not even my shoes, and I felt rumpled, disheveled, disoriented.

The church was dark. I gazed at our house and pictured Charley inside. No doubt he was spreadeagled over the bed. He was something to try to sleep with. I spent half the night pushing him back onto his side. Sometimes I just gave up and slept on top of him. Once when I was perched up there he turned and capsized me onto the floor. We laughed about that for weeks. I wished I were in bed with him now, jabbing him in the ribs, telling him to move his legs off me.

I walked along the Oostanaula, the ancient path smooth under my deerskin moccasins. Reflected stars broke on the surface of the moving water like icicles falling from limbs and shattering on the ground. I heard the familiar rustle of the forest—birds and small animals alarmed by the interloper. I hoped the snakes had retired for the winter.

I was comfortable in the forest, even at night. I had never lived anywhere except in our village, and the path was as familiar as my hand to me. For a moment—just a moment—I wondered if I should keep walking, leaving everyone behind, ending up a thousand miles away in the midst of some strange tribe where no one knew me and I knew no one. I could teach the children and the adults the ways of civilization, found a newspaper, build a capital that reminded me of Baltimore, be remembered as a Nancy Ward of transition from the old ways to the ways of the whites.

A flash of orange touched a tall tree in front of me, then another, and another. And then orange flashes flitted among the trees, and I turned and looked back toward our village and saw that the sky was turning orange, and then a brighter orange. I was perhaps two miles from home, but I ran, and when I lost my breath I stopped and panted until I could breathe, and then I ran again.

I was close enough to hear the fire, smell the smoke, see the orange sparks being carried into the sky by the breeze, hear the people clamoring and shrieking in confusion.

I burst into the clearing and saw that Charley's church and school were burning. The freshly sawed heart pine was roaring like some fantastic animal made of flame, and the villagers shielded their faces with their arms, unable to even throw water from the buckets they held in their other hands. Thwarted, they one by one backed away and watched in silence as the buildings burned.

Charley apparently had given up early. He stood beside The Bull, his arms folded across his chest, his lips pursed. Across the clearing stood my parents, Staring Otter hanging on his crutch, looking as old as the mountains.

I walked to Charley's side and put my arm around his waist. He pulled me to him and kissed me on the forehead. Neither of us spoke. I was afraid I might utter some word that would drive us further apart, and I suppose he was afraid he might do the same. It was simply a time for silence. I saw Strong Hickory, leaning against a tree, gazing stonily at us. I looked straight ahead, though the brightness of the fire hurt my eyes.

"I saw a white man ride away on a black horse," The Bull said. "I couldn't see his face. Probably a gold miner or a Georgian having a little fun. The bastard."

Charley and I stood there until the roof caved in, dropping the copper steeple, launching a great shower of sparks. Finally, the light that the fire cast on the surrounding trees began to creep down, down, down their trunks, and the heat dissipated, and the fantastic animal diminished. What was left was a blaze so tame and level that it might have been intended to roast pigs.

I felt Charley's sweat on my arm and side, heard his breath, no longer panting but even and resigned. Finally, he spoke: "I have to go wash. Come with me."

I stood on the bank of the Oostanaula as he stripped naked in the winter wind and dived into the black water. I was concerned when he didn't surface immediately, but then his head popped from the flow, and he was sputtering and gasping against the cold. He stood on a sandbar and with his hands rubbed his face and body furiously, and then he plunged beneath the river again, and the soot and dirt and sweat and even blood were gone.

"Don't put those dirty things back on," I said when he was on the bank, and I gave him my wool coat. He wrapped it around him and smiled at the thought of what he must look like.

"Let's go home, Nancy," he said. And we did.

CHAPTER 15

Nancy, wake up," Charley said.

I didn't know if the words were real or if I was dreaming. I had only just gone to sleep, and it was impossible that the morning light already could be falling across our bed.

"No," I said, burying my face under his arm. But then I remembered the fire and being up most of the night and going back to our cabin, and I was jarred into wakefulness.

"Charley?" I said, sitting up in the bed. "The church burned. Your church burned to the ground."

He kissed me on the forehead. "Get up and get ready," he said. "It's Sunday morning. We have services on Sunday morning."

"But your church burned."

"We still have services on Sunday morning. Get up."

"Charley?"

"What?"

"I love you."

"I love you, too. Get up."

"Services can wait a few minutes," I said, and I pulled him under the covers. He didn't resist.

Later I fixed a breakfast of cornbread and bacon and cider. I couldn't swallow a bite, but Charley dug in. "I didn't eat all day yesterday," he said. "I was too nervous."

"Charley, do you really want a divorce?" I asked.

"We'll talk about it later," he said. "I want to go over my sermon. Obviously it will require some changing. Somehow a sermon on the opportunities afforded by a new church building and school isn't appropriate this morning." He managed a grim chuckle.

"Do you think it was a gold miner?" I asked. "Or maybe some mean, drunk Georgian?"

"I don't know," Charley said, gazing out the window. "But I do know the Cherokees are going to lose their land. The whites want it too badly, especially now that they know it contains gold, and there are so many of them. Some way, they will take it. We can't win."

"Oh, no," I protested. "There are too many good whites to let that happen, too many in sympathy with the Cherokees. Just the other day I was reading an editorial in *The Boston Courier,* and it declared ..."

"Boston is a million miles away," he said. "Ten million. Milledgeville is next door. I've got to work on my sermon." He left to walk in the forest.

Charley's sermon that morning was the best I ever heard him preach, perhaps because he didn't have much time to prepare. He stood beside the smoldering ruins of the church, and the people of the village sat in the dirt in front of him. "I want you to smell the smoke and hate it but not hate the one who set the fire," Charley said. "It's all right to be angry, but not to hate the person who did this. And that will be more difficult for me than for anyone else."

When his sermon was ended and he issued the invitation, everyone was startled to see The Bull, their village chief, step forward. "I would like to be a Christian," he said. "May I join the ranks of the Christians?" On this morning, the morning his beloved church burned, I saw an expression of the most profound satisfaction on the face of my husband.

"Did God will this fire?" The Bull asked after the service.

"I don't like to think of life as a huge puppet show with God constantly working the strings," Charley replied. "It wouldn't have much meaning that way. But I can't answer your question. Perhaps he did. Sometimes I think ministers believe they know more than they do. I believe we are called upon to live as nearly like Christ as we can, and beyond that I confess to ignorance in many matters."

Sweet Melon, The Bull's wife, and Strong Hickory, his son, stood away, waiting. "Join us," Charley said, lifting his arm, and Sweet Melon came to accept a hug. Strong Hickory came, too, glancing at me and then at the ground. Charley patted him on the back with his other hand. "I heard you caught a huge fish the other day," my husband said, and the nervous boy nodded.

We heard the syncopated sound of a fine horse's gait, and we saw Bartholomew Bramlett's buggy approaching. His black driver stopped the vehicle and assisted his master in getting out. "Good morning," Bramlett said, his voice flat.

"It is a good morning, in spite of the fire, Bartholomew," Charley replied. "The Bull has given his life to Christ."

"I am glad," Bramlett said. He shook The Bull's hand. "Congratulations." He waited a proper moment and then told Charley:

"I heard about the church and school. I am sorry. My men will be here tomorrow morning to begin building anew."

He turned to me. "Don't be upset, Mrs. Marley. I am true to my word. I wouldn't be here today except for the fire, and I won't be back after today. This will be my final visit to your village. I won't attend your husband's services or see him or talk to him again. But I would like to rebuild the church and school if that is all right."

"Bartholomew ..." Charley began, but the little man raised his hand to command silence, boarded his buggy, and rode away.

My contention that Bartholomew Bramlett built the church to buy his way into heaven fell and shattered at my feet, like a mishandled china platter. If that had been the case, he would have considered his admission into the hereafter paid for, and wouldn't have to pay it twice.

"I was wrong, wasn't I?" I whispered.

"You were wrong," Charley said.

He told The Bull he would baptize him in the Oostanaula the next Sunday. "I went swimming early this morning," Charley said. "It wasn't cold. In fact, I've almost regained the feeling in my feet and hands."

I told The Bull I was happy that he had surrendered to Christ. I felt hypocritical speaking the words. Here I was welcoming him into the Christian life, I who might have driven Bartholomew Bramlett away from it forever. I didn't deserve a husband who could counsel others not to hate the person who torched his church. But I hoped I could keep him.

We went home, and Charley slipped out of his confining white man's clothes and into buckskins. "I'm tired," he said. "Very tired."

"I know you are, darling," I said. "Your wife alone is enough to make you tired."

He ignored the remark and broke off a piece of cold cornbread, poured syrup over it and ate it without a plate.

There was still the matter of my walk with Strong Hickory along the Oostanaula to be discussed, and since we seemed to be clearing the air, I brought it up. "You must hate me because of what happened that day with Strong Hickory," I said. "I know how embarrassing it must have been for someone to tell you about it."

Charley sat on the bed and motioned for me to join him. He took my hand. "You lead a weird life, Nancy Swimmer Marley," he said. "You're a young Indian girl whose life is anything but the life of a young Indian girl. I want to think the pressure was too much, your childhood sweetheart was there, he represented the old comfort and simplicity of childhood you hadn't felt in awhile, and you walked with him and kissed him—and that's all it was. I know you love me, Nancy. Am I correct about what happened?"

"Yes," I said. "That's all it was. But I'm not sure I kissed him. I know I tried not to. I'm sorry, Charley. I'm so sorry. Forgive me."

He kissed me long and tenderly and then, sitting on the bed, he tucked my face into his neck, even laughed. "I'm not sure what trying not to kiss someone means," he whispered, "and I'm not sure I even want to know. Anyway, let's leave it at that. It's all forgotten and forgiven." Then he added: "But it damned sure better not happen again."

Bartholomew Bramlett's wagons and men rambled into our village at dawn the next day. I was up and about in anticipation of their arrival, but Charley still slept.

"Hello, Mrs. Marley," said the pudgy white foreman, sweeping his broad-brimmed hat extravagantly. "Nice day to build a church, ain't it?"

"Good morning, Mr. Rodham," I said. "I want you to take me to see Mr. Bramlett."

"All right. Some day I will."

"Now."

"I just came from Mr. Bramlett," he sputtered. "I've got two wagonloads of rock to unload, and then we've got to load the ashes and burned rocks and get started on the pillars."

"Surely these men can do that without you," I said. Five black slaves listened intently to the insistent Indian girl-woman.

"It's ten miles to Mr. Bramlett's place," he protested.

"Then we'd better get started," I said. "Here, I'll help you unload the rock."

I ignored his wails and lifted a huge rock from the wagon bed, took two steps on buckling legs, tossed it to the ground, and reached for another. "All right, all right," he said. "My God, Mrs. Marley, you'll bust a gut. Here, you men get these rocks off this wagon, get this mess cleaned up and get to work on the pillars."

"Thank you, Mr. Rodham," I said.

Charley joined us, yawning but appearing refreshed by a good night's sleep. "Mr. Rodham is going to drive me to Mr. Bramlett's," I announced. "I must talk to him."

Charley hesitated, then he nodded. "I'm glad," he said.

I knew the answer, but I couldn't leave without clearing it up. Never go to bed without making everything all right, my mother used to say when I was little, for you might not wake up. I couldn't get into the wagon without making everything all right, for I might not come back. I whispered: "Charley, you don't really want a divorce, do you?"

"No," he answered. "At least not until I learn to make my own carnuchee."

"But you were serious about it, weren't you? Serious enough to mention it to Bartholomew Bramlett."

"I was serious," he said. "If I am going to be a minister I must minister to everyone, and I must do it as I see fit. I can't exclude someone because my wife doesn't happen to like him."

The warning was clear: "I'll always feel that way, Nancy."

He helped me onto the wagon seat, and I felt a splinter snag the dress Harriet Boudinot had given me, but I didn't care. Rodham shook his head in exasperation and commanded the horses to retrace their steps to Bartholomew Bramlett's plantation.

The wagon banged over the road, lurching and twisting. It wasn't sprung like a buggy; it was made for work, for hauling heavy loads. "Not exactly a carriage for a queen," Rodham said, breaking the silence after fifteen minutes.

"I'm not exactly a queen," I replied.

We rode for another fifteen minutes in silence before I said, "You don't like me, do you, Mr. Rodham?"

"It ain't my place to like you or dislike you," he answered.

"From what you've seen of me, you shouldn't like me," I said.

"Look," he began, "I know it sounds strange, but Montgomery's my friend. I didn't appreciate you calling him a black bastard—which is what you were going to do if you hadn't caught yourself and come up a little short. Mr. Bramlett doesn't treat his slaves like you think of slaves being treated. They're more like hired hands. I like that."

"I know this sounds strange to you, too," I said, "but I was very upset with myself for saying what I said to Montgomery. It just came out. I despise slavery, and I despised myself for speaking to a slave the way I did that day."

The pudgy man didn't answer. He groaned as he reached under his seat and retrieved a goatskin. He threw back his head, hoisted the skin, and squirted water into his mouth. "Sorry I can't offer you a drink," he said, sticking the cork back in the neck.

"Why can't you offer me a drink?" I asked.

"Out of this thing? Maybe you ain't a queen, but you're a lady."

"Give it to me," I said. I uncorked the skin, raised it, aimed the opening at my mouth, pressed the sides—and a stream of water blasted the tip of my nose.

Rodham guffawed, but for the first time I thought I saw affection in his eyes. "I'll say this for you: you'll try. It takes practice. Don't give up."

This time I over-corrected and hit my chin. "Keep trying," Rodham urged, and on the third attempt I got it right.

"Deer jerky?" Rodham asked, removing a packet from underneath the seat and unwrapping the paper. "If you'll battle that old water you'll probably battle this stringy mess."

It was stringy. And tough. And salty. And bitter. After I finally got it down I asked for a second piece, and Rodham roared and slapped his knee. "So bad it's good, ain't it?"

The rest of the trip was cordial. We chattered about everything under the sun. Rodham even told some jokes that stopped just at the edge of off-color. I expected he could be quite a character in a tavern full of men. While I had him talking, I suggested: "Tell me about Mr. Bramlett."

"Bartholomew? Well, he's different, to say the least. We're kin. He's three-quarters Cherokee, and I'm four-quarters white. We had the same grandfather.

"Grandpaw Bramlett was a trader with the Cherokees and Creeks and Choctaws who, frankly, had two wives. I mean at the same time. One was an Indian woman who lived in the Cherokee Nation, and the other was a white woman who lived on the Georgia coast. Wasn't no problem. The arrangement seemed to suit everybody concerned.

"Grandpaw had twenty-four children by those two women and two more Indian women he took a fancy to. Nobody seemed to get upset about the two extras, either.

"He loved his young'uns, and one summer he got his wives and sweethearts and as many of his children and their wives and husbands and their children together as he could, and we all camped for a week at a place he had on the Chattahoochee River. There was way more than a hundred folks there. It was a beautiful spot with plenty of flat land, and we swam and fished and raced and played ball, and all the little white children and little Indian children got to know each other.

"Now, I don't feel like I'm talking out of school when I say Bartholomew ain't the handsomest fellow you ever saw. Well, he wasn't no pretty little boy, either, and the other children stayed away from him. They'd rip and roar, and there'd be little Bartholomew standing off by himself.

"I felt bad for him, and I played with him. I had to coax him into swimming and racing and such, but he finally did. He clung to me the rest of the week and I couldn't go get a drink of water without li'l ole Bartholomew was there looking up at me. I was probably eleven and him nine, and that's a pretty big difference when you're young'uns.

"Well, when the week of camping was over we all went up and hugged Grandpaw Bramlett's neck and went our separate ways. I sure never expected to see my cousin Bartholomew again, and I forgot about him.

"When I was twenty-five and farming a little piece of rocky ground near Augusta, a well-dressed white man rode up on a big, fine horse and asked if I was Pepper Rodham. I said sure, and he said he'd like to talk to me, and I motioned him to follow me and my mule over to the shade of a water oak."

The thought of shade and the drink of water that must have awaited him that day caused Rodham to hush for a moment while he fetched his goatskin from under the wagon bench. He pushed it toward me, but I shook my head, and he again went through the ritual of squirting liquid into his mouth.

"Anyway," Rodham said, brushing his lips with his shirtsleeve, "the fellow told me he was Bartholomew Bramlett's agent in Augusta, and Bartholomew would like to talk to me.

"I shrugged and said all right and waited. He didn't say nothing, and finally I told him to bring Bartholomew on. 'He wants you to join him at his home in the Cherokee Nation,' the man said.

"I laughed and told him I was busy, that if Bartholomew wanted to see me he could come to Augusta. The fellow never smiled, just said, 'It will be worth your while to do as Mr. Bramlett asks. A coach will be here at daybreak tomorrow.'

"That irritated me a little, but my curiosity got the best of me, and I said I'd be ready. Sure enough, at daybreak this beautiful coach came rolling up with a black driver dressed like he was going to heaven. The white fellow wasn't with him. In fact, I never saw him again.

"Well, off we went, headed for the Cherokee Nation. There was all sorts of fancy foods and wine in the coach, and I made the best of it. Riding along like a king sure beat working in the field.

"We stayed at folkses' homes along the way, quality folks that done business with Bartholomew. There was baths and nice beds and great suppers, and they treated me like I was somebody. The black fellow said the agent sent a rider ahead to make the arrangements. It seemed Bartholomew didn't leave a stone unturned—and over the years I sure learned that was true.

"I was enjoying being pampered, but finally the trip ended. We came around a bend, and there, sitting on top of a hill like Jehovah's own house, was Bartholomew's mansion. Bartholomew even had a little black boy stationed at the bend so he'd spot us and run and tell Bartholomew I was here. Bartholomew greeted me on the veranda, and I'll have to admit my first thought was that the homely little boy had grown up to be a homely little man.

"We said our howdies, and a servant showed me to my room. A tub of hot water was already drawed, and it felt mighty good. There was even some soap from Paris, France. It was pretty sissified and perfumey, but I didn't care.

"Bartholomew guessed that I didn't have a lot of duds, and the truth was I was down to my last outfit, so when I got through bathing, the servant brought in an expensive suit of clothes and helped me get dressed.

"I went down and we sat on the veranda and drank some wine that was from Paris, France, too, and after some small talk Bartholomew said he wanted to thank me for playing with him that time when we was boys and Grandpaw Bramlett had us all camping, and he wanted to see if I'd like to be the overseer of his plantation. Just like that.

"I couldn't believe it, but you better believe I said yes before the words were hardly out of his mouth. I'd have to go back home and try to sell my little spread and my stock and take care of all the loose ends, I said, but I'd be back in a few weeks.

"He just laughed and waved his hand, palm down, in this way he had that says everything's taken care of. 'My agent will handle it,' he said. 'Do you consider a thousand dollars a fair price for all of it?' A thousand dollars? I nearly fainted because it wasn't worth half that, but before I could answer he reached into his coat pocket and handed me a pouch that contained a thousand in gold.

"I've been his man ever since. I live a good life, all because I treated a little boy like he was somebody, and he never forgot it."

I told Rodham that was quite a story, but I resisted the urge to question him about Bramlett. I wanted to converse with the plantation owner myself, form my own opinions.

We talked about everything under the sun. Rodham was amused by me, amused by life. I liked him. He was intelligent but unpretentious, a tobacco chewer who read good British novels.

When we tired of talking we hushed and gazed at the scenery, foothills just ahead of us, blue mountains in the distance, creeks and rivers coursing the land with sweet waters, ancient forests majestic in height and breadth. And hidden in the earth and the flow was gold. The Cherokee Nation was rich and gorgeous—so rich and gorgeous, some said, that it was doomed.

I asked Rodham if he thought it was true, and he said he didn't know. "But if you want to see gorgeous, wait about another half mile. I've seen Bartholomew's house a thousand times, but I still get excited."

We didn't speak again until Rodham said, "This is it," and we climbed a rise and rounded a bend and began our descent into a valley, and suddenly revealed to me was a house unlike any I had ever seen or have seen since. It was a two-storied mansion of marble—not white marble but pink marble. Even the pillars that supported the roof of the front veranda that ran the width of the house were pink. For a moment I imagined I had somehow entered a fairy realm.

The house was built on a knoll in the valley, across from a wide stream that watered hundreds of acres of pasture and cultivated land. It was surrounded by a fine lawn that was bright green even though we were in the midst of winter.

"A sight, ain't it?" Rodham said.

"A sight," I agreed.

The driver stopped the wagon and motioned to a black boy who was repairing a fence. "Run to the house and tell Rachel to tell Mr. Bramlett that Mrs. Marley is coming to visit, that we've just pulled onto the plantation. Now, what'd I say?" The boy repeated the message, dropped his tools and sped toward the house.

A few minutes later, Rodham stopped the wagon in the semi-circular drive in front of the house. Bartholomew Bramlett was on the porch, dressed in shiny boots and velvet pants and a claw-hammer coat, all as black as if he were going to a funeral, and a lacy white shirt and white silk scarf. The clothes on his back were worth more than everything the average Cherokee owned.

Rodham helped me down from the wagon, grasping my waist and lifting me as if I were a light sack of feed, and I was embarrassed when my knee cracked. My back was stiff and my bottom raw from the ten-mile trip in the punishing work-wagon, but I tried not to wince.

"Mrs. Marley," Bramlett said. "You honor me and my home with your presence."

"How are you, Mr. Bramlett?" I replied. They were the most cordial words I had ever spoken to him.

The hard leather heels of his boots tapped extravagantly as he walked down the pink marble steps. He extended his hand, palm up, and I gave him mine. He kissed it. I was afraid he noticed that I held my breath for a moment. Bartholomew Bramlett was so ugly that I, even on this mission of apology, couldn't help it.

"I have caused your Mr. Rodham a day of inconvenience," I said as Bramlett, still holding my hand, led me to the steps. "Thank you, Mr. Rodham."

"It was my pleasure," Rodham said, and he re-boarded the wagon and snapped the reins, and it lumbered off behind the house.

Bramlett led me into a mansion that was majestically furnished, stunningly appointed.

A winding staircase of exquisite workmanship rose from the foyer like a lily from a meadow. I gazed at the rainbows in the crystals of a fine chandelier, the burning candles of which were light blue to match the imported wallpaper.

We entered a parlor so magnificent that it might have been lifted directly from a home of European royalty. Mahogany pieces were polished to a mirror finish, and the chairs and couch were covered with needlepoint that depicted scenes of pastoral beauty. Around the edges of a huge Oriental rug peeped hardwood floors that were so lustrous they appeared wet. A massive tapestry that covered more than half of one wall portrayed St. George slaying the dragon. Shelves on another wall held hundreds of leather-covered books. Floor-to-ceiling windows let in gray light of the murky winter day, but a blaze in the arched fireplace toasted the room.

"It's beautiful," I said as Bramlett sat me on the couch and took a chair covered in burgundy leather. He smiled, placed his fingertips together over his chest and waited.

"I have come to thank you for rebuilding Charley's church and to invite you to attend services," I said, speaking too rapidly, eager to have the embarrassing words out of my mouth. "I misjudged your motives, and I apologize. It is my Christian duty to tell you this and to stop interfering with your seeking Christ."

A slight smile creased his extraordinarily broad face, and I knew he realized I was reciting a statement I had silently rehearsed during the wagon ride.

"I thank you for your kind consideration," Bartholomew Bramlett replied, "but I think it best that I stay away. I don't relish the role of a fly in the ointment. You and your husband can pursue your work more effectively without my presence. Perhaps Christianity is not for me, after all."

The last words pierced me like an arrow, and I was about to say no, no, Christianity is for everyone, when he added, "Certainly my pursuit of it has been unrewarding," and I felt twice stabbed because I had been an even more committed opponent than the arsonist.

"Please," I said. "Charley will conduct a service in the village Sunday morning. I want you to be there."

Bramlett pulled a silken cord that hung from the wall, and a black woman who appeared to be about his age, mid-thirties, entered the room, smiling and holding a silver service. She began pouring, and her smile broadened when Bramlett said, "Rachel makes the best tea in the land."

It was hot and bitter, the way I liked it, and I didn't tame it with cream or lemon. Neither did Bramlett. He savored the aroma and the taste, looking past me at St. George, not speaking.

"Please come," I repeated, forcing the words.

Bramlett lowered his gaze from the tapestry and directed it to my eyes, but he didn't immediately speak. Finally, he said, "Did you really think I was trying to buy my way into paradise?"

"That's what I thought."

"I may have many faults, Mrs. Marley, but I am not a stupid man. I have read every word in the Bible at least three times, thoughtfully, inquisitively. I know one can't purchase passage into heaven, no matter how much money one has." There was an accusing edge to his words that he immediately tried to soften with a smile and the tendering of more tea.

I hadn't merely misjudged him, I thought, I had seriously underestimated him. I, a minister's wife, had not read every word in the Bible. I had read all of the New Testament (even Revelation), but I hadn't the patience for more than a rifling through the pages of Leviticus, Numbers and Deuteronomy. They made me nervous, gave me a headache.

"I was wrong about you," I said. "I know that. I am saying I am sorry, thanking you for building the church the first time and for rebuilding it and inviting you to regularly attend my husband's services."

With that, I felt I had performed my Christian duty. If he said no, so be it; I had tried.

He stared at me for a moment, then he said, "Thank you, I will."

I know that down deep, in the pettiest part of me, I hoped he would say no. On Judgment Day I could rightly plead that I had done my best to rectify a mistake, and the decision to stay away was his. But he said yes, and I truly hoped Bartholomew Bramlett would ally with the living Christ.

We didn't speak for two or three minutes. My mission was completed, and he waited for me to say I must go home. But curiosity was devouring me. I knew how uncouth I sounded, but I said, "I would like to see the rest of your house."

"Certainly," he said, obviously pleased. "Come with me."

The tour must have lasted an hour, for Bramlett discussed the origin and acquisition of every piece of furniture, every mirror, every rug, every piece of glassware. He had selected most of it during trips to Europe. Some items he had found in New York and Boston and Philadelphia and Savannah and Charleston. The most remarkable component of this fantastic home, the pink marble itself, had been quarried in the Cherokee Nation.

"And you live in this house all alone?" I couldn't help asking.

Bramlett smiled at my inquisitiveness. "With Rachel, my housekeeper, and Randolph, my butler," he answered. "Randolph is off today. He is quite a hunter, so I expect some unfortunate rabbit is even now in the sights of his shotgun."

A slave with an off-day? A slave with a shotgun?

Bramlett noticed my quizzical expression, and he said, "My people have every Sunday off, and each gets another day every two weeks. As I told you before, they aren't mistreated."

But, of course, I couldn't bring myself to just let it ride. "Your people, as you call them, are slaves," I told him, "and when I said I was wrong about you I didn't mean about your owning other human beings. That is a terrible thing."

Bramlett sighed. "And what would you have me do?" he asked.

"Free them."

He pulled the silken cord, and Rachel, a stunning, erect woman, entered the parlor. "Yes, sir?"

"You're free," he said.

"Sir?"

"You're free. Mrs. Marley said I should give you your freedom. You're free, Rachel. Please thank her."

The woman looked at me as if I were insane, a hand on her hip adding to the expression of incredulousness. "No thank you," she said.

"This is ridiculous, Mr. Bramlett," I said. "You wouldn't really free her. You're just …"

"Oh, I assure you I am giving her her freedom—if she wants it," Bramlett said.

"Who the hell are you to pass judgment on him?" the housekeeper said, and I was as stunned by the words as if they had been a club that struck me between the eyes. I glanced at Bramlett, hoping, I suppose, that he would reprimand her, but he was grinning.

"I should want the freedom to leave this house and go live in—what?—a tiny log cabin?" she continued. "That's probably what you live in—a log cabin."

"Thank you, Rachel," Bramlett said. "Mr. Rodham is in the barn, and I wish you would take him some of your hot tea."

She glared at me as she left the room. I was so confused, so taken aback, that I couldn't look into her eyes, so I averted my gaze to the window.

"I got the impression she didn't want her freedom," Bramlett said, a look of mock seriousness on his face.

He couldn't do this to me. "She's hardly a typical slave," I said. "Being your housekeeper isn't like picking cotton twelve hours a day in the boiling sun."

"My people don't pick cotton twelve hours a day," he said. "But you're quite right. One person shouldn't own another."

Had I heard him correctly?

"This business of owning slaves is, indeed, a vexation," he said. "But let me tell you how I got into it."

It was time for me to go home. Charley would be worried, but I had to hear this. "Go ahead," I said.

"My grandfather Bramlett was a white trader who made a lot of money, but he had so many children that no individual got much when he died. Besides, he lived to be very old. His son—my father—was half white, half Cherokee, and he ran a tavern. We weren't rich, by any means, but we had more than the average Cherokee family. By watching grandfather and father, I saw that money could be made if one was industrious and smart. I learned about business by attending school in London, a chapter of my life arranged by my grandfather Bramlett who, I believe, always favored me because I was a shy, miserable child.

"I realized the land was the key. The whites desperately wanted our land—yet our land was free to us for the asking, and for the most part it merely provided a home for deer and other game. As you know, individual Cherokees don't own the land—it belongs to all our people—but it's there for the individual to farm, and that makes it even better, for one doesn't have to buy it.

"I found the richest unused land available, here in this valley, and began clearing it. I got a loan from my father and bought three black slaves, and they helped me. At first we cleared and planted fifty acres. Then fifty more. Then I bought more slaves, and we cleared a hundred more acres. Then more slaves. Then more land. And so on.

"I learned about a couple of roads that were going to be cut through the Cherokee Nation, and I built four inns to accommodate travelers, give them a place to eat and drink and sleep. I opened stores along those roads. I acquired the rights to three ferries. I developed a system of buying hides from the Cherokees and selling them to the whites.

"Wagonloads of corn left my plantation for the surrounding states. My men drove hogs and cattle along those roads. It was nothing for two thousand hogs to be in a drove, traveling ten miles a day, consuming forty-eight bushels of corn in a day.

"More and more workers were required, so I bought more and more. I was never comfortable with it, never felt it was truly the right thing to do. But I treated them well, and there isn't a man, woman or child on my place who would rather be a slave elsewhere. In an ideal world there would be no slavery, but we don't live in an ideal world, and if one must be a slave, one is better off here than anywhere else. My conscience may not be perfectly clear on the matter of my being a slave-owner, but I am not haunted by any memories of mistreatment."

I had been plenty rude already, so there was no need to stop now. "Have you ever been married?" I asked.

"No," he said, "I have never been married. I tell myself that I have been so busy that I never had time for a wife. But I have mirrors in my house. I suspect no woman would have ever had time for me."

It was a touching admission, and I suppose my surprise in his confiding in me showed on my face, for Bartholomew Bramlett recovered and laughed heartily, as if he had meant it as a joke, and said, "Randolph should be in with his rabbits any minute. I'll have Rachel prepare them for supper if you will stay."

He knew, of course, I wouldn't, and when I got to my feet he summoned Rachel, who gave me an icy look before she alerted Rodham that I was ready to go home. I was glad when the overseer brought Bartholomew Bramlett's fancy carriage around to the front of the mansion, because I don't believe my butt would have survived another ten miles in that work wagon.

CHAPTER 16

The Cherokees were the Principal People. We lived at the center of the earth. Of course. And a bullfrog could jump from New Echota to Augusta.

Even the most intractable traditionalist, even the staunchest champion of custom—even a Staring Otter—had to realize what we really were: a people tiny in number and matched against the governments of Georgia and Andrew Jackson.

There were between sixteen and eighteen thousand persons in the Cherokee Nation; the United States was approaching twelve million.

Justice? The word came to have a forlorn sound as the white torrent spread toward us like a flood-gorged stream erupting from its banks and bearing down on fragile cornstalks that clung to cropland.

Prominent voices would plead for us—those of Edward Everett, Daniel Webster, Ralph Waldo Emerson, Henry Clay, Sam Houston, David Crockett, Theodore Frelinghuysen, John Howard Payne—but words were powerless against the determination of Jackson and the Georgians.

In his first address to Congress, in December of 1829, President Jackson said he would initiate and shepherd through Congress a bill providing for removal of the Southeastern Indian tribes to lands west of the Mississippi River. We should emigrate voluntarily, the Chicken Snake said, "for it would be cruel and unjust to compel them to abandon the graves of their fathers and seek a home in a distant land."

Go voluntarily, but go. If we didn't, the U.S. would uphold Georgia's claims of jurisdiction, and we would be absorbed into the state.

Delighted with Jackson's words, the Georgia legislature passed a Cherokee code that embarrassed even some of its citizens who desired to see us driven off to the West.

It declared that an Indian couldn't testify against a white in a Georgia court. No Indian contract was valid without two white witnesses. We couldn't dig for gold in our own land. No Cherokee could deter another from selling or ceding land to the whites or from enrolling for emigration or moving to the West. Banned were meetings of the Cherokee National Council and other political assemblies on Georgia soil unless they were held to negotiate land cessions.

This new outrage, like the earlier restrictive measures, would take place on June 1, 1830—just six months into the future.

My eyes brimmed when I read in *The Cherokee Phoenix* the words of Edward Everett of Massachusetts, who in later years would share the platform at Gettysburg with Lincoln.

He told the House of Representatives that white villains "have but to cross the Cherokee line; they have but to choose the time and place, where the eye of no white man can rest upon them, and they may burn the dwelling, waste the farm, plunder the property, assault the person, murder the children of the Cherokee subjects of Georgia, and though hundreds of the tribe may be looking on, there is not one of them that can be permitted to bear witness against the spoiler. When I am asked then, what the Cherokee has to fear from the law of Georgia, I answer, that, by that law, he is left at the mercy of firebrand and dagger of every unprincipled wretch in the community."

So blatantly discriminatory was the code that even *The Georgia Journal* of Milledgeville, the capital, wrote: "We cannot omit to express ourselves decidedly hostile to the law excluding Indians from the privileges of testifying in our courts. It is unjust and inexpedient and should be repealed."

Example after example of assaults against innocent Cherokees became common knowledge. Elias reported in the pages of *The Cherokee Phoenix* the case of a farmer whose horses were turned out, and while he chased them the white men entered his cabin and beat his wife into unconsciousness. A Cherokee, Elias noted, "cannot be a party or a witness in any of the courts where a white man is a party. Here is the secret. Full license to our oppressors, and every avenue of justice closed against us. Yes, this is the bitter cup prepared for us by a republican and religious government—we shall drink it to the very dregs."

White gold miners who didn't strike it rich stayed on in Cherokee country. After all, it was a pleasant place of rich pasture lands, herds of cattle and sheep, fields of cotton and corn, orchards that hung heavy with fruits. They would squat and farm Cherokee land. Or they would merely steal. Of course, their presence was quite illegal, but so what?

Some intruders called themselves the Pony Club, and they took Cherokee horses, cows, anything they could make off with. They would for now be patiently content with small stuff, for when Georgia's Cherokee code took effect, it would be a simple matter to fake a bill of sale and take an entire farm.

Of course, there was Governor George Gilmer's untrained, callous Georgia Guard to enforce the law. The best thing an Indian could do if he saw a member of the Georgia Guard approaching was hide behind a tree.

Even when he fought back it turned out poorly.

Whites moved into deserted cabins on a strip of land that both the Cherokees and Georgia claimed. The Cherokees appealed to the federal government, whose representatives found no basis for the Georgia claim and who suggested the Indians throw the whites off the land.

Perhaps old Major Ridge was merely trying to look fierce. Perhaps he was reverting to the ways of his youth. Whatever the case, he stripped to the waist, adorned his body with red paint, pulled a buffalo head—complete with horns—over his own, and led a war party into the disputed territory.

The Cherokees rounded up the eighteen white families—injuring no one—and ordered them to leave. Then they burned the houses, which didn't belong to the whites, anyway.

The white newspapers, of course, portrayed Major Ridge as a villain turning women and children out into the cold. Whites threatened to burn down the homes of Major Ridge and John Ross, the principal chief, and armed Indians stood guard at both places for a few days. Nothing happened.

"Such has been the excitement produced by the outrage," Governor Gilmer declared, "that it has been with the utmost difficulty that the people have been restrained from taking ample vengeance on the perpetrators." There were a few rifle skirmishes, but nothing that could really be called a battle.

I visited Elias and Harriet at their home, and she answered the door with her forefinger on her lips. "Shhh," she said. "He's very upset. He has been trying to write an editorial all day. It has to be exactly right. He's talking to himself, yelling, praying in a loud voice."

She walked me to the community spring in front of their house, and there we stood in the cold for nearly an hour. She wouldn't even invite me inside. She shook her head when I asked her what was wrong.

Finally the front door opened and Elias stood on the porch. His coat and shirt were askew and his hair was a mess, as if he had been raking himself with his fingers. "Harriet, come here, please," he said.

We followed Elias into his study where he sat behind his desk, straightening his clothes. "See what you think," he muttered, handing his wife a sheet of paper. "Oh, you can read it, too, Nancy," he added, as if he had just noticed my presence.

I realized why Elias Boudinot was upset. He had written an editorial criticizing his uncle, Major Ridge. It had been excruciatingly painful to scold the Cherokee hero and statesman.

Elias saw the raid as an unfortunate, unwise incident, although the whites bore their share of the blame:

"It has been the desire of our enemies that the Cherokees may be urged to some desperate act—thus far this desire has never been realized, and we hope, not withstanding the great injury now sustained, their wonted forbearance will be continued. If our word will have any weight with our countrymen in this very trying time, we would say, forbear, forbear—revenge not, but leave vengeance to Him 'to whom vengeance belongeth'."

Harriet told me a few days later that Elias felt better when his uncle told him, "You are right."

Congress passed Jackson's Indian Removal Bill on May 28, 1830. Theodore Frelinghuysen of New Jersey rose in the Senate to champion the Indians with a speech that made him famous throughout the North, gained him the title of the "Christian Statesman," and led to his nomination by the Whigs as vice president. "Do the obligations of justice change with the color of the skin?" he asked. "Is it one of the prerogatives of the white man, that he may disregard the dictates of moral principles when an Indian shall be concerned?" But the bill passed.

The people thus had decided, through their elected representatives, that the proper and Christian thing to do was uproot their red brothers from their Eastern ancestral homes and dispatch them to unfamiliar lands across the Mississippi River.

The bill did not prescribe force. It appropriated funds to facilitate the migration and provided for territory west of the Mississippi to be guaranteed to the five Southeastern tribes—the Cherokees, Creeks, Chickasaws, Choctaws and Seminoles—"as long as they shall occupy it," in exchange for their lands in the East. Separate treaties with each tribe would have to be signed. But the message was clear. The federal government, which occasionally had been an ally of the Indians, was telling them to move.

The Cherokees, who had fought beside Jackson at Horseshoe Bend, had been betrayed by the Chicken Snake, but still they weren't giving up.

I thought it pathetic when Principal Chief John Ross reminded his people of a clause in the Removal Bill which said: "Nothing in this act shall be considered as authorizing the violation of any existing treaty between the United States and any of the existing tribes." Any attempt to oust us would be contrary to the treaties of Hopewell and Holston, which had guaranteed our territorial integrity and independence—guaranteed them forever and ever. So what if there was a Removal Bill? So what if Georgia was threatening to annex the Cherokee Nation? We had but to stand strong and wait for justice to win out.

Of course. And the Cherokee were the Principal People, we lived at the center of the earth, and a bullfrog could jump from New Echota to Augusta.

Jackson didn't miss a trick. Government annuities, due the Cherokees for previous land sales to the U.S., had been paid directly to John Ross for deposit in the national treasury. The Chicken Snake said that from now on the money would be distributed to individual Cherokees at the Indian Agency at Tellico.

That meant some Indians would have to travel more than one hundred miles to collect forty-two cents. The Cherokee government would be crippled—but it could not be said the U.S. didn't pay its debts. Nosiree.

Georgia's series of confiscatory laws became effective on June 1, 1830, but Governor Gilmer thought it best to tread softly. Even in his state the oppression of the Cherokees was creating some resentment.

He settled for stationing units of the Georgia Guard at key locales in the Cherokee Nation, particularly in the gold fields. The militiamen were a nuisance more than anything else, undrilled, ignorant bullies, all of whom put together didn't have a fraction of the character of an Elias Boudinot or a Charley Marley. They were at their best kicking or shoving old Indians who didn't respond to orders quickly enough or plying normally sober Cherokees with liquor and then arresting them for being drunk.

Three of them rode into our settlement one day, and they immediately spotted Staring Otter who, with the support of his crutch, was dragging his useless leg across the grassless area in the center of the village. I was sweeping the front steps of Charley's new church, the one Bartholomew Bramlett had built on the site of the short-lived sanctuary that was destroyed by fire.

They dismounted, and one of them said in a loud voice so that everyone could hear, "I swear I believe that's the feller who grabbed my tobacco pouch out'n my pocket in New Echota yesterday. Ran so fast I couldn't even get a hand on his shirt tail."

"Sho' looks like him to me," another agreed.

"Hell, you can see the speed in them legs. Probably one of them ball players. That's how he learnt to snatch your tobacco, snatching the ball in that webbed thing and running down the field, nobody able to get near him."

Staring Otter ignored them and shuffled on. Until one slapped a hand over his crutch, forcing him to a halt. "He'd a-been gone then if I hadn't grabbed him," the guardsman said. "He's so fast, that's the only way to stop him, grab him before he gets up his speed."

One of the others kicked my father's crutch from under his arm, and he sprawled in the dust. "Can't be too careful with this feller," he said. "He's so quick he'll jerk loose and tear outta here before you know what's happening. We couldn't catch him even on horseback."

Charley was downriver, fishing. So were the other men. I ran from the porch, and just as the guardsman who had sent Staring Otter to the ground looked up, I hit him across the face with my sedge broom.

It didn't hurt him, but it shocked and embarrassed him. "Why you goddamn Cherokee whore-lady," he screamed.

The others broke into raucous laughter. "Whore-lady?" the oldest, a man of perhaps fifty, said. "Damn if that ain't a new one on me."

I gazed at the guardsman, my useless broom drawn back. I wasn't afraid. I looked beyond his yellow beard and saw a youthful, innocent-looking face—and recognized him as the gold miner who had rubbed my face in the dirt on the road to New Echota.

"You bastard," I said.

"Tell him, girl!" the oldest one shrieked.

"Whore-lady'll knock your head off with that broom, boy!" the third guardsman, a tall, skeletal man who looked like he had lived a hard forty years, warned.

There was no sign the boy recognized me. He pulled a knife from his boot and said, "Or I might cut her'n off."

I don't know why I wasn't afraid, but I wasn't. "Do you remember the day you stopped me on the road, the day you were so upset?" I asked him, and I saw the recognition come to his eyes. "You said you had to go home to a drunk father and a whoring mother, and you were real upset because they would curse you because you hadn't found any gold."

"You crazy," he said. "I never saw you before."

"You pushed my face in the dirt and said you guessed I knew who was boss. And you tried to get me to say it, and when I wouldn't you almost cried. You begged me to say it, and I finally did. Do you know what I said about you after you rode off—such a pathetic coward disappearing over a hill on a poor half-dead horse you were mistreating? I said ..."

"Goddamn it, let's get out of here," he screamed, looking into the sky as if he were trying to spot a destination behind a cloud.

"Wait," said the oldest militiaman, laughing. "I want to hear the rest of this story."

"Goddamn it, let's get out of here," the boy screamed again, his face scanning the sky. Then he broke for his horse as if he were being pursued by a band of warriors, and he leaped into the saddle and struck the animal on its neck with his fist until it galloped away.

The other two, dismayed, watched as he and his horse followed the bending road out of sight, and then his dust cloud settled to earth.

"Always knew he was a little bit crazy," the skinny one said. "Must be a lot crazy."

"Well?" the oldest one said, looking at me as he helped Staring Otter to his feet.

"Well?" I said, slipping my shoulder under my father's arm and taking his weight.

"Well, what did you say when he rode off the other time?"

"I said, 'You bastard, you didn't even have enough guts to rape me and kill me'."

"Let's go," the skinny one said, almost in a whisper, and without another word or even a glance back they mounted their horses.

"And you two are gutless bastards, too," I shouted, but already they were riding, their eyes on the horizon.

His fifteen-year-old daughter helped Staring Otter, former warrior, to his feet. "You couldn't help it," I said.

"No," he answered. "I couldn't help it. That is precisely the point. When I could have helped it, I didn't."

"What?"

"They have won, the whites," he said. "The old prophecy of the conjurors is coming true—they will drive us from our homes and to the West. Better that I had died when I fought beside Jackson. Better that I had cut his throat and then silently suffered the torture of the whites until I was dead. I have told you, I was close enough to him to have done it."

"Yes, you have told me."

"He was sick and wounded, braced against a tree. I was on my horse. I could have killed him. I could have changed the future."

"You couldn't have known," I said. "He was an ally then."

"I could have killed him, like I would kill any chicken snake."

"But you couldn't have killed Georgia."

"Perhaps another president would have beaten back Georgia."

Charley's religion—my religion—told me not to hate the whites, not even the bullies who had humiliated my crippled father. But it was becoming more and more difficult. Suddenly I wanted to be in the church, alone.

The copper steeple was turning a flat brown, but the rest of the new sanctuary was a fresh white so brilliant that in full sunlight you had to shade your eyes when beholding it. I walked my father home, and then I ran to the church and bolted inside and knelt at the altar and prayed for forgiveness—that I be forgiven and that I have the heart to forgive.

Bartholomew Bramlett had his men remove every charred fragment of wood, every ash, every blackened foundation stone before they began construction of the second church. "He doesn't want anyone to be reminded that the first one was destroyed by fire," Pepper Rodham had explained.

The replacement church was a replica of the original. The dormitory, though, was a bit larger than its predecessor, for Bramlett said, "There must be many potential scholars out there. Let's make more room for them. Perhaps if we demonstrate our faith we will be rewarded."

If there were many out there, they stayed out there; they didn't flock to the school that Charley named Bramlett Academy. Four little boys moved into the dormitory, and a boy and two girls who lived in the village attended classes.

I was impressed that Bramlett replaced the church and dormitory that burned. It seemed to expose as false my cherished theory that he was trying to buy his way into heaven. He wouldn't have had to pay twice.

But still I tolerated him more than I liked him. I sighed when Charley sounded me out on naming the school Bramlett Academy, but I did not protest. "Well, he did build it," I said noncommittally.

Bramlett and Pepper Rodham attended services every Sunday morning. "Come, Levi," Bramlett would say, and the liveried black man who drove the buggy the ten miles from Bramlett's plantation would enter the sanctuary and take a seat, not on a back pew but beside Rodham. I suspected that was done for my benefit.

Bramlett always had Sunday lunch with us, though he usually brought a feast of venison, pork, beef, vegetables, pickles, cakes and pies with him. I had only to heat the food, and we ate lavishly, frequently inviting other parishioners to join us. Occasionally I insisted on cooking—not because I wanted to, but because I was embarrassed to always be feted—and on those Sundays there was a noticeable lack of enthusiasm at mealtime. Charley pretended to be coughing, but he was really laughing when, on a day I had cooked a venison roast to leather dryness, Levi said, "Pardon me, ma'm, but I just ain't hungry. Ain't felt good lately."

Charley taught the children, and so did I. But their eyes sparkled when Miss Sophia Sawyer made her weekly appearance. She was a Moravian missionary who operated a one-teacher school in the courthouse in New Echota. She lived with Samuel and Ann Worcester, and among her pupils were Eleanor Boudinot and Ann Eliza Worcester. I asked her to come to our school on Fridays, and she did, bringing copies of the *Youth's Companion,* from which she read stories that caused the children to shriek with delight. She not only taught them about heaven but about the heavens—for she was well versed in celestial phenomena.

Miss Sophia was an old maid who believed right was right and wrong was wrong and compromise was compromise. Years before, she had accepted black children for schooling at a mission, but her superiors, worried about what the Cherokee chiefs would think, reprimanded her. So she went to the slaves' houses and in those fly-infested hovels she taught them to read.

Once, after her pupils at Bramlett Academy had been particularly receptive and she had experienced a teacher's great reward—the satisfaction of knowing she had imparted permanent knowledge—she told me, "This is a new era in my life, when angels love me."

I was amused by her rhetoric, and I asked her what she meant.

"I was kicked out of the Brainerd mission school and sent to the mission school at Haweiss and kicked out of there and sent to the Worcesters. The missionaries said I was fiery and intractable and not cut from the missionary mold. After all, I used magazines instead of the Bible to teach English, and I laughed and ran with the little Cherokee children to the swimming hole, where they stripped naked and plunged beneath the water. I wished I could join them in the stream but, of course, I couldn't.

"Samuel Worcester himself recommended I be moved from Brainerd to Haweiss, but I don't hold it against him. I feel only delicacy and tenderness for him. I love him and his family. My faith has grown, and I have been rewarded with my own little school in New Echota, which I can operate as I see fit, because I'm my own boss. Some day I shall walk the streets of the new Jerusalem and associate with glorified spirits and understand the mysteries. My soul will be expanded."

I felt she was asking me something, and I thought I knew what it was. "You may teach the children here as you see fit, too," I said.

"Good," she said.

Sophia Sawyer lived an emotional life. If she had been a man, I thought, she would have been a booming preacher, moving from church to church because she made parishioners angry, but doing whatever good works she could manage before the forces of discretion and circumspection could throttle her.

She smiled crookedly and looked over my shoulder while framing another question. "Suppose I brought a black child to your school?" she asked. "I consider slavery a great sin, and I believe every child has a right to an education."

"So do I. Bring a pink and green child if you like."

"We'll get along fine," she said.

⫸⟶ • ⟵⫷

CHAPTER 17

ouncil time in New Echota. I loved it. When the tribal council met, the people came from all points of the Cherokee Nation, and the normally sleepy village pulsed with life. It still wasn't Baltimore, but it wasn't just a wide spot in the
New Town Road, either.

"I'm going to stay with Harriet and Elias during council," I told Charley. "I
couldn't stand to miss it."

"Have a good time," he said.

"They invited you, too."

"I know. I don't want to go."

The one-time magician and wearer of a British red coat with a .69 caliber hole in
it had taken a turn toward a more serious, more reflective life. Concern over the
removal crisis was a factor, but there was more. Being in the company of Samuel
Worcester influenced Charley toward a deeper spirituality, toward a genuine convic-
tion that his mission was more important than his life. The Cherokees' calling
Worcester The Messenger was a simple yet eloquent tribute, and it touched Charley,
for he remarked it often. Charley wanted to be remembered as a messenger.

My husband didn't have time for the fun and frolic of council time. He would
stay home and read the ponderous new books about Christianity that had arrived
from Boston, and then he would get down on his knees in his new church and pray
for an hour at a time.

Fine—but a great social gathering swirled around council time, and I would be
in its midst.

Harriet, Ann Worcester, Sophia Sawyer and I sat on Harriet's veranda and
watched the Cherokees arriving. Most immediately visited the communal spring
that was scant yards in front of us. When the flow of Indians was interrupted, we
giggled at our curiosity and ran to the backyard for a different view.

Thousands came. They arrived on horseback, in carriages and wagons, and
some walked. Most dressed like white men, but a few mountain warriors were in
buckskin, and some patriarchs were wrapped in blankets. Frock coats and beaver
hats proclaimed the prosperity of mixed bloods. Most women wore colorful skirts
of printed calico that belied the gravity of the times.

Boys brought blowguns and bows and arrows and headed for the woods, away
from the adults. They shrieked as they slid down a steep bank covered with dead
leaves and pine needles and plunged naked into a smooth-bottomed swimming

hole on New Town Creek. It was October of 1830, and the water was cold, but so what?

The shouts of families that hadn't seen each other in months echoed across the village. Women hugged each other, and men clasped the shoulders of other men.

The people pitched camp in and around New Echota, and the night sky was illuminated by campfires and torches. We listened to the beat of drums and the voices of chanters and pictured the dancing feet that pounded the dust everywhere, and we smiled.

Ann and Sophia went home, and Elias went to bed, but Harriet and I stayed up late into the night, laughing, chattering about everything under the sun. She was telling funny stories about her children when I felt a sudden bolt of sadness. My shoulders ached from the weight of it.

"Harriet, we can't keep having council in New Echota, can we?" I said, my voice trembling.

"I don't see how," she said. "This council is being held in defiance of Georgia law. I don't know if there will be a raid by the militia. I hope not. Forbear and revenge not, Elias writes, but I don't believe thousands of Cherokees who are having a good time would turn the other cheek in this instance. But the Georgians and Jackson seem to be getting their way, so perhaps they will just ignore the council as a minor annoyance."

The next day I was playing doodle bugs with baby Mary in the dirt of the back yard when I heard a familiar voice: "Mrs. Marley. What a beautiful child."

Bartholomew Bramlett sat on the back seat of his black buggy with the red spokes. He wore his wide black hat with the white feather from the tropical bird. Levi, the driver, appeared seven feet tall in his top hat.

"Mr. Bramlett, Levi, this is Mary Boudinot," I said. Mary recoiled at the sight of the ugly little man, burying her face on my hip, occasionally peeking out. Bramlett laughed, as if it were a joke on him.

"Editor Boudinot's child, I presume?" Bartholomew Bramlett said.

"This is their home. They are friends of mine," I said, lifting my chin. "Elias isn't here, but Harriet is. Perhaps you would like to meet her." It gave me great satisfaction to call such important persons by their first names.

His master gave Levi permission to walk around the village, and I led Bramlett to a rocker on the veranda. I called Harriet and introduced them.

"I admire your husband's work, and I admire your courage and devotion to righteousness," he said. She was speechless.

"I know the story of how you were persecuted for marrying an Indian, and I know how you have dedicated your life to the Cherokees."

Harriet smiled broadly and actually reached out and patted Bramlett's hand. "Thank you," she said. "Thank you so very much. Thanks." This overworked refugee from Connecticut felt appreciated.

"Bartholomew is a friend of ours," I said, feeling hypocritical, but pleased to call by his first name a man who had so captivated Harriet.

We rocked and talked, the three of us, Harriet intermittently humming until Mary finally dozed off into a nap.

"Do you think there will be trouble?" Harriet asked Bramlett. "Do you believe Georgia will break up the council?"

"No, no," Bartholomew said. "An emissary from Jackson will make another plea—threat is a better word—during council."

During our brief acquaintance I had noticed something about Bramlett. He seemed to know what was going to happen before anyone else did. Once I mentioned that to Charley, and Charley said, "He didn't get rich by not keeping abreast."

Bramlett's authoritative manner drew out Harriet's confidence. "Mr. Bramlett," she asked, "is there a chance the Cherokees can save their land?"

"Do you want an optimistic answer or an honest one?" he said.

"An honest one."

"No more chance than Mary's doodle bug house of dirt has in the next rainstorm."

"John Ross is hopeful," she said.

"John Ross is a good man," Bramlett answered. "So was Simon Peter. They say they crucified him upside down."

"But if we win in the Supreme Court ..." Harriet was pleading for a shred of hope.

Bramlett held her to her choice of an honest opinion. "I think Georgia would laugh at the Supreme Court," he said.

"But Georgia couldn't just laugh at the Supreme Court of the United States," Harriet begged.

The Cherokees had retained William Wirt, a Baltimore lawyer, to represent them in a test case they hoped would epitomize their conflict with Georgia. He had been attorney general of the United States under Monroe and Adams before Jackson dismissed him.

The Hall County Superior Court in Gainesville, Georgia, had convicted of murder a Cherokee named Corn Tassel, sentencing him to hang. The Cherokees considered Hall County within their nation, so they claimed jurisdiction. Wirt drafted an appeal. For the first time, American Indians took their plea for justice to the United States Supreme Court.

The Cherokees desperately wanted something good to come of this. If they could win one battle against Georgia, perhaps they could win others. "Georgia can't just tell the Supreme Court of the United States to go to hell," I blurted, and Harriet clasped her hand over her mouth and gasped.

Bramlett was shocked by my vulgarity, too. Maybe he took it as a signal that we didn't want answers that were too honest after all, for he said, "Well, perhaps it can't."

Elias arrived, and I introduced him to Bramlett, and they retired to Elias's study to talk politics. Harriet and I rocked on the porch, not speaking, trying to overhear what they were saying inside, but all we could detect was a grave tone.

When Bramlett left, he bade Harriet and me farewell with a broad sweep of his plumed hat. "If you see my man Levi, I would appreciate it if you would tell him I am exploring the village and that he should find me," he said cheerily.

"An interesting man," Harriet said when he was gone.

"Very interesting," Elias agreed.

And informed.

Day after day, a white man stood in the background at the council house and listened to the proceedings. He was said to represent the U.S. government. Cherokees whispered their speculations about his mission. I heard about him and peeped inside. He stood with his arms folded, his eyes always on whoever was talking. He looked like a statue, I told Harriet.

Finally, he stated his mission to the Indians. The members of the two houses of the Cherokee General Council—the National Committee and the National Council—assembled in front of the council house on a mild day, and John Lowrey was introduced to them. He was a United States agent, and John Ridge translated his message into Cherokee.

The U.S. government wanted to eliminate the difficulties that existed between the Cherokees and Georgia, he said. It would "promote the future peace and happiness of all concerned."

But if anyone's ears perked up, it was useless perking. He said the same old thing. The U.S. wanted to enter into a treaty with the Cherokees and exhange land west of the Mississippi for our land. But there was a disquieting addendum, a threat: whenever Georgia decided to enter Cherokee territory to survey it, Jackson would not interfere.

The Cherokees gave their customary reply. They long ago had decided never to cede another foot of land. All they asked was that the federal government protect the rights that had been guaranteed to them under the old treaties.

I stood beside Lowery's buggy and waited for him. "Take that answer back to the Chicken Snake!" I shouted as he assumed his seat behind his driver, but he barely gave me a glance. I suppose I sounded like an idiot, but it made me feel good.

Bramlett had known of the emissary, had known of his threat before it was made. Did that mean he was right about the hopelessness of our cause, even about Georgia spitting in the eye of the United States Supreme Court? I doubted we had a chance, either, but hearing it when it wasn't idle speculation was chilling.

Despite the grave atmosphere, the session of the council produced a moment that caused Elias, Harriet, Major Ridge and me to celebrate. John Ridge, the major's son and Elias's cousin, was chosen president of the

National Committee. That meant he was second in authority to John Ross, the principal chief.

"Some day John himself will be the principal chief of the Cherokees," Major Ridge pronounced. "He will lead us to success against Georgia." We drank a toast of apple cider, and the old warrior said New Echota looked just like Baltimore.

The council ended, and I went home to Charley. I walked, refusing a ride in several buggies that passed. It was a warm autumn day, so I pulled my shoes off and felt the soft dust of the road under my feet.

I peeped through the window of the church and saw Charley standing behind the pulpit, rehearsing a sermon. He held the Bible high with his left hand, pointed to an imaginary sinner with his right. As always, his gestures were unnatural, planned. But I loved him, and I flung the front doors open and bounced down the aisle into his arms.

He tossed the Bible onto a table and hugged me until I couldn't breathe. Then we went home and locked the door and stayed in our cabin for half the day.

Georgia did laugh at the Supreme Court of the United States.

Two months after the council, Jackson made his second annual address to Congress. He announced that the Choctaws and Chickasaws, two of the Five Civilized Tribes, had made treaties for removal to the West. Their example, he believed, would influence the remaining tribes to "seek the same advantages."

He made it clear that the United States government would not interfere with the right of Georgia or any other state to expel the Indians within its boundaries. Move or be annihilated, he said, "as one by one many powerful tribes have vanished from the earth."

A week later, on December 12, 1830, the Supreme Court cited the State of Georgia to appear before the bench and show cause why a writ of error should not be issued in the Corn Tassel murder case.

Charley was excited. Our right of appeal had been established, and that could lead to a major victory. "I believe this is the beginning of the Cherokees being permitted to remain in the land of our ancestors, in this beautiful country that God gave us," he shouted from the pulpit.

Members of his congregation nodded and smiled and chattered among themselves. My mother hugged me. But I remembered Bartholomew Bramlett's prediction. And I could picture Georgia politicians smiling at Jackson's latest reassurance that he would be no roadblock to their ambitions.

And one day Charley burst into our cabin with tears streaming down his cheeks. My big ball player was sobbing. "Georgia not only ignored the citation," he said, bewildered, "it hurriedly hanged Corn Tassel to show its contempt for the Supreme Court."

Senator Wilson Lumpkin's words to Andrew Jackson: "Georgia is not accountable to the Supreme Court or any other tribunal on earth."

So that ended that.

No matter what the political climate, no matter what evil threatens a people, there still exists a certain routine to life. So we tried to dismiss Jackson and Georgia from our minds as we celebrated Christmas, 1830.

We exchanged gifts. I gave Charley a silver bookmark that was engraved with the words of John 3:16. I ordered it from Philadelphia through an exchange paper. Harriet let me tend to her children to earn the money. I loved them, and it wasn't work. I still wasn't pregnant with a child of my own. Good.

Charley had been the dominator in a couple of Ball Plays, and some spectators who had won money on the outcome gave him a few dollars. He bought me a new pair of lace-up shoes from a trader's wagon. His heart wasn't in the Ball Play—and it troubled him that many missionaries were aghast that a minister would compete in the frolic—but he felt obligated to the village and its team.

My gift to Harriet and Elias was service. After I made enough money to buy Charley's present, I donated my time to them. "Your keeping these children while I try to tend to Elias and his kinfolks and friends is the best gift of all," Harriet said.

I would know many heroes in my lifetime, but in my estimation, none would ever equal Harriet Gold Boudinot. She gave up home and family to marry an Indian and move to a faraway land to serve God. Her service was not as direct as she had hoped and believed it would be. She was a background figure in the army of the Lord. She would bear three sons and three daughters in less than nine years, and a seventh child would be born dead. Her home would be tumultuous with visitors and Indian relatives, and her role would be that of helpmeet to an important historical figure. She frequently was tired out. But she kept the faith, insisting it was God's will, not hers, that mattered. She would do what was required for the greater good, even if that were merely changing a baby's soiled underpants.

My mother and grandmother attended church regularly, but they didn't accept Jesus Christ as their savior. My father went one time, said Charley didn't know what he was talking about, and never went again. The women and I exchanged homemade gifts, but Staring Otter refused to participate in the Christmas festivities, so I didn't give him a present, and he didn't give me one.

It was difficult to concentrate on the birth of the savior. When Georgia's laws were extended throughout the Cherokee Nation, John Ross and Major Ridge had advised Indian sheriffs and courts to execute Cherokee laws as usual. But Georgia declared such enforcement a crime punishable by imprisonment. So lawlessness overwhelmed our land.

At one time Elias estimated in the *Phoenix* that thieves had taken some five hundred head of cattle and horses from the Cherokees. They leveled fences, burned down houses, murdered and raped.

They poisoned the Cherokee Nation with whiskey. Barrel after barrel was brought in, and the unhappy Indians were susceptible to drunkenness to a degree never before seen in the land. Emboldened by drink, the Cherokees fought each other and fought the whites. Gambling became a diversionary, ruinous disease. Cherokees didn't understand the Georgia laws and frequently ran afoul of them. So they were locked up in filthy jails.

Elias despised liquor. He had observed the Cherokees' weakness for it and their degeneration when they associated with whites—even peaceful whites—bearing whiskey. Once he wrote in the *Phoenix*:

"Among us, it has been a wide spreading evil. It has cost us lives and a train of troubles. It has been an enemy to our national prosperity, industry and intellectual improvement. Even at this day when it is generally conceded that we are the most civilized of all the Aboriginal tribes, we see this enemy of all good stalking forth in triumph, carrying desolation and misery into families and neighborhoods."

Charley agreed. "The whites are destroying our people, and the people are destroying themselves," he told me. "We missionaries can't just stand by and watch the result of our labor with the Indians obliterated."

So, four days after Christmas, the Moravians, Baptists, Congregationalists and Presbyterians spoke up for the Cherokees. They met in New Echota, with non-denominational Charley Marley in their company, and drew up a manifesto in defense of the Indians.

Their statement mentioned the advances of the Cherokees. It didn't give all credit to the missionary influence; in fact, it applauded the federal government's role in civilizing the Indians. The missionaries had no political motives, they said; they were speaking only from moral ground. Removing the Indians or subjecting them to their white neighbors would result in disaster for the Cherokees, "arresting their progress in religion, civilization, learning, and the useful arts." The manifesto was signed and sent to Boston, where it was published in *The Missionary Herald*.

Resolutions, yes. A resolution against Georgia had all the force of a mosquito against the thick hide of a charging bull. The Georgia legislature, annoyed, passed a law that no white man could remain in the Cherokee part of Georgia after March 1, 1831, unless he took an oath of allegiance to the state and secured a permit from the governor. The law was aimed at the missionaries. If they broke it, they would go to the penitentiary for four years. *Draft a resolution about that, you interfering Northerners.*

All right, we'd try the Supreme Court again. William Wirt, our lawyer from Baltimore, demanded an injunction to stop Georgia from extending its laws over the Cherokee Nation, from intruding on our territory, from violating in any way our sovereignty.

Chief Justice John Marshall sympathized with us. The Indians, he said, "are acknowledged to have an unquestionable right to the lands they occupy, until that right shall be extinguished by a voluntary cession to our government ..." But he ruled the court didn't have jurisdiction because we had sued as a foreign nation and we weren't a foreign nation.

Georgians were ecstatic. Nothing stood in their path. The Georgia Guard looked the other way while their countrymen bullied, raped and robbed their way through the Cherokee Nation. They sang with a Robert Burns lilt as they went about their mischief:

Go, nature's child.
Your home's the wild;
Our venom cannot gripe ye
If once you'll roam,
And make your home
Beyond the Mississippi.

Persecuting the Cherokees wasn't merely profitable; it was great fun. Two Georgians set a cornfield afire and perched on a fence and whooped and hollered while a Cherokee housewife attempted to extinguish the blaze. Three members of the Georgia Guard interrupted a baptismal service by riding into the river and declaring themselves to be so moved that they had to baptize their horses.

What was really funny, they thought, was an aged Indian becoming so despondent that he hanged himself from a tree in his yard.

I was sweeping Harriet's veranda when a half dozen white horsemen rode up to the house. The tied their mounts to the banister and bolted inside, without a word to me, without knocking. I followed them into Elias's study, where he sat open-mouthed, thoroughly bewildered by their intrusion.

"Boudinot, if I don't stop reading lies about the Georgia Guard and Andrew Jackson, I'll have you whipped," bellowed their leader, who I later learned was Colonel Charles H. Nelson.

He shook a copy of *The Cherokee Phoenix* in Elias's face. "You call Andy Jackson 'our false and faithless father.' I ought to burn your house down for that.

"Only one thing keeps me from binding you to a tree and taking a whip to your back: I know you're the one who's false. I know an Indian wouldn't have the talent to write an editorial like that. Someone else wrote it—probably that Worcester fellow. But you'd better use whatever influence you have to keep libels like that out of the newspaper."

One of the guardsmen spat tobacco juice on Elias's desk, on his papers. And for good measure, he spat the wad that was left in his mouth on Elias himself. The six guardsmen thundered out of the house, mounted their horses and galloped away.

Elias was shaken, but he tried to laugh it off. "At least he said it took some talent to write it," he remarked in a shaky voice. "I appreciate the compliment."

I was glad Harriet was visiting at Ann Worcester's house. She had burdens enough on her without having to experience that visitation.

"What will you do?" I asked Elias.

"I'll do the only thing I can do," he said. "I'll continue to write editorials criticizing the Georgia Guard and Andrew Jackson."

I wet a cloth and cleaned the tobacco spit off Elias's desk and his papers and his coat sleeves. It was the least I could do.

CHAPTER 18

Perhaps the fatigue and depression that weighed upon us like anvils only made it seem so, but the winds of March, 1831, were more punishing than any other, before or since, that I can remember. They tore across the flatland of New Echota like blasts from Greenland.

"Never have they cut to the bone like this," Sophia Sawyer agreed.

"I don't believe they blew this chillingly in Connecticut," said Harriet, and though we knew that had to be an exaggeration, our misery welcomed the company.

On February 27, tiny Jerusha Worcester had been born to Ann and Samuel. The child was ill, and so was Ann, who had experienced a difficult labor. Jerusha's two sisters, little Ann Eliza, four, and Sarah, two, were a double handful.

Samuel had chosen to defy Georgia's new law that demanded white men in the Cherokee Nation take an oath of allegiance to the state and secure from the governor a license to remain.

Samuel was torn by the dilemma.

The Georgia Guard was humiliating and degrading the Cherokees. Georgians were robbing them, and the Cherokees were powerless to stop them. The now unregulated sale of whiskey was accelerating the Indians' predicament and their despair, getting them into all sorts of trouble. The chances of the Cherokees' winning appeared bleak.

"I can see rational reasons to accept Jackson's offer, to exchange our land for that in the West, to pack up and move," Samuel told Charley and me as the three of us stared into the glow of the fireplace at the Worcester home.

"But I have tried to teach faith. Is abandoning your home—abandoning the fight against evil—an example of faith? I think not. I think the Cherokees should stay and fight. I think I should stay and fight. I must stay and fight."

I was overwhelmed by his bravery. I stared at tall, thin, thirty-three-year-old Samuel Worcester as if I had never seen him before. Behind that delicate—even frail—face there was much of what God expected (or at least hoped for) from us all. But this spell of admiration didn't prevent my silently thanking God that my missionary Charley Marley wasn't a white man.

Harriet, Sophia Sawyer and I took care of Ann, her baby, her other two daughters and the household. Harriet, of course, wasn't much help because her own children required attention. Sometimes I wished she would just go home, because she was as much a part of the problem as the solution, but she regarded Ann as a sister and wanted to be at her side.

At least the house was comfortable—certainly by Cherokee standards it was. The American Board of Commissioners for Foreign Missions had given him eight hundred dollars to build it and Samuel, an accomplished carpenter, had done much of the work himself.

Closets were rare in those days, but he was innovative, and he had built three into his home. Thank goodness, for when the mess got to be too much for us, Sophia and I would just shove it into a closet.

The house itself was the New Echota missions station. The Worcesters lived on the first floor, but four second-story rooms were occupied by boarders, including Sophia Sawyer's Cherokee students. Five to ten boarders might be living up there at any time. An outside stairway provided private access to the upper floor—which also served as post office and church—but the place frequently was in a state of commotion, and I would throw up my hands and go outside and lean against a cedar tree until I regained my composure. It stood just twenty feet from the raucous house, but it was staunch and calm, and somehow it restored those qualities to me—and, yes, I know that sounds silly, but that's the way it was. It worked, which was all that mattered.

On March 12, 1831, just before sunset, our fears materialized. Buffoons of the Georgia Guard arrived in New Echota to arrest Samuel Worcester.

I call them buffoons because if the episode hadn't been so serious, I would have laughed. It was as if a circus had arrived in town. As I stood alone on the front porch and watched their approach, I thought that all that was missing was a corps of painted jesters dancing at the front of the procession.

First appeared a wagon transporting a massive drum. A bumpy-faced militiaman who didn't look a day over fifteen was beating it wildly, first on one side, then on the other, swinging the sticks as if he were trying to slay some wounded but still dangerous animal. He must have known how ridiculous he looked, for when I shook my head at the sight he started laughing.

Next came an equally young fifer, strutting and playing a piece that was intended to be martial but that sounded more like the accompaniment to a jig. His eyes crossed when he gravely looked at the tip of his instrument.

Twenty-five mounted guardsmen followed, their bayoneted muskets at ready, as if they were about to challenge the forces of Napoleon.

This was the party that had come to arrest a thin, tired missionary who was caring for a sick wife and new baby.

The detail stopped in the front yard, and the leader of the horsemen dismounted and asked me if Samuel Worcester lived there. I recognized him as Colonel Nelson, the guardsman who had chastised Elias.

I didn't answer. I just stared at him. He cursed me and pushed past and was about to open the front door when Samuel stepped outside. "Let's talk out here," the minister said. "My wife and child are ill."

"Mr. Worcester, you are under arrest for failing to take the oath of allegiance to the state of Georgia and failing to acquire a license to remain on Cherokee land," Nelson said.

"Do you have a warrant?" Samuel asked.

"No," Nelson barked, "but I have twenty-five armed men."

Samuel's smile was almost cordial. "Well, I don't suppose my Cherokee brethren have an army to do battle with these soldiers," he said. "The Supreme Court declared we aren't a foreign nation."

Even the martinet colonel appreciated the little joke. "It wouldn't have mattered what the Supreme Court declared," Nelson said evenly. "If the verdict had gone the Cherokees' way, Georgia wouldn't have recognized it. We would have sent ten thousand troops into Cherokee country to enforce our laws if necessary."

The front door opened, and there stood Ann Worcester, pale, haggard, supported by Harriet Boudinot and Sophia Sawyer. Four-year-old Ann Eliza and two-year-old Sarah peered from around the skirts of the adults. Ann approached the colonel, and when she stopped, her face was so close to his that he took a step backward. "Samuel, we tried to get her to stay inside," said Harriet.

"You've come to take my husband?" Ann asked Nelson.

"Yes, ma'm. I'm sorry."

"You aren't sorry," Sophia blurted.

Ann was determined not to cry. She stood as straight and tall as she could. "God be with us all," she said. "And may he forgive you."

"You may say your goodbyes," Nelson told Samuel.

Harriet and Sophia and I went to the kitchen and left Ann and Samuel and their children alone in the living room. Armed guardsmen surrounded the house and peered into the windows, as if they were afraid the minister would flee into the forest. Yes, I would say buffoons was an accurate term.

After about five minutes, Ann called us. Samuel led a prayer, told us goodbye, and joined the guardsmen. Ann didn't watch their departure—which was celebrated by drum and fife. She went to her new baby's crib, and there, looking down at the ill Jerusha, she began to cry. But she wouldn't let us comfort her, and we left her alone. When she joined us in the kitchen her head was high and her eyes were dry. "The children want cornbread and milk for supper," she said. "If you would fix it for them."

Colonel Nelson and his men arrested Samuel Worcester at New Echota, John Thompson at High Tower and Isaac Proctor at Carmel. The missionaries were marched to Lawrenceville where they were to appear with their attorneys in Gwinnett County Superior Court.

I was hanging out clothes I had washed when a buggy stopped at the Worcester house. I recognized the freshly painted red spokes.

"Mrs. Marley, how nice to see you," Bartholomew Bramlett said as he stepped from the vehicle. "I wish it were under other circumstances. I heard about her husband's plight, and I have come to offer assistance to Mrs. Worcester, monetary and otherwise."

The man I had once despised was welcome. Who wouldn't be pleased to see a wealthy plantation owner at the home of a sick woman whose husband had been spirited off by the Georgia Guard?

What I wasn't pleased to see was his housekeeper. "You remember Rachel, don't you?" he said. Rachel glared at me without a word and, for my benefit, edged over beside Bramlett until their arms touched. She was a beautiful woman, in her mid-thirties, whose very posture asserted her independence, even if by law she wasn't independent. She stood as straight as a soldier at review, chin up, ample chest out.

I took them inside, seated them on a couch in the living room, and brought Ann in to meet them. She was almost past walking, but she insisted they not see her in bed.

Bartholomew offered money. "I couldn't take cash unless I could repay it, and I don't know that I could repay it," Ann answered.

"I can appreciate your attitude," Bramlett said. "But these are perilous times. We aren't allowed to dig in our own gold fields, Jackson won't pay the $6,000 annuity to our government, and the U.S. denied our application for a loan. The Cherokee government is in financial trouble, and wealthy individuals such as myself are helping to bear the costs. There is no difference in aiding a government in need and a family in need. In fact, I like to think we're all one big family."

Ann sighed and gazed out the window, as if expecting an answer from the forest. "Damn, woman," I thought, "bury your pride and let the man help you. Your husband may not be back for years—if ever."

"I brought Rachel so that she can care for you and your children," Bramlett said. "She is very good. She takes charge and doesn't have to be told what to do."

"That won't be necessary," I piped up. "We're getting along fine. Mrs. Boudinot and Miss Sawyer and I are enjoying seeing after Mrs. Worcester and the children." Now whose pride was at the ridiculous point?

Sophia frowned at me and said, "Maybe it would be good if ..." But I insisted I was feeling wonderful, that we didn't need outside help. Rachel glared at me.

There was a knock at the door. "I'll get it," I said, and when I opened it my scream of joy awoke little Jerusha.

There stood Samuel. "Is this the Worcester residence?" he said cheerily. I grabbed his shoulders and pressed my face against his chest.

Samuel bounced into the living room and hugged and kissed his wife. "The Lord has delivered the captive!" Sophia shouted, and before she caught herself she danced a few jig steps.

Samuel sat beside Ann on the couch, the excitement momentarily restoring her vigor and even her color. "What happened?" she asked.

He explained that it all was very simple. He and the other two missionaries appeared before the court, and the judge noted that they were in charge of U.S. government funds for the benefit of the Indians and that they were U.S. postmasters. Since they were federal employees, they were not subject to Georgia law. Cases dismissed.

He had walked the sixty miles from Lawrenceville to New Echota, and here he was back home, less than a week after he had been arrested.

"There is nothing more for ministers of God in the Cherokee Nation to fear," Samuel said. "The ruling was a vindication of our work among the Indians, a signal that it is to continue. Praise the Lord."

I walked Bartholomew Bramlett and Rachel to the buggy. Without a word she took her seat and gazed straight ahead. Bramlett spoke softly to me. "Nothing more for ministers of God in the Cherokee Nation to fear," he repeated Samuel's words. "Oh, if that were only true."

"It isn't true?" I asked.

"A government that ignores the Supreme Court of the United States isn't likely to be put off by a technicality," Bramlett said. "The Georgia Guard will be back for Mr. Worcester. My offer still stands, so when it happens, Mrs. Worcester has only to get in touch with me, and I will render whatever assistance I can. This is no time to bear hardships because of pride. You know where I live, Mrs. Marley. Please help me to help her."

"Nancy," I said. "Call me Nancy."

A smile instantly linked the little man's dark eyes. "Thank you," he said. "If you will call me Bartholomew."

Rachel sighed, Bartholomew said goodbye, and Levi, the driver, set the buggy in motion.

The neighbors heard that The Messenger was home, and soon the yard was filled with celebrating Cherokees. "With the Lord at our side, we have won a great victory," Samuel told them. He knelt on the porch, and they knelt on the ground, and he led them in prayer.

"Let it be so, dear God," I whispered, but I doubted that it was.

And it wasn't. First, Governor George Gilmer got an assurance from the federal government that it did not consider the missionaries its agents simply because they handled federal funds. Still, as postmasters they were employees of the U.S. Postal Service. What to do about that?

No problem. Gilmer asked Jackson to fire them, and the Chicken Snake did.

The governor wrote Worcester, Butler, Thompson and other leading missionaries a letter, stating that he wanted to spare them imprisonment. The Georgia Guard would delay their arrests until they had time to leave the state.

Some prudently went to North Carolina and Tennessee, leaving their missions in the care of female teachers, who weren't affected by the law. Samuel Worcester, though, stood strong. He would not leave his sick wife and baby, nor would he bend to Gilmer's threats.

He wrote to the governor, informing him that he would remain at New Echota, "and if I suffer in consequence of continuing to preach the gospel and diffuse the written word of God among his people, I trust that I shall be sustained by a conscience void of offence, and by the anticipation of a righteous decision at that tribunal from which there is no appeal."

On July 7, 1831, a detachment of the Georgia Guard again arrested Samuel Worcester. He told its leader, Sergeant Jacob Brooks, that his wife and child were ill, and he could not leave them. The sergeant said he was under orders, and the next morning Samuel fell into line behind the baggage wagon for the march to Camp Gilmer outside Lawrenceville.

A new surge of arrests had begun. The procession picked up other guards and prisoners along the way. A minister who was riding in the other direction, who was a resident of Tennessee, was added to the parade and forced to walk in the center of the road where the mud was deepest. A Cherokee gold miner was chained to the wagon. Dr. Elizur Butler was chained by the neck to a horse.

Samuel and the others had been treated with some courtesy during the episode in March, but it was different this time. Brooks not only railed against his prisoners but against all ministers and religion itself. He was a profane man who could barely speak a sentence without cursing.

Samuel never forgot a taunt that Brooks repeated over and over: "Fear not, little flock, for it is your Father's good pleasure to give you the kingdom." Samuel was able to hear the words quite apart from the one who was speaking them, and they gave him solace—hardly the result that Brooks had intended.

They arrived at Camp Gilmer on July 10. "This is where all the enemies of the state of Georgia will have to land," Brooks told them. "There and in hell." During the days to come, more captives arrived, until there were about a dozen, most missionaries and all white, except for the Cherokee gold miner.

On Sunday Samuel asked if he might hold services in the jail for the prisoners, members of the Georgia Guard and local residents. Request denied. "If your object be true piety," Colonel Nelson said, "you can enjoy it where you are."

On July 23 the captives went to Gwinnett County Superior Court where they were indicted and released, pending trial in September. Again Samuel Worcester walked home. The sixty miles between Lawrenceville and New Echota were becoming quite familiar.

Ann still ran a fever, and little Jerusha had never enjoyed a day in which she wasn't ill. This time there was no claim of victory for the ministers of God on the lips of Samuel Worcester. He was told of a letter that Governor Gilmer had written to Colonel J.W.A. Sanford of the Georgia Guard: "If they are released by the courts, or given bail and return to their homes, arrest them again." He could not help his wife or child if he were in jail, so Samuel reluctantly crossed the border into Tennessee. He would stay at the Brainerd Mission until his September trial.

I was neglecting my husband, but he understood. I spent more nights in the Worcester house than in my own. Harriet, Sophia, and I were ground down to the bone. Finally, I gave in. I spotted Pepper Rodham at a store in New Echota and told him, "Tell Mr. Bramlett to send Rachel."

And I didn't care what Ann thought about it: "Tell him to send some money and food, too."

Levi and Rachel arrived the next morning. He tipped his hat to me, but she didn't acknowledge my presence. She unloaded packages of food from the buggy and carried them into Ann Worcester's home. Then she hoisted more packages and took them to the smokehouse.

Bramlett was right, she didn't wait for instructions. She reorganized everything we were doing and, a model of efficiency, cared for Ann and her children. She ordered Harriet and Sophia and me around as if she had been white and we had been black. "Go home," she told Harriet—and things did quieten down once Mrs. Boudinot and the little Boudinots were out of the way.

She intimidated Sophia Sawyer's heretofore noisy Cherokee students, and she intimidated Sophia Sawyer, who began asking permission before assuming the simplest chore. She even intimidated John Ross, the principal chief of the Cherokees. He was whistling absentmindedly as he stepped onto the porch, intending to pay Ann a visit. "Shut up!" Rachel rasped at him from the front window. "We finally got that baby down, and you're going to wake her up. No, Mrs. Worcester is not asleep, but we don't need any chatting in the house right now. Come back later."

Rachel's presence at the Worcester home enabled me to spend days at a time with Charley, and for that I was grateful. I found him struggling to keep Bramlett Academy operational. He was preaching, teaching, cooking, disciplining, wiping noses, washing clothes and linens. The seven pupils—four who lived in the dormitory and three residents of our village—took most of his time. I wasn't there to teach my classes, and Sophia had ceased her Friday visits that propelled the children into such delicious flights of imagination and inquisitiveness. When I returned I found them bored, argumentative, discouraged.

"Thank goodness for Bartholomew Bramlett," Charley said. "And thank goodness for you. These children are driving me insane."

"You'd do better to thank goodness for Rachel," I said.

"Well, Bartholomew sent her. That's what I meant. But, yes, thank goodness for Rachel. Thank goodness for anybody or anything that will help me out of this mess."

I laughed. "You don't consider those shirts washed, do you? If I were the pupils I'd wonder why you even bother to get them wet." The children's and Charley's dingy clothes, draped over limbs of bushes, flapped in the wind.

I bored into the tasks at hand, pleased to rescue Charley. Teaching the children arithmetic and geography was a welcomed diversion from caring for a sick woman and child.

Then one day Rachel walked into my classroom—the auditorium of the church—without knocking, without speaking. She took a seat on the backmost pew. The children stared at the black stranger and whispered and giggled, but a stern word from me reclaimed their attention, and we completed the lesson.

I sent the students out to play, and Rachel walked to the front of the church. "I want you and your husband to teach my children," she said.

"Your children?"

"I have two sons, ten and eleven."

"I had gathered that you didn't like me," I said.

"I don't."

It was the answer I had expected. "I'm not certain why you don't like me," I said.

"Because," Rachel answered, "you came into Mr. Bramlett's home that day and criticized me as if you—really just a girl—knew everything and he was some terrible, inferior person. I don't like impudent people."

"Then why do you want me to teach your children?"

"I would prefer that Miss Sawyer teach them at New Echota, but the Worcesters' household doesn't need any more disruption, any more trouble. It is against Georgia law to teach black children. Miss Sawyer told me you once told her she could have black children in your school if she wished."

I had said that—before I had actually witnessed the Georgia Guard arriving at a person's home, arresting him without a warrant, and marching him sixty miles to jail for violating the laws of a state that didn't even have jurisdiction.

"Why do you feel your children need schooling?" I asked, stalling while I weighed the situation in my mind.

"I can't read and write," Rachel said. A tiny smile creased her face. "I learned big words like impudent from listening to Mr. Bramlett talk about you. I've never thought it mattered whether I could read and write, for my life seemed to be laid out for me. I would live comfortably in a big marble house and run it for a wealthy Cherokee.

"But the Georgians are going to take it all. I realize that now. For a long time I had heard Mr. Bramlett and his friends speak of the peril, but I dismissed their fears from my mind, saying Mr. Bramlett wouldn't let that happen. But the other day I saw white men on his plantation, and I asked him what they were doing, and he said they are dividing the Cherokee Nation into farms for the Georgians when they take over."

It was true. Talk about impudence: white surveyors were moving through the nation with axe and chain, surveying our lands, blazing trees and leaving strange marks on the blazes. They were sectioning the Cherokee Nation into plots of one hundred and sixty acres—forty acres in the gold fields—eventually to be distributed by lottery to Georgians.

"I now believe they will force us to move west of the Mississippi River," Rachel continued, her voice rising and her eyes widening.

"Who can say what's over there? Everyone knows the spirits of the dead go west. They say the Mississippi is a thousand times wider than the Oostanaula. Perhaps it is in that huge river that the Uktena, the magic serpent, lives. It is as big around as a tree trunk, its scales glitter like fire, and there are horns on its head. I heard of a man who merely smelled the Uktena's breath and died. Yet we must cross the Mississippi. When you make a great journey such as that, you invite evil spirits to attack you.

"Perhaps there will be no slavery there. And if there is, perhaps it will soon be abolished. I am told that there are those in the North—called abolitionists, in fact—who vow to destroy slavery.

"Perhaps none of us will survive the trek. Perhaps all will. Perhaps some will and some won't. Perhaps my children will and I won't. Perhaps Bartholomew Bramlett will continue to be a wealthy important man, and our lives won't change so drastically in the West. Perhaps he will be just another poor Indian, barely able to care for himself, much less anyone else.

"In such tumultuous circumstances I believe my children will have a better chance if they can read and write, if they are educated, if they have weapons of the mind to bring to bear on whatever we encounter."

It was a mixture of Cherokee and black superstition, the Christian religion, nonsense and commonsense. I saw another side of Rachel, the composed systematic keeper of an educated man's household who repeated such words as tumultuous. The myths of field hands and the old Indians had registered with her, too.

"You suggest the Cherokees are being punished for enslaving blacks, yet you defend Bartholomew Bramlett," I challenged her.

Rachel's aloof practical demeanor returned instantly. "He is different," she said.

"What does Mr. Bramlett think about your children attending school here?" I asked, still stalling.

"I haven't mentioned it to him. But since you lectured him on how the color of a person's skin is of no consequence, I'm certain he will approve of black children being taught along with Indian children."

"What will your husband say?"

"My husband is dead. And that's all you need to know."

"I'll have to talk to Reverend Marley," I said. "He is in charge of the school. I don't know if we can take your children. It is against the law, after all."

"You think Mr. Bramlett should free his slaves, though the law says he is entitled to them."

At that moment I didn't feel at all noble. I felt cowardly. But I was correct in that I would have to discuss it with Charley. And he was visiting a member of his congregation who was ill.

"I'll tell my husband what you said and give you an answer," I repeated, and without another word, Rachel turned and left the church.

>>>→ • ←<<<

CHAPTER 19

Sophia Sawyer touched my elbow, and I stopped, and we watched a bird disappear into one of the gourds that hung like little moons over the Worcesters' garden.

"Nancy, would you like to be a purple martin?" she asked.

"Not particularly," I said.

"Imagine the view they have of the world."

I shrugged.

"Oh, Nancy," she insisted, "it's a beautiful world, and they are beautiful birds. See how the sunlight brings out the color of their feathers?"

A post was erected in the center of the garden, and it supported two crossarms from which hung a dozen gourds, the homes of the martins. I considered them ugly birds, not pretty ones. Humans provided them a place to live, and they worked for the humans. I saw nothing remarkable in the arrangement—but Sophia did.

"We couldn't be having our walk today if it weren't for the purple martins," my companion said.

"Oh, Sophia, what are you talking about?" I asked in the bewildered tone I reserved for her.

"They eat thousands—no, millions—of insects that would be pestering us right now. They gobble mosquitoes like children gobble peaches. I haven't been bitten a single time."

"I know that," I said, "but of course we could have our stroll if there were no martins. People walk all the time where there are no martins."

But Sophia Sawyer loved the world and its wonders. And she saw wonders where no one else did. What was commonplace to most was phenomenal to her. She reached for the sun with one hand and the moon with the other. She believed we were to love God and one another on this marvelous earth, and if it sometimes wasn't as marvelous as it was supposed to be, then it was our job to try to make it marvelous again.

"Sophia, what are you doing?" I asked as she dropped to her knees, but already she was praying.

"Thank you, God, for your wonderful purple martins," she said. "Thank you for your birds that eat the insects that would attack our gardens, for your beautiful martins that chase the crows and the hawks from our food."

I bowed my head and waited. When she finished, I offered her my hand, and she lifted herself to her feet, her knees popping. "Getting old," the tall, angular spinster said.

"You'll never get old," I told her. "Let's walk beside the creek. That is, if you don't think the insects will carry us off. By the way, I'll bet the poor insects aren't offering thanks to God for the purple martins."

The path beside New Town Creek was as old as the Cherokees, I supposed. No doubt it had afforded a pleasant stroll to some ancestor of mine two hundred years before. The limbs and leaves of tall trees created a canopy and shut out the light, and it was as if one were disappearing into another world, leaving troubles and fears behind.

"Oh, I love the red maple most of all," Sophia said, stopping to pat the trunk of a tree. "It gives color to the forest, red flowers in the spring, scarlet, orange and yellow leaves in the autumn. It feeds its buds and seeds to the squirrels and birds, its leaves and twigs to the deer, the sugar from its sap to humans. And look, the muscadine vine with its purple fruit climbs almost to the top."

At least she didn't stop to say a prayer of thanks for the red maple. But she did demand: "All right, I have named my favorite tree. Which is your favorite, Nancy Swimmer?"

Oh, I suppose her delight was infectious. I thought about the question and, with some genuine excitement in my voice, said, "The black cherry. I love the tart black fruits and the gorgeous white flowers, and my father once made a magnificent table from the fine-grained wood—but mostly I like the tea that comes from the bark, because it always makes me stop coughing."

Sophia shrieked at the sight of a beaver dam. The water was normally two feet deep, but the barrier of mud and sticks increased the depth to five feet. "Just think," she said, "an old orange-toothed, paddle-tailed fellow is right there in his lodge, right in front of us, waiting to come out tonight and eat his supper of bark and twigs. I wish I could leap into the water and come up inside his house. I think I will."

"Sophia," I yelped, "that thing might bite your nose off."

"Just teasing," she said.

We walked on, stopping under a shagbark hickory, hoping to find a few nuts the squirrels and other animals hadn't opened, but they had devoured them all. I tossed a shell into the creek and said, "Sophia, I have a problem. Rachel wants to put her two sons in Bramlett Academy."

"Where's the problem in that?" she asked, as sincerely as a songbird greeting the sun.

"It's against the law. The Georgia Guard might close Charley's school. They might even close his church. They might throw Charley in prison. You've seen them in action. You know what they're capable of."

"But we don't recognize Georgia law," Sophia said. "This isn't Georgia. This is the Cherokee Nation."

I spoke the words: "Sophia, I'm afraid."

"Being afraid is no disgrace," she said. "Everyone is afraid. The disgrace is in letting fear direct you to do the wrong thing. And I know you won't do that."

"What is the right thing?" I asked.

"Oh, you know what the right thing is, without asking me. The right thing isn't submitting to an evil law that doesn't apply to us. The right thing is taking Rachel's children into your school."

I didn't answer. My thoughts swirled like the water before us. I began to walk, and Sophia followed me. But she couldn't go far without stopping to investigate and marvel at something, anything. "This river cane has so many uses," she said. "Arrow shafts, blowguns, baskets, mats. The deer and rabbits love its tender leaves. God does provide."

I hugged her. "Oh, Sophia, I love you more than the rabbits love leaves," I said.

"I know you'll do the right thing," Sophia answered, and she took my hand and led me to a pool of clear water in a bend of the creek. We stood on a steep hill, and the clean sandy bottom was visible below us. It was a favorite swimming hole of children, and rocks had been removed from the banks for use in the construction of New Echota.

"Now I'm going to do the right thing," Sophia said. "Remember, I told you how the missionaries at Haweiss didn't like it because I delighted so in the naked little Indian children plunging into the swimming hole, and how I wished I could have joined them? Well, I'm going to do something I've always wanted to do. I'm going to take off my clothes and go swimming in a creek—and so are you."

It should have seemed like the craziest thing in the world, but it didn't. An assortment of protests danced through my mind—someone would see us and our reputations would be ruined, we'd break an ankle descending the steep hill, a snake would bite us, the frigid water would make us ill—but I dismissed them just as quickly. "All right," I said.

Lanky Sophia Sawyer and I stripped and, naked as stones, we slid down the leaf-covered hill as if we were playing in snow, and we leaped from the edge into the shallow water. It was cold, but not too cold, and we frolicked like children. We splashed each other, and we had a contest to see who could hold her breath the longest. I don't know why we weren't embarrassed or afraid, but we weren't.

We were wet, muddy, and disheveled when we slipped back into our clothes, tugging at twisted garments that clung to our damp skin. We set out for the Worcester house, eager to see the look on Ann's face when we presented our matted hair and wet blouses and squishy shoes.

But Rachel was tossing a pan of water out the back door when we got there, and she barely seemed to notice our unkempt condition. "Thank goodness you're back," she said. "I didn't know where you were. Hurry."

We found Ann Worcester on the bed, on her hands and knees, over the figure of her baby. Little Sarah and Ann Eliza stood in the corner, hugging each other, crying. "Jerusha is so hot," Ann said, "and she doesn't seem to be aware of anything."

"We'd better get word to Mr. Worcester," Sophia said.

"I'll ask Charley to ride to Brainerd and tell Samuel his daughter is dying," I whispered.

The baby's eyes blinked, and then her unbroken gaze at the ceiling informed us Jerusha Worcester had escaped this world without learning how hateful it can be. Gently, Rachel closed her eyelids and said, "Ask your husband to tell Mr. Worcester his daughter is dead."

Elias conducted the funeral at the New Echota cemetery. It was a small plot on a hilltop, a few feet nearer to God. A neighbor had carved into a fieldstone the information that Jerusha Worcester had been born on February 27, 1831, and had died on August 14, 1831.

We waited as long as we could, but Samuel and Charley had not returned from Brainerd. I kept looking over my shoulder at every sound as Elias spoke, because I knew all manner of evil could have befallen them.

"Amen," we said, and our group began the short walk to the Worcester home, Elias supported the faltering Ann Worcester in the brutal summer heat. Two neighbors lowered the tiny pine box into the ground, and in the distance we heard shovelfuls of dirt hitting its top.

In the yard and on the porch of the Worcester home were sprawled members of the Georgia Guard. At least they had enough respect not to boom their drum during the funeral. Colonel Nelson tipped his hat and said, "Sorry to hear about your baby, Mrs. Worcester."

Ann's wail raised chill bumps on my back. "He's not here," she screamed. "He's not coming."

"Well, we know he is coming," Nelson said calmly.

"Do you people have no feelings?" Elias demanded. "Can you arrest a man on the day his daughter is buried?"

"I'm just a soldier following orders," Nelson told him.

"You're just a bastard," Rachel said.

He raised his fist, but Elias stepped between them. "If you want to hit somebody, hit me," he said.

Nelson dropped his arms to his sides. "This ain't the time and place," he said, "but I'll keep that in mind. I should have bullwhipped you that day I came to your house."

We went inside, and Rachel tried to get Ann to go to bed, but she insisted on sitting in a rocker that faced a front window, watching for her husband.

He arrived an hour after his child's funeral. Through the terrible heat he and Charley rode stumbling, lathered horses that had no more speed in them.

"You're under arrest for trespassing on Georgia soil," Nelson said before Samuel's feet touched the ground.

"I've been freed until my trial in September," the haggard missionary said. "You can't arrest me again."

"Yes, I can," Nelson declared.

"At least let me see my wife," Samuel pleaded.

"For a few minutes. But hurry. We've got to get on the road."

Nelson looked at Charley and said, "You, get my men some water. They're thirsting to death."

To which Reverend Charley Marley replied: "Get it yourself, you son of a bitch. But don't get it out of the Worcesters' well."

Nelson's hand went to the butt of his pistol, and I gasped. But he didn't draw the gun. "I'll remember you, big fellow," he said. "You and Boudinot. I'll see you down the road." And he walked away.

I don't know why he didn't arrest Charley and march him to Lawrenceville. I believe it was because he was, indeed, a big fellow, and it was simpler to ignore the remark than to try to guard him for sixty miles. It was one thing to command a thin missionary, another to command the best ball player in the Cherokee Nation.

Ann had maintained her composure when Samuel was arrested before, but this time she went to pieces. "My baby is in the ground, and my husband is going to prison," she cried as the militiamen led him away. He had been allowed fifteen minutes alone with her.

Any question I had about whether Charley would take in black pupils at Bramlett Academy was answered on that day. And if Rachel could call Colonel Nelson a bastard to his face, I could welcome her children. After she got Ann Worcester to bed I said, "Rachel, your sons will be most welcome at our school."

She didn't smile, and her voice remained hard, but she did at least say, "Thank you."

Samuel was marched to Lawrenceville where he stayed in jail for nearly a month before going to trial on September 15. He and ten other missionaries were told by the judge that it was "the duty of every Christian to submit to civil authority." They were sentenced to four years' hard labor in the penitentiary.

Governor Gilmer desired no martyrs. When they reached the Milledgeville Penitentiary they were told that anyone taking the oath of allegiance to Georgia or moving from the state would be pardoned.

Nine of the eleven accepted the offer and were freed. Samuel Worcester and Elizur Butler refused.

Many times I've put myself in their place. I've thought how adamant I was in arguments against slavery, but how I balked when Rachel asked me to accept the danger in teaching her children. It's one thing to angrily debate philosophy, something else to hear the jail doors closing.

And Samuel and Dr. Butler did hear the jail doors closing. Samuel told me later how officials argued with them for hours, all the time opening and shutting the prison gate, the clanging of the steel reminding them they would lose their freedom. But they remained fast, and the Cherokee cause had its martyrs.

They were issued prison clothing and thrown in with murderers and thieves—who treated them with respect. They were fortunate in that the penitentiary had been destroyed by fire earlier in the year, and it had been reconstructed into four large chambers. There was plenty of light and ventilation.

Perhaps through the sympathy of someone in authority, their "hard labor" wasn't hard. Samuel became a cabinetmaker, Dr. Butler a cobbler. They were allowed to preach on Sundays to the other inmates and to a few citizens who came to hear them, whether out of curiosity or sincerity.

"God has given me a cheerful heart," Samuel wrote to Charley and me. "I try to view this as an opportunity to serve him. There is great consolation in knowing Christians everywhere believe in what we are doing."

Once again the Cherokees turned to the Supreme Court of the United States. William Wirt asked the gentlemen to consider the case of Samuel Worcester vs. the State of Georgia. A white man's constitutional rights had been violated, Wirt claimed. And in this case resided hope for the red man. We waited.

The persecution of the Cherokees ranged from arrests of missionaries to gratuitous annoyances. I was at Harriet's when Elias came home and slammed his fist against the wall. "Tarvin won't give me the exchange papers," he cried.

"He can't simply withhold them," Harriet said.

"Well, he is simply withholding them."

William Tarvin had replaced Samuel Worcester as postmaster of New Echota. He had been a whiskey trader, and he was more interested in supplying drink to the Indians, which was illegal, than in seeing that the mail service was handled efficiently.

When Elias protested in the pages of the *Phoenix*, Tarvin began to keep back letters and packages. Supplies and exchange papers were delayed or "lost," and publication of the newspaper became problematical.

The exchanges were a key source of news for the little paper—and once Strong Hickory found a package of them in New Town Creek. He took them to Elias who spread them out to dry. Tarvin said he had no idea how that could have happened.

I wrote more and more feature stories for the *Phoenix*. In a time of national peril, they weren't topical, but they filled space. And perhaps a story on Sophia Sawyer's study of the stars helped some Cherokee get his mind off his trouble.

Rachel and her two sons arrived at Bramlett Academy in a work wagon driven by Pepper Rodham. It was loaded with food for our students and for Ann Worcester and her children and for the Boudinots, who always struggled on Elias's meager salary. Bartholomew sent a handsome tuition for Rachel's boys, as well as money for Ann.

A shotgun was propped against the seat, between Rodham and Rachel. "Just in case some Pony Club trash was in the mood for a bite of ham," Rodham said.

I wondered how he had managed to remain in the Cherokee Nation without signing an oath of allegiance to Georgia. Or perhaps he had signed one. I asked him.

"Bartholomew has influence," Rodham answered. "He can't perform miracles, but he can handle simple briberies. But it's probably only a matter of time until someone high enough up the ladder hears about me and I have to leave."

"Or you could simply sign it and ignore it," I offered.

"Mrs. Marley, it's called an oath," Rodham said.

You just never know about people. I, the preacher's wife, was suggesting a person's word before God didn't matter; Pepper Rodham, a rough-cut plantation overseer whose beard was streaked amber with tobacco spit, said it did.

Rachel introduced her children. Peter, eleven, and Thomas ten, stammered their rehearsed greetings and thanks to Mrs. Marley and Reverend Marley for accepting them in Bramlett Academy. Charley wasn't present, but they thanked him anyway.

They wore clean, ironed clothing, oiled shoes and new straw hats. Each held a carpet bag containing his belongings.

I led them to the dormitory, which was upstairs over the single classroom (which I never used because I preferred the airy, high-ceilinged, more comfortable sanctuary of the church itself), and showed them their beds. The Bull had built two new ones, and now there were six in a row, plain wooden frames crisscrossed with ropes that supported cornshuck mattresses. At the foot of each was a chest that Charley—no carpenter—had made.

"Mamma ...," Thomas said, pleadingly.

"It's a wonderful school, my children," Rachel blurted. "Your stay here will be rewarding."

"But I don't want ..."

The four little Cherokee boys who lived in the room bounded up the stairs, one swinging a basket of fish that dripped murky water on the floor I had swept half an hour before. They stopped and stared at the two black children.

"Peter and Thomas are moving in," I said. "They will be your new school-mates. Tell them your names."

"Do you like to fish?" the Cherokee with the basket asked after the introductions.

"Yes," Peter said.

"Come see what we caught," the Cherokee said, and all six bounded down the steps and into the yard, where he turned the basket upside down and fish flopped in the dust.

Rachel and Pepper Rodham and I stood at an upstairs window and watched the boys as they became more and more antic, stretching their arms to illustrate fish tales.

"They'll get along fine," I said.

"Children usually do," Rachel said. "They haven't yet been taught not to."

Charley had been helping my father with repairs on the roof of his cabin. He returned at sunset to find six boys at the supper table, already fast friends.

"Rachel wept when she left," I told him. "I couldn't imagine Rachel ever crying."

"I got your father's roof fixed," Charley told me. "He is so obstinate. He insisted he could do it himself. If he had got up there he would have fallen and broken his neck."

"Thank you," I said.

"A strange thing happened," Charley said. "Usually he would stick his hand in fire rather than ask me for anything, but he asked me to organize a Green Corn Festival. He said he wanted to see one more Green Corn Festival before he dies."

And so, for the first time in several years, there was a Green Corn Festival in our village. The summer ritual commemorating the new corn had been the greatest of ceremonies, not only of the Cherokees, but of other tribes. It was a time of dancing and merrymaking but also of solemnity. But the old ways were passing, and more and more, throughout the Cherokee Nation, the Green Corn Festival was being neglected.

I was glad Staring Otter had proposed a Green Corn Festival and pleased that he asked Charley to organize it. During the hectic present, a touch of the past would be welcomed. And I hoped that he and Charley would become better friends.

"Not the Black Drink," Charley said that night in bed. "Surely not the Black Drink."

"You know Staring Otter," I said. "He will insist on the Black Drink."

"I'm going to sleep," Charley said, and he groaned and turned over.

The Black Drink was a tea brewed from a holly plant. It caused vomiting. It was a gift from the Great Spirit, and its use purified both body and soul.

Charley asked my father and The Bull, our village chief, to meet with him, and they agreed on a four-day Green Corn Festival. That was a victory of sorts for Charley, because sometimes they lasted eight days.

Charley was visibly touched when he returned home from the meeting. "Staring Otter suggested that I perform the sacred fire and corn ritual," he said. "I had assumed old Hidden Snake would do it. But your father said I was a priest, and he wanted me."

So the Green Corn Festival began. The women swept out their houses and threw away broken and worn out pots, and the men repaired and cleaned the council house. The people fasted for two nights and a day and, indeed, swallowed the Black Drink. The noise was awful as the emetic sent the people rushing to privacy behind their cabins.

On the third day Charley conducted the most sacred part of the festival, the fire and corn ritual. Four small logs were placed in the form of a cross, and on each was placed an ear of corn. Charley knelt beside them and, in the sand at the center of the cross, twirled a fire drill while he prayed to the Great Spirit. First there was smoke, then a blaze. Charley took the four ears of corn and placed them in the fire as an offering of thanksgiving for another year. All the household fires in the village were extinguished and new ones were ignited from the fire that Charley had started.

It was a time of forgiving one's enemies, of forgetting grudges, even of pardoning crimes. I cried and so did my mother when Staring Otter took Charley's hand and said, "You have done well by my daughter. I am sorry I have not done as well by you."

The fourth day was spent in dancing and feasting and having a good time. The women danced in the afternoon and the men that night. Tied to our legs were terrapin shells that contained pebbles, and they rattled like angry rattlesnakes. Rawhide had been stretched over a couple of iron pots to fashion drums.

As those things go, I'm sure our Green Corn Festival wasn't much, but I hated to see it end. "I don't expect we'll ever see another one," I told my husband. And we didn't.

CHAPTER 20

I had only to look into Major Ridge's eyes during his periodic visits to New Echota to see the streets of Baltimore.

He allowed his imagination to take flight. This old warrior, this white-haired statesman, was like a little boy when he walked the beaten earth of the tiny Cherokee capital. His smile told me he was reminding himself that some day New Echota would be a wonderful city of cobblestoned streets with a gas light on every corner. He used to remind others, but the dire circumstances of the Cherokee Nation had rendered that metamorphosis so improbable that he never spoke the words any more.

"Major Ridge is going to visit Elias and Harriet," I told Charley. "She invited us to come for supper. Would you like to go to Baltimore? I mean to New Echota?"

It was not a mean-spirited joke; it was spoken with fondness.

I loved the Major, and I lavished attention upon him. He was a Cherokee hero. He did not apologize for or explain his owning slaves. The bundle of inconsistencies that was Nancy Swimmer Marley ignored that.

He was flattered by the story I wrote about him for the *Phoenix*. In his sixties, he was also flattered by the attention of a pretty young girl. "If I were sixteen I'd swim the Oostanaula River with my hands tied behind me to get to you," he would say, always careful to laugh.

Charley didn't mind our flirtations. He knew they were harmless, even amusing.

The Major was a robust man with a big chest, a no-nonsense face and curly, snowy hair. Harriet was a fine cook, and he ate heartily of the bounty spread before us, which centered around exquisite smoked fish that Bartholomew Bramlett had sent by Pepper Rodham when he brought Rachel's children to our school.

"It's almost time for October council," Major Ridge said. "You're terribly busy during council, aren't you, Mrs. Boudinot?"

Harriet said only, "Yes, I am."

The question made everyone else at the table uneasy, for holding a council meeting in New Echota clearly was against Georgia law. The Cherokees had successfully defied the state in 1830, but Georgia had become more aggressive in the year since, and Charley and I had agreed that a gathering at New Echota in 1831 probably would encounter resistance.

"Can the council meet again in Georgia?" Charley asked Major Ridge.

"A nation can't abandon its capital in the face of the enemy," the Major said, his tone mildly chastising Charley for the suggestion of any other possibility.

"I think it might be a mistake to meet here," Elias commented.

But the major didn't answer. He pushed his chair back, thanked Harriet for a wonderful meal, and said, "Mrs. Marley, I'm going for a stroll. Would you care to accompany me?"

I glanced at Charley, who grinned and pretended to pick at something on his plate. "Yes, I would," I said.

The night was pleasant, with just enough chill in the air to clear one's head after such a sumptuous supper. There was no moon, and the only light was from the windows of the few houses in New Echota. I took Major Ridge's arm and hoped I wouldn't step in a hole.

"Why, I believe we have been magically transported to Baltimore," he remarked.

I tried to think of a reply, but before I could speak he laughed and said, "I know the people joke about me comparing New Echota to Baltimore. It's all right. I make no apologies. I'm not an insane man. A man must have his dreams."

"They mean no harm," I said. "They love you. They think it's admirable that one of the great Cherokees dreams majestic dreams."

"My immediate dream is to see the upcoming council meeting in New Echota. I believe it will happen." The certainty that had been in his voice at the supper table was missing as he spoke only to me.

"I pray you are right," I said, adding, "if it is for the best."

"It's difficult to keep our hopes alive, isn't it?" Major Ridge said.

"Sometimes."

We took a long walk that night. After we got back to Harriet's, Major Ridge said, "Let's don't talk about politics. Let's talk about your religion, Reverend Marley. As you perhaps know, I am not a Christian. But my wife Susanna embraced the faith of the Moravians and was baptized on November 14, 1819."

Charley was delighted at being given the opportunity to witness to Major Ridge. He hoped the Cherokee leader was on the verge of making a decision for Christ. I stood back while Charley, Elias and Harriet shared their faith with the legendary chief. I thought Charley, bless his heart, tried too hard. The three-person assault overwhelmed the Major, and his receptive mood passed.

Major Ridge was not converted that night, but he would be in 1832. He became not a Moravian, as Susanna had, but a Presbyterian. I like to think that the example of Charley's faith that evening at the Boudinots' was instrumental in his decision, but I don't know.

The council of October, 1831, was not held in New Echota. It was convened in Chatooga, Alabama, at a camp meeting site. The delegates sat on logs under a brush arbor rather than on benches in a clean, comfortable council house.

His son John Ridge and his nephew Elias Boudinot convinced the Major and other chiefs that some members of the General Council would resign rather than go to New Echota and that there would be serious trouble between the people and the Georgia Guard if the militia tried to arrest the Indian leaders. It was better to cross the state line.

One could either find melancholy in the young men dissuading the legendary old chief or be pleased he was not intractable when he saw he was mistaken. I aimed for the latter but hit the former.

I went to New Echota on the day the council convened in Chatooga. I walked the street of the nearly deserted village and wept openly. I saw it for what it was, not a potential Baltimore but a small Indian town that had had its moment in history and that now was slipping into the nondescript ranks of a thousand other villages. It had, indeed, been a place of dreams, but the Georgians and Andrew Jackson had sounded reveille.

For once the Georgia Guard didn't get the message. The same militia that somehow knew Samuel Worcester was headed home on the day of his daughter's funeral didn't know the council had been moved. Would-be raiders galloped into New Echota, eager to break up the meeting, only to find there was no meeting.

"Where is everybody?" an officer demanded of me as I took garments off Harriet's clothesline.

"At Chatooga, across the state line," I said. "You've made a trip for nothing."

They searched buildings and houses and finally rode away, cursing.

It wasn't much as victories go, but at least a satisfied sneer replaced my tears. For a moment, anyway.

Out of the Chatooga Council came the appointment of John Ridge and two others as a delegation to Washington City to present the Cherokees' grievances to the federal government and the authorization of a journey to the North by Elias Boudinot to raise money for the *Phoenix*. The newspaper was a key to Cherokee survival efforts, but it was badly in need of funds.

Elias's brother, Stand Watie, served as editor during his absence. He was a stocky, bowlegged man, forceful but without the writing and editing skills of Elias. It was while he was in charge that I realized the newspaper was Elias.

John and his group got no satisfaction from Secretary of War Lewis Cass, so John joined Elias, and they were successful in raising funds and exciting sympathy in Philadelphia, New York, New Haven and Boston.

Samuel was in prison, and Elias was in the North. Charley was at home, thank God, as another Christmas came and went. I slept in his arms all Christmas Eve night, and the next morning I refused to allow him to get up and preach his Christmas sermon. He didn't resist too strenuously at first, but after an hour he began to wonder if I was serious, and he tore himself away with an uneasy smile. If I had been as big and strong as he was, I would have kept him in bed all day.

On January 8, 1832, my seventeenth birthday, I told my husband I wanted a special present. I wanted to have a baby. I had stopped taking my stoneseed, the plant that Cherokee women relied on to prevent pregnancy. He tried to talk me out of it, but finally he gave up and he complied. To be certain, I saw to it that he complied three times that night.

I wanted a baby because I was a woman, and women want babies. Certainly there was no logic to having a child at that time. But would there ever be? The future of the Cherokees was dim, but there was no reason to think it would be any more promising five years hence. Or ten years hence.

God knew what he was doing when he imbued women with the maternal instinct. If it had been left up to logic, the human race would have died out long ago. I watched Ann Worcester care for a sick baby at three a.m. I watched Harriet Boudinot wipe a dirty fanny with one hand and stir soup with the other, and I watched Rachel illegally send her boys to school when there might be big trouble because of it, and all that made me want to be a mother. There's no explaining it.

When I was certain I was pregnant, I told Charley. He was happy because I was happy. But even though he never said so, I know Charley would have preferred to wait, considering the uncertainty of the political situation.

Then I crossed the village square to tell my mother and father and grand-mother. Staring Otter met me at the door and whispered that I should be quiet. He motioned me inside the cabin in which I grew up and nudged me toward my mother.

Rain had been crying. "Your grandmother is very ill," she said. "She is unconscious, barely breathing."

Plum died within minutes. She hadn't even been sick. She had gone to the woods and gathered pine fat lighter the day before. She had washed the glass windows in Charley's church, and I had considered telling her I thought I was pregnant, but I decided I should tell Charley and my parents first. Now she would never know. At least not on this earth.

Staring Otter was crushed by her death. I think it was because he read his own mortality in her passing. She was sixty-two but she seemed healthier than he. He turned to the old Cherokee customs of death, and refused to let Charley preach a Christian funeral. Mother gave in to him. So Charley and I conducted our own Christian memorial at our cabin.

Plum was laid out in her best clothes, and her most valued belongings were placed beside her. Her favorite cup and saucer and a vessel of salt were on the bed. I don't know why, but Staring Otter said it was mandatory. Perhaps he didn't know why, either.

The body wasn't placed in the coffin for two days. She was never left unattend-ed. Neighbors always watched. They must keep witches from stealing her liver, Staring Otter said.

Plum was buried in our village cemetery, on a hillside, and her relatives were required to bathe in the Oostanaula River. Charley said he absolutely would not allow me to plunge into the water in February, that I might lose the baby. I was afraid, too, but I did as my father had requested. Charley was furious, but I suffered no ill effects.

Old ashes were scattered over the yard, and smoke from burning pine boughs filled the house. Seven days after the burial, relatives and neighbors danced to speed Plum's spirit on its way.

It wasn't until after the dance that I finally got around to telling my mother that I was pregnant. She hugged and congratulated me, but her smile was forced. It wasn't the best time. A grandmother had died, and she would become a grandmother.

I left it for her to tell my father. He never mentioned it to me.

Charley was solicitous to a fault. He was afraid for me to walk up steps, move a chair, pull a dress over my head, get angry with a student, cook a meal.

"I'm not an invalid," I told him. "Here, I'll show you." I pushed him down on the bed and jumped on top of him, and soon Charley realized that, indeed, I was a quite healthy young woman with a healthy appetite for lovemaking.

My getting pregnant had eliminated our fear that I might get pregnant, and we tarried in bed nearly every morning. We were embarrassed on a cold, blustery March mid-morning when The Bull pounded on our door and shouted our names.

We tugged on our clothes and opened the door, and Charley said, "What's wrong?"

"Nothing's wrong," our visitor said. "Everything's right. We won."

"What?"

"Worcester versus Georgia. The United States Supreme Court decided in our favor! The news is spreading over the nation!"

The Supreme Court had ruled as unconstitutional the law that had imprisoned the missionaries and along with it Georgia's entire Indian legislation. The court said the Cherokee Nation was "a distinct community, occupying its own territory … in which the laws of Georgia can have no right to enter but with the assent of the Cherokees …"

The Bull hugged us both, taking my breath. He shouted an ancient war cry and bolted from our house to tell others. I grabbed Charley by the neck and began to dance. "It's wonderful!" I said over and over.

Charley patted me on the back, but I could feel the restraint. "What's wrong?" I asked.

"It's great news if it leads to the results one would expect," he said. "But remember, Georgia is obstinate. It defied the Supreme Court by hanging Corn Tassel."

"Not this time," I said, angry with my husband for dampening my enthusiasm. "You know Georgia can't just pretend this ruling didn't happen."

I rushed to New Echota to tell Ann Worcester, but she already had heard. She and Harriet and Sophia Sawyer were on their knees, offering thanks to God, when I arrived.

"My husband is coming home from that awful prison," Ann said as she embraced me. "Samuel is coming home to his wife and children."

Elias Boudinot and John Ridge were in the missionary rooms of the American Board of Commissioners for Foreign Missions in Boston when they learned of the court's decision.

Elias wrote to his brother, Stand Watie, acting editor of the *Phoenix*, a letter calling it "glorious news. The laws of the state are declared by the highest judicial tribunal in the country to be null & void. It is a great triumph on the part of the Cherokees …"

John Ridge, on the other hand, sent a dispatch to Watie saying the decision was cause for satisfaction but advising "the contest is not over" and warning of the "nefarious hypocrisy" of Chicken Snake Jackson.

Throughout the Cherokee Nation, our people celebrated the court's ruling. They strapped tortoise-shell rattlers to their ankles, dug feathered headdresses out of trunks and danced all night. At the Ball Plays, the gambling was wild and the games even wilder. There were feasts at which hidden whiskey kegs were produced—and to hell with the Georgia Guard.

Ann Worcester flew into house cleaning and chattered about cooking her husband's favorite foods. Every time there was a noise outside she would rush to the window to see if it was Samuel.

But nothing happened. The noise never was Samuel. Her husband and Elizur Butler remained in jail.

They remained in jail because Wilson Lumpkin, beginning his first term as governor of Georgia, vowed "determined resistance."

Andrew Jackson's reaction to the court's ruling: "John Marshall has made his decision; now let him enforce it."

News of Jackson's attitude became widespread, and John Ridge and Elias Boudinot went to Washington City. John secured an audience with the president, asking him point-blank whether the power of the United States would be used to execute the court's decision and knock down Georgia's Indian code.

No, Jackson said it would not. He advised John to tell his people their only hope of relief was to abandon their country and remove to the West.

John spoke of broken treaties and broken promises, but the Chicken Snake had heard it all before. He didn't care then, and he wasn't about to start caring now.

When John and Elias returned home the fire was gone from their eyes and their voices. Ann Worcester pleaded with them to help her obtain the release of her husband from prison, but they said they had no idea what to do.

Samuel Worcester remained in the penitentiary, the length of his sentence—four years—stamped on the front of his white cotton shirt as a badge of dishonor. But for all anyone knew, his term could last forever, for it was clear the Supreme Court's decision wasn't worth the ink in which it was written.

Georgians, of course, were delighted by their governor's refusal to obey the court's ruling and by Jackson's attitude in their favor. They were invincible. Soon now they'd be chasing these frog-eating, wolf-eating Cherokees out of their state and taking the land for themselves.

After all, the Choctaws were already leaving Mississippi. They had ceded their lands, like Indians were supposed to do, and they were the first of the five major tribes of the Southeast to move west. Could the Cherokees be far behind?

Some Georgians heard there was a missionary school up in the Cherokee Nation that had taken in a couple of little black boys, so they reported it to the Georgia Guard, like concerned citizens should. The guard said they'd by-God put a stop to that outrage.

See, what more evidence could you want? Those Cherokees simply had no regard for the law.

CHAPTER 21

The baby that grew in my belly changed the way I regarded the children at Bramlett Academy.

I had always loved them, always worked toward their best interests, but now I saw them in their relationship to their mothers. I realized that women had suffered to carry and birth them and done without to provide for them. I realized a person is the result of magic and therefore magic himself. I realized that I was charged not only with doing my best by a child but by his mother, too.

And father, of course. But it was the mothers who were on my mind. I was sick every morning. No Black Drink was required to make me throw up. Charley held my head in a cold, wet cloth while I vomited until there was nothing left, and then I retched some more.

Charley and I drew even closer. My big, strong man of God always had revered life. He would rescue a bug from a mud puddle, tell the students not to disturb an ant bed. Now life had a new, more profound meaning to me, too, as a new person took shape inside my body.

We had decided to name the baby Nancy or Samuel. I wanted Charles, but my husband wouldn't have it.

"I've never liked my name," he said. "I don't know why, but I don't. There is no one I admire more than Samuel Worcester and Elizur Butler. They are heroes, and I want my son's name to come from a man who is a political prisoner in the penitentiary in Milledgeville."

"You want to call him Samuel?" I asked.

"No," Charley said, "I want to call him Elizur."

I shrieked. "You'll not name a son of mine Elizur!" But Charley's laugh told me it was a joke.

"Samuel Marley," I whispered. "All right, if you won't consider Charles."

Once I got my legs under me in the morning, I survived the rest of the day. I taught the children English and Sequoyah's syllabary and geography. I let each of them feel my belly and told them to remember. It would change, and we would all monitor its expansion.

Peter and Thomas, Rachel's sons, adored me and I them. They were bright boys who eagerly took on the first formal lessons of their lives. They got along fine with their Cherokee schoolmates.

Sometimes when the thought occurred to me that they were slaves, that they were by law the property of another human being—even one who treated them well—I felt inexorable despair for humankind. I was crushed by the darkest pessimism. What if my child were going to be born a slave, perhaps even taken from me and sold? How did God's world get in this condition?

Rachel visited them frequently. Pepper Rodham would bring her on the work wagon or she would ride with Bartholomew Bramlett in the formal buggy. The boys loved the school, but they always wanted to return home with their mother. Sometimes they cried when she left. I would come up with some activity, perhaps read from a book or tell a story, and they would be pacified.

Once when Rachel was visiting, Thomas, the ten-year-old, showed her my growing belly, insisting that she touch it. Then something dawned on him and he asked, "Mrs. Marley, how will the baby get out?"

I swallowed hard and was about to explain, "the doctor will open a little door in my belly and Nancy or Samuel will come through there," but Rachel said: "A man, or a boy like you, has a penis, but a woman has an opening where your penis is. It's called a vagina. The baby will come out there."

"Do you have a vagina, Mamma?" Peter asked.

"Yes. That's how you and Thomas got out."

That satisfied him, and he asked how his pony was getting along at home.

That's when I promised myself I would tell my child the truth about sex and conception and birth. A door in my belly, indeed!

I was gratified when Rachel told me the children's excitement at acquiring knowledge had rubbed off on her, and Bartholomew Bramlett and Pepper Rodham were teaching her to read and write English and Cherokee.

During one of the Friday visits that the pupils so eagerly anticipated, Sophia Sawyer taught the children to draw the constellations. I favored the church sanctuary for my classes, but she preferred the classroom under the sleeping quarters. "It's a school room," she said, "and this is school."

Charley was in his cubbyhole of an office in the church, preparing his sermon. I was cleaning the sanctuary, and I could hear him talking to himself, occasionally raising his voice to emphasize a point. "Hallelujah!" I shouted, and he chuckled.

There had been no rain, and the road was hard, and I heard the hoofbeats approaching from outside the village. I stepped into the sunlight as nine mounted members of the Georgia Guard halted their horses. Behind them came a supply wagon driven by a black man. "Whoa!" he shouted, and the team stopped some twenty yards behind the riders.

"Goddamn it, Nathan," one of the guardsmen shouted, "bring that goddamn wagon up here so we can get a drink."

The black man snapped the reins, and the horses, obviously too spirited to be pulling a wagon, leaped forward, causing the supplies to tumble and scatter over the wagon bed.

"Goddamn, you turn that water barrel over and I'll make you eat it," the guardsman, a private, said, and the others laughed.

Charley stepped outside, and so did Sophia. She pushed the children back, telling them it was nothing, to sit down and read page so and so.

"Can I help you?" Charley asked the man in charge, only a corporal.

"Y'all got two nigger boys going to school here, ain't you?" the corporal demanded.

"We have two black pupils," Charley said.

"Well, hell, you hadn't heard that's against the law in Georgia?" the corporal said, as if he were speaking to an idiot.

Sophia couldn't stand it. "This isn't Georgia," she blurted. "This is the Cherokee Nation."

"No, ma'm," the corporal snapped. "This here is Georgia."

"Not according to the Supreme Court of the United States," Sophia said, her voice rising.

"We pay about as much attention to the Supreme Court of the United States as we do that piss ant," the corporal said, grinding his toe in the dirt.

Charley squeezed Sophia's arm before she could speak again. "No harm is being done by these black children going to school and learning to read and write," he said. "We hope you will just let them be."

The guardsman who had cursed the wagon driver now told him to stand up. The black man was lanky and, though he appeared to be in his late twenties, balding. He gazed at the ground, embarrassed and frightened. Until then I hadn't paid him much attention, but now I knew I had seen him somewhere before. I noticed Charley staring at the man, and I knew he, too, was trying to place him.

"Nathan's been in my family ten years. He can pick two hundred pounds of cotton a day or snake logs for sixteen hours and do it all again when the sun comes up," the private said. "He can't read and write, but he's a pretty good nigger, ain't you, Nathan?"

The black man was staring at Charley as hard as Charley was staring at him.

"I said ain't you, Nathan?" the private demanded.

"Yes, sir," Nathan said.

By now the nine children had spilled out of the classroom into the yard, and they were bug-eyed.

"Well, there's the two little niggers right there," the private said. "Nathan, tell these little niggers you're happy without reading and writing, and they don't need to read or write neither."

Nathan looked into the eyes of Rachel's sons for the longest without speaking. "Nathan!" the private demanded.

Nathan said, "I'm happy. You don't need it."

"So get them out of this school before we bullwhip all y'all and them, too!" the private shouted, grinning and looking around at the other guardsmen for approval.

Peter and Thomas began to cry, and they hid behind me. The other children were terrified. They ran to Charley and Sophia.

The private delighted in seeing them scattered. "Nathan, bring me my bull-whip!" he yelled.

Peter and Thomas gripped my legs so tightly they left bruises. They screamed for Rachel.

"Hell, I ain't even got no bullwhip," the private chortled. "Imagine how they'd run if I really did."

For the corporal, the glorious assignment under his command had gone awry. "Leon, you son of a bitch, shut up!" he yelled.

"Don't call me no son of a bitch," Leon said.

"By God, I may just be a corporal, but you're just a private. Shut up."

Leon gazed at the ground and sulked, his lips moving silently.

"I joined the Georgia Guard to be a soldier, not to be no boogerman to little children," the corporal said to everybody and to nobody.

"I don't give a damn who goes to your school or what hell I catch about it when I get back to the post," he said, directing his words to Sophia. "We're leaving."

He commanded his men to follow him, and they rode off into the shimmering heat.

But the damage was done. That night Peter and Thomas slipped out of the dormitory and walked the ten miles home to Bartholomew Bramlett's plantation, to their mother and to the man who owned them. Their brief matriculation at Bramlett Academy had ended.

Charley petted me. He saw me in a new light. He always had loved me, but now he thought of me as an instrument of God's intent that we be fruitful and multiply. I was contributing a person to the endless flow of mankind. He had helped, but I was the vessel itself.

"This child is someone's great-great-great-grandson," Charley said as he rubbed my swollen feet at the end of a day. "This child will be someone's great-great-great-grandfather. I had never thought of it exactly that way. You and I do God's work with the few people we reach here at the church and the school, of course, but how many people will be reached by our making this child? How many will the lives of our son and his offspring reach, offspring that would never exist if we hadn't made him? He represents one of how many generations? Perhaps he will become a great preacher. Perhaps he and I are links in a chain of clergymen, as Samuel Worcester is a link in a chain of clergymen.

"Oh, Nancy, I know this sounds strange, but I almost wish I could be a woman for nine months. God must especially love women."

"Then I wish he'd do something about my backache," I said. "Besides, how do you know it will be a boy? Instead of a son who becomes a great preacher, you may be the father of a daughter who spends her life cooking venison and sweeping the yard for some old man like Staring Otter who believes in witches."

"Then she'll be a woman preacher," he said, "and her husband can cook for her."

Though I felt bad much of the time, we had great fun during my pregnancy. Lifted to a new level of awareness, we celebrated not only with expansive philosophical discussions but physically—with long walks in the woods, with wading in the Oostanaula, with inspired lovemaking.

And three or four times we combined two of those activities.

"Let's do it right here," Charley said as we stepped carefully along the slanting, sandy bottom of the river until the water touched our armpits.

"My darling, I always thought you were insane," I answered, "but now I know it. People walk along this path all the time."

"We've never done it under water," he said.

"And we aren't going to now."

"Well, just a kiss then."

But, as frequently happened on dry land, kissing Charley led to other things. Charley was a great kisser. And before you knew it, the Marleys no longer could say they hadn't done it under water.

We made love in the woods, Charley hastily piling up a pine straw mattress and rolling his shirt for my pillow. It's a wonder we weren't discovered. I have no idea what we would have said if we had been.

Maybe it was part of our new "flow of mankind" consciousness. I don't know, but it was fun. What could be more natural than making love wherever the notion struck you? That must have been the way it happened right after the Great Buzzard created the mountains and the valleys.

I can't believe two people have ever been more in love than Charley and I were that summer. We loved with a love that was at once as intense as the glow of a blacksmith's embers and as sweet and tender and golden as a perfect peach.

Sometimes at night, after Charley had gone to sleep and I couldn't get comfortable, I was paralyzed by the thought that it would end.

And I was right.

Two weeks after the Georgia Guard's intrusion into our village, the private returned. He wore no uniform, just the rude clothing of a frontiersman. I was sweeping the yard around around the church. "Good morning, ma'm," he said pleasantly. "I'd like to see the preacher, to apologize for the other day."

"Come in," I said.

"Aw, I'm in a hurry. I'll just say my piece and be on my way. If you'd ask him to come out."

I went to Charley's office and told him, and he smiled and said, "Well, how about that?" He followed me into the morning sunlight and greeted the man.

But my husband stepped back when the rider, still on his horse, pulled a shotgun from a scabbard. "So I finally meet the man who killed my brother," he said. "You lousy son of a bitch."

"What are you talking about?" Charley said.

"You know what I'm talking about. My name is Leon Cadwallader. You bushwacked my brother, Lorenzo Cadwallader."

"He was going to kill some of my neighbors and take their young daughter," Charley said. "I didn't have a choice."

"Don't matter why you killed him—you killed him."

"Man, I couldn't just stand there and watch him murder innocent people," Charley said.

"My brother's life's worth all the Indian lifes in Georgia," Leon Cadwallader said. "And nigger lifes, too, for that matter."

The private was enjoying it. "Wondering how I found out, ain't you?"

"Not really," Charley said.

"My nigger, Nathan, told me. He protected you for a long time, but he finally give in.

"When it first happened he claimed him and Lorenzo was hunting, and they camped for the night, and he woke up the next morning and Lorenzo was gone, and he never saw him again. Claimed he didn't have no idea what happened. I always had my doubts, but I guess I believed him.

"One day Nathan couldn't get them damn wild horses stopped, and a wagon wheel ran over my foot and cracked my toe. I started to kill the son of a bitch right there, but I didn't.

"My toe wouldn't stop hurting, and a few nights later I downed a bate of whiskey trying to ease it. I got drunk, and I got mad about the wagon wheel, and I got mad about Nathan being so damn halfhearted when he told them little niggers they didn't need to read and write, and I got some of the boys to help me tie him to a tree, and I cut a sapling and whupped him til there weren't much left to whup.

"He begged and he begged, but I didn't pay him no mind. Finally he started saying if I'd quit he'd tell me something I'd like to know. I said, hell, he didn't know nothing I didn't know, and he said, yes, sir, it was about my brother Lorenzo. So I stopped, and he told me you was the one that done it. I was so mad because he had kept it a secret all that time that I beat him some more and, well, I guess I overdid it, because Nathan died.

"Anyway, we're rid of a worthless nigger, and we're going to be rid of a worthless Indian."

Leon Cadwallader lifted the muzzle of his shotgun, and Charley curled into a ball and put his arms over his face. I was standing to the side, and I ran toward the horseman, swinging my fists, but he kicked me in the belly with his stirruped foot, and as I hit the ground I heard the shotgun explode, and when I looked up my Charley was drenched in blood, as totally red as if he had been painted with red paint, and he was motioning to me to back away from the private, and the shotgun exploded again, and Charley crumpled to the ground, and his only movements were death twitches.

The State of Georgia did nothing about the murder of my husband. Cherokee officials, including John Ross and Major Ridge and John Ridge, protested, but Georgia said its investigation revealed that Charley Marley, Cherokee, had become infuriated by the efforts of Private Leon Cadwallader of the Georgia Guard to enforce the law against black slaves being schooled, and when Private Cadwallader politely asked the minister to see that the law was obeyed, the minister attacked him with a knife. Private Cadwallader had no choice but to fire his shotgun.

Although the minister's wife, Mrs. Nancy Swimmer Marley, joined in the attack on the duly appointed guardian of the law, the State of Georgia, in its magnanimity, would take no legal action against her.

Sophia told me the baby I lost in the dust beside my dead husband during my fifth month of pregnancy was a boy. She and The Bull saw to it that Samuel Charles Marley was buried in our village cemetery alongside his father, their names scratched onto the same slab of fieldstone.

CHAPTER 22

I stopped functioning as a human being. Without Charley, I had no identity. Mrs. Marley, the missionary's wife, the opinionated young woman, the teacher, the friend of important people, ceased to exist. I didn't revert to being Nancy Swimmer, average Indian girl. I cared for nothing, had no interest in anything or anybody.

I returned to my parents' cabin to live. It wasn't because I desired to. Nor did I mind. Nor did I desire to stay in my house. Or mind staying in it. It simply didn't matter to me where I lived. Or whether I lived.

Staring Otter and Rain came and got me. "You can't be like this," my mother said, finding me naked in bed in the middle of the day, unwashed and unfed, the cabin a mess. She wrapped a blanket around me and called The Bull, and he draped me over his shoulder and carried me to their house, my mother leading the way, head high, my father dragging his leg at the rear of the procession, his eyes to the ground.

Strong Hickory came to visit. He whispered that he loved me. I told him that was nice. Not because I felt anything from hearing the words but because I seemed to recall that in this case that is what a person would say.

"Let's take a walk," he said. "Let's walk by the river. It will be great fun. It's a fine day."

I remember that he was speaking to me as one would speak to a child, as I spoke to the children at the school when I wanted to make something sound better than it really was.

"Thank you," I said.

He waited, confused. Finally: "Well?"

I smiled and pulled the blanket up around my neck and turned my back to him and my face to the wall and said, "Thank you for a nice day," and he sighed and left.

Harriet and Elias and Ann and Sophia visited, but none was able to penetrate what I call my inorganic state. It was as if I were a rock or a cloud or a waterfall. I wasn't distraught. I didn't have the capacity to be unhappy or happy. I just existed.

"You must trust that the Lord's ways are not our ways," Harriet said.

"Thank you," I replied.

Of all people, it was Major Ridge who started me on my way to recovery. "Let's take her to my house," he told my parents as he concluded a visit.

"Nothing else seems to work. Perhaps a total change of scenery and situation might be of benefit."

He had a fine new buggy that had been delivered from New York City, even finer than Bartholomew Bramlett's, driven by a liveried black man, and in it we made the trip of some thirty miles from our village to Ridge's Ferry. But it could have been the rudest work wagon for all I cared. After trying without success to carry on conversations with me, he gave up.

"Well, we're here," Major Ridge said, as the buggy stopped in the front yard of a lovely two-storied, white, weatherboard home. Huge water oaks shaded us, and I could see the limbs of pecan trees overhanging the back part of the house. The Oostanaula River was only one hundred and fifty yards from the house, flowing slowly and evenly, like time.

His wife Susanna and their twenty-three-year-old daughter Sally were surprised to see Major Ridge come riding up with a seventeen-year-old girl, of course. They were even more surprised when I acknowledged our introductions with only a faint smile. "Sally, please take Nancy to the guest room," he said, and the puzzled young woman took my arm and led me upstairs.

A few minutes later, Susanna, briefed on my situation, came to my room and told Sally she would take over. I know Sally was glad to hear it.

The Ridges never pushed me, never insisted I do anything. Sally read to me in my room, and sometimes in the mornings, before the day's heat reached its full fury, we would sit beside the Oostanaula in chairs fashioned from willows and talk. At first our conversations weren't conversations at all; they were monologues, with Sally speaking and me choosing to hear or not hear. But she patiently drew me out, and I began to communicate with her.

Major Ridge operated a ferry at his home. Indians and whites, in wagons and buggies and on horseback and afoot, were floated the eighty yards or so across the river. Some ignored us, some nodded, others stopped to chat. It became a game with Sally and me: when we spotted someone approaching, we made up a story about him. "He is an Englishman," I told Sally as a thin white man with intelligent eyes whistled a tune. "He stole the queen's priceless jeweled necklace and stowed away on a ship to America. Her agents have almost caught him several times, but he once again has given them the slip, this time ducking out the back door of a church in Augusta. That's why he is so happy."

She said that was her favorite story of all we had made up. What she didn't say was that it told her I was returning to the real wold. When I arrived at Ridge's Ferry nearly two weeks before, I couldn't have formulated such a simple plot; nor would I have tried to.

When we returned to our rooms that afternoon, I stood before a full-length mirror and regarded Nancy Swimmer Marley. I squared my shoulders, raised my chin and told myself it was all right to cry.

I sprawled across the bed, buried my face in a pillow and wept so furiously that pain clamped my shoulder muscles into immobility. I screamed Charley's name and cursed Leon Cadwallader, and when I couldn't cry and scream and curse any more, I took a bath and put on one of Sally's prettiest dresses and went downstairs for dinner.

I greeted Major Ridge and Susanna and Sally at the table, and I joined in their conversations. I told them I wanted to see the farm. I asked Major Ridge if he remembered a humorous anecdote from the newspaper story I wrote about him. I asked them if they believed John Ridge ever would become principal chief of the Cherokees.

They were startled, for I had rarely spoken at meals, or any other time, during my stay at Ridge's Ferry. I caught their covert glances at each other and Major Ridge's nod at Susanna.

His nod signaled what I believed to be true: I was back.

"Charley would have loved this apple pie," I said. "It was his favorite, but I never did learn to make a decent one. Some day I'll see that bastard Leon Cadwallader dead for taking Charley away from me."

Susanna and Sally gasped. Major Ridge laughed and slapped me on the shoulder. I thought the notion of pure, unadulterated revenge appealed to this man who may have been dressed in expensive clothes from Philadelphia but who in olden days had been a semi-naked warrior slicing off scalps.

I slept soundly, and I was up long before daylight. Susanna and Sally were still asleep when I joined the Major for coffee on a side porch. He greeted me with a continuation of his laughter of the night before.

"I want to thank you for taking me in," I said. "I'm all right now. I'm not certain I ever would have been if I had stayed in our village."

"You are welcome here," he said. "Your husband was a Cherokee hero—and, besides, you more than paid your room and board when you shocked Susanna and Sally by calling that guardsman a bastard." He laughed so that he spilled coffee on the front of his shirt.

"Your home is beautiful," I said. "I can appreciate it now, whereas I couldn't when I arrived. Tell me about it."

Major Ridge poured himself another cup of coffee, sipped it thoughtfully as if he were judging a fine burgundy, and said, "I've often reflected that the house is like me—civilized on the outside, rough-cut on the inside."

I smiled inquiringly, and he explained: "Originally it was a log house—bigger than most, but still a log house. I had the pretty sawed weatherboards put on later and had them painted white.

"The foundations measure fifty-four by twenty-nine feet. There are eight rooms on the two floors, ceiled and paneled with hardwood, and outside are two kitchens and a smokehouse. There are four brick fireplaces. There are verandas in front and back, and over the front porch is a balcony supported by turned columns, with a glass door opening onto it. There are thirty glass windows, faced in walnut.

"There are sheds and cribs and stables, and there are cabins for thirty servants. On two hundred and eighty acres of open land I grow corn, cotton, tobacco, wheat, oats, indigo and potatoes. There's a vineyard and nursery and orchards of peach, apple, quince, cherry and plum trees. There are cows, swine and sheep—the sheep mainly because Susanna enjoys weaving.

"The ferry boat is big enough to float a wagon and its team, and just up river I have a trading post that does a prosperous business, and I have a toll road.

"It is a fine plantation.

"I tell you all this not to boast but to illustrate that a place and a person can be alike—plain, hewn logs on the inside but grown to quality on the outside."

"It's a wonderful place," I said. "I noticed you called them servants."

"All right, slaves. Susanna won't call them slaves. She insists on servants. But you are right, they are slaves."

He wasn't apologetic. He looked me in the eye. I told myself I was a guest in the house of a family that had treated me with loving care, and to just shut up. And I did.

The Major gazed out over the Oostanaula, shimmering in the light of the rising sun. "I hate to give it up," he said.

"Give it up?"

"My son John is coming today. So is my nephew Elias. We have decided the time has come for the Cherokees to remove."

I couldn't have been more shocked if he had told me he was going to leap over the sun. What was I hearing? Major Ridge and John Ridge and Elias Boudinot had fought Chicken Snake Jackson and Georgia for the Cherokees' God-given right to retain their homeland, and now they were saying we should surrender our country and move to lands across the Mississippi River? Was I hearing a man who had lost his mind? Was I hearing the voice of treason? What was I hearing?

"I can't believe my ears," I blurted.

"I shouldn't have mentioned it," Major Ridge said. "What activities do you and Sally have planned today?"

I knew what he meant. He meant that he should have kept quiet because of my mental condition. "I'm all right," I said. "You can talk to me. I just don't understand why you would say such a thing."

But the conversation was over. Major Ridge got to his feet and said he had to go to his trading post to be sure he hadn't been shorted in a load of goods from Augusta. He said he hoped Sally and I had an enjoyable day.

And under normal circumstances we would have. We walked along the river, rode horseback and read the Bible. She was probably lonesome, for she confided female things to me. But all I could think about was Major Ridge's pronouncement that it was time for the Cherokees to give in to Jackson and Georgia. I kept an eye out for John and Elias. If the Major wouldn't talk to me, perhaps they would.

It was an excruciating day. John and Elias didn't arrive until late afternoon. John materialized the earlier by half an hour, but he chatted with his mother and sister. He and his father wouldn't talk politics until the editor of *The Cherokee Phoenix* reached Ridge's Ferry.

I sat in a willow chair on the lawn so I would spot Elias at the earliest possible moment. When I did, I ran to him. He got off his horse and hugged me, obviously wondering if my condition had improved.

"I'm all right," I said. "I came back to the world. I cried my eyes out and raved against the man who murdered Charley, and I'm all right."

"Thank God," he said.

I didn't delay. "Elias," I said, "the Major told me you and he and John have decided the Cherokees should remove."

He shook his head in disgust. "He shouldn't bother you with such as that. We're just in the talking stage. Have you and Sally been having a good time? She's quite an energetic young woman."

I hated it when men did that. "Elias, this is me you're talking to—Nancy. You trusted me to write stories for your newspaper. Do you suddenly feel you can't talk to me about anything more important than sewing? I want to know."

He sighed. "What did my uncle tell you?"

"Just that you three have decided we should leave our homeland. Then he was sorry he had spoken, and he wouldn't say anything else."

"There's just no point in worrying you with it," Elias said.

"I'm seventeen years old," I rasped. "I know that's young for a white girl, but it isn't young at all for a Cherokee. Surely you haven't gotten so white that you don't remember that."

Instantly I wished I had the words back—the part about his turning white, I mean.

"I haven't gotten white at all," Elias said, rolling back his shirtsleeve and proffering his dark arm. "I have dedicated my life to the welfare of the Cherokees, and now my life is taking a turn that may cause most of them to hate me. But I must do what I think is best for my people. The irony is that many of them will say what you just said—that I have turned white."

"I'm sorry," I said. "I didn't mean that. Tell me."

"I'll talk to the others about it," he said, and he led his horse to the house where he handed the reins to a black man. I followed, like a scolded puppy.

Sally and I sat on the front veranda and watched the shadows grow long in the twilight. The men talked for more than an hour, and I was surprised when Elias summoned me to Major Ridge's study, where the Major and John waited.

Elias seated me on a huge, horsehair-stuffed couch, and Major Ridge said, "I remarked that you are the widow of a Cherokee hero, and I meant it. Be assured that is the only reason you are in this room with us. I should have kept my mouth shut this morning, but I didn't, and that is that. We will make an explanation to you, but we must have your promise that anything said here today will not leave this room."

"I promise."

The Major nodded to John, who began:

"I talked to Jackson after the Supreme Court ruled against Georgia's Indian code and ordered the missionaries to be freed. He said the U.S. would do nothing against Georgia. He said the Cherokees' only hope is to remove to the West.

"I knew then that we had lost. A few thousand Cherokees can't defeat a state and a nation that have no regard for treaties and laws. We are being offered money and land across the Mississippi River, and we must accept while we can still get it. The Georgians are going to take our homeland if they have to murder us family by family in our doorways. We are in a rotten position—but never will the terms be more generous than they are now."

I gazed at this man who sat under a portrait of himself. In the portrait he held a quill, as if he were writing. When he was a child his parents had begun preparing him for the service of his people, and he had never wavered from that charge. I hated to admit it, but he had to be right.

"Could we just stay and voluntarily become citizens of Georgia?" I asked.

"Nancy, they hate us," Elias interjected. "We are of a different race. Perhaps you would fare better, but they would swallow up the uneducated Cherokees and take everything, either by cheating or by stealing. The Cherokees would become drunkards and beggars, as poor and miserable as the once-mighty Catawbas have become in their midst. We must remove and live as one people across the Mississippi. As long as we continue as a people in a body, with our internal regulations, we can go on improving in civilization and respectability."

John Ridge rose to his feet and gazed out the window at the first dark. "John McLean is a justice of the Supreme Court and a friend," he said. "McLean believes our cause is lost. One by one, our friends in the U.S. Congress are telling us the same thing. The American Board of Commissioners for Foreign Missions is advising us to remove."

So even the organization that had sent Samuel Worcester and other men of God to us had decided there was no use.

Major Ridge smiled at me, like a father smiling at a daughter. "John returned home from Washington City to find me exulting in the decision of the Supreme Court," he said. "He told me my hopes were false. Sure enough, the missionaries are still in prison and Georgia's surveyors still roam our land with ax and compass. John and Elias have convinced me it is time to go."

"But why do you tell me to be silent?" I asked Elias. "If you believe this, why not say it?"

"John Ross assures the people they will win, that they will not have to leave their homeland," Elias answered. "The principal chief is tremendously popular, and what he tells them is what they want to hear. We, on the other hand, will be bearers of ill tidings. Already there are rumors that we have been bought by the whites. Speaking prematurely can only cause us to lose our influence."

"Or lose something else," Major Ridge said with an ominous laugh that brought no response from the other two.

I wanted to say that John Ross was right, that we should cling to the land of our ancestors. We couldn't just announce we were leaving for some unknown country west of Arkansas and give it away. We should stay, and right would triumph. Law would triumph. Old treaties would triumph.

But, except on paper, the Cherokees hadn't won any battles in this pitiful little war, and I realized the Ridges and Elias were right. The time had come to admit defeat and get the best terms we could get. Maybe I didn't know all the details, but I knew if these three were saying it, it had to be true.

"I accept your judgment," I told them. "It is very difficult to do so, but you are wise men, and I know you love your country. But doesn't John Ross also love the Cherokees?"

"He does," Major Ridge said. "He is a good man, and he has been a capable principal chief. I fought at his side at the Horseshoe and stood at his side in government. We aren't contending that John Ross doesn't love his people or that he is insincere in what he is saying. But now there is a serious difference of opinion. Our estimation of what should be done is correct and his is mistaken. We must overcome John Ross and remove."

So it had come to this. It had been Cherokee against white, but now it was Cherokee against Cherokee as well.

CHAPTER 23

Courtship. There is no other word for it. Strong Hickory began a courtship when I returned to our village.

At seventeen, he had become a man. His shoulders were broad, his legs muscular, his eyes penetrating. His voice was deep but pleasantly melodious. He still preferred a breechcloth to confining white-man's clothes, but I will admit I was more attentive than embarrassed, as I had been when the nearly naked adolescent used to bounce up to my door on spindly legs.

My parents were delighted to find the deadened girl who had departed for Ridge's Ferry was, upon her return, functioning more or less normally. I grieved for Charley, and there were times when I cried until I thought I would become hysterical, but my inorganic state had passed. It is better to feel sadness than to be incapable of feeling anything.

I told Rain and Staring Otter I would spend the first night with them. The sun was setting when I arrived at our village, and I didn't want to be alone in the cabin Charley and I had shared. I would go home in the morning.

Before I could empty my carpetbags on the bed in the room that had been mine since I was a little girl, I heard Strong Hickory shouting his arrival. Rain opened the door, and he said, "Nancy is all right, isn't she? I saw her smiling and talking to the man who drove the buggy."

"Yes, she is much improved," Rain said. "But see for yourself. Nancy!"

I entered the room and said, "Hello, Strong Hickory."

He grabbed me and kissed me on the mouth, which was stunning to say the least. "I couldn't sleep for worrying about you," he said.

"I am much better," I told him. "I am fine."

He ate supper with us. Rain's vegetable stew was familiar, reassuring, as was the presence of my parents and my childhood sweetheart. There was still sanity in the world; you just had to return to the familiar to find it.

Strong Hickory was solicitous, trying to get me to eat more, asking if I was comfortable, patting my hand. Staring Otter smiled approvingly at Rain, for a proper Indian was being attentive to his daughter. This lad could don a deer head and skin and creep to within mere yards of venison on the hoof. He didn't wear a clawhammer coat and quote from the white man's Bible.

The four of us chatted at the table after supper. Strong Hickory and Staring Otter swapping tales of bear hunts and other adventures. I knew what Strong

Hickory was doing; he was establishing himself as a favored candidate for son-in-law. I was amused and put off at the same time.

He even offered to help Rain clean up from the meal, a suggestion so transparent that she laughed and told him to get on outside with my father and me, that she had been doing her housework since before he was born, and she didn't need his aid.

There were two benches, made from logs, behind our cabin. Staring Otter sat in the center of one, so there would be no room for me. I took the other one and Strong Hickory sat beside me, our legs touching. I moved over as far as I could until there was six inches between us. "Perhaps we could take a walk by the river tomorrow, the way we used to," he suggested.

That was too much. "No," I said, "we can't. My husband just died—or didn't you hear? I am a widow who is in mourning."

"I'm sorry," Strong Hickory said. "I only meant …"

"I know what you meant. The answer is no."

But I couldn't help being flattered. Strong Hickory had always loved me. And the feeling I had for him when we were growing up had never completely disappeared.

Fond. That was a good safe word. "I've always been fond of you, Strong Hickory," I said, "but the earth over Charley's grave is still raw."

That soothed his hurt feelings, and he behaved in a proper manner the rest of the evening. Which wasn't long, for after a half hour of remarking on the clarity of the stars and the fullness of the moon, I told the two men goodnight. I had been through an ordeal, and I needed rest, I said. I excused myself and went inside.

"Can you believe that Strong Hickory already is inviting me to walk by the Oostanaula with him?" I said to my mother. "I'm going to bed."

"He never stopped adoring you," she said. "You were married, but he would tell us he still loved you. Once he had to leave because he didn't want us to see him crying."

"Charley's body is barely cold in the earth," I protested.

"Strong Hickory is an impulsive young man who needs a wife," Rain said. "He would be a good husband. I know you are grieving for Charley, but you might want to consider that you will need a man to bring home venison and fish for your table. A woman does not stop getting hungry just because she lost her husband."

Incredible! I think my parents would have married me off that night.

"Don't worry," I said, "you and Staring Otter will never have to support me."

It was a hateful remark, and I apologized. But as soon as I did, I realized there was another side to that coin. Rain may have been considering the day when I—and my husband—might have to support them. Anyway, I said I was sorry, and we changed the subject.

"How are Major Ridge and his family?" she asked.

"They are well. They have quite a plantation, and I don't see how he finds time to do all that he does."

"Nancy, we hear disquieting things about the Major," my mother said. "And about his son John Ridge. And about your friend Elias Boudinot."

I froze. "Oh?"

"We hear that the three of them have been bribed by the whites to tell the people that all is lost and we must remove. They will become rich, and we will lose our homeland."

"Major Ridge is already rich," I said, "and perhaps John is, too."

"You have heard these rumors?"

"No," I lied. "But those three men would not take bribes. They are patriots whose lives have been dedicated to the wellbeing of the Cherokees."

"I don't know. Everywhere we go, we hear these stories. It's hard to believe there is nothing to them."

"It's easy for me to believe there is nothing to them," I said. "I am going to bed. Goodnight."

I retired too early. I woke up shortly after midnight and tossed and turned for two hours before I went back to sleep. Then I slept too late, and I required four cups of coffee to get on track.

It was midmorning when I stood before Charley's church. It gleamed white in the light of the ascending sun. But it was empty. The school had closed because, except for Sophia Sawyer on Fridays, there was no one to teach. I opened the front door and a blast of summer heat escaped. It probably hadn't been opened since Charley's death.

I gazed at the pulpit where my devoted but untalented preacher had stood. I was shocked, because I realized I was having difficulty remembering his face, remembering his voice. Tears coursed down my cheeks. I knew I couldn't have Charley back, but I had to retain his image, his sound, in my mind.

I heard footsteps and turned to see Strong Hickory. He wore a homespun shirt and white-man's pants that I knew belonged to his father, The Bull. At least he had enough respect not to appear in a breechcloth.

"I'll leave if you want me to," he said.

I wiped my tears with the sleeve of my blouse and said, "No, you don't have to leave. You may have a seat." I joined him on the front pew, and we stared straight ahead at the walnut cross on the wall behind Charley's pulpit.

"He must have been a great preacher," Strong Hickory finally broke the silence.

"He was a very ordinary preacher," I said. "He was a great pastor. He was a great man. My life would have been very much the poorer if I had never known him."

"I don't suppose I behaved very well last night," Strong Hickory said, "but I was excited to see you, to see that you had recovered. I'll always think of you as my girl."

"It's all right," I said. "I know I hurt you when I married Charley. But I did marry him, and he has just been murdered, and we shouldn't be talking like this."

"For awhile I hated him for taking my girl," Strong Hickory said. "But I loved you so much that I told myself it was not right for me to hate something you loved. So I made myself stop hating him."

I was touched that he would admit it. "Jesus says we shouldn't hate anyone," I said. "You did right to stop hating Charley." But my words didn't ring true in my own ears, for I wondered if I could stop hating Leon Cadwallader, the man who killed Charley. Sometimes I hated him so fervently my stomach ached.

"Do you really believe Jesus was murdered and then flew away?" Strong Hickory asked.

"Yes. I believe that God so loved the world that he gave his only begotten son to save us."

"I've never understood that part," Strong Hickory said. "How that saves us."

"Neither have I."

"If God loves you, why didn't he knock the gun out of that guardsman's hands that day? Why did he let an innocent man get killed?"

"I don't know."

"Nancy, can you prove your Christian religion to me? If you can I might become a Christian myself."

"No, I can't prove it. You have to accept it on faith."

It was a conversation that had been repeated for nearly two thousand years.

"Nancy, I don't want you to be angry with me," Strong Hickory said. "I want you to be my girl again. Just tell me how long I must wait, and I will wait."

I appreciated his honesty. "I don't know how long," I said. "For now we can be friends, but nothing more. Perhaps that's all we can ever be. I just don't know. When I do know, I will let you know."

"All right."

So we talked about other things. His mother had a persistent pain in her shoulder, caused by chopping down trees for firewood, he said. His father was burning out a log to make a new canoe. I met some interesting travelers at Major Ridge's ferry, I said. There was a crow at the Ridges' house that would eat from my hand.

"Nancy, you should be careful around the Ridges and the Boudinots," he said. "I know the Boudinots are your friends, but be careful."

I pretended I didn't know what he was talking about. "What do you mean?" I asked.

"The whites are paying Boudinot and Major Ridge and his son to influence the Cherokee people to give up their land and move to the West," he said.

"Where did you ever get such an absurd idea?" I demanded.

"Everybody knows it. I've heard lots of people say it."

"Everybody knows the Great Buzzard made the mountains and valleys, too," I said, "but it's still an absurd idea. Elias Boudinot and the Ridges are loyal

Cherokees who wouldn't accept a penny from the whites to do something they don't believe in."

"All right," Strong Hickory said, not wanting to risk angering the object of his courtship. "If you say so."

"I'm going home," I said, careful to smile. "And Strong Hickory, I appreciate your friendship."

He left the church pleased, encouraged in his suit. But unconvinced of Boudinot's and the Ridges' innocence.

In the next few days I learned that rumors of a sellout of the Cherokee Nation by the three leaders were as epidemic as smallpox once had been, and in July of that year, 1832, in a meeting of the General Council at Red Clay, in Tennessee, the battle lines were at least scratched, if not drawn.

Ross opened the sessions with an appeal to the Cherokees to "continue constant and be sensible and true to their own interest." Eyebrows were raised when he said, "A man who will forsake his country in time of adversity and will cooperate with those who oppress his own kindred is no more than a traitor and should be viewed and shunned as such." He named no names.

A representative of the U.S. presented a proposal for the Cherokees to remove. John Ridge and Elias Boudinot said it should at least be considered—a suggestion that struck the council with the force of a tornado. It was, of course, rejected. The U.S. had ignored all other guarantees and treaties, so why take seriously any more?

The meeting was held in Tennessee so as to be outside the reach of the Georgia Guard. Since Georgia had warned the Cherokees not to exercise governmental functions, the council decided to suspend elections. That meant John Ross would continue indefinitely as principal chief.

The Ridges and Boudinot were angry. John Ridge considered himself the most qualified man in the Cherokee Nation to be principal chief, and now he was being denied the opportunity to run for the office. The split between the Ridge and Ross factions grew wider. In time John would agree with Governor Wilson Lumpkin's opinion: "Ross, when compared with such men as John Ridge and Elias Boudinot, was a mere pygmy."

I was very lonely in the cabin I had shared with Charley, and I didn't want to stay with my parents, so whenever I was invited—which was frequently—I stayed with Harriet and Elias. Ann Worcester had recovered from her illness, but Samuel continued to languish in the penitentiary, so she was a regular overnight guest at the Boudinots' home, too. As I have said, Harriet was a saint.

We three women were cleaning house on a brutally hot August day when Elias asked us to join him in his study. Ann and I exchanged puzzled looks, but we could tell Harriet knew what this was about.

Elias sat behind his desk and gazed at the floor, as if he didn't know how to begin. Then he picked up a piece of paper and shook it, as if it were repulsive to him.

"This is a letter to John Ross," he said. "I am resigning as editor of the *Phoenix*."

He couldn't, I thought, any more than an arm or a leg could resign from a person. He had been the paper's editor for four years—its only editor. I could no more imagine the *Phoenix* without Elias than I could imagine water without wet.

"Ross has ordered me not to present any but the anti-removal point of view in the newspaper," Elias said. "There must be what he calls 'unity of sentiment and action for the good of all.' I cannot, of course, continue as editor under those conditions."

I wanted to cry. My voice cracked when I protested, "But isn't there something ...?"

Elias shook his head and read us a portion of his letter:

"I could not consent to be the conductor of the paper without having the privilege and the right of discussing those important matters—and from what I have seen and heard, were I to assume that privilege, my usefulness would be paralyzed, by being considered, as I unfortunately already have been, an enemy to the interest of my beloved country and people. I should think it is my duty to tell them the whole truth; I cannot tell that we will be reinstated in our rights when I have no such hope."

Harriet left the sofa and stood by Elias's side, her hand on his shoulder. "My husband is being presented as a traitor and a coward," she said. "It is easy to urge the people to remain stalwart, to tell them they will prevail, to assure them they will somehow keep their homeland. It isn't easy to tell them the truth—that they have lost, that they had best leave now. Elias is a man of courage and honesty, and he is being persecuted because of it.

"Please understand that Elias is not siding with Georgia and Jackson. They have betrayed the Cherokee Nation, and he knows that, of course. He is simply saying the cause is hopeless, and we must be realistic."

I had never seen Harriet so angry. As for myself, I was profoundly sad.

"Elias gave birth to the *Phoenix* as surely as I gave birth to my children," Harriet said, her voice rising. "He guided it like a boat on turbulent waters. He raised money to keep it going. He made it interesting and successful. Now he is resigning because he has been ordered to deny the Cherokees all viewpoints on a life and death subject. Sometimes I wish I had never heard of this terrible land."

Harriet raised her hand, and before anyone could speak, she said, "I didn't mean that last part. God led me here, and I accept whatever he has in store for me."

Elias put his arm around his wife's shoulders, and she nestled her head against his neck. It was an uncommon public show of affection for the daughter of New England.

"They say kings of old used to kill the messenger who brought bad tidings," Elias said. "I suppose I am such a messenger.

"There are five hundred and fifty surveyors carving up the Cherokee Nation so that it can be presented, piece by piece, to Georgians, just as their politicians promised, but the people laugh at the surveyors and make jokes about the strange marks they cut on trees. John Ross tells the Cherokees to be staunch and patient, and everything will work out fine. And, bless their hearts, they believe him. No wonder they hate me.

"But I can't do otherwise. I can't say peace, peace when there is no peace. The Georgians are going to take our homes and drive us into the forests and caves. We must remove to the West while we can still make a decent deal with the Chicken Snake."

If there had been a shred of doubt in my mind that Elias was right, it disappeared there in his study. I knew how much he loved the *Phoenix*, and he was surrendering it rather than surrender his honor. I reached for his hand, and I kissed it.

Harriet said she would accept whatever God had in store for her in this terrible land. I wondered what he had in store for me. Widowed at seventeen, I faced the very real problem of supporting myself. I could grieve for Charley and curse his unpunished murderer, but I had to be practical and put food on the table.

I loved Harriet and Elias, and they loved me, but I couldn't continue to stay overnight with them. They were hospitable, but they had their own problems. Since he was losing his job, they certainly didn't need another mouth to feed, even on a part-time basis.

Our neighbors had given us food so that Charley could devote his time to studying the Bible and preparing sermons, but that merely meant he was a paid preacher. Now Charley was gone, and there was no obligation to feed me. I'm sure they reasoned that my parents lived there in the village, and I could move in with them. Despite being lame, Staring Otter sold bows and hunted and fished, and my mother had a garden. And The Bull, who had induced the other villagers to help us, knew that his son loved me, and he probably saw marriage to Strong Hickory as a solution.

But I couldn't live with my parents. I had come too far under the influence of Charley Marley and the Boudinots and the Worcesters. I loved my father, but I could not return to evenings of listening to him warn about Raven Mockers who steal the hearts of the dying and eat them to add years to their own lives.

The students of Bramlett Academy had fled when Charley was murdered, and I doubted any of them could be persuaded to return to school, certainly not to a school with a seventeen-year-old female in charge. Besides, with all the turmoil in the Cherokee Nation, few parents wanted their children to be away from home.

My problem was temporarily solved when I returned to my village the next day.

Sitting against a shady oak that grew beside the church was Pepper Rodham, snoring away. I spoke his name, and he leaped to his feet, declaring he wasn't asleep.

"Mr. Bramlett sent you some food and clothes," he said, nodding toward a loaded wagon. "And cash." He reached into his shirt and withdrew a leather pouch that was heavy with gold coins. "Here."

I wouldn't insult the intelligence of either of us by reciting a spiel about how I just couldn't accept money from Mr. Bramlett—and then accepting it. "Thank you," I said. "I need it."

"He knows you do. That's why he sent it."

"I suppose he won't be surprised that I took it," I said.

"He wasn't sure. He thought you would."

"Mr. Rodham, would you like to sit a spell in the church?" I asked.

"Yes, ma'm. That would be soothing."

We took a seat on a back pew to be near the door, hoping a breeze would offer some relief from the August heat. "Say a prayer, why don't you?" Rodham whispered.

The man always surprised me. I did say a prayer. I prayed for him and for me and for Charley's soul and for the Cherokee Nation. And then I thought I should pray for his boss, too, so I included Bartholomew Bramlett, petitioning the Lord to watch over the ugly little man in the pink marble house, though I didn't use those words.

Pepper Rodham smiled sheepishly, and I knew he wanted to tell me something. "What in the world is it?" I asked, grinning myself.

"Bartholomew said if you took the money and goods to tell you that he would like to call on you the day after tomorrow, say at two p.m., at your home. He awaits your answer."

I was shocked. Stupidly, I asked, "You mean he just wants to be certain that the widow of one of his old friends is doing well, don't you?"

Rodham chuckled. "He just sent you a sack of gold and a wagonload of food, so he knows you're doing well."

Pepper Rodham and I looked into each other's eyes for the longest, both of us grinning. Finally, I said, "Tell him I'll receive him at two p.m. the day after tomorrow."

CHAPTER 24

And so Bartholomew Bramlett came calling on the widow Marley.

I asked myself why I permitted this visit, and the answer might as well have come from the Tower of Babel.

Certainly I wasn't physically attracted to Bramlett. God forgive me, but I never saw an uglier man.

Certainly it wasn't because he had a cheerful personality and would cause me to laugh away my troubles.

Certainly I knew I was guilty of impropriety. Charley had been dead less than three months, and I was encouraging the attention of one man while I had scolded another—Strong Hickory—for offering his.

Was it because he was wealthy, and wealth fascinates everyone, especially when it has been accumulated by an Indian? Was it because he was a wayfarer in life, seeking for meaning, studying the Bible and Shakespeare and the Greeks and people's faces?

I didn't know, but here he was, climbing down from his buggy, knocking on my door, sweeping a new wide-brimmed black hat with a new white feather, and saying, "Hello, Mrs. Marley. It's nice to see you."

I invited him in, and he sat in Charley's rocking chair. As always when he had visited Charley and me, he showed the courtesy of not glancing around the cabin, which would have fit in one room of his huge pink marble mansion.

Bramlett had eaten in our cabin many times after church services, but on those occasions he had really been Charley's guest. One would expect near poverty from a minister. Our circumstances even gave me some feeling of superiority over this rich man. We were concerned with matters of the soul; he was concerned with accumulating wealth. But now he was my guest, and my pride was pinching.

"Mr. Bramlett," I said with a sigh, "let's get out of this tiny place and go sit in the church. I know you must be uncomfortable in these cramped circumstances."

"I'm quite comfortable," he said. "But as you wish."

We walked to the church, and I knew the villagers were watching—from windows, from cracked doors, probably from around corners. So what? They had seen Bramlett's buggy when it arrived, and they might as well get an eyeful now.

We sat on the front pew, a few feet from the pulpit in which Charley had preached to both of us.

"I counted your husband as one of my best friends," Bramlett said. "He was an exceptional person."

"He liked you," I said.

"And how are you getting along?"

"Fine. I appreciate the things you sent."

"How are your parents?"

"Fine. Just fine."

The silence in the church hung as heavy as the heat. This was ridiculous, I thought—this man calling on me, my allowing him to call on me. We had nothing to say to each other.

Then Bartholomew Bramlett sighed deeply, squared his shoulders, and said, "There is something I must tell you, Mrs. Marley, before we go any further. After I have spoken, you have only to request it, and I will leave, and you will never hear from me again."

Even in speaking this cryptic message, his voice was as monotonous and inflectionless as ever.

"What?" I said, giggling nervously. "What is it?"

"The original church. The one that burned. I burned it."

At least I knew he wasn't joking, because I had never heard him joke. "What?"

"I burned it. Or I had it burned. Mr. Rodham set the fire on my orders."

I didn't know how to answer. All I could say was, "What?"

"It was very important to me that you accept me," Bramlett explained. "I admired your husband, and I believed that he was to be an instrument of my salvation. I knew you did not like me, and I was becoming a wedge between a husband and wife."

He began coughing. He covered his mouth with a handkerchief. It seemed it would take forever, and to expect patience of me at that moment was too much. "But why burn a preacher's church if you loved him?" I demanded. "Are you insane?"

He tucked the handkerchief inside his coat and patted his watery red eyes with the back of his hand. "No, I'm not insane. What I did was calculated."

He coughed again. "Go on, man," I insisted.

"You said I was attempting to buy my way into heaven by building a church for your husband," Bramlett continued. "I thought that if I built one, burned it, and built another it would be obvious that you were wrong. If I were buying my way into heaven, my admission would have been paid with the first church. That's why I did it."

I waited for more, but there was no more. It was a simple plot—and one that had worked.

I thought of the terror I experienced when I saw the flicker of the flames on the trees. I thought of Charley covered with soot, numbly watching his prized new church burn. I thought of our neighbors furiously working against hope to extinguish the blaze.

I also recalled my husband, who had said he wanted a divorce, holding me and kissing me as the church disappeared in the flames. I recalled Charley and me lingering in bed the next morning. I recalled that fire being the instrument of our reconciliation. Maybe we would have gotten back together anyway, but maybe we wouldn't.

I laughed. I looked into Bartholomew Bramlett's startled eyes and laughed until I cried. "That's the funniest thing I ever heard," I said.

He was speechless. I don't think he could have spoken at that instant if his life had depended on it.

"You went to all that trouble and expense to convince me you were serious," I said, as much to the universe as to him.

"Yes."

I couldn't stop laughing. I saw Bartholomew Bramlett as a human being, in this mess called life with all the rest of us, wanting to be loved and accepted and pulling a crazy stunt to ensure it.

But, of course, it wasn't crazy. It was brilliant, and it was daring. Who else would have gone to the trouble and expense? Who else could have even conceived it? Bramlett wasn't entirely like the rest of us. No wonder he had become wealthy.

"I was afraid you would be furious," he said, his shoulders relaxing for the first time.

"I think Charley would be flattered," I said. "Once he got over the shock." I laughed again.

Bramlett actually smiled. "I hope you will be a wee bit flattered yourself," he said. "While it's true that I needed your acceptance to work in harmony with your husband, I also liked you and simply wanted us to be friends."

"All right," I said. "We are friends."

"Do you think God is angry with me?" Bramlett asked.

"I hope He has a sense of humor, or we're all in trouble. I think He'll understand. After all, you built the second dormitory a little bigger than the first, didn't you?"

"Yes. You're perceptive. That's why I made it larger. I suppose we all try to buy off God at one time or another, in one way or another."

I was fascinated. "When did this idea occur to you?" I asked Bramlett.

"Before I ever built the first church. But it was not the reason I built the church. Even if I had known I would die before the first church was completed, I still would have built it. I wanted your husband to have a church."

"What did Mr. Rodham think?" I asked.

"I told Mr. Rodham I wanted him to build a church, burn it down and immediately build another one on the same site. That was all he needed to know, probably all he wanted to know. He trusts me explicitly."

Should I have been furious? Should I have chased Bartholomew Bramlett from our village, exposed his plot? Well, I wasn't and I didn't. I was, indeed, flattered.

We talked for two hours, about everything under the sun. We gossiped and laughed and bet a potato pie on a Ball Play that was coming up in Oothcaloga. "I hope I lose," he said, and we laughed some more because we knew he meant he'd rather eat a pie he furnished than one I cooked. If God wasn't angry about his church being burned, I suppose He could tolerate us making a small bet in His sanctuary.

Bramlett said it was time for him to go home. I couldn't believe he had been there nearly three hours, but that's what his gold watch said. The time had passed quickly. "Mrs. Marley, I would like to call on you again," he said.

"I would enjoy that," I told him.

I walked him to his carriage. Levi, the driver, in top hat and black coat, had survived the heat by sitting in the shade of a tree and swapping stories with a villager.

Bramlett and I looked back at the church, gleaming white against the dark forest. "It is beautiful, isn't it?" I said. "I hope that services will be held again some day."

"So do I," Bramlett said, and then he took his seat and said goodbye, and he and Levi began the ten-mile trip home.

Strong Hickory stopped me before I reached my cabin. "Nancy, what are you doing?" he demanded.

"What does it look like I'm doing?" I answered. "I'm going home."

"You know what I mean. What are you doing spending the afternoon with that old man?"

"Well, it's my afternoon, isn't it? I suppose I am entitled to spend it any way I choose."

"Your husband's body isn't cold yet."

Now that made me angry. "That didn't stop you from chasing me," I said. "Why is it so important to you now?"

"I wasn't chasing you," he said.

"Well, in any case, you sure didn't catch me," I shot back.

"You like them old, don't you?" Strong Hickory sneered. "This one's even older than the preacher. He must be twice as old as you."

"A little more than twice as old," I said. "I wish his father were alive. I'd be after him. His grandfather would be even better."

This was ridiculous, standing in plain view of all the snoops in the village, swapping insults with a jealous boy who wore only a breechcloth and moccasins. "Oh, go put on some clothes, and maybe you'll look old enough to interest a woman," I got in the last barb before I stormed away.

A week later Bartholomew Bramlett called on me again. He brought me a beautiful Bible, expensively and surprisingly covered in tan leather, rather than black. Stamped in gold in the cover was "Nancy." There was no last name. Such a gift wasn't available in the Cherokee Nation, of course, and I knew he must have sent someone to Augusta for it. Probably Pepper Rodham, arsonist and right-hand man.

This time we remained in my cabin. "Mrs. Marley, I am quite comfortable," Bramlett said when I suggested we go to the church. "I feel as I did when I visited historical sites in Europe. This was the home of a great man, the Reverend Marley. I can feel his presence, as I felt the presence of Shakespeare at his home. Your husband was not a materialistic person, and this is where he lived and how he lived. I expect if we could visit the houses in which Jesus lived we would find them just as modest."

I started to speak, but he held up his hand and continued, "I believe that at this moment I realize for the first time just what a materialistic person I am. While I was accumulating the things of the world, your husband was serving God and other people and acquiring a desirable wife. He must have been much happier in this cabin that I have been in my marble mansion."

The part about the desirable wife embarrassed me. I looked at my shoes and said, "You are kind, Mr. Bramlett." I wondered if it meant anything. Did he toss it out there to see how I would react? Bartholomew Bramlett hadn't piled up his treasures on earth by being naïve and not measuring his words.

I supposed that to stand being in my dreary little home this man who was accustomed to opulence had to indeed look upon it as some kind of historical relic. It was made of hewn logs. Only at your peril did you walk across the splintery slab floors barefoot. The walls were naked except for a framed oil painting of Jesus someone had given Charley. The chimney didn't draw quite right, and there was a smoke smell in winter.

Neighbors had made the austere furniture for the three rooms: a dining table, four straight chairs, a bed with a cornshuck mattress, a desk for Charley's work.

While Bramlett was extolling the virtues of the simple life, I was thinking that I must escape it. It was one thing to live in poverty as the wife of a preacher who was performing the work of God; it was another to be a poor widow. Maybe I would have starved to death for Charley's sake, but I wouldn't starve to death just to be starving to death.

I think I was beginning to answer my question as to why I had permitted Bartholomew Bramlett to come calling.

The next day my parents invited me to eat supper with them. I was afraid I knew the reason. I was right.

"Nancy, everyone is talking about you," my father said before the food was even on the table.

"Really? Why?" I asked.

"You know why. Your husband is barely dead, and you are seeing this man. Your husband was a beloved leader, a person the villagers looked up to. They are disappointed in you."

That was too much. "You never looked up to Charley," I blurted. "Why, you tried to run him out of our settlement. Beloved? You never even liked him, much less loved him."

"Nancy, I stand with your father on this," Rain said.

"On this? On what? A friend of Charley's—which is more than my father ever was—has visited his friend's widow. What is it you believe? That Bartholomew Bramlett and I are diving into the bed where Charley and I slept? Is that what you believe?"

My voice was approaching a shriek, but Rain said calmly, "It's too soon, Nancy."

Of course, I knew it was too soon. But I also knew that if I told my father I had changed my mind and wanted to marry Strong Hickory that very instant, then too soon wouldn't matter. It was too soon, but what was really killing him was that I, who had married a mixed blood who preached the white man's religion, was again seeing a non-traditional Cherokee. No doubt he found Bramlett even more objectionable than Charley, for in every way he lived as a white man.

"The Bull and Sweet Melon have always loved you," my mother said. "But they are distressed by your conduct. And The Bull, after all, is our village chief."

I couldn't believe this was happening. The Cherokees always had been live-and-let-live people. They were non-judgmental, perhaps to a fault. Divorce and remarriage were easy and commonplace. Some men had more than one wife. And now I was the village's number one topic of conversation?

"What The Bull is, is Strong Hickory's father," I said. "Strong Hickory and I grew up as sweethearts, and it's killing The Bull and Sweet Melon because I won't marry an Indian who goes naked and believes life's greatest accomplishment is to kill a bear. Well, I won't. I never will. I want more from life than that."

"Strong Hickory is a good boy," my father said

It was useless. "I'm not hungry," I said. "I have work to do at home."

"Don't leave," Rain said, but I was already out the door.

The truth was, I was hungry. I went home, and I reached upon a shelf and took down a gorgeous potato pie. Bartholomew Bramlett had lost our bet on the Ball Play, and he had paid up. "Rachel is the best baker in the Cherokee Nation," he had said as I had cut two slices. And, indeed, it was a tasty production.

I sat there alone by candlelight with my triangle of pie and tried to honestly assess myself.

I loved Charley. I could never love anyone else the way I loved Charley. But it was Charley himself who had shown me there was another mode of living besides the traditional Cherokee way. I could never go back to that life. I could never live with a man who, like my father, would look you in the eye and tell you the Little People were as real as that tree.

I wasn't trying to be disrespectful of my late husband. Some nights I still cried myself to sleep for Charley. But the powers of evil were closing in on the Cherokee Nation. Time was a luxury. Three months hence there might not even be a Cherokee Nation. Where would we all be when winter came? One had to make things happen—or at least allow them to happen.

I wasn't in love with Bartholomew Bramlett by any stretch of the imagination. But he did represent that other life, the one that included the Boudinots and the Worcesters and the Ridges. He was thirty-seven years old, and I was seventeen, but I could relate to him much easier than I could relate to Strong Hickory, who was my age.

It was settled. I would continue to see Bramlett. I had no idea whether anything would come of it. I didn't know whether I wanted anything to come of it— or if he did. We were simply two people getting to know each other, I told myself, and in my Bible that was no sin.

Good old Elias stayed on at the *Phoenix* for a month after his resignation to allow Principal Chief John Ross to appoint an editor. The pool wasn't large, for Ross needed someone who not only was a competent editor but who shared Ross' views against removal to the West. Many of the educated Cherokees, though, knew the cause was lost and didn't fall for Ross' hollow reassurances. They were lining up with the pro-removal Ridge-Boudinot faction. Ross finally chose his brother-in-law, Elijah Hicks, who was anti-removal but hardly a newspaper editor.

Hicks did enjoy the power of the position, though. He wrote an editorial accusing Elias of being unpatriotic.

Elias and Harriet were livid. He wrote a reply and walked the few yards from his house to the office of the *Phoenix*. He slammed it onto Hick's desk and demanded he print it, which Hicks agreed to do.

Elias defined patriotism as not only the love of country but of people. Our lands were about to be seized, he said. He could not pretend there was nothing to worry about when the Cherokee Nation faced death. The country was going to be lost, but the people could still be saved.

But the words of John Ross fell more pleasantly on the Cherokee ear. The land could and would be rescued, he told them. So the mass stood behind him. Elias and the other advocates of removal found themselves overwhelmingly outnumbered when the General Council convened in October, 1832, in Red Clay, just over the state line in Tennessee.

At Red Clay the principals in the removal fight took their sides, split as distinctively as groups on opposite banks of a raging river.

John Ross set the tone of the meeting with an anti-removal speech.

John Ridge offered a resolution to send a delegation to Washington City with the authority to make a treaty of removal. It was defeated, and the council sent some majority leaders—with Ross as chief counsel—to handle the affairs of the Cherokees with the U.S.

Cherokees were openly calling John Ridge, Major Ridge, Elias Boudinot and their allies traitors. Elias found himself hated by his people and by the whites. The Georgia Guard frequently rode through New Echota, shouting insults regarding Boudinot's being married to a white woman. They were especially gratified on the occasions when they saw Harriet outside or on the porch and could make her the direct target of their filth.

Ann Worcester had recovered from her illness, but she was depressed. Her baby had died, her husband remained in prison, and her friends were being cursed. Who knew when the words would turn into actions?

Harriet and I were helping Ann with her chores when a fine carriage stopped in front of the Worcester home. The black driver opened the door, and a white man got out. He looked familiar. I thought I had seen his picture.

"Good afternoon, ladies," he said. "Isn't it a beautiful day? This morning I told my driver we would have rain before noon, but I couldn't have been more mistaken, and I certainly am happy that I was wrong. I am Governor Wilson Lumpkin. Is either of you Mrs. Worcester?"

We were scouring the front porch. We brushed the hair out of our eyes, and each waited for the other to answer the governor. The ogre stood before us, smiling as if we were friends. We stared at him until finally Harriet said, "I'll tell her you're here. Come in."

Curiosity was eating us alive. Harriet and I continued to go through the motions of washing down the porch, but we were trying to hear through the open parlor window. We couldn't make out what Lumpkin and Ann Worcester were saying, though, and we frowned and shook our heads in frustration.

After fifteen minutes, Ann showed the governor out. He kept saying, "I wish you would reconsider," but he was cordial in his goodbyes to the three of us. "Yes, ladies," he declared, "an absolutely gorgeous day."

His carriage rumbled off, and we turned to Ann, hating to question her and hoping she would volunteer an explanation.

She did. "He said he wanted to pardon Samuel, but that he must ask for it. He wanted me to persuade Samuel to request a pardon."

"What did you tell him?" I asked.

"I told him the decision was Samuel's, and I would not attempt to influence him. But, oh, Nancy, I do so want him home."

At that moment I was overcome with a heart-rending loneliness. No doubt Samuel would come home some day, and Ann would have her husband back. But Charley would never come home. I would never know the love and security of his strong arms again.

The man who kept Samuel from Ann had just walked into the missionary's house, as blithely as if he lived there. I pictured the man who killed my husband going about the routine of his life in a manner just as carefree. Leon Cadwallader had murdered with impunity.

I knew the law would never punish him, and so I had tried to forgive him in order to banish the awful animal of revenge that was nourishing itself by plunging its teeth into my heart and mind. I prayed, and I read the appropriate verses in my Bible, but I hadn't been able to do it. Then when I pictured Samuel Worcester's tormentor, Wilson Lumpkin, chatting about the weather, I stopped trying.

CHAPTER 25

The wheels of the Georgia lottery began to turn on October 22, 1832, and the state started giving away land that it did not own, Cherokee land.

Georgians swarmed into the Cherokee Nation like buzzards to a dying deer, seeking the parcel they had drawn, either a 40-acre gold plot or a 160-acre plot for homesteading or any other use.

No Indian could testify against a white man in Georgia court, and certainly the Georgia Guard had no objection to violence, so while some of the new owners never came at all and some simply came to satisfy their curiosity, others evicted Cherokees by whatever means struck their fancy. Indians were robbed and whipped and raped. Some were charged rent to remain on property they had farmed for years, to continue living in cabins they had built with the sweat of their brows.

The homes of Major Ridge, John Ridge and Elias Boudinot were exempted from takeover. They were the leaders of the removal faction, and it was to Georgia's benefit not to disturb them. Of course, this favored treatment only caused the majority of Cherokees to hate them all the more. They considered it evidence their enemies had been bought.

Bartholomew Bramlett had avoided taking sides in the removal controversy, yet he was allowed to remain on his plantation. I wondered why.

"Bribery," he said, smiling. "I bribed the Georgians not to steal my hearth and home."

That reinforced my opinion of him as a man of expediency. He could get things done—or he could prevent their being done. In these turbulent times he would, I thought, be a good husband for an attractive, intelligent, ambitious—but dirt-poor—young woman.

Certainly the lottery was ripe for crookedness. The wheels had hardly begun to spin before they were stopped and an investigation was launched into the methods of Shadrach Bogan, the commissioner who supervised the lottery in Milledgeville. It seemed that his friends and relatives were drawing some of the most desirable property. What a coincidence.

Bogan was kicked out of office and his civil rights suspended for twenty years. A Georgia newspaper called it "one of the most stupendous frauds ever practiced on any community." I thought it trivial compared to the fraud Georgia was practicing on the Cherokees.

Bramlett continued to call on me. Strong Hickory glared at him, once even yelling oaths at the perplexed man. My parents never mentioned Bramlett again, but they adopted a stiff attitude and withheld affection from me. The other villagers treated me like a stranger.

I visited Bramlett's home, once spending the night after a party, on another occasion staying for three days. It was all quite proper, with Rachel a chaperone and me sleeping in a bedroom at the other end of the house.

The Rachel who had been grateful for my taking her children into Charley's school resumed being the Rachel who resented me. I didn't care. I was tired of worrying about what others thought of me.

It was as if Bramlett's plantation were in Europe or Arabia or on Mars. When I returned to my tiny cabin in an ordinary Indian village, on earth, I felt as if I were locked in a box. The man owned tablecloths that were worth more than my house.

I began to suffer attacks of panic in the cabin. I thought of Charley's body in a coffin under the ground, and I wanted to push the walls of my house away from me. I had to get outside, no matter how cold it was, no matter if it was raining, no matter if it was midnight. I wished I were in an expansive high-ceilinged bedroom in Bartholomew Bramlett's mansion.

I sought refuge in the church. It was much larger than my cabin, and the several glass windows that Bramlett's men had acquired in Augusta let in light. I considered moving in. Why not? It was mine.

But it was the house of God, and I didn't feel right about making it my house. I had been reading about the magnificent temple of Jerusalem, and I couldn't imagine a young woman saying she owned it and was going to turn it into her house.

Perhaps there would never be another sermon in the church, but I kept it clean. I swept it and dusted the pulpit and pews and broke up the nests that dirt daubers built under the eaves. I was outside washing the windows one day when three horses galloped up.

I stopped in mid-wipe, and the water ran down my arm and off my elbow. Leon Cadwallader rode between two other members of the Georgia Guard who didn't look any older than sixteen. He reined his horse and tipped his hat, and they glanced at him and then tipped their hats.

"Just riding through," Cadwallader said to me. "Thought I'd stop and show the boys where I killed that Indian that tried to kill me."

"You sorry son of a bitch," I said.

"Seems like you was lots fatter last time I seen you. What happened?"

"You killed my child, too," I said. "Tell the boys how you kicked a woman in the stomach and caused her to lose her baby. They'll be impressed."

"Wasn't none of me," he protested. "I save my kicking for worthless Cherokee men."

"Get out of our village, all of you," I said.

"Say you're sorry for lying about me." Cadwallader spoke the words evenly, purposefully.

I saw Strong Hickory striding across the village square. When he reached my side he took my hand and said, "What's the trouble?"

"It's up to her whether there's any trouble," Cadwallader said. "She owes me an apology, and I'm by-God going to get it."

"He's the son of a bitch who killed Charley and my baby," I said. "But go home, Strong Hickory. Here, I'll go with you."

"Ain't nobody going nowhere," Cadwallader said, but the words were barely out of his mouth when Strong Hickory ran for him, aiming to wrest him from his saddle.

But the Georgian was too fast for him. He drew his pistol and pointed it at Strong Hickory, who stopped short. The toe of Cadwallader's boot was touching Strong Hickory's belly. All five of us stopped breathing, suspended in time.

Then Cadwallader looked at me and grinned. "Say you're sorry for lying about me."

"You son of a bitch," I said.

He jabbed Strong Hickory with the pistol, touching the opening of the barrel to his forehead. "Say you're sorry for lying about me."

"I'm sorry I lied about you," I said.

"You mean, 'I'm sorry I lied about you, sir,' don't you?"

"I'm sorry I lied about you, sir."

"That's better. You heard that, didn't you boys? I'd kill this frog-eater anyway, but hell, if you kill one the officers question you forever, and you have to sit there while they write out all them papers. It ain't hardly worth it. Let's get out of here."

And away they went, Cadwallader forcing a raucous laugh, his young companions too frightened to laugh.

My words lingered in my mouth, as bitter as the Black Drink. I believe that if the gun had been to my head instead of Strong Hickory's I wouldn't have spoken them, but I don't know.

Strong Hickory was trembling, pulling air into his lungs with difficulty. "I shouldn't have stopped," he muttered. "I should have pulled him off the horse." But there was no fire in his words.

"Thank you for trying to help," I said lamely, engulfed in defeat.

I couldn't say no when he asked me to walk with him beside the Oostanaula. We did, and he tried to kiss me, and I wouldn't let him, and he became angry and hurt and ran away and left me alone. I walked another mile by myself and sat on a log and watched the flow of water until twilight before I went home.

Bartholomew Bramlett came the next day. He was coy and stammered a lot and avoided eye contact, and I thought I knew what was about to happen. I was right. He asked me to marry him.

Then he began apologizing for his age and his appearance and his methodical manner—and I stopped him and said, "I will marry you."

Then I heard him swallow hard when I added, "If you will have a man killed for me."

I simply could no longer exist on the same planet with Leon Cadwallader. I explained to Bramlett what had happened the day before. "I suppose there is a way to get almost anything done," he said.

Three days later Pepper Rodham arrived at my cabin in a work wagon. "Let's take a ride," he said.

Perhaps two miles outside the village he whoaed the horse, and we walked another half-mile into the woods, through a tangle of briers and undergrowth as forbidding as fire.

"Here," Rodham said, and we stopped beside a pile of fresh dirt. A black man held a shovel at his side, like a soldier at inspection.

Lying on its back in the grave was the corpse of Leon Cadwallader. His throat had been cut from ear to ear. I said, "Thank you." Pepper Rodham nodded and took me home, and for most of the night I stared at the embers in the fireplace.

A Christian ceremony at his mansion—our mansion—united thirty-eight-year-old Bartholomew Bramlett and his eighteen-year-old bride. A few of his friends attended, as did Harriet and Elias Boudinot, Ann Worcester and Sophia Sawyer. My mother came but not my father. I didn't invite anyone else. Rain was pretty in one of Sophia's old dresses, but she was intimidated by the place and the people, and though I suggested she spend the night, she said she must get home to take care of Staring Otter, so Levi took her in the carriage.

A white Methodist minister from Tennessee, a friend of Bartholomew, officiated. A few days earlier he had baptized Bartholomew, who said the widow of a Christian minister should have a Christian husband. I wanted to ask him if he truly believed, but I thought that was between Bartholomew and his God, that for once I should just keep my mouth shut.

My father didn't ask me to also have a traditional Cherokee wedding, as he had when I married Charley. But I wouldn't have done it anyway. I wasn't a traditional Cherokee, and there comes a time when you have to live your own life. Staring Otter simply grunted and shook his head in disgust when I invited him to my wedding.

Rachel served at the reception and refused to even look at me. Her jaw quivered in anger every time she walked by me, the wine glasses on her silver tray tinkling against each other. I knew what I had always suspected was true: she was in love with Bartholomew. Her boys, Peter and Thomas, dressed in dark green velvet suits, saw to any needs of the guests. They were cordial with me until their eyes met the glare of their mother's, and after that they were merely polite.

I was a slaveowner. I who had despised Bartholomew Bramlett because he owned slaves was now the mistress of those same slaves.

The guests left in order of the distances they had to travel, the last—quite drunk—finally, mercifully, retiring after dark to one of the apartments in the huge guest house behind the mansion. Bartholomew took my elbow, and we entered the grand parlor in which we had talked the first time I'd set foot in his house. He sat in his favorite burgundy leather chair, I on the couch. The flames of the myriad candles reflected in the windows, mirrors, furniture, and even the finely polished floors. It was as if we were in the midst of a fire that could not harm us.

Bartholomew sighed, smiled wanly and said, "I hope to make you happy, Mrs. Marley."

Old habits died especially hard with this man who was such a model of rectitude. It was the third time that day he called me Mrs. Marley. "I mean Nancy," he said.

"And I hope to make you happy," I said.

Oh, when you really think about it, there have been stranger couples. We shared some things. We voraciously sought after knowledge. We were Cherokees who appreciated our heritage, but for whom the old ways had been replaced by civilization. We cherished the memory of Charley Marley. We were Christians, though Bartholomew was too honest not to admit his faith blew in the winds of introspection and circumstance like a willow leaf.

And we shared murder.

But I can truthfully say that I never agonized over my part in the execution of Leon Cadwallader. There was no law in the disintegrating Cherokee Nation, and he never would have been punished for killing Charley and my baby. Bartholomew and I became the instruments of justice. My new husband agreed with my reasoning. If we were wrong I hope God forgives us, but we never believed we were wrong.

We talked for perhaps an hour, about everything under the sun, killing time, as embarrassed as any newlyweds on their wedding night. Then Bartholomew said, "It has been a long day. Are you ready to retire? I think I'll take a bath."

I nodded, and he pulled a silken cord that summoned Rachel. He told her to prepare two tubs, and without a word she left the room.

I thought heating the tub must be a nightly ritual, for within five minutes Bartholomew said, "Well, I'm going to get that bath. I think yours will be ready at the end of the hall, my dear."

And it was. In a large bathroom on the second floor a copper tub of soapy water awaited, so warm that Rachel must have been heating it even before her master ordered it. She stood expressionless, a towel and washcloth over her arm. "Shall I help you undress?" she said.

"No, thank you."

"Shall I return and bathe you?"

"Good lord, no."

"Shall I help you into your nightclothes?"

"Of course not," I said. "I've managed to undress and bathe and dress myself for eighteen years, Rachel, and I will continue to do so without your help."

"Will that be all?"

"Go to bed, Rachel."

I took my bath and put on the frilly lace robe and matching nightgown that Bartholomew had bought for me. He was already in bed, reading, when I entered the master bedroom that was almost as large as the church he had built. He placed his book on the bedside table, turned back the covers and said, "Come to bed, my dear."

Then came a surprise. Bartholomew Bramlett was an adroit, enthusiastic love-maker. I had expected a tentative thirty-eight-year-old virgin. He wasn't tentative, and obviously he was no virgin.

Before I dozed off, I felt much better about my marriage. It was not simply a marriage of convenience; it was a marriage of passion—or at least more passion than I had expected of either of us.

As the cold winds of January, 1833, blew across the Cherokee Nation, Samuel Worcester and Elizur Butler asked Governor Wilson Lumpkin for pardons. He granted them, and they were freed from Georgia's penitentiary at Milledgeville. They had been there a year and four months.

The decision to ask for pardons was one agonizingly reached.

Attorney William Wirt wanted to file an appeal with the U.S. Supreme Court that would force Chicken Snake Jackson to either move against Georgia in the matter or refuse to move. But clergymen, educators, lawyers and Georgia statesmen pressured the missionaries. They feared for the federal union itself if the courts issued a demand of release that Georgia would not obey and Jackson would not enforce.

Samuel and Dr. Butler said they would remain in prison if that was what the American Board of Commissioners for Foreign Missions wished, but the board finally decided there was no use for its missionaries to continue their martyrdom, that they should request pardons. It suggested to Chief John Ross that the Cherokees should give up their country and remove to the lands west of the Mississippi. The board was simply joining other friends of the Cherokees, in Congress and elsewhere, in concluding that their cause was hopeless.

Bartholomew sent his carriage, with Rodham driving, to Milledgeville to bring Samuel home. The two men returned in silence. Rodham said Samuel slept much of the way, frequently crying out.

I gave Samuel two days with Ann and the children before calling on them in New Echota. They were my old friends, Bartholomew said, so he would stay home and allow me time with them. But I coaxed him into accompanying me, and Levi donned his top hat, covered my husband and me with blankets, and drove us in the same carriage that had brought Samuel home from prison.

It was a visit that would change Bartholomew's life.

The spirit was gone from New Echota. The homes and public buildings were neglected, the forest that had been beaten back to create a Cherokee capital had ceased its retreat and was now advancing upon the settlement. Even Elias Boudinot's home was in disrepair, paint flaking, a porch railing hanging, a window broken out and plugged with old copies of the *Phoenix*.

The rail fence was down at the Worcesters', and the roof had blown off the smokehouse. Old mud was caked on the front steps and porch, Ann not bothering to sweep it off.

She led us into the living room, and I wasn't prepared for what I saw. Samuel had always been a thin man with delicate features, but now his bones threatened to pierce his skin. His shirt looked to have been sewn for a much larger person, his skin was gray, his eyes were as dead as stones, and his hair was the texture of straw.

"Nancy and Mr. Bramlett, how good to see you," Samuel said. "Excuse me for remaining in my rocker, but I am very tired. There's nothing wrong with me that a little freedom won't cure, though."

He was weak, but he wanted to catch up on all that had happened during his imprisonment, so Samuel and I talked for two hours. And, yes, I was curious about prison life—which in Samuel's case turned out to be more boring that horrible. "No one ever struck me or really mistreated me," Samuel said. "It might have been more interesting if someone had."

Bartholomew remained silent and stared at Samuel, as one might a strange plant or cloud that formed a picture. Finally, after more than an hour, he said, "It is incredible that in this day and time a state and a president could have such low regard for the law that, without even being embarrassed about it, they could allow a man of God to languish in prison, though he had committed nothing that could be counted a crime in a civilized country."

He said nothing more except, when our visit had ended, to wish Samuel and Ann well and tell them he would be sending a wagonload of supplies to their home.

We had traveled a few hundred yards when Bartholomew ordered Levi to stop at the Boudinots' house. When Elias came to the door my husband said, "I apologize for intruding, but it is important that I talk to you."

I joined Harriet in the living room, and Elias closed the door of his study behind Bartholomew and himself. The men spent nearly three hours in seclusion, an unplanned delay that forced us to travel the last few miles home in uncomfortable darkness.

My husband had asked the former editor of the *Phoenix* to explain to him all he knew of Cherokee politics. Elias had convinced Bartholomew that we must treat with the U.S. and abandon our homeland for the new country across the Mississippi. The alternative was racial oppression too horrible to contemplate. The proud Cherokees would be reduced to objects of contempt and abuse if they remained in reach of the whites. They were as totally excluded from the protection of the law as was a squirrel in the sights of a rifle.

Elias also told him that anyone publicly advocating removal could lose his life at the hands of those Cherokees who believed Chief John Ross' assurances that the Indians could win and keep their lands.

Which, unfortunately, was most Cherokees.

CHAPTER 26

Bartholomew Bramlett's adulthood had been spent in the pursuit of money and knowledge, and he had accumulated wealth in both categories. Yet, he was a melancholy man who had experienced little joy.

"Is this all there is to life?" he used to ask himself almost daily. I know, because after we were married he told me he did.

He found Christianity, and it consoled him, but never perfectly, for there were too many questions he considered unanswered. He simply couldn't believe everything in the Bible really happened, and he was too honest to say passages that were obviously meant to be taken literally were not supposed to be taken literally. If two bears didn't actually kill forty-two children because they teased Elisha about his bald head, why say they did?

He took a wife and received companionship and devotion, if not the sweet, romantic love of poetry. I do know I brought him many happy moments.

But the visit to New Echota on a bleak January day infused in him the need to be remembered as something more than a learned fellow who got richer than anyone else in the Cherokee Nation. He wanted to help his people. He wanted to save them from the whites who were demanding their lands.

He appreciated the irony of the situation. To argue that the Cherokees must surrender their homes to the whites and remove to the West required courage, but the masses considered it the cowardly viewpoint. Bartholomew was about to become a great patriot, and in doing so he would be labeled a traitor.

"I've always ignored politics," he told me as we stood before a crackling fire in the parlor of our home. "I always considered it a trifling business for pompous men. But this is not the time to leave it to others.

"I gazed at Samuel Worcester and was ashamed of myself. That white man went to prison for the Cherokees. I wouldn't even accept a seat on the General Council.

"I listened to the reasoned, impassioned arguments of Elias Boudinot for removal. He lost his job as editor of a newspaper because he believed he had a right to present his viewpoint.

"Nancy, he believes patriotism not only is love of a country; it is love of the people of that country. He knows the Cherokees must remove, that they can only preserve their character as a people by relocating to the West. He loves the ground of the Cherokee Nation—the hills, the valleys, the rivers, the forests—but he loves his people more. He believes a living man is more important than the soil which holds his dead ancestor.

"I intend to take the side of removal. I will do whatever I can to help Elias Boudinot, Major Ridge and John Ridge present their viewpoint and implement it. They are good, honest men. They aren't selling out the Cherokees, as so many have charged. They are trying to prevent their being obliterated, trying to promote their only chance to survive as a meaningful, vital people.

"Of course, it is more rousing to declare that if we stay and put our faith in Chief John Ross we somehow will magically triumph over Georgia and the United States. That is what Boudinot and the Ridges are up against. Ross tells people who want to keep their land that they can keep it; the removal faction tells them they can't."

Like most new zealots, Bartholomew dashed fervently and indiscreetly into his cause. He uncharacteristically rode horseback to the office of *The Cherokee Phoenix* in New Echota to place an order for handbills urging removal. Elijah Hicks, John Ross' brother-in-law who had replaced Elias as editor, refused to print them, but my normally calm, deliberative husband cursed him and created such a disturbance that Hicks accepted the order.

They were printed in Cherokee and English, and they explained why removal was the only answer. He would ride through the Cherokee Nation and tack them to trees and taverns and stores and ferries, he said. Would I like to accompany him on his first sojourn?

Why not? It was a pleasant, cool day, and Levi drove the open carriage along a road north of the plantation. Every quarter-mile or so, Bartholomew would tell him to stop, and he would leave a handbill on a tree.

After an hour or so of this, six turbaned, buckskinned Indians on horseback galloped up beside us. They slowed to our pace, and their leader held up one of the handbills. He stared at Bartholomew without expression. Then he crumpled the paper and tossed it into our carriage. Without a word, they sped ahead of us and out of sight. "Bastards," Bartholomew said. "I wonder how many of my handbills they tore down."

A mile ahead the road bent around a hill that was topped by a pine thicket. We reached the apex of the curve, and a stone struck the seat beside Levi. "What was that?" Bartholomew shouted, but the words were barely out of his mouth when another stone hit his shoulder, and another landed in my lap. Then came a barrage. The rocks struck the carriage and my husband and me. It was as if the pine thicket were a monster spitting stones. "Turn around, Levi, and head home!" Bartholomew commanded, and Levi spun the carriage, got the horses pointed back toward the plantation, and began to whip them desperately.

"Are you injured?" Bartholomew asked me when he was satisfied we weren't being followed.

"I don't think so," I said. It wasn't until we were home that I realized that the excitement had masked the pain from a half-dozen bruises on my back and legs and arms.

Neither Levi nor the horses had been hit. The only targets were the Cherokee who counseled removal and his wife. "I'm all right," Bartholomew protested, but he wasn't all right. His scalp was lacerated, his ear was torn, and a cut ran diagonally across his forehead. He joked that the tragedy was that his favorite hat with the tropical feather was ruined, but I didn't laugh. There was nothing funny in this.

I bathed his head, and then I almost fainted when Rachel, the plantation doctor, sewed up four wounds while he bit into a strip of rawhide and gripped the back of a chair.

"I'm sorry that I got you into this," he said that night as he inspected my bruises. "I never dreamed anyone would do such a thing."

"I know you wouldn't do anything to hurt me," I said. "At least you know now not to put up anymore handbills."

Bartholomew drew back and poured himself another glass of pain-killing brandy. "Oh, but I can't stop because of this," he said. "I have a duty to spread the word."

And he didn't stop. I begged Bartholomew not to return to the road, but it was no use. This circumspect, logical man had found excitement in his life. There was danger in his cause, and he thrived on it. Almost daily he would leave home on his chestnut stallion, the handbills stuffed in a saddlebag. At least take Pepper Rodham with you, I cried, but he insisted on going alone.

Usually he met no opposition, but one day he returned displaying an arrow that someone had shot at him. It had torn his pants and scratched his leg, and he had caught it against the saddle and saved it for a souvenir. Once he proudly displayed a split lip that an antagonist had given him in a tavern, explaining that he had broken the attacker's nose, causing him to flee. As a boy he had never won a fight, Bartholomew confided. Now he had. He was delighted.

He began making speeches in behalf of removal. He would ride into a village, tie his horse, plant himself in the most public place and begin his oration. A crowd would gather, and some would listen attentively and others would curse and threaten him, sometimes shouting him down.

When he failed to come home after one such trip, I sent Rodham to look for him. They were riding double on Rodham's horse when they returned in the darkness.

While Bartholomew was making one of his speeches to the villagers, someone had poisoned his horse. The horse fell dead a mile outside the village, and Bartholomew had walked all but two of the eleven miles home when Rodham found him.

He was exhausted, and after a half hour of ranting, he went to bed.

I was alone in the parlor, which was dark except for the flicker of the flame of a single candle when a voice startled me: "You're going to get him killed."

Rachel stood in the doorway, as straight as a pine, her eyes narrowed. "What in the world are you talking about?" I asked.

"Your friends are the ones telling the Cherokees they must move west. He knows them through you. He wouldn't be involved in this if it weren't for you."

I was furious. "I haven't told him to ride about the countryside endangering himself," I blurted. "On the contrary, I've asked him to stay home. I've told him a rich plantation owner is the last person the average poor Cherokee would trust anyway. He won't listen to me."

"Maybe they'll kill him, and then you'll have this big house and plantation to yourself, and you can marry a man your own age," Rachel said.

"Goddamn you," I said, leaping to my feet. It was an oath I had spoken perhaps twice before in my young life.

"Does Mrs. Bramlett require anything before I go to my room for the night?" Rachel said evenly. "With her permission, of course."

"Yes, Mrs. Bramlett does," I hissed. "Mrs. Bramlett requires you to sit in that chair and tell her why you hate her."

"Slaves aren't permitted to hate their mistresses," Rachel said, spreading her skirt over the brocaded chair.

I breathed deeply, trying to compose myself, and said evenly, "I want an answer. Why do you hate me?"

Rachel took a deep breath, too, no doubt pondering whether to pass a point of no return. She decided to do it. She said: "I hate you because you married the man I love. I'm a better woman than you are, and I would be a better wife for him. He loved me until you came along."

I was speechless. At least I fully realized how thoroughly wrong I had been when I had suspected I was marrying a thirty-eight-year-old virgin.

"Go on," I said.

"He would have married me if I had been white or a Cherokee," Rachel said. "He would have married me anyway if the Cherokees hadn't had a law against a Cherokee marrying a black slave."

"Where did you come from?" I asked her. "How did Bartholomew acquire you?"

"As settlement for a debt," she said. "A Cherokee owed money, and the marshal held a sale of his belongings—corn, fodder, horses, oxen, a wagon, a loom, two rifles, furniture and me and my husband Vernon and our two boys. One was a year old, the other was in my belly. The marshal shoved us up on the auction block and said he'd sell Vernon and me together or separately, he didn't care, he just wanted to get out of there and go fishing. He asked the audience their pleasure, and several yelled, 'Sell them separately.' They began bidding on Vernon.

"I was crying and holding onto Vernon and cursing the marshal, saying I couldn't live without my husband. The marshal slapped me, and Vernon tried to hit him, but his men grabbed Vernon and me. They drug me and my baby off the block and into a storeroom. One got all excited, and he told the other one to hold me down on some feed sacks. The other one didn't want to, but I guess the one doing the ordering was his boss, so he did. I could hear them bidding on my husband while he raped me, and I hoped he would to ahead and kill me right then and there, because I couldn't bear the thought of living in one place while Vernon lived in another one.

"But suddenly the door opened, and the marshal was standing there, and he kicked the man in the ass who was raping me and said, 'Get her out there. A fellow just stopped the bidding and bought both of them for twice what they're worth.'

"That was the first time I laid eyes on Bartholomew Bramlett, nine years ago. I found out later he couldn't stand to see Vernon and me separated, so he simply stepped up on the block and announced he was buying us both. He named a price he knew no one would challenge. 'My name is Bartholomew Bramlett,' he said to Vernon and me, as proper as if he was introducing himself to the king and queen. 'I'm pleased to meet you.' He even took off his hat, all polite like, and he chucked the baby under the chin.

"He completed the paperwork and led us out to an enclosed carriage. Levi was perched up on the driver's seat, and we wondered where we were supposed to ride. We couldn't believe it when Bartholomew motioned us inside with him. But there we went, the five of us, off to his plantation.

"We didn't know what to make of the way he talked to us. He said we would be treated well, more like folks on a payroll than slaves. If we had any problems we were to let him know."

My husband's noble rescue of the family vied in my mind with his having made love to this slave who regarded me as a romantic rival. I wasn't sure at that moment whether I admired him or was angry with him. Unexplained so far was the fate of Vernon—and curiosity was eating me alive.

"It had rained every day for a month, it seemed like," Rachel continued. "It started again right after we left. I felt sorry for Levi, being outside, on top of the carriage, but I was glad we were inside.

"The creeks and rivers were all up, some out of their banks. Levi came to a stream, and the bed of the bridge was covered by an inch of water. He stopped the horse and asked Bartholomew whether to go on. There was nothing to the eye to indicate danger, so Bartholomew told him to proceed. He asked Vernon to get on top with Levi and keep an eye on the edges of the bridge and help guide him across. Later he told me he was just showing Vernon right off that he had confidence in him, because Levi could see the bridge fine.

"The carriage got halfway across, and the bridge collapsed in the middle. The swift water had undermined the pilings. The horse and carriage stayed on the bridge, though the water rushed in on us. Through the side window I saw Vernon fall off the top and into the water. I screamed that he couldn't swim, and Bartholomew himself shoved open the door and swam into the flood, trying to rescue him.

"But Vernon disappeared immediately in the muddy water. Bartholomew dove for him time and again, but he finally had to give up. Levi got me and the baby out of the carriage and onto the bank. I was hysterical, and I sat under a tree in the rain and the mud, and Bartholomew put his arm around me and tried to comfort me.

"The horse was hurt bad, so Levi shot it, and for some reason I stopped crying when I heard the explosion. I got to my feet and said, 'What now?' and Bartholomew said, 'We walk home,' and we walked the three miles to the plantation. Bartholomew sent some slaves back to the creek, and they found Vernon's body snagged in a tree nearly a mile downstream."

Rachel calmly looked me in the eye. I was angry with myself because my chin was jerking, and I was squeezing my hands together as I fought to keep from crying. "The rest?" I said.

"Bartholomew felt like Vernon's death was his fault because he had told Levi to cross the stream, even though I told him no one could have known the bridge would fall. He felt guilty because he had bought Vernon and me, but if he hadn't we probably would have been separated. He retired the old woman who was his housekeeper and put me in charge.

"I was a pretty young widow, and Bartholomew was a lonely man. One thing led to another, and for several years we made love. We didn't for, oh, the last five years or so before he married you, but I never stopped loving him.

"He is a complicated person. He never forced himself on me. He didn't have to. But I know he wondered if I was doing it just because he was my master. He'd remind me I wasn't bound to do it, and I'd tell him I knew that, but it worried him. One day he just said, 'Why would a woman go to bed with an ugly man if she didn't feel she had to?' I tried to tell him looks didn't have much to do with how a woman felt, but he didn't believe me.

"The other slaves knew, and they laughed about it themselves, and it got back to Bartholomew. Once I saw a girl peeping in the bedroom window, but I didn't tell him. One of his rich friends joshed him about it so much that Bartholomew stopped seeing the fellow.

"One day he called me into his office and told me it just wasn't proper, and we wouldn't go to bed together again. I tried to put my arm around his shoulder, but he got up and walked to the window and looked out, and that was the end of it.

"But I know he didn't really stop loving me until he married you. I could feel the change, just like I can feel when a sweet breeze stops blowing."

I got to my feet and said, "Good night, Rachel." She nodded and left the room.

Now what did I do? Could I continue to live in the house with a woman who was in love with my husband? Should I ask Bartholomew to sell her? He wouldn't do that. He wouldn't even sell field hands, because he was afraid they wouldn't be treated well. Should I ask him to remove her from the house and assign her other duties? Then she would hate me even more, if that was possible, and she would still be on the plantation, perhaps agitating the other slaves against me.

For the time being I did nothing. Except vow to rid this place of slavery some-how, some way. Even under the best of conditions—the conditions that prevailed on Bartholomew Bramlett's plantation—it was an evil device. It mocked God by assigning one human dominion over another, though he had created them equally. It disregarded the human heart, which might be the biggest sin of all.

If Bartholomew and Rachel had been in love, and if they had wanted to marry, the community of humankind should have blessed their union, I grudgingly told myself. Instead, because of unnatural laws and mores, it could not be.

Of course, I reminded myself, if not for slavery, Bartholomew and Rachel would never have even known each other.

How to cleanse this plantation of slavery? There was work to be done, and it was the slaves who had to do it. The place couldn't be allowed to grow up into weeds. They couldn't be sold into God knows what kind of life on other farms. Anyway, if they were told they were free, they wouldn't leave. Where would they go?

And, I asked myself, was It really the desire to cleanse the plantation of slavery that was keeping me awake as I lay in the bed beside Bartholomew and gazed at the moonlit clouds passing by my window? Was it perhaps the desire to cleanse the plantation of Rachel?

It was well after midnight when I dozed off, and the sounds and light of the morning awoke me two hours short of a decent night's sleep. My head felt as heavy and as dead as an anvil. My poor wounded husband was up and dressed and supervising life on a plantation with a pink marble house.

I slipped into a gown and stood in a window and gazed at the western horizon. Would we really have to give all this up and move in that direction some day? Would a massive and incomprehensible evil prevail as the white Georgians, by sim-ple might and disregard for law, dispossess the Cherokees? Was Bartholomew right? Were the Ridges and Elias right?

Or was John Ross right? He was, after all, the principal chief, the leader of our people. Perhaps he knew more than anyone else about our politics. Perhaps he could delay the proceedings until the election of 1836, and perhaps Henry Clay, a friend of the Cherokees and Jackson's political arch enemy, would contest the Chicken Snake and occupy the White House, and we would be allowed to remain in our homeland. Jackson had crushed Clay in the election of 1832, but perhaps it would be different another time.

I lowered my eyes from the horizon to the forest that bordered the grounds of the plantation, and I recoiled at what I saw. Indians, some two dozen of them, stood in the tree line. They were wrapped in blankets up to their eyes.

They had seen me before I had seen them. Their eyes were focused on me. They didn't move. They might as well have been stone monoliths.

I didn't have to be told why they were there. I knew. They were reminders to Bartholomew Bramlett of the ancient blood laws of the Cherokees. Their presence affirmed that the unauthorized disposal of Cherokee land meant death.

CHAPTER 27

I rode horseback over the plantation, sitting man-style in the saddle, seeing to this and seeing to that. It was mine, and I was going to have a say-so in its operation, at least when my husband was away—which was most of the time now.

But even when he wasn't away from me in body, he was away in mind and spirit. The sexual side of our marriage withered. It wasn't that Bartholomew was incapable in bed. He just wasn't interested in bed.

Bartholomew Bramlett was a complex person. We had made love satisfactorily at first, until he had immersed himself in the public welfare, and then that changed. Perhaps somewhere deep in his mind something told him his transformation from what he called a "self-absorbed life" to one of service required that he abandon pleasure, for that was exactly what he did. He not only gave up sex (oh, he joined me in an occasional session when, I suppose, the pressure became intolerable, but such interludes were rare), he gave up other comforts, such as hearty meals and parties and fine clothes and specious friends and, though he despised riding horseback, the use of his carriages and buggies and Levi.

I have read that many driven, accomplished men have voracious sexual appetites. Well, it wasn't that way with Bartholomew. So I occupied my thoughts with the plantation.

I didn't pretend to know how to run a huge farm, but I knew that a table left out in the rain would ruin, that a fence trampled down by a bull invited cattle to escape, and a tree that had fallen across a shed two months before should have been removed.

"Now, Mrs. Bramlett, you just leave the plantation to me," Pepper Rodham said when I returned from the first of what he came to call my inspection tours.

My only comment was to tell him what I had seen and add, "Those things need to be taken care of, Mr. Rodham." He smiled a patronizing smile and nodded.

When, a week later, they hadn't been taken care of, I rode to the slave quarters, summoned a huge, middle-aged man named Harry from an interlude with his new teen-aged wife, and told him to make right what was wrong.

"Uh, I best ask Mr. Rodham first," he said.

"I am the wife of Mr. Bramlett, the owner of the plantation," I told him. "Surely you remember that, for when he brought me here he assembled you all and introduced me. You don't have to ask Mr. Rodham before doing what I tell you."

"Uh, maybe I best ask Rachel then," Harry stammered.

I was furious. Not at him, but at Rachel and my husband. The slaves knew they had slept together—probably thought they still did—and in their minds she was third in command on the plantation, behind Bartholomew and Rodham. In her mind she probably was second in command.

"I own Rachel," I said in one of the truly ignoble moments of my life. "I own you. It had better all be finished by nightfall."

I returned to the mansion, ignored Rachel's snide, "Good afternoon, Mrs. Bramlett," went to my bedroom, got out of my riding pants and boots, sprawled across the bed in my underwear, and gazed at the ceiling.

Months after Rachel's confession that she had been my husband's lover, she and I were at a stalemate. We spoke perfunctorily. I imagined sarcasm in her every clipped sentence, but I had no solution to the problem of her presence.

Bartholomew traveled constantly, speaking on behalf of removal, tacking up handbills, meeting with important men, Indian and white. He even went to Washington City. He had found his reason for being, and his young wife felt assigned to the background.

She had to have something to do, so she looked after the plantation.

Bartholomew insisted that his slaves not be treated as slaves but as hired hands. His overseer, Pepper Rodham, also was his friend, relative and confidant. Consequently Rodham never heard a harsh word from his boss. Those two situations led to laxity on the plantation. The slaves were not treated as hired hands; they weren't required to work nearly as hard as hired hands would have been. If that was how Bartholomew felt, it was fine with Rodham, an easy-going sort of fellow anyway. The slaves never heard a harsh word from him, either.

Because of my husband's talent for bribery, Rodham remained in the Cherokee Nation without taking an oath of allegiance to Georgia, and we kept our plantation, though "fortunate drawers" in the Georgia lottery were occupying other Cherokees' homes—including Principal Chief John Ross'. For all I knew, we might be kicked off the place the next day, but as long as we were there, I felt the plantation should operate efficiently. It made a lot of money as it was, but it could make more.

And, as I said, I didn't have anything else to do but tighten up the operation of the farm.

Naturally, in the minds of Rodham and the slaves, I became the villain.

"There must be eight or nine acres of good bottomland in that bend in the creek," I told Rodham. "Why don't we clear it and plant corn?"

"Oh, I don't know. We just never did."

"Well, do it. I hate to disturb those four fellows I saw fishing a minute ago, but maybe they can put their poles down long enough to do a little work."

My image became that of the stern mistress of slaves. I who detested slavery was conveniently assigned that slot by Rodham, Rachel and the workers.

Once I made the mistake of muttering about some slackers to Rachel. "Why, Mrs. Bramlett," she said, "the day I met you, you were criticizing Mr. Bramlett for working slaves, and now you don't think they work hard enough."

"Get out!" I screamed.

"Just making conversation, ma'm," Rachel said cheerily.

She didn't look back when I slammed an expensive vase against the wall.

That night Bartholomew returned from a two-day conference of removal advocates at John Ridge's. I threw myself into his arms and begged him to stay home more. "I love you, Nancy," he said, "but I'm afraid I'll be staying home less. These are the times that are crucial to the future of the Cherokees. Some day there will be time for us to relax and be together when we've built a new home for ourselves west of the Mississippi."

"I've got to talk to you about Rachel," I said. "She …"

"Not now, darling," he said. "I must go over this entire stack of papers before I go to bed. Just relax and read your Bible and your Shakespeare and let Rachel run the household. She's good at it. You don't have to worry yourself with it. I saw the glass on the floor, and I know it was one of your favorite vases, but I'm sure Rachel didn't mean to break it. Don't be angry with her. She will get around to sweeping it up. I'll replace it with one just like it."

I had to get away from that place. "I want Levi to drive me home in the morning," I said.

"Home?"

"To visit my parents and friends for a few days."

If my husband had complained that he had been away and wanted me to stay with him until he left again I would have. But all he said was, "All right. I'll call Rachel and have her tell Levi."

"I'll tell him myself," I said. He nodded and buried himself in his papers.

I was still awake when he came to bed. He sighed as he slid under the covers. I pressed myself against his back, ran my fingers through his hair, but soon he was breathing heavily and irregularly, a certain sign he was asleep.

There was room for a wife in Bartholomew's parlor, but not in his bedroom. His "calling" was his new lover. I think I would have felt better if I had been challenged by a mistress rather than a cause.

The next day, despite Levi's silly protests that I might somehow be injured, I insisted on sitting beside him on the driver's seat as the carriage rumbled away from the house. I wanted to see what was literally ahead of me, perhaps because I certainly didn't know what was figuratively ahead of me.

When we reached the village I ordered Levi to put me and my two carpetbags out in front of Charley Marley's church. "Now go home," I said. "I'll send word when I want you to come back for me."

It was a crisp November day, but I welcomed the cold air into my lungs. I gazed at the church, its once-brilliant whiteness dulled by time. I looked across the square at the cabin Charley and I had occupied. Now I owned slave houses that were bigger. I saw my parents' cabin, where I had grown up, and the cabins of neighbors I had always known. At least the malignant hand of the Georgia lottery hadn't yet grasped my old village.

I went inside the church. Though unused, the interior was clean and undisturbed. I sat on the front row and imagined Charley in the pulpit—poor, frustrated, sweet Charley, with his rehearsed gestures and uninspiring sermons. If he could be here now, I thought, I would gladly sit on that hard bench and listen to him preach forever.

I thought someone might have seen me arrive, might come to the church to welcome me, but only the scampering of a couple of field mice broke the silence. So after perhaps half an hour alone with my thoughts, I crossed the square to our cabin, to the home Charley and I had shared.

I opened the door and was startled to see a thin young woman in Charley's old rocker, nursing a baby. "This is my house," I said, feeling ridiculous in my fancy Philadelphia velvet dress that cost more than all the money the girl would see in her lifetime.

"You are Nancy Swimmer," the frightened squatter said. "The whites came to take our home, and when we wouldn't leave, the Georgia Guard shot my husband, and his arm was crushed. We ran away and came here, and your parents said we could stay in your cabin. Do you want us to leave? We can't pay you any money, but my husband is fishing, and he will return home soon, and when he does he will give you a fish. Here, I made a terrapin shell rattle for my baby. You can have it for your baby. Do you have a baby?"

"No," I said. "I don't have a baby. You are welcome to stay. I don't need a fish or a rattle."

My father was out back of my parents' cabin. I watched him string a bow with bear gut, his lips moving as he recited goodness knows what to himself. He looked older and more defeated than ever. I hadn't seen him in nearly a year. "Father," I said.

I was delighted when he pushed himself to his feet and hugged me. "My daughter," he said excitedly. "Welcome home. Let's go inside. Your mother is making some of her wonderful cornbread."

Mother shouted when she saw me. She raced across the room and hugged me. "Can you stay a few days?" she asked.

"Yes," I said, "a few days." Perhaps more than a few. It was good to be home—and this humble cabin, not my pink marble mansion, felt like home.

Rain and I chattered like birds. She told me the gossip from the village. Even Staring Otter joined in. When they wanted to know about my life on the plantation, I reversed the conversation. "There really isn't much to tell," I said. "Very little happens there. Are you selling many bows, Father?"

I ate Mother's cornbread, and it tasted better than any of the fancy recipes I had had in the pink marble house. "I suppose you noticed we bought a cow," she said, pouring me a cup of rich, yellow milk.

She laughed and shook her head. "A trader told me just today he'd trade me out of that cow, and when I told him no he said I'd take a pair of comfortable moccasins for her when the time came to march to the Mississippi. I told him I heard yesterday that John Ross almost had this thing settled, that we wouldn't be moving anywhere. He just chuckled and went on."

"Your friend Boudinot had better watch his step," Staring Otter said. "He's still preaching that foolishness about the people giving up their land and moving west. The other day some men stood at the edge of the woods in front of his house, wrapped in blankets up to their eyes—their way of reminding him what could happen to someone who tried to fleece them out of their land."

I tried unsuccessfully to stifle a gasp. When I failed, I coughed on purpose. "This cornbread is so good, I'm going to choke myself eating it so fast," I said.

"How does your man feel about these scalawags who think they know more than John Ross?" my mother asked. At least the question told me that Bartholomew hadn't visited this village yet.

"Let's not talk politics," I said. "I'm just delighted to be home. I missed my parents."

"Strong Hickory misses you," Mother said. "He told me the other day how he'd like to see you. He said it was strange, but even with all the years you two had known each other it was getting so he couldn't remember your face. He said he couldn't get it exactly right in his mind, that he'd like to see you and get it fixed in his thoughts again. The boy's loved you all his life, and he still hasn't stopped."

I didn't change the subject. Directly after my marriage I would have, but now I didn't. I remembered how I had stood in the church and been unable to recall my poor murdered Charley's face, and I felt a rush of sympathy for Strong Hickory. "How is he?" I asked.

"Well, I was hoping you wouldn't ask," Mother said, "because I didn't want to upset your visit. But he's in jail, at Camp Benton. He was helping a friend drive some hogs on the road toward Nashville, and he drank some whiskey, and got into a fight with a couple of Georgia Guards. Whipped them both, the way it's told. Nobody was hurt bad, but they locked him up. They won't tell The Bull anything. They just laughed at him when he asked how long his son would be in jail, when his trial would be, whether there would even be a trial. He's been in there four days now."

"Those people could kill him," I said. "He's at their mercy. There are no laws to protect the Cherokees. Where is Camp Benton?"

I could see the sadness in Rain's eyes. "The Spring Place Mission Station is now called Camp Benton," she said. The Georgia Guard took it. They converted the chapel into a courthouse and the missionaries' house into a tavern. People say every kind of vice imaginable goes on there. The commander of the guard, Colonel Bishop, took Rich Joe Vann's mansion across the road."

Moravian missionaries had established their school at Spring Place in 1801, thirty-two years before. Elias Boudinot and John Ridge had attended school there, and many times Elias had regaled Harriet and me with stories of their school days. It was a place sacred to Moravians and Christianized Cherokees, and now the Georgia Guard had desecrated it.

I excused myself and got some gold coins and a quill and ink and paper out of my carpetbag and went to my old cabin. The girl who lived there was again startled to see me, and so was her husband, who had returned from fishing, but I calmed their fears and told them I needed a table and a chair so I could write a message.

When I was finished I sized up her husband. His left arm hung limp at his side, but his legs looked strong. I handed him more money than he had ever seen in his life and asked, "Would you like to earn these gold coins?" He nodded, and I gave him the message and told him to take it to Mr. Bartholomew Bramlett, who lived in a huge pink house north of there. He had to leave immediately and not stop until the message was delivered.

He didn't have a horse, he said.

I gave him another coin and told him to rent one or buy one, but to get on the road, for he had a long ride ahead of him. And when he returned the cabin he was living in would belong to him and his wife. He thanked me, kissed his wife on top of the head, and left.

I returned to my parents' house, and we talked into the night. I continued to dodge questions about Bartholomew and politics. I couldn't concentrate on what was being said for worrying about Strong Hickory. He might disappear and never be seen again, and no white man would give it a second thought. Official Georgia hadn't cared that Charley Marley had been brutally murdered, and it wouldn't care if Strong Hickory were murdered.

The next morning I walked to New Echota, as I had done so many times in years past. It was nice to be alone on the road, to feel the cold wind that rattled the limbs of the skeletal trees, to watch the flow of the Oostanaula under a blanket of dead leaves, to gaze at the pewter sky that hid the sun. I wondered how it would be to live completely alone, to never see or hear the voice of another person. Probably not so bad.

I reached New Echota and found it to be more disheveled than when I had visited there ten months before—when Bartholomew had talked with Elias and become caught up in the need to "make my life count for something," as he phrased it.

The bleak, unrepaired buildings reflected the spirit of the people. No one even bothered to sweep the debris of winter from their yards. To be the capital of the

Cherokee Nation was now like being the heart of a dying person.

I knocked on the Boudinots' door and Harriet answered. She graciously welcomed me, but there was no light in her eyes. The normally neat Elias needed a
shave, his hair was uncombed, and there was an ink stain on his shirt.

We rocked by a fireplace, and the Boudinots said they were getting by. Elias's
ally in the removal cause, the considerate Bartholomew Bramlett, sent food, of
course. Some friends had remained at their side, but most Cherokees considered
Elias a pariah. "Merely knowing you are right isn't very nourishing stew in that situation," he said.

"They stand in the forest in their blankets and gaze at our house," Harriet said.
"All the old stories I heard as a child come flooding back, stories of Indians scalp-
ing whites, burning their homes, killing their babies. I tell myself these are the
Cherokees, my people, but I can't get the images out of my mind. That's so silly,
isn't it?" She got up and walked to the window to regain her composure, to hide
her tears from me.

"They come to my house, too," I said.

Harriet began to wail, and she embraced me. "Oh, Nancy," she said. "Little
Nancy." There wasn't really much else to say.

I spent the night with the Boudinots. The Worcesters and Sophia Sawyer took
supper with us. We were able to manufacture a few laughs by telling old stories,
but then the laughter would stop, and silence would return.

"And how is Rachel?" Ann said. "She was such a help to us."

The last thing I needed was to be reminded that Rachel existed—that, indeed,
she and my husband were alone in the luxury of that pink mansion, doing goodness knows what. But, I told myself, Bartholomew probably was too busy with his
"cause" to realize Rachel was in the house—or, for that matter, that I wasn't.
Anger began to replace moroseness, and it felt better.

"Nancy?" Harriet said, "Ann asked you a question."

"Oh, I'm sorry," I blurted. "Uh, how is Rachel? Rachel is fine. So are her
children."

It was not a satisfying visit. I was pleased to be returning to my village the next
morning. "Thank you, Elias," I said when he offered to take me on horseback,
"but I'd really rather walk. I always enjoyed that walk."

I spent much of the day in Charley's church. Just sitting on the front pew,
where I'd always sat during his sermons, reliving our life together, remembering
the handsome, exciting magician who had come to our village that day a million
years ago to dazzle a young girl, remembering the educated man who taught me
so much, remembering the strong, talented ballplayer in a breechcloth, remembering how he looked on our wedding day.

Remembering the great lover.

Mother came and got me for supper. I'm afraid I wasn't very good company. I
was aching for Charley. I was afraid to speak, afraid I would go to pieces if I did.

I was sweeping the yard with a brush broom the next morning when I heard: "Nancy, thank you."

Strong Hickory looked good. He was a man full grown, lithe, handsome despite the bruises on his cheeks and the cut on his forehead. His buckskin pants and homspun shirt were filthy after the fight and imprisonment, but he looked good.

"You're welcome," I said. "What happened?"

"They locked me in a shed and stationed a guard outside the door," he said. "A dead Indian's body was tied to a rafter. The odor was awful. But that's why they left him there. They gave me some water, but only a few pieces of bread, and I slept on the wooden floor.

"Last night an officer opened the door and said, 'You're lucky, boy. You know somebody who knows Bartholomew Bramlett. That rich bastard slipped somebody something to get you out of here. You ought to get on your knees and thank him, because we was going to starve you till you'd rather pick up a rattlesnake than hit another guardsman, much less two.'

"I told him I hated Bartholomew Bramlett. He said, 'Well, that ain't my affair. All I know is he paid you out of here. So get.'

"I shouldn't have said that, Nancy. The part about hating him, I mean. I appreciate him getting me out of there. But he took my Nancy."

"Go get a bath and some clean clothes, and we'll walk beside the river if you want," I said. The shock of my invitation illuminated his tired eyes.

Strong Hickory returned fresh in sweet-smelling, soft, white cotton pants and shirt his mother had boiled in a black pot. He was barefoot, and his raven hair was tied with a small piece of yellow ribbon I had given him ten years before. We did walk by the river, and when he tried to kiss me I let him. And then we left the path and entered a grove, and on a blanket of pine straw with only the clouds above us, my childhood sweetheart and I made love for the first time.

CHAPTER 28

I wasn't proud of what I had done. I was the widow of a minister, and I had committed adultery. But I was also the eighteen-year-old wife of a man who thought a bed was merely a place to rest up between forays on behalf of those whom he had now come to call "my people."

The next day, at dawn, before Strong Hickory had a chance to come to my parents' cabin, I paid the young man with the ruined arm to drive me home in a wagon I borrowed from a neighbor.

When I arrived, Bartholomew kissed me—on the forehead—and asked me if I had a nice visit. "Yes," I said. Very nice, I thought.

That night I almost confessed to Bartholomew what had happened.

I was awake, listening to him wheeze and mumble unintelligible words in his sleep. I was gazing out the ceiling-to-floor window beside our bed when a light blazed across the sky. Then another. Then the blackness was inscribed with a multitude of white streaks. I had read of meteor showers, and Sophia Sawyer, the amateur astronomer, had explained them to me, but I was terrified. I feared the end of the world had come, and I didn't want to be judged by God immediately after having made love in the woods with a man who wasn't my husband.

I grasped Bartholomew with such panic that my fingernails cut into his arms. I buried my face in his chest. "What? What is it?" he blurted.

We sat on the edge of the bed and watched the meteors. "We know it's a natural phenomenon," Bartholomew said, removing the arm he had placed around my shoulders, evidently considering his civilized, reasonable wife had been sufficiently consoled, "but what must my people be thinking?"

"To hell with your people," I said, the urge to tell him about Strong Hickory burning out like the meteors. I slipped on a robe and went downstairs to the parlor and read for the few hours until daylight. When I heard Bartholomew's boots stomping around upstairs I returned to our bedroom. We passed on the stairs.

"I'm going to Head of Coosa," he said. "I'll return tonight."

"I'm going back to bed," I said. "I hope to sleep until noon. Tell Rachel to see that I'm not disturbed."

"Nancy …," he said, but I slammed the bedroom door.

The Cherokee Phoenix reported that "the world was literally striped with fire," but that the meteor shower was an explainable astronomical event. Many Cherokees thought it was a bad sign, though. They wondered if John Ross could really pull them out of the mess the whites were making of the Indians' lives. For some, their confidence in Ross was seriously shaken that night for the first time.

After I got up sometime after 1 o'clock, I asked Rachel if she had seen the display. "No, ma'm," she answered, not looking up from the clothes she was folding. "I was sleeping like a baby. I heard about it. Just a few shooting stars. Don't be scared."

Damn it. I knew better than to even speak to the woman. One would have thought she was the mistress and I was the slave. I didn't want to be either one. I hoped that whoever brought the first shipload of black slaves to these shores was burning in hell.

"I'm not scared, Rachel," I blurted. "For goodness sake."

"Oh, good," Rachel said.

I was furious. I was sick of her patronizing me. But I was afraid to ask Bartholomew to sell her or send her to the fields. He not only wouldn't do it, but in a showdown he might choose Rachel over me. Certainly he made love to her longer than he made love to me.

And, my confused brain reminded, who was I to be judging anyone? I had just been unfaithful to a husband who had provided me with every luxury I could imagine.

So I took my frustration out on others. I put on my most severe riding clothes and boots and told Pepper Rodham to have all the slaves assembled in front of the main barn in thirty minutes.

"You serious?" he asked, but I didn't dignify the question with an answer.

Seventy-four slaves lined up, men, women and children, apprehension on the faces of some, amusement on the faces of others. Rodham purposely took his place alongside the blacks.

"I am Mrs. Bramlett," I said. "In case some of you have forgotten." A titter came from the backmost of the three rows.

"There is a general laziness among the people on this plantation. That is going to be corrected. You are well fed, you are housed, and you have clothes on your backs. You must earn all that. You must work harder than you now work.

"It isn't entirely your fault. My husband is a good man. Mr. Rodham is a good man. Perhaps they are too good for their own good. My husband likes to think of you as employees, but you don't work as hard as employees would. There will be some changes made. I just want to you understand what is happening and why.

"I have several ideas on how to improve efficiency around here. Mr. Rodham will meet with me and then with you to pass on my wishes. Thank you. Mr. Rodham, would you please join me in Mr. Bramlett's study in the house?"

The meteor shower was duplicated in Rodham's stare as he faced me across Bartholomew's desk and received his orders from one he must have regarded as an obnoxious girl. His eyes spit fire. I did feel a surge of authority and command as I sat in my husband's huge leather-covered chair, my hands spread on top of his expansive oak desk. I could understand the appeal of power, of being one who helped decide the future of the Cherokee Nation.

But I knew it would never have replaced sex in my life.

"Will that be all?" Rodham asked when it was apparent I was finished. He held a long list of orders, some requiring arduous work.

"Yes. Thank you."

"You know none of this is going to matter, don't you?" he said. "The Georgians are going to swoop in here one day like buzzards and take this place. We'll all be living in caves."

"Probably," I said. "Until then, we all will do our best—me, you, the blacks. Or perhaps we will get a miracle and the Cherokees will not have to move."

"I'm going to protest to Bartholomew, of course."

And he did. While I eavesdropped outside the room. "Oh, just humor her, Pepper," said my husband. "I'm away a lot, and this keeps her busy. Do what she says. She does have some good ideas. Now leave, for I have a lot of work."

It wasn't a rousing endorsement, but it would do.

At night, lying awake in my bed, I considered my relationship to the slaves. The uncompromising girl who would have unlocked the gates of slavery and freed every black on the grounds had been replaced by a woman who was ordering them to work harder. But, I told myself, I was simply being realistic. I still hated slavery, and I did wish it would disappear, but it was more difficult to undo an evil than to create it.

Still, I was a slave mistress. And there was a time when I never would have believed that could be my role.

The plantation was not in immediate danger of takeover. At first, Bartholomew had protected it from the Georgians with bribery, but since he had become a force for removal of the Cherokees to the land beyond the Mississippi, bribery had not been necessary. Governor Lumpkin had simply placed the plantation off-limits. The whites were not to touch it. Similarly protected were the homes of Boudinot, the Ridges and others. Cherokees who were being evicted from their modest homes hated us all the more as they observed our favored treatment.

Bartholomew had even received a letter of appreciation from Chicken Snake Jackson. Thank goodness the people couldn't see that.

A week after I had returned from visiting my parents, I was in Bartholomew's study going over the books when Rachel came in and said, "There's a boy here to see you. I tried to get him to leave, but he says he's a friend." There was a smirk on her face and vinegar in her voice when she spoke the last word.

"Hello, Nancy," Strong Hickory said, so adoringly that the walls must have noticed. Rachel stood there until I told her that would be all. And to shut the door behind her.

"You shouldn't have come here," I said. "This is crazy." But he took me in his arms, and the woman who was so firm in running the plantation wasn't firm under his insistent kisses. I didn't resist when he led me across the room or when he took off my shoes and lifted my legs onto the couch. I knew Rachel might be listening outside the door, but I pulled Strong Hickory down to me and dismissed Rachel and everyone else from the planet.

Later, as I gazed out the window at a gray sky, Strong Hickory's arms around my waist, I whispered, "You can't come to my home again."

"I know," he said. "There's a cabin a few miles from here. It belonged to a cousin of my father who died. I'm claiming it. Meet me there in three days."

He sat at Bartholomew Bramlett's desk and took his quill and paper and made a map. He drew a homey cabin with smoke curling from the chimney and light pouring from the window and children playing in the yard.

I did meet him at his cabin. And I met him again and again and again and again. I rode horseback, like a man, and we hid my mare in a log shed at the back of the cabin, a structure Strong Hickory had built for the purpose.

Without explanation I saddled my horse every few days and rode away to be with Strong Hickory. Pepper Rodham and the slaves watched as I passed by them and out the front gate.

How could anyone know what was going on? With seventy-five persons, besides Bartholomew and me, on the premises how could someone not know?

One day I returned from a tryst to find Bartholomew in the kitchen, eating a piece of apple pie that Rachel had baked. "Where have you been?" he asked.

"Riding," I said. "I am becoming quite a horsewoman in your absence. I enjoy riding. It's relaxing."

"Relaxing?" he said. "I can't imagine anything less relaxing than bouncing along on the back of a horse."

"I mean it's relaxing to be alone with your thoughts."

He wasn't supposed to be at home. He had left that morning just before I did. He had said he was going to Major Ridge's for two days.

"Ridge became ill," Bartholomew explained. "A rider intercepted me after I had ridden less than a mile to tell me not to come. When I returned you had gone. Ridge should be feeling better tomorrow, and I will leave then."

"I hope it's nothing serious," I said, nervously trying to make conversation.

"If it were serious he wouldn't be seeing me tomorrow, would he?" Bartholomew said. His eyes peered into mine, as if he were trying to find something hidden in my skull.

He knew about Strong Hickory, I told myself. I knew he knew.

But then he put his arm around my shoulders and pulled my face to his chest. "Nancy, you are as sweet as this apple pie," he said. "I don't know what I would do without you. I won't tell you that you can't ride, but please be careful out on the roads. These are terrible times. People hate me. They might do you harm. You have brought so much joy to my life."

It was sad. Bartholomew Bramlett didn't know what joy was, but at least this rare demonstration of affection told me he was not suspicious of me.

I took his arm and led him from the kitchen, but when he saw that I was headed for the bedroom he said, "You must try some of Rachel's pie. I never tasted better. I have to go speak to Rodham. I'm glad you had a nice ride, Nancy."

I was at Harriet's house in New Echota on a February day in 1834 when Ann Worcester entered without knocking, weeping, a piece of paper crumpled in her hand. She handed it to Harriet, and I looked over Harriet's shoulder, and we read that Samuel Austin Worcester was ordered by William Springer, the Cherokee agent in Georgia, "to evacuate the lot of land number one hundred and twenty-five in the fourteenth district, of the third section, and to give the house now occupied by you up to Colonel William Harden, or whoever he may put forward to take possession of same."

The Worcesters were dispossessed. The eviction notice was as perfunctory as an invoice.

"You'll move in with us," Harriet said. "As long as we have a home, you have a home."

Ann ran her fingers over a sheaf of hymns lying on a table in the parlor. Samuel Worcester and Elias Boudinot had collaborated on the translation, and Elias was fond of calling the result "the first Cherokee book ever published."

"They have worked so hard," Ann said. "We all have worked so hard. And now everything is unraveling."

"We must ask God to lead us and follow His leadership," Harriet said. "Sometimes when He closes one door He opens another."

Ann was consoled, and she hugged Harriet. The Puritan mystic who had surrendered a comfortable New England life to marry a Cherokee and bring the news of Christ to his people had a gift for consoling the heartsick.

Later it was her husband she was consoling. On May 31, 1834, *The Cherokee Phoenix* ceased publication. John Ross's brother-in-law, Elijah Hicks, who had replaced Boudinot after Elias's resignation a year and eight months before, had no talents as an editor, and the *Phoenix* had stumbled and finally collapsed. The first Indian newspaper was a part of history.

Elias was no longer the editor, but it was he who had breathed life into the *Phoenix,* who had looked on so proudly when the first sheet of the first number, dated February 21, 1828, had been lifted wet from the press, and he grieved at its passing.

I remembered Ann Worcester's words: "Everything is unraveling." Indeed, everything was unraveling. Confusion, animosity, the struggle for power between those urging removal and those insisting on resistance—those were depressing days, frenetic days.

John Ross met with Chicken Snake Jackson, and the president offered three million dollars and good land in the West in exchange for the homeland of the Cherokee Nation. Why, the gold on Cherokee land was worth twenty million, Ross countered. And he asked a legitimate question: if Jackson couldn't protect the Cherokees against Georgia, how could he protect them in the West?

Andrew Ross, John's brother, who had little authority, signed a removal treaty with the U.S. that was so ridiculous the Senate rejected it.

John Ross suggested the Cherokees stay on a part of their land, amalgamate with the whites and be under state jurisdiction. Major Ridge protested that the Indians quickly would be swallowed by racial prejudice and reduced to beggary.

John Walker, Jr., a removal advocate who had made his bid to represent the nation, was assassinated.

John Ross investigated the possibility of moving the Cherokees to Mexico.

The Cherokees voted for the impeachment of council members Major Ridge, John Ridge and David Vann. The Major was crushed by the people's denunciation of him, but Ross didn't prosecute the charges, thus never giving the three a chance to clear their names. They resigned from the council and called a meeting of their own at John Ridge's house.

That meeting lasted for three days and resulted on November 27, 1834, in the formation of a Treaty Party, a group dedicated to removal of the Cherokees to the West. "Now it's official," Bartholomew told me when he returned home. "Only eighty-three Indians were there, but that number included most of the educated Cherokees."

"Education isn't much protection against a knife in the back," I said, but he wasn't listening.

As he became more deeply immersed in politics, in saving his people, he hardly seemed to know I existed.

Strong Hickory knew I existed. I not only rode to his cabin every day that Bartholomew was away from home, I sometimes went when he was at the plantation. I felt abandoned by my husband, and I had become increasingly indiscreet. The slaves smirked as I rode by them. They knew I was being unfaithful to Bartholomew. They despised me anyway, and this just gave them more reason to hate me: the wife who made them work was cuckolding the husband who didn't.

"Why don't you leave him?" Strong Hickory begged. "You don't love him."

"I can't leave him," I said. He is in a crucial stage of his life, and I can't leave him."

Oh, I'm sure devotion to Bartholomew was part of it, but the main reason I didn't leave him was because I couldn't exist as the wife of a traditional Cherokee, living in a tiny cabin and working crops and dressing hides. I couldn't go back to that life. The Boudinots and Charley Marley had shown me something more, and I wouldn't return.

Strong Hickory knew that. Neither of us said it, though, for to speak the words would shatter our system of idyllic trysts in a tiny cabin in a cedar grove.

Bartholomew accompanied other members of the Treaty Party to Washington City, where they would present their case, and I saw Strong Hickory every day. "You're going to wear that horse out while your husband's off serving the nation," Pepper Rodham said venomously. "We may have to get you a younger one, so you won't miss a day. Of riding, I mean." I ignored him. He wanted me to feel like a whore, and he succeeded.

John Ridge wrote a message for Congress stating the intentions and beliefs of the Treaty Party. On February 4, 1835, Henry Clay of Kentucky, the staunch friend of the Cherokees, read it to the Senate. Even he admitted that the Cherokees must move west. After that, I couldn't understand how anyone believed we had a chance of staying on our lands.

"Sir," Clay said to the presiding officer, "it is impossible to conceive of a community more miserable, more wretched. Even the lot of the African slave is preferable, far preferable, to the condition of this unhappy nation. The interest of the master prompts him to protect his slave, but what mortal will care for, protect the suffering injured Indian, shut out from the family of man?"

The three-way struggle among the Treaty Party, Ross's National Party and the U.S. continued.

The U.S. and the treaty men began negotiating a "preliminary treaty," but Ross countered with a proposal to sell the Cherokee lands for twenty million dollars. Jackson labeled the offer mere filibustering.

All right, Ross said, then he was willing to let the U.S. Senate set the sale price. Five million dollars, said the Senate. But then Ross began crawfishing, so the U.S. resumed negotiations with the Treaty Party.

That led to a provisional agreement, in accord with the Senate's assessment. The Cherokees would receive $4,500,000 for exchanging their lands in the East for thirteen million acres in the West. They would receive an additional eight hundred thousand acres in the West, worth five hundred thousand dollars, to make the sum total five million dollars. They would get a perpetual annuity for schools, as well as subsistence and other benefits. It was at that time, of course, merely a piece of paper.

On a spring day in 1835, Samuel and Ann Worcester and their children departed for the West. The Cherokees couldn't win their battle against the whites in the East, Samuel said. Therefore, he would be settled when the others arrived. Various Cherokees had migrated west since the 1790s, some because of dissatisfaction with the federal government's civilizing policies, and they were called the Old Settlers or the Cherokees West. Worcester would get to know them, and he would minister to the Eastern Cherokees when they crossed the Mississippi. Samuel told Elias that when the Boudinots removed, the men would resume their intellectual and spiritual collaboration in the West, but their voices trembled when they spoke their assurances.

"I can bear to see you go only because I know I will join you," Harriet said to Ann, but Ann couldn't answer, and each sobbed on the other's shoulder.

Bartholomew and I stood on the porch of the Boudinots' house while the Worcesters waved goodbye. They would travel in Bartholomew's carriage to Ross' Landing on the Tennessee River where they could board a boat. Pepper Rodham, the driver, nodded to my husband that all was well for the trip, but he ignored me.

I wept as the carriage pulled away. Bartholomew put his arm around my shoulders, and I was surprised to see that he was crying, too. "It's terrible for them," he muttered. "Can you imagine how it will be for the mass of Cherokees?"

At that moment the human aspect, the tragedy of removal was branded into Bartholomew Bramlett's brain. It affected actual men, women and children; it wasn't just something to be drawn up on paper and argued for or against. If one family's departure could be so depressing, what would it be like when thousands of Cherokees exited the land of their ancestors, destined for who knows what?

Levi drove us home. We rode for perhaps half an hour before my husband spoke. "I sat there in his office in Washington City and drank coffee with him," he said. "He talked about the weather and about farming. He asked if I had any good horses. He invited me to visit him and see his horses when he's at his home near Nashville. Perhaps we could fish, he said. Fish.

"When you ponder the evil in this, you think he must be some scaly monster from hell, a serpent who breathes fire, but he's just an old white-headed man who laughs and cries and eats and sleeps and blows his nose like you and me. A man can do much harm to so many other people. Just a regular man. That makes evil all the more sickening."

"What?" I asked. "Who?"

"Jackson," he said. "Andrew Jackson. The hero of Horseshoe Bend. The hero of New Orleans. The Great Father. The president of the United States."

I didn't answer. I didn't know what to say. I drew nearer to Bartholomew, hoping to comfort him. I pulled our blanket over his shoulders, but he didn't seem to notice. It was springtime, but in an open buggy I welcomed the cover.

"He shouldn't live," Bartholomew said. "He shouldn't serve his term and then just go home to the Hermitage and live out his days in comfort while poor Indians suffer."

"I love you," I said. I meant it. I didn't know him, but I did love him.

Finally, a few miles from our home, we rounded a bend, and I wouldn't look at the cabin where I had been meeting Strong Hickory for more than a year.

Bartholomew gazed at it. "In some ways I have been a poor husband to you, Nancy," he said. "I wish it were otherwise."

So he had found out. I was mildly startled, but not shocked. "In other ways you have been a very good husband to me," I said.

I patted him on the knee, but he again set in on talking about Andrew Jackson.

CHAPTER 29

I wondered if the dead could look down upon us from heaven. Perched up there where everything was perfect, where they didn't always have to be worrying about what sin they were committing, could they spy on us mortals and shake their heads in disgust when we messed up?

Was Charley Marley watching as I slipped into the expensive riding clothes Bartholomew bought for me, and an hour later as I removed them to have sex with another man?

There were times Charley had reminded me he was not just my husband, he also was my pastor. There had been times when I reminded myself of that, too. Charley was never one to say I had done right when I had done wrong.

What would he say now? I wondered if he had acquired in heaven some extraordinary depth of understanding that would cause him to say, "Nancy, a twenty-year-old woman has needs, and Bartholomew doesn't even attempt to satisfy yours. He hasn't for a long time now. So you are justified in what you are doing." Or I wondered if he would simply say, "Nancy, you are acting like a whore, and I'm disappointed in you. So is God. You were a preacher's wife, girl."

As I lay in my young lover's arms at our cabin I decided that if I was whoring, I was whoring against him, not Bartholomew. It wasn't my husband who was being wronged when I slept with Strong Hickory. It was Strong Hickory who was being wronged when I kissed him goodbye and left him alone in the little cabin and returned to the cold pink marble mansion. I wasn't having sex with Bartholomew, but what I was doing was worse; I was taking his money not to have sex with him.

"He knows, and he didn't strangle you?" Strong Hickory said when I told him of Bartholomew's remarks when we passed the cabin. "That's all he said?"

"That's all he said," I assured him. "He's on a crusade. His mind is on higher matters than me."

"There are no higher matters than you," Strong Hickory said, kissing my eyes.

A funny thought popped into my mind, and I smiled. "When the knights of old would go on a crusade, they would fit their fair ladies with chastity belts. Bartholomew doesn't care enough to buy me a chastity belt."

"What?" Strong Hickory said.

"Nothing."

"I ought to kill him," Strong Hickory growled. "I ought to stick my knife in his belly, and then I'd have you all to myself."

"Oh, shut up," I said, and I got out of bed and began dressing. "Don't ever make an ignorant remark like that again."

"Come back to bed and I won't."

Well, if your husband won't even protest your adultery, it is flattering to have your lover offer to kill for you. So I did get back in bed.

Bartholomew was at home when I got there. He sat in a rocker on the veranda, inspecting the hilly vista before him. "Nancy, my dear," he greeted me. I'm sure he knew where I'd been, but he stood and kissed me on the cheek and asked me to join him. How could he kiss me when he knew Strong Hickory had been kissing me minutes before? I felt revulsion for him. I was right when I said it was Strong Hickory, not Bartholomew, I was whoring against.

Rachel brought us hot tea. Always there was Rachel. She, too, knew where I had been. Everyone on the plantation knew where I had been. Rachel smiled sweetly, sympathetically, at Bartholomew. She looked at me as if I were a centipede crawling across her skirt. "Lemon? Cream?" she asked curtly, as if she might have been speaking to the centipede. She knew I took neither, but it was an opportunity to remind me of her disapproval by the tone of her voice.

"Bartholomew, you must sell Rachel," I demanded, the words surprising even me.

"What?" he stammered.

"Rachel must go. You should be able to get a good price for her and her boys."

"Why, Rachel is like that big oak yonder. She is part of the place."

"Rachel is an insubordinate slave," I said. "Rachel acts as if I were a pile of cowshit, something distasteful, but something she has to put up with."

Rachel stood as still as a statue. Her smirk had disappeared. Her mouth was open in amazement.

"Rachel is a beautiful woman," Bartholomew blurted. "If I sold her I couldn't sleep at night for thinking about what might be happening to her."

"You know what's happening to me, and you don't have any trouble sleeping," I said. "That's all you want to do at night, sleep."

"I'll have to ponder this," Bartholomew said. "I'm terribly busy right now. Jackson is at the Hermitage, and I'm going to accept his invitation to visit him. I'll be leaving before daybreak tomorrow."

I knew he was stalling. I'll have to ponder this. It was what he always said when he didn't want to deal with something. But at least I had Rachel at bay for the time being. No acid words were coming from her mouth. "May I be excused?" was what she said.

And I was genuinely impressed that my husband was going to be the house guest of the President of the United States. It was hard to be angry with a husband who was about to leave for the Hermitage.

"What do you think it will be like?" I asked Bartholomew, breaking the tension.

"I think it will be a big white mansion that houses a little white man," he said. "Little in his regard for his red brothers, that is."

"What will you talk about?"

"I'm going to talk to him about his lack of regard for his red brothers," Bartholomew said. "I don't think we'll have time to talk about much else."

I thought it a cryptic remark. "You said you'd talk about horses, even go fishing," I reminded him.

"There won't be time for that," Bartholomew said.

I wanted to talk about his visit to the Hermitage, share his excitement—but he wasn't excited, and he kept changing the subject. Finally, I hushed, and he said, "What do you think is over those hills, Nancy?"

"I know what's over those hills. The village where I lived as a girl. The Oostanaula. New Echota."

"And it goes on and on, this round earth," he whispered, "until it comes back to us. So you and I are over those hills."

"In a sense, yes."

"No, not in a sense. In actuality. You and I are over those hills."

"All right."

"Evil is that way," Bartholomew said, still holding a full teacup. "You can't escape it. No matter how far you ran, you would come upon it again. We must try to stamp it out, not run from it. Our Christian God—Charley's Christian God—isn't in charge of this world; Satan is. But we must try to make it more habitable for God's people. We must do what we can."

There was profound sadness in his voice—confusion, fatigue. He was forty years old and looked sixty. I thought the man needed a good session with a woman in the worst way, and I said, "Bartholomew, let's go to bed."

"We're over those hills yonder," he said. "It seems so weird, but it's true."

We didn't say anything else for nearly an hour, and then I went inside and read a book.

I slept fitfully that night. I kept waking up and feeling disoriented and dropping back off to sleep. It was nearly nine a.m. when I finally got up.

On my bedside table was a sheet of paper, folded, with my name on the outside. I'd read it later. I had to have a cup of coffee.

I took the paper with me to the kitchen. Rachel wasn't there, and I didn't call her. I didn't want to see her anyway, and I didn't want her to see me so disheveled in my nightclothes, not on that particular morning.

I wouldn't have sold Rachel. She was a beautiful woman, and I couldn't have stood the thoughts of what might have happened to her in the hands of a cruel master, either. But she didn't know that, and for the time being, I thought, she could just squirm.

I made my own coffee, strong. The aroma squared my shoulders, and the taste cleared my head. I unfolded the piece of paper and began to read. It was from Bartholomew, and it said:

"My Dearest Nancy,

"It is after eleven o'clock, and the only sounds are the night sounds of the forest. You are sleeping soundly, I hope. So is most everyone else on the plantation. I will soon go to bed and sleep my usual three or four hours. I will order myself to get up very early and, as you know, I can will the hour of my awakening. It is a handy, if amusing, talent.

"I have lied to you. It is not a lie of commission, but one of omission, like the sins Charley used to talk about on those hopeful Sunday mornings when the church was new, when the copper steeple still reflected the sun and the smell of paint still burned our nostrils.

"I told you I was going to the Hermitage to visit Andrew Jackson. That is true, but there is more. I am going to assassinate the president. A small pistol will be hidden in my armpit and another behind my knee when I enter his home.

"I will, indeed, lecture him about his lack of regard for his red brothers, and then I will shoot him.

"I will not, of course, be able to escape. I will be shot—either by Jackson's men or by myself. I promise you one thing—I will not be taken alive.

"What purpose will this serve? It will rid the world of an evil man, which to me seems a sufficient purpose. But it also will call worldwide attention to the plight of the Cherokees. John Ross will denounce me as a Treaty Party fanatic, and the Ridges and Elias and my other colleagues will say my deed did not reflect their wishes, but the world will notice.

"Eliminating Jackson, of course, will not save the Cherokees from removal to the West. Jackson's man Van Buren will become president, and he will merely carry out the Chicken Snake's wishes in that regard. Anger among the whites may even speed removal."

Then there was a space, and the note continued in a more agitated scrawl.

"Nancy, I was very tired, and I intended to finish this letter this morning. I made the mistake of leaving it on my desk. I thought Rachel was asleep with everyone else, but she had been watching from outside the door while I wrote it. When I left the room she read it.

"Rachel then demanded that I take her with me. She said she would reveal my plans if I didn't. I told her she faced death if she accompanied me, but she said she didn't care. She said she wouldn't want to live if I were dead.

"I see no alternative but to allow her to go with me to the Hermitage. God help her.

"Please believe that after you and I were married I was never unfaithful to you with Rachel.

"Nancy, I treasure my more than two years as your husband. I failed you in physical ways, but I always loved you, and your sweet face will occupy my final thought as death reaches out his dark hand for me.

"Your husband,

"Bartholomew."

I was as immobile as if I were dead. I couldn't put the letter down. My eyes were locked on Bartholomew's signature. I don't think they even blinked. My husband, who had once been the most logical and pragmatic and unemotional of men, was on his way to the Hermitage to kill the President.

When I could move, I screamed and threw the letter onto the floor. I told myself to run to my horse and ride to Strong Hickory and bury my face in his chest and shut out the world. I made it to the door, barefoot and in my nightclothes, willing strength into my arms so I could lift my saddle onto the back of my mare. But a reprimand from somewhere in my mind stopped me. At least have enough decency not to be in the arms of your lover when they kill your husband, it said.

I sat back down and took deep breaths and tried to compose myself. I couldn't just sit there and tremble. I had to do something. But what could I do?

Bartholomew had a huge head start, and I probably couldn't catch up to him. And if I did, then what? I couldn't physically stop him. I couldn't scream to bystanders that they must help because my husband was going to assassinate Andrew Jackson.

I could tell Pepper Rodham. If he could reach Bartholomew he could try to reason with him. It was unlikely that would be successful, but if it wasn't, Rodham could perhaps restrain him. But Bartholomew had written a private letter to me. He had trusted me. He would despise us both if we somehow thwarted his mission. And he probably would just attempt it again.

But I did run to Rodham. He was in the kitchen of his house, too, also drinking his morning coffee. He motioned for the shrieking woman before him to sit at the kitchen table, and then he read the letter.

When he was finished Rodham gazed out the window for what seemed forever, then he said, "Say a prayer for him. That's all we should do."

"That's all?"

"If he wants to kill Andrew Jackson, let him kill Andrew Jackson. Let Cousin Bartholomew have his way and go down in history."

"But we can't," I whimpered.

"Of course we can," Rodham said calmly. "That's some good jam Rachel made, and I baked the bread myself. It's warm as can be. Spread some and have breakfast with me."

"But why?" I asked.

"What happens if we stop him? Then he hates me and he hates you and he hates himself. He set out to complete this monumental act, and he didn't succeed.

A young slip of a wife and an overseer who isn't half as smart as him brought him down. Just let him go. Let him have his moment that children will learn about in school a hundred years from now."

"Is he insane?" I asked Rodham.

"We're all insane, to one degree or another. He simply found a cause, and took control of his life. There are worse things."

A certain calm comes with inevitability. I wasn't composed enough to eat bread and jam, but I did take a cup of coffee.

"So we just wait?" I said.

"We just wait."

When I had swallowed the last of the bitter coffee I said, "Do you hate me, Mr. Rodham?"

He shrugged and answered, "I wouldn't say hate. I didn't like the way you took over the plantation."

"There was much that needed to be corrected," I said.

"Maybe. But the way I looked at it, Bartholomew was just getting wealthier and wealthier, and the slaves were happy enough, and I was happy enough, and it seemed to me you could have been happy enough. What more could you have wanted that you didn't have?"

"I could have wanted a plantation that ran efficiently and produced as much as it should," I said.

"Should. Damn if that word doesn't cause more trouble than most any I can think of."

I was sorry I had asked him if he hated me. I could have taken it if he had said he hated me, but he was just brushing me off, like someone brushing a ladybug off his arm, not because he hated it but just because that's what one did with lady-bugs.

Rodham smiled and said, "Mrs. Nancy Swimmer Marley Bramlett, I knew that young girl who despised slavery so, and then I knew that young woman who took her frustrations out on the slaves. I knew that minister's devoted Christian wife, and then I knew Bartholomew's wife who was always riding away from here to crawl in bed with another man. I think you've got a lot of hypocrite in you."

"Damn you," I said. It was all I could think to say.

"Aw, I think the good in you outweighs the bad by a long stretch," Rodham said, drinking his coffee, his voice still just a dull buzz. "I think the good Nancy would whip the bad Nancy pretty handily if you could figure a way for them to arm wrestle. But you are an exasperating female."

"May I remind you that you work for me, Mr. Rodham," I stammered, because I couldn't think of anything intelligent to say.

He chuckled and patted me on the shoulder and said, "Well, maybe you should go report me to your husband. I expect he'll want to fire me."

I stammered some more. "I can fire you myself."

Rodham smiled that infuriating smile of his again and said, "It ain't going to matter after they kill Bartholomew. With him gone, your plantation won't be protected, and neither will I. Remember, I'm a white man working in Cherokee country against Georgia law. When Bartholomew and all his efforts toward getting the Cherokees to go west cease to be, the whites won't have any more use for you and me than for those coffee grounds. They'll swoop in here and take everything, including the rouge off your cheeks."

"Good day, Mr. Rodham," I said, and I returned to the mansion and flew into washing windows, dusting and mopping to try to occupy my mind.

The house was as clean as an angel's thoughts when, as sunset approached, I heard a knock on the door.

Two teenaged members of the Georgia Guard stood there, hats in hands. "Are you Mrs. Bramlett?" one asked in a shrill voice.

"Yes."

He couldn't look me in the eye. He looked over my shoulder and said, "I have the unpleasant duty of reporting that your husband has been killed."

Even though I suspected what was coming, the words took my breath. I nodded.

"Him and a nigger woman. We have their bodies on that wagon there, under that canvas."

I hadn't expected to ever see Bartholomew again. I assumed the authorities would keep the body of a man who killed—or attempted to kill—the president.

"And the President?" I muttered.

"Ma'm?" the boyish spokesman said.

"The President. How is the President?"

"The President of what?"

"The President of the United States."

"I don't know," he said, cocking his head quizzically. "I guess he's fine. Where do you want the bodies?"

Where indeed?

I had them take Bartholomew to the master bedroom and Rachel to her room. I gasped at the sight of my husband's body. He had been shot at least a dozen times.

The guardsmen stood with their arms behind them and their heads down as I wept. Finally, the spokesman took two steps forward and patted me on the shoulder. "I'm sorry," he said.

I dried my eyes and asked, "You don't know the President's condition?"

"No'm," he said.

The other one nudged him and said, "Tell her about Hosmer and Siggers."

The boy straightened himself and recited: "Our captain said tell you that your husband was a brave man, that he served his people well in urging them to remove to the West.

"Jed Hosmer and Emerson Siggers are the ones that killed him and the nigger. They are well known anti-removal men. They was headed the other way when they passed your husband on the road just this side of the Tennessee line. They recognized him, and they got to picking at him, and he fought back, and they shot him and the nigger.

"Nobody would have known who done it, but they went to a tavern and got drunk and started bragging about it. Somebody told our captain, and we arrested them."

He grinned and nudged the other boy, urging him to tell the rest, to share in the story. "They tried to escape," the other said, winking at me, "and some of the fellows had to shoot them."

"My husband wasn't shot at the Hermitage?" I said. My mind was too befuddled to grasp that Nashville was several days away.

"The Hermitage? That's Andy Jackson's house? Oh, no, ma'm," the spokesman said. "This happened right near the state line, on the Georgia side. That's why we're handling it."

I began to cry and laugh, simultaneously, hysterically. My poor, poor husband. He hadn't even gotten out of Georgia on his quixotic mission, much less to Andrew Jackson's home. My poor, poor Bartholomew.

Andrew Jackson himself sent me a message of condolence. I still have it. I keep it and Bartholomew's last letter in the same envelope. On a piece of pea-green stationary, the Chicken Snake wrote:

"My Dear Mrs. Bramlett:

"Please accept my condolences in your hour of bereavement.

"Your husband was a farsighted, earnest representative of the Cherokee people. I am sure that when the current crisis has ended and they have time to reflect, all will regard him fondly and with gratitude and respect.

"Certainly he had my gratitude and respect. Moreover, I counted him a personal friend. As he no doubt told you, I had invited him to the Hermitage, and I was looking forward to his paying me a call some day. I shall always regret that he never set foot in my home. I'm sure I would have enjoyed the visit.

"I'm sorry I was not able to attend his funeral, but the business of state was pressing, as I'm certain you understand.

"Sincerely,

"Andrew Jackson."

CHAPTER 30

Bartholomew had been dead eight days when six work wagons stopped in the half-circle driveway in front of my house. Ten scruffy white men, each armed with a shotgun, set their brakes and stepped down.

I was sitting in a rocker on the veranda reading. "Hidy," one said. "We want your slaves."

"What?"

He repeated himself, as matter of factly as before.

"By whose order?" I asked.

"I guess by this here's order," he said, patting the shotgun.

"You mean you're just going to steal them?"

"Yes'um."

"The quarters are over there, behind those oaks," I said.

Pepper Rodham was right, I was a hypocrite. My slaves were probably going away to a worse life than they had experienced on the plantation, and I feared for them, but I was instantly pleased to no longer be a slave mistress. A burden was being lifted from my conscience, even if I would feel guilt because I experienced such relief.

The whites marched the women from cabins and the men from the fields and herded them in front of the mansion. I had allowed Rachel's two sons, Peter and Thomas, to continue to live in her room in the big house, but they had been fishing with other boys in the creek that ran through the slave quarters, and they were rounded up, too. When they tried to run to me, two of the white men caught their shoulders from behind.

Rodham joined me on the porch. I continued to rock, and he put his hand on the back of the chair and watched, not protesting. He wasn't a man who wasted words, and he knew anything he said would be wasted. The white man assigned the slaves to the six wagons, mixing the men and women and children, trying to prevent two men from sitting beside each other. A white man sat at the back of each wagon. The whites made sure their cargo saw the shotguns, as well as the holstered pistols at their sides. The slaves were frightened but silent.

When they all were in place I walked to the edge of the porch and said, "People, you are being kidnapped by these men. There is nothing I can do about it. I assume you will be taken to another farm or farms, or perhaps you will be sold. I just don't know. I had never even seen these thieves until a few minutes ago. I appreciate your loyalty to my husband and I wish you well."

"Good luck," Rodham said.

I didn't know anything else to say.

"Good day, ma'm," the spokesman for the kidnappers said, and the wagons rolled from the driveway and onto the road and around a bend and out of sight.

"Well, I guess I'll be off to Augusta," Rodham said. "You won't be needing me any more. I think I'll start this afternoon and get a few miles in before nightfall."

He was surprised when I hugged him. But I wanted him to remember me as fondly as possible. "Thank you," I said. "For everything. You are a good person."

Dear, sweet Harriet Boudinot had assured me she believed Georgia would allow me to remain in my home until the exodus to the West began. After all, Bartholomew had been a leading advocate of removal. But I knew better, and so did Rodham. We didn't even have to speak the words. Bartholomew was of no further use to them, and the plantation of the richest man in the Cherokee Nation would be a prize plum. I knew I would be evicted.

It happened two days after the slaves were stolen, ten days after my husband was murdered. A "fortunate drawer" in the lottery, who coincidentally was the brother of a politician, showed up to claim the house and land.

He was accompanied by a man of the green bag with a sheaf of official papers who did the talking, but he didn't need the lawyer. I was reconciled to being kicked out. "Help yourself," I said, and I went upstairs and packed a few clothes.

"Where are the slaves?" the lawyer demanded when I came back down. His client, a thin little man in his fifties whose glasses threatened to fall off the end of his nose, nodded vigorously, but he didn't speak.

"We've never had any slaves," I said. "I've always done all the work myself. I plowed the fields, planted, harvested."

The little man looked desperately at the lawyer, who roared, "Impertinence!"

"You're too late for the slaves," I said. "Some other thieves beat you to them a couple of days ago. They herded them into wagons at gunpoint and drove away with them to God knows where."

"My client is not a thief!" the lawyer thundered as if he were trying to impress a jury. "He is quite within the laws of the State of Georgia."

"To hell with your client, and to hell with Georgia," I said wearily.

"Tell him to enjoy his newfound wealth. I never really understood why anyone would build a pink house, anyway."

And with that I climbed onto my horse and rode up to the knoll where I had buried Bartholomew and Rachel side by side. I kneeled on pine needles, said a prayer and told them goodbye. Then I headed down the dusty road to Strong Hickory's cabin.

He had asked to move in with me after Bartholomew's death, but I wouldn't let him. Now I was moving in with him. His house was tiny, and the chimney didn't draw well, and the puncheon floors were full of splinters, but at least it wasn't pink.

I washed Strong Hickory's clothes, cooked for him, worked his garden and kept his house. Yes, I even tanned the hides he brought home—not because I had to, but because it gave me something to do. I dressed in homespun, because to have worn the fine clothes Bartholomew had bought me would have been absurd in that setting.

My father was delighted. His daughter, in his mind at least, was a traditional Cherokee woman who had caught herself a traditional Cherokee man. He laughed and made jokes and patted Strong Hickory on the back when we visited. At last he had himself a real son-in-law after enduring those two radicals, Charley Marley and Bartholomew Bramlett.

Except that the fellow in the breechcloth wasn't really his son-in-law. Strong Hickory asked me to marry him, but I said no. I loved him—I especially loved the fact that he loved me so ardently—but I still wasn't going to take a traditional Cherokee as my husband. Staring Otter was able to assign that little fact to a corner of his mind.

Strong Hickory hunted, and I gardened and picked berries and gathered the other fare the woods had to offer, and we ate well. Bartholomew's wealth had been mostly in crops and cattle and his house and its furnishings, but there had been gold, too, and I had dug it up from the yard of the mansion and buried it in the yard of Strong Hickory's cabin. We didn't splurge. There was little to splurge on, and I didn't want to call attention to myself as a rich widow, not with brigands roaming the Cherokee country, men who would as soon kill an Indian as crack a walnut.

If the comforts of the plantation were missing, the comfort of being in the arms of a hot-blooded man was not. Strong Hickory and I drew on mutual passion, and we were as contented as Cherokees could be in that tempestuous era.

With Bartholomew dead, I was out of the mainstream of Cherokee politics. I visited Elias and Harriet Boudinot occasionally to keep up with what was going on, and I learned that Elias and John Ridge and others of the Treaty Party were determined to force an agreement of removal between the Cherokees and the U.S. into being—even if it was fraudulent.

They were working with a Jackson henchman, Reverend John F. Schermerhorn, a retired Dutch Presbyterian minister from New York whom the Ross supporters nicknamed the Devil's Horn. The first time I ever saw Schermerhorn, at New Echota, he patted me on the rear. Elias was embarrassed, and Strong Hickory was about to strangle him, but I talked my lover into forbearing, since these were historical times and the reverend might even be an historical personage.

His persistent but clumsy attempts at seduction had Cherokee women shaking their heads in amazement and amusement. One couldn't argue with the Ross people when they called him a buffoon.

But he got his treaty.

When a legitimate council at Red Clay in October, 1835, failed to produce a treaty, Schermerhorn called a meeting of his own for New Echota in December, audaciously declaring that any Cherokee who failed to attend would be considered in agreement with whatever transpired. He promised free blankets and subsistence money to those who would come.

A tiny percentage of the Cherokee population showed up, and many of them seemed more excited about the prospect of getting blankets than about politics. "Ross told them to stay away," Elias said as he and Harriet and Strong Hickory and I ate supper at the Boudinots'. "But it won't matter. A treaty will be signed."

I had convinced Strong Hickory of what I believed, that the Cherokees' only chance to survive as a people was to escape the Georgians and move West, but I couldn't look him in the eye and tell him this treaty was anything more than what it was—a bogus document contrived by a group of men who simply declared themselves to represent the Cherokees, just as he and I might declare ourselves able to fly.

This was a dirty piece of work, and seeing Elias and Major Ridge involved in it made me uncomfortable. Yet, I believed the ends justified the transparent means.

"This is what Christians do?" Strong Hickory asked as Elias explained the treaty over the sparse meal that Harriet had prepared.

Elias and Harriet didn't like Strong Hickory, but for my sake they had invited us to spend a few days at Christmas with them. They were put off by his loud, intractable devotion to the old ways. They found him boorish. They didn't approve of my living in his cabin without benefit of matrimony. They didn't answer.

I knew Strong Hickory's barbed question really was aimed at me. I had tried for years to convince him to become a Christian. Any time he could catch me in something (except having sex with him) that might be un-Christian, he wanted to discuss it.

"This treaty doesn't sound like a very Christian piece of work," he persisted.

Harriet was tired, worried, probably ill. She put her napkin over her eyes and began to weep. The best Christian I had ever known was listening to her husband being insulted by a rude guest. She was close to the breaking point.

"Go home," I told Strong Hickory.

"Now?"

"Now."

"It's late."

Harriet had invited us to stay the night—in separate bedrooms. It was after eight o'clock. "Go home anyway," I said. "I'll be there in a few days. I'm going to help Harriet with the house, with her children."

Harriet straightened up, wiped her eyes and said, "Oh, no, I don't want you to go, Strong Hickory. I'm just weary. I'll be fine."

"Either you go or I'll go," I said calmly. "And if I go it will be to my parents' house, not yours."

"Oh, no," Harriet said, but Strong Hickory shrugged, and he went upstairs and got his things and got on the horse that had brought us and headed into the night.

"I'm sorry," Harriet said.

"Don't be. He can be a terrible lout when he wants to be."

I made my protesting hostess go to bed. I played with the children and then made them go to bed, too. I washed the dishes and cleaned up the house, and when I looked at the clock in Elias's study it was after one a.m.

He sat on a worn purple sofa in the room where he had written his most brilliant editorials. The flame of the oil lamp was low. He motioned for me to join him.

"She is worn out," Elias said as I flopped on the other end of the sofa. "She could be in New England, living a comfortable life, but she is in the Cherokee Nation, bearing the insults of people she only wanted to help. Just today some Indians shouted curses at her when she was hanging out clothes."

"Strong Hickory can be a fool," I said.

"At least he wore clothes tonight," Elias said, and we laughed. I think we both sensed we should retire on that small note of levity, for we simultaneously said, "Well, I'm going to bed." We laughed at that, too.

I slept like the dead. It was nice not having to listen to Strong Hickory's snoring for a change.

The next evening, that of December 29, 1835, a committee of twenty that was formed "to represent the Nation" repaired to Elias's home to hear read a final, formal treaty which they would discuss and then sign. My friends Elias and Major Ridge were among the number.

I was in the bedroom above the parlor. I could hear the rise and fall of voices. I moved the corner of the rug back and plastered my ear to the floor, but I couldn't understand anything.

So I put on my shoes and coat and slipped outside and pressed the same ear to the fogged-over glass of the parlor window. The cold wind blew up my nightgown and took my breath.

I couldn't hear any better from there, and I was about to go back inside when a pair of hands grasped my ribs and a voice yelped, "Got you, Nancy!"

Elias guffawed and said, "I couldn't resist it."

"You scared me to death," I said. "I don't know whether I'm more frightened or embarrassed."

"Someone spotted the outline of a head at the window and motioned to the rest of us," he said. "We thought it might be a spy from the other side."

I was mortified. "I don't know what to say. You caught me."

"It's all right. Don't worry about it."

So I went back to my room. But I couldn't sleep, and I put on my clothes, and when I heard the meeting breaking up I went downstairs. It was after midnight.

The Treaty of New Echota had been signed. It would cede all Cherokee lands east of the Mississippi to the United States for five million dollars, and land in the West would be made available to the departing Indians. The terms were essentially those that had been written into the provisional treaty in Washington the winter before—essentially those that had been turned down at the legitimate Cherokee council at Red Clay in October.

I stood in the hall and watched the solemn men file out of the house, their eyes straight ahead as if they could see far away, into the darkness.

Old Major Ridge was the last to leave. He stopped and patted me on the head, a vacant look on his face. For a moment I wondered if he recognized me. Then he said, "Nancy Swimmer, I have signed my death warrant."

Andrew Jackson was graciously hosting John Ross at the White House when a note from the good reverend, Commissioner John F. Schermerhorn, was handed to the President. It said:

"I have the extreme pleasure to announce to you that yesterday I concluded a treaty. Ross, after this treaty, is prostrate. The power of the Nation is taken from him as well as the money, and the treaty will give general satisfaction."

Jackson curtly informed Ross of what had happened and showed him the door.

Of all the treaties that had been negotiated with the Indians, this one was the most ridiculous. It didn't "give general satisfaction." Many white Americans were embarrassed that their government could be involved in such a sorry transaction. Daniel Webster, Henry Clay, Edward Everett and David Crockett stood against it in Congress. John Quincy Adams called it "an eternal disgrace upon the country." If he had still been president, the Treaty of New Echota no doubt would have been scrapped.

But he wasn't president. Andrew Jackson was. The Senate approved the treaty by one vote, and Jackson proclaimed it law. The last of the Cherokees were to be on their way west in two years.

I turned twenty-one on January 8, 1836, less than two weeks after the Treaty of New Echota was signed. My mother wanted to celebrate, but I wouldn't allow it. It was no time for celebration. I believed the treaty was necessary, but I wasn't happy about it. An amputation may be necessary, but it isn't desirable. Who would want to celebrate a birthday a few days after having a leg removed?

"You've lived a lifetime in twenty-one years," Harriet said.

"Or two," I said.

Had it really been seven years since I married my gorgeous Charley Marley? Was I really twice widowed? Had the girl who was born into an ordinary Cherokee family really squeezed her way into a white lifestyle and a luxurious mansion only to be living now in a hut with her unlearned childhood sweetheart?

Had the girl who hated slavery really become a slaveowner?

But musing about the past was a luxury best enjoyed in a civilized country. Spurred by the treaty and the sure knowledge the Indians must leave, Georgians swarmed into the Cherokee Nation like a plague, raping women, killing men, stealing livestock and evicting families. Some charged Indians rent to stay in cabins they had built with their own hands.

John Ross was not prostrate, as Schermerhorn had written. He told the people to ignore the treaty, which he insisted was null and void, and he continued to seek legal redress.

The Chicken Snake dispatched General John Ellis Wool and seven thousand federal troops to occupy the Cherokee Nation. They were to keep down violence, but their presence also was to "overawe the Indians and frown down opposition to the treaty."

Wool had been a career officer for twenty of his fifty-two years, but his heart was torn by what he found. He wrote to Secretary of War Lewis Cass:

"If I could, and I could not do them a greater kindness, I would remove every Indian tomorrow beyond the reach of the white men, who, like vultures, are watching, ready to pounce upon their prey and strip them of everything they have or expect from the government of the United States. Yes, sir, nineteen-twentieths, if not ninety-nine out of every hundred, will go penniless to the West."

John Ross sent a memorial of protest to Congress—with Wool as the messenger—and Jackson reprimanded the general for delivering it. It was "insulting" to him and to the people of the United States, and since there was no longer a Cherokee Nation, there certainly was no leader of a Cherokee Nation.

One early summer day a blond young man from Augusta rode up on a gray horse, greeted Strong Hickory and me with a nervous smile, and said he had come to claim his one hundred and sixty acres. He believed this was the right plot of land.

"Then claim it," Strong Hickory said, taking his stance before the doorway of our cabin, squaring his shoulders and placing his hands on his hips.

"What?" the young man said.

"Claim it. As soon as you kill me, it's all yours."

"But I have this paper," the man said, his voice quivering.

"Fine. Claim it," Strong Hickory said as if they might have been discussing the cloudless day.

"But I didn't come to kill anybody," the man said, this time choking on his words. "They just said y'all would be leaving for the West anyway, and this place was mine since I drew it in the lottery." He gulped hard. "I'm an advertising salesman for a newspaper, not a killer."

I walked to Strong Hickory's side, looked deep into his eyes, and said in a low voice. "If you kill him, they will hunt you down and shoot you. If you don't give the place to him, they will put you in prison. How can I get along without you?"

He gazed at the young man for a full minute, then he said, "You are lucky. This was almost your last day on earth."

So we left. We stayed a few days with my parents while Strong Hickory and The Bull and some other villagers felled some trees and built us another cabin in the forest.

But many trees were being cut down in the Cherokee Nation in those days. They were used to build pens in which to imprison the Indians before we were dispatched to the West. Tall logs were placed picket style in the ground to create stockades that were open to the weather. When the time came we were to be herded into those "forts," and those who survived disease and exposure would begin the trek toward the Mississippi.

Harriet Boudinot would never make the trip. She would remain in the Cherokee Nation.

In less than nine years she had given birth to three sons and three daughters. In May of 1836 her seventh baby, a boy, was born dead. Her strength failed steadily, and on August 15 the Raven Mockers, those witches of Cherokee legend who draw their sustenance by stealing the lives of others, visited the Boudinot home.

I was there when Harriet died. She was just thirty-one years old. She suffered terribly during her illness. She feared she hadn't done enough for Jesus, that her faith hadn't been strong enough. She had done more for Jesus than anyone else I ever knew. Her faith had been strong enough that she had endured the bitterness of family members and friends to marry an Indian and leave New England to serve the Cherokees in the South.

I knew one thing—if Harriet Boudinot didn't make it to heaven, there was no hope for the rest of us.

She died on a hot summer afternoon. An hour and a half later I stood on a knoll strewn with acorns and hickory nuts and watched the body of Harriet Gold Boudinot lowered into the ground. Nearby was the grave of Jerusha Worcester, who had lived less than six months, and the grave of Chief Pathkiller, who had lived eighty-five years. I wondered which one was the most fortunate.

"We seek rest beyond the skies," the inscription on Harriet's tombstone eventually read. I hoped we would find it, for there was precious little anywhere else I had ever been.

CHAPTER 31

On an evil night when lightning made incisions from heaven to earth and rain drummed the copper steeple and my heart was empty, I prostrated myself before the pulpit in Charley's church and in total darkness prayed—no, begged.

I envisioned the Cherokees freeing their two thousand black slaves and asking God for mercy. He granted it, for the example of the Indians' humanity softened the hearts of the Georgians, and they freed their own slaves and returned the Cherokees' land and bade them remain in the country of their ancestors. Red man and white and black would live in harmony forever.

But that wasn't what happened, of course. What happened was that Lewis Ross, the brother of Principal Chief John Ross, realized that the arduous work of clearing the land and building homes and planting crops in the country across the Mississippi would create a rich new market for slaves, so he bought five hundred more blacks in Georgia and sent them west.

At dusk, as the storm clouds had built on the horizon, I had been robbed. The same polite bandit who had led the kidnapers of my slaves appeared at the cabin Strong Hickory and I shared. He was accompanied by another man. "Good evening, ma'm," he said. "Looks like a bad 'un brewing, don't it. Hope that dead pine yonder don't blow over on your house. I want your gold, ma'm."

He explained that it had dawned on him that the widow of Bartholomew Bramlett would have some gold hidden away somewhere, and he wanted it, please.

"I don't have any gold," I said.

"I'll start with the little finger of your right hand and slice them off one by one until you tell us," his companion said, drawing a huge hunting knife.

"Paulas likes to cut people," the leader said. "I never got no kick out of hurting anybody myself. Live and let live, I always said. But everybody's different, and one thing I learned in life is that I can't make everybody else be like me. You better tell him, 'cause he'll surely delight in chopping off your fingers."

"That dogwood," I said. "Four paces back this way from that dogwood."

Paulas dug down three feet, and his shovel thudded against the iron box that held my gold. He shoveled furiously, and he grunted as he lifted the box from the earth. "Damn," he whispered when he opened it, "ain't that pretty. But I thought there would be more than this, rich as that old Indian was. Where's the rest buried?"

"That's all there is."

"Give me your hand," he said, drawing his knife from its scabbard.

"You'll just have to cut," I said. "There's no more."

"She's telling the truth," the polite one said. "Let's get."

"Not before me and her goes in that cabin for a little fun," Paulas said. "Might be two kinds of stabbing goes on."

"Me and the gold's leaving," the other said, the voice hard now.

Paulas analyzed the challenge, got on his horse and said, "Well, you're so anxious to go, let's go, but you can just wrestle the gold without no help, asshole."

The polite one sighed and tied the box with its heavy contents to his saddle, trying three times before he finally got it balanced on a blanket on his horse's back. "Goodbye, ma'm," he said, and they rode toward the storm clouds.

Strong Hickory and some friends were on an overnight fishing trip. I said a prayer of thanks that he hadn't been at home, and as I spoke the words I was overcome with a profound yearning. I had to see God, actually lay eyes on Him. I felt the panic of one searching the forest for a lost relative. I had to find my lost God. He had to acknowledge me.

He had to explain to me why He had made a world in which I could be twice widowed, a world in which his noblest creation, Harriet Boudinot, could die young, a world in which the whites could drive the Cherokees from their homeland. A world in which a person could enjoy amputating the fingers of another person.

So I ran through the woods to Charley's church and threw myself upon the floor and screamed for God to appear. He didn't, and finally I got up and wiped my eyes and walked home in the rain and thunder and lightning and wind and said that, logic be damned, I would be the last Cherokee to leave Georgia.

Major Ridge, John Ridge and Elias Boudinot were among the first to leave. Elias was accompanied by his new wife, a woman named Delight. Hundreds of members of the treaty faction, of course, wasted no time in heading for the new land beyond the Mississippi.

The Ridges and Elias had invited me and mine to accompany them. My parents, like so many Cherokees, still believed that John Ross would produce a miracle, so they sat tight. Strong Hickory knew better, but his parents, too, begged us not to leave. I had hoped I could change their minds, convince them that traveling with these people of means now would be preferable to falling in with the masses later. But after facing Paulas and his knife, I rejected common sense and obstinately vowed to stay where I was.

Major Ridge traveled by boat, John Ridge and Boudinot by carriage. They arrived none the worse for wear. In fact, Rollin Ridge, John's son with a literary bent, would one day describe the trip as "a zestful voyage of discovery among new flora and fauna." The journey by water took about a month, the journey by land about seven weeks. They settled in the vicinity of Honey Creek, in the northeast corner of the Cherokee lands.

The clock that had been wound by the Treaty of New Echota ticked—but traditional Cherokees ignored it. May 23, 1838, the deadline for voluntary removal, two years from the day the Chicken Snake had signed the treaty into law, arrived, and the Indians spoke not of leaving but of how handsome their knee-high corn was.

John Ross had stood with the thousands who lined Pennsylvania Avenue on March 4, 1837, watching the Chicken Snake and his successor Martin Van Buren pass in a carriage, headed for the Capitol and Van Buren's inauguration. Perhaps he even took some crumb of satisfaction in having outlasted Jackson as chief of a nation. But my decision to remain wasn't grounded in any hope that Ross could win out, or least of all, that Van Buren wouldn't be as implacable as Jackson on the removal question. Jackson was too old and ailing to consider a third term, but Van Buren was his hand-picked successor. My decision to remain was strictly one of obstinacy.

Still, I wasn't prepared for what happened.

Van Buren appointed General Winfield Scott to command a roundup of the Cherokees in Georgia, Alabama, Tennessee and North Carolina. He was a huge man who had faced Indians in the War of 1812, the Black Hawk War of 1832 and the campaign against the Seminoles of Florida in 1836. He loved military pagentry and so was called "Old Fuss and Feathers."

Scott had at his command seven thousand U.S. regulars and volunteers, including a regiment each of infantry, cavalry and artillery. He established headquarters in New Echota.

Numerous "forts" had been erected across the Cherokee Nation. They were simply open stockades made of vertical logs. The Indians would be imprisoned in these pens until they could be forwarded at regular intervals to emigration depots and thence on to the land beyond the Mississippi. Resistance by force, Scott warned the Cherokees, could lead only to bloodshed, perhaps war.

The presence of uniformed soldiers was wonderful, some of the more ignorant Cherokees guessed. The U.S. must have dispatched guardians to protect them from the Georgians.

But it was not wonderful. The soldiers swooped down upon the Cherokees like sharp-beaked birds upon harmless butterflies. Wherever a Cherokee was found, he or she was taken.

Children at play in the woods were whisked away to forts, their hysterical parents left to wonder what happened to them. Husbands were abducted from the field, never to return to their families. Wives cooking supper were prodded with bayonets and marched to stockades, their men coming home to find warm coals and uneaten food but no mates. Old people too sick to walk were left behind, unattended, to die. The bodies of those who perished marching to forts were dumped on the roadside for the buzzards.

A frightened boy bolted from his captors, and when he didn't respond to the order to halt, he was shot in the back. Well, hell, the assassin later said, how could he have known the lad was deaf and couldn't hear the command?

Frequently Cherokees on the march to the pens turned for one last glimpse of their homes and saw them burning, torched by the looters who followed the soldiers. Panicky Indians who knew the soldiers were on their way made bad bargains with whites, selling their cattle and other belongings for pennies. Some white scavengers dug up graves and robbed the dead of valuables that had been buried with them.

Word of the outrages spread, and those Cherokees who hadn't been arrested waited their turn. "We need to stay close together," Strong Hickory told me. "At least when they take one of us they will take us both."

A boy came to our cabin and said Staring Otter wanted to see us. We walked the half-mile through the forest to his cabin.

He was old, sick, cadaverous, lethargic. He could barely maintain control of his crutch. It was almost as if it were going to push his shoulder out of socket when he put his weight onto it. He couldn't have walked to New Echota, much less to Oklahoma.

We entered the cabin and found my mother and father seated at the supper table. She was weeping, but he was smiling, his head held high. "I love you, Nancy," he said mysteriously. "Strong Hickory, you have been a good husband for my girl. Now please come with me."

Mother and I and the man Staring Otter had made himself believe was my husband followed him up a rocky slope behind my parents' house. It was slow going, but he refused our help. We arrived at a cave that had served as a fox den, probably for several generations. It was barely large enough to accommodate an adult. When I was a little girl I had crawled in there in moments of stress and imagined it to be my mother's womb and me safe and yet unborn.

Except for a slit perhaps a foot wide, the entrance was sealed with rocks. More stones were piled outside. "Goodbye," Staring Otter said. He kissed his wife on the lips and kissed me on the cheek. He patted Strong Hickory on the shoulder.

Then he threw his crutch down the hill and sank to his knees and pulled himself into the cave.

We looked at Mother. "This is his tomb," she explained. "He wants to stay here, in the land of his ancestors. He wants you to finish sealing the entrance, Strong Hickory."

"I won't do it," Strong Hickory said, shaking his head frantically.

I could barely breathe. Strong Hickory would have to remove my father from the cave, I thought. The words were forming on my lips when I remembered Pepper Rodham's telling me we must not try to stop Bartholomew in his quest to assassinate Jackson. Indeed, I thought, why should my father be buried in the new land across the Mississippi? Or, what was more likely, along the trail that led to the Indian territory? If he wanted to remain in his homeland, he should remain.

A calmness came over me. "I will do it," I said, and I began edging the rocks into the opening. I smiled at my mother, and she wiped her tears and nodded, and each knew the other understood.

Strong Hickory watched with his mouth open, wringing his hands. When I placed the last stone I said, "Let's wait in the village, at Mother's cabin. She and your parents and you and I will be together when the soldiers come."

They arrived the next day, on foot, whooping and hollering, banging on cabin doors with their rifle butts. They assembled all the villagers inside Charley's church. We sat on the pews, as if we were attending a service—and I realized it was, indeed, Sunday morning. The soldier in charge stood in the pulpit and counted heads, his forefinger jabbing the air, his lips silently moving.

Finally, he said, "You are lucky. You have only to march to Fort Wool at New Echota. Many other Cherokees have had to walk much farther. You will not be allowed to take anything with you, for there is no time. You Cherokees ignored the law of the land for many months, and now this must be done on a hurry-up basis. It's your fault, so I don't want to hear any whining about it.

"We will march out of this church and directly to New Echota. No one will return to his or her cabin. Anyone trying to do so will be judged as attempting to escape. The penalty for attempting to escape is fifty lashes. That goes for man, woman or child."

Mother gripped my arm. Staring Otter had left her what he considered his finest bow. Evil spirits would be so impressed by its beauty and strength that they would stay away from her, he had said. It was in her cabin. She had to have it.

We were ordered from the church, and the march to New Echota began. "Do something," she whispered. "It's by the fireplace. It would only take a moment to get it."

As we neared her cabin, I turned to a young soldier walking beside me and whispered, "I just started, uh, you know, bleeding. Please let me run inside my cabin and get some cotton."

He was uncertain. "Oh, go ahead, I guess," he said.

In seconds I returned to the line, the bow in one hand and cotton in the other.

"What's this?" an officer yelled. "You ran away to get a weapon?"

"I went to my cabin to get cotton because I am bleeding down there," I said. "I picked up the bow because it has sentimental value to my mother, not to use it as a weapon. I don't have an arrow. That young man gave me permission."

The officer took the bow, splintered it over his knee, and glared at the young soldier. "Three minutes ago the lieutenant was telling them they couldn't take anything with them, and you're already countermanding his orders?" he roared.

The young soldier's lip quivered. "I didn't tell her she could do it," he said. "Not me. She's lying."

The officer ordered the Cherokees to halt. "Prepare to administer punishment," he told another man. Fifty lashes. This woman here. For attempting to escape."

"Yes, sir," he said. He led me to a tree, and with the help of two others forced my arms around it and tied my wrists. My cheek was against the bark, and he tore the blouse off my back.

"Everyone must watch," the officer said.

I heard Strong Hickory scream and the officer say, "Blow his brains out if he takes another step."

And so they horsewhipped me. I still have the scars on my back. I am told they stopped after nineteen lashes because the young soldier began bawling and admitted he had given me permission to enter the cabin. When I regained consciousness I was lying on the ground in the stockade at New Echota, my head in Strong Hickory's lap. He had covered my nakedness with his shirt, and he was rocking back and forth, stroking my hair and crying.

Fort Wool was an enclosure that I estimated to be one hundred and twenty-five feet square—and there was plenty of time for estimating. The log walls appeared to be sixteen feet high. In each corner was a raised guardhouse. There was no shelter except for what we could fashion from brush and limbs and canvas and cloth that the soldiers gave us.

A slow stream that was perhaps a yard wide flowed through the pen, and that was our supply of water for drinking and bathing. There were no provisions for sanitation. The excrement of hundreds of persons simply piled up, and the stench was awful. The ground smelled as if it were made of urine.

Each prisoner was given a daily ration of pork and flour, but few had cooking utensils. We ate the pork raw or poorly cooked. Fire was valuable, to be conserved, protected at all costs. Some sympathetic officers permitted the women to go outside the walls during the day to search for fruits and greens and medicinal herbs for babies. I have subsequently been told the conditions were much the same in other "forts."

The roundup of the Cherokees began on May 26, 1838, and was completed on June 20. It was said that fifteen thousand Cherokees were imprisoned.

Many of them despaired of their lives ever improving. Whiskey was smuggled in for those who could buy it, and drunkenness and brawling were common. Strong Hickory broke the jaw of a man who tried to drag me to his tent. Some young women sold themselves to the soldiers. They would leave the stockade and return a half hour later, eyes downcast, money in their hands to buy enough putrid brandy to induce an alcoholic stupor. Not all the soldiers paid; some simply chose their women and raped them.

An army doctor rubbed my lacerated back with a foul-smelling grease, and after three visits it got well. All I had to do was allow him to fondle my breasts. Strong Hickory would have killed him if he had known. Maybe he would have killed me, too, but I had to have treatment.

A white minister visited Fort Wool and conducted services. He received permission to baptize three Cherokees, two women and a man. When I told him I was the widow of a minister, he asked an officer if I might assist in the sacrament.

I led them to the swimming hole on New Town Creek in which Sophia Sawyer and I had once cavorted. I wanted to plunge beneath the water and magically resurface in that happier day.

But participating in the baptisms strengthened my spirituality, even if an armed guard was watching. When I said my prayer that night, I felt for the first time in weeks that God was really listening.

The heat was unrelenting, the food frequently spoiled and toilets non-existent. Dysentery, pleurisy, bilious fever, measles and whooping cough ravaged the stockades. The very young and the very old were most susceptible. Dr. Butler, the missionary who had been imprisoned with Samuel Worcester, estimated two thousand Cherokees died in the pens.

My mother was one of them. She died of the disease of heartsickness. She and Strong Hickory and I slept on pine straw under a narrow strip of canvas, and one morning I awoke to find her lying on her back, drenched in blood, her arms crossed upon her chest. She had found an arrow point and cut her wrists while we slept.

Two soldiers picked up the dead each morning, and when they arrived I asked them if they were Christians. They were, they said. Methodists. I told them I wanted Rain to have a Christian funeral. Their sergeant wouldn't allow it, they said. There were so many dead Indians, and there wasn't time for a service for each one. But they promised me they would dig an extra deep grave for Rain so the animals couldn't get at her, and one of them would speak a few words from his Bible, and the other would say a prayer, and they would scratch her name on a flat rock and drive it into the ground as a headstone. They later told me they did all that. I don't know whether they did or not.

Forced emigration—by water—began on June 6, 1838. One group survived without loss of life a scary trip over dangerous rapids, a trip in which a flatboat crashed. Another group had to switch to overland travel when its flotilla was grounded near Little Rock, and seventy of its eight hundred and seventy-five members perished from disease, exposure, fatigue and lack of water. Some hastened their departure from this earth by eating green peaches and green corn during a stop.

A crippling drought grasped the South that summer. Wells and springs dried up, and in some areas finding drinking water was a problem. The level of rivers subsided dramatically, and by the middle of June the upper Tennessee ceased to be navigable.

A strange thing happened. John Ross proposed to General Scott that subsequent emigration be conducted by the Cherokees themselves, on an honor system. Scott agreed, and in July he awarded the contract to conduct removal of the Indians to the Cherokee council.

It was a mark of the love most Cherokees had for John Ross that they never blamed him for their troubles, though it was obvious that if he had yielded earlier on the subject of removal much of their misery would have been averted. Now under tribal management, they were no longer prisoners in the stockades, and when Ross asked the people to present themselves for removal in October they agreed that they would.

But it was a relative freedom. Many had nowhere to go, so they remained in the stockades. Accompanied by his parents, Strong Hickory and I returned to our village, only to find every cabin burned. Charley's church was a heap of ashes, too. But the area was familiar, and we camped there. Strong Hickory and I swam naked in the Oostanaula and even managed a few laughs. I did not go to Staring Otter's tomb. I didn't even mention it, and neither did Strong Hickory.

>>>→ • ←<<<

CHAPTER 3 2

The Cherokees would travel to the new country by land. That was fine with them. The superstitious ones considered rivers and creeks to be paths to the underworld. Perhaps the Uktena, the serpent with supernatural powers, lurked in the next pool. Hadn't the earlier unfortunate experiences of those Cherokees emigrating by river been warning enough? If not, there were the more than three hundred Creeks who were killed when the steamboat that was transporting them up the Mississippi River collided with another craft and sank.

Besides, west was the direction taken by the spirits of the dead, and if one must go west, why tempt fate by traveling on water?

Not only did the Cherokees have faith in John Ross, so did General Winfield Scott. He assisted the chief and his men in assembling what they would need for the journey—six hundred and forty-five wagons, five thousand horses and oxen and standby vessels for river transportation for the seriously ill.

In the Cherokees' minds, Ross's intervention had rendered the exodus a movement of the Cherokee Nation rather than a march of individual prisoners. Ross packed their governmental records, their resolutions, their written laws, their beloved constitution. Their heritage would travel with them. Scott recognized a "unanimity of feeling" among the Cherokees and "an almost universal cheerfulness since the date of the new arrangement."

I've always believed Boudinot and the Ridges and the other members of the Treaty Party did right in fashioning the fraudulent Treaty of New Echota. They acted in what they perceived to be the best interests of the Cherokees. But I never felt that viewpoint required me to hate John Ross. I believe he, too, had the same motive, the welfare of the people. He believed that principle would win out—but he was wrong. So when he took over the removal of the Cherokees I changed my mind about being the last one out of Georgia. When he called, I came.

We assembled at Rattlesnake Springs, two miles from the Cherokee Agency in Tennessee. An area of perhaps ten square miles was choked with tents, wagons, oxen, horses and people. Smoke from campfires curled upward, pleasant to sight and smell. Children who couldn't comprehend what lay ahead frolicked among the wagons—children who would never reach the place that one day would take its name from the Choctaw word for "red people," okla-homma.

Strong Hickory and I had no wagon, no horse, no ox. We took no belongings except a small tent he fashioned of canvas and a few articles of clothing, including four pairs of comfortable deerskin moccasins each. We believed that to travel light was to travel right, that it was our best chance of surviving this murderous parade of nine hundred miles. His parents, The Bull and Sweet Melon, felt the same way.

The plan was for thirteen separate groups of about a thousand persons each to start for the new land in intervals of three or four days. Only the very old, the very ill and the very young would ride in the wagons; their space had to be utilized for cooking utensils, blankets, fodder for the horses and other necessities.

The first group started at noon on October 1, 1838, on an exodus that also had been or would be marked by the moccasin prints of Chickasaws, Choctaws, Creeks and Seminoles. It was a bright, sunny day. The wagons were in line, flanked by mounted braves chosen to keep the column and the people in order. Accompanying each detachment was a white physician and a contractor who was responsible for provisions.

A bugle sounded, and the first caravan, about a quarter-mile in length, began to move. Strong Hickory touched my arm and pointed to a man on a horse. Going Snake, his head white from eighty winters, was astride his favorite pony, and he broke from the ranks and to the front. He was a chief of the Cherokees, old, overcome by superior might—but still a chief of the Cherokees. I hoped I could hold my head as high, maintain my pride during what I knew would be a death march.

Three days later the second contingent, including Strong Hickory and his parents and me, left Rattlesnake Springs. Its leader was John Ross's brother-in-law, Elijah Hicks, the man who had replaced Elias Boudinot as editor of *The Cherokee Phoenix*. At the head of the column rode White Path, another venerable chief. Though ill, the leader of White Path's Rebellion of 1828 refused space in a wagon.

We crossed the Hiwassee River and proceeded northward. I struck up a conversation with Hicks, enjoying the advantage of knowing all about him while he had no idea I was a friend of Elias and the Ridges. He was cordial, intelligent. He told me all thirteen caravans would travel northwestward through Tennessee by way of Murfreesboro and Nashville, then through Kentucky and across the southern tip of Illinois into Missouri, then either westward through Springfield, Missouri, or southwestward through Arkansas, depending on the weather and other conditions.

"No doubt some groups will catch up to others and even pass them," he said. "Groups will send back warnings and reports of progress to those behind."

"How many will die?" I asked.

The question startled him. "I hope none will die," he said.

"I didn't ask how many you hope will die," I replied, oddly offended by his answer. "I asked how many will die."

"God only knows," Elijah Hicks said.

Fifteen days later, when we camped for the night after passing Nashville, Hicks stepped from his tent as I happened to be walking by. His lips were quivering as if he were about to cry, and he was breathing heavily. I was surprised he remembered me, but the agitated leader said, "You wanted to know how many will die. This should give you an idea. It's a message I'm sending to those who follow."

Written in Sequoyah's symbols, it said members of his group were suffering from lack of clothing, and he feared scores of them would inevitably fall victims of disease and die before reaching their destination.

"Indeed, when they passed through Nashville, forty or fifty were on the sick list, and four or five were afterward buried near the city."

I had seen men digging some of the graves. A woman held her dead baby in her arms, alternately screaming to the heavens and cooing to her child while her weeping husband shoveled the earth. In my mind's eye I could see Andrew Jackson, a few miles away in the Hermitage, old and ill but warm and comfortable, perhaps standing in front of a glowing fireplace, pouring a snifter of brandy. The procession kept moving, and the aggrieved left their dead in the earth and caught up as best they could.

Hicks handed the message to a brave who waited astride a pony. The rider nodded and galloped away. Hicks said nothing else to me and returned to his tent.

Strong Hickory and I slept under the stars when the weather permitted, in our tent if the night was chilly or if rain was falling. When raised, it formed an inverted V, barely three feet high. Inside was just room for us to lie side by side. Strong Hickory had thought to bring another piece of canvas to put on the ground, or we would have had to lie on one of the blankets we drew from the supplies in the wagons, and usually we needed both for cover. His parents bedded down in a similar arrangement, and each morning Sweet Melon would complain that she didn't sleep at all.

Our caravan overtook and passed the first one. There was a little good-natured teasing among friends in the two groups, but very little, for this wasn't a foot race among children. If any caravan couldn't keep up, it was because of misfortune, which might include illness, death, broken wagons or simply fatigue.

We reached the Cumberland River, south of the Kentucky border, having marked twenty-one days and two hundred miles on the road. My legs were as heavy as stumps. I was young; I could only imagine how the older ones felt.

A man stood in the seat of a wagon and shouted for the Cherokees to gather around. "What can they do to us if we just break up and disappear into the forest?" he asked in a pathetically desperate voice. "Let's do it."

Indeed, some already had. There were intermittent reports that individuals, couples, families had simply left the caravan to seek whatever lay beyond that pine grove or over that hill or across that stream. I noticed many heads nodding when the man suggested a mass mutiny.

So did Elijah Hicks. "We'll camp here," he shouted. "We'll take an extra day of rest before we move on."

Hicks and I became friends. I suppose chatting with a pretty young woman was a diversion. I had even told him of my friendship with Elias Boudinot and that I was the widow of a minister and of Bartholomew Bramlett. He knew of Bartholomew, "a worthy adversary," but not of Charley. Rather than turning him against me, his new knowledge of my background piqued his interest.

He showed me another message he was sending to the caravan behind ours. It read: "The people are very loath to go on, and unusually slow in preparing for starting every morning. I am not surprised at this because they are moving, not from choice, to an unknown region not desired by them. I am disposed to make full allowance for their unhappy movement."

I told The Bull about the message. The chief of our villagers had earned respect among other exiles with his sound judgment and his willingness to help those around him. When the Cherokees had had time to rest, he addressed them from a perch in a tall tree, telling them that a breakup of the caravan would only bring another roundup. We must keep our faces to the West; we must complete this journey. The murmurs I heard were murmurs of assent.

White Path was failing fast. He was forced to accept a place in a wagon, and though Hicks tried to keep it secret, the news spread. He died a few days later, and he was buried beside the trail near Hopkinsville, Kentucky. A wooden slab marked his grave, but there should be more, said The Bull. So beside it he erected a pole with a white flag. It would be a shrine for those Cherokees following us.

Hicks did stop the procession to bury White Path. "His history is the history of our nation," Hicks said in a brief eulogy. He asked me, a minister's widow, to say a prayer. I kept it brief, too, and then we moved on.

Hicks feared that the death of White Path would further dispirit the people. They were saddened, of course, but they remembered the old chief's courage, and his example seemed to energize them.

I was glad we were in the first caravan. The only graves we saw were those we dug. Each day the groups behind us were visited with the grim reminder that this was a death march of inconceivable proportions. I could only imagine the horror of being a sojourner in one of the backmost caravans.

The Bull was a robust man given to a little inoffensive boasting about his physique. On a cold, rainy day a wagon became stuck in the mud.

"Move," he said impatiently to a little fellow who was among a trio trying without success to lift a back wheel. The driver cracked his whip, and the wagon lurched forward. The Bull, red-faced and panting, fell flat on his belly in the mud, but he was laughing when he got to his feet. Then he winced, grasped his chest and fell again. The single doctor in our caravan arrived a few minutes later and, with no more emotion than if he had been commenting on the weather, pronounced him dead. But, then, he had pronounced many travelers dead since we had left Rattlesnake Springs.

Strong Hickory and I had to tear Sweet Melon from her husband's grave. She wanted to stay, to lie on the earth that covered him and die in that godforsaken spot.

She couldn't walk, and we requested a space for her in a wagon, which Hicks granted. "I don't suppose one more is going to matter," he said. So many were sick that room had to be made for them by removing fodder from the wagons. Then there were delays when some of the hungry horses fell ill from eating poison ivy.

Sweet Melon wouldn't speak, wouldn't eat, wouldn't even drink water. She had no wish to live, and in that condition she was easy prey for pneumonia. Four days after The Bull's death, she had joined him in what we Christians hopefully call Paradise. We buried her and six others that day, including an emaciated woman who didn't have the strength to survive the birth of a baby boy.

Our caravan came to a stop somewhere in Kentucky, the trail blocked by six armed white men. Hicks spoke to them, and then he turned to those of us at the front of the procession and said, "They say their boss owns this land. He wants seventy-three cents a wagon and twelve cents a horse for us to pass."

"He might just take that pretty gal instead," one of the men said, nodding toward me and laughing. Strong Hickory stepped toward him, cursing, but the men raised their rifles, and I grabbed his arm. "They'll shoot you for sport," I said. "Don't leave me alone."

Hicks paid them some forty dollars and we moved on.

I taught myself to think pleasant thoughts, to picture beautiful mountain scenery, to invent waterfalls and glorious flowered hillsides populated by the Little People. I was at Harriet Boudinot's table, feasting on turkey and a multitude of vegetables rather than our daily diet of pork and bread. I was delighting in intelligent conversation among the Boudinots and the Worcesters, and Sophia Sawyer was making us laugh, and Major Ridge was dazzling us with heroic tales. Once I learned to manipulate my mind in such a fashion, I could march toward oklahomma in a virtual trance.

One bright, fragrant spring day I was in Charley's church, and he was preaching with the magnificent force of a prophet when a voice said, "Well, if it isn't Mrs. Nancy Bramlett."

My fantasy evaporated, and I turned to see Pepper Rodham. He was smiling, he had lost considerable weight, and he appeared healthy, ruddy. "How are you making it, Nancy?" he asked.

"I'm making it," I said. "Strong Hickory hasn't been feeling well. One of the guards is an old hunting friend, and he is letting him ride his horse for awhile. He lost his father and his mother. What in the world are you doing here?"

"Well, as you know, I went back to Augusta. But I wasn't happy there. Things were too tame. I had grown used to the Cherokees, maybe even used to the turmoil. One morning I just woke up and said, 'I'm going west with the Indians.' And that's what I'm doing. I arrived late at Rattlesnake Springs, and I began traveling with a group that's fourth in line behind this one. I was doing all right, with nobody but myself to worry about, so I stepped it up, and here I am. Between the walking and the awful food, I've lost some of that belly. Had to cut three new holes in my belt. When we get to wherever it is that we're going, I'll never eat pork again."

I was pleased to see him. We had both loved Bartholomew Bramlett, and his presence reminded me of the days when I dressed in silk and ate from fine china on a table imported from France. "Bless you, Pepper," I said. It was the first time I had ever called him by his given name.

"You haven't taken over the caravan?" he said, grinning.

"No," I said. "I'm better at running plantations."

He gazed at me for the longest, and then he said, "Nancy, are you with, uh, that same boy?"

"He's a man, not a boy. The same one, yes."

"I guess maybe, back there on the plantation, I didn't try to understand," Pepper Rodham said. "In fact, I guess maybe I tried not to understand."

"It doesn't matter whether you understood or not," I said, not angry at his bringing up the subject of my infidelity. "I understood."

"Nancy, like I said, I'm by myself and I'm doing fine. If I can help you in any way I will."

"Thank you," I said. I patted his hand.

Strong Hickory's forehead was alarmingly hot. He was doubled over with pain in his belly, and we lagged farther and farther back in the procession. He refused a space in a wagon, though, stumbling on and insisting he would be fine. But I saw desperation in his eyes when he said, "Nancy, let's have a wedding."

"All right," I said.

"A Cherokee wedding."

"All right."

That evening, when the caravan stopped, we were married. A stranger assumed the role of Sweet Melon and gave Strong Hickory a blanket and a piece of rancid bacon. Another stranger, assuming the role of Rain, gave me a blanket and some flour. Strong Hickory and I approached each other, and when we were face to face I folded his blanket with my own, my pledge that we would share a bed. I gave him the bowl of flour as a promise I would bake bread for our family. He presented me the bacon, his vow to provide meat. Elijah Hicks pronounced our blankets joined. Strong Hickory forced a smile, but a bystander had to grab him to prevent his falling.

A young Methodist preacher had left his home in Nashville to join our caravan. He had been overwhelmed by the sight of the suffering Cherokees, and he said he could not remain in his comfortable home and his comfortable church while others were driven from their homes like animals. If he were there, Jesus would throw in with the Cherokees, he said, and so the young preacher would, too.

He cried a lot. The son of a minister, he had led a sheltered life, been educated in the East, and always assumed that life was more or less theory, not really sweat and pus and excrement and injustice and heartbreak. But preaching funerals by the roadside every day had taught him more about evil than all the lectures he had ever heard. Trying to offer solace to the dying who couldn't even understand his language gave him a point of view that wasn't available in school books. Yes, he cried a lot, but he was also there for anyone who needed him.

I noticed him observing our Cherokee wedding, and I told Strong Hickory, "I want a Christian wedding, too."

"But I'm not a Christian," he said.

"I want a Christian wedding, too," I said.

"All right."

He had never performed a wedding, the young preacher said, but he supposed he could. Yes, of course, he could. He said some words and pronounced us married in the eyes of God.

Icy rain pelted our caravan that night, but Strong Hickory still refused to accept a space in a wagon. "Give it to someone who is sick," he said. The doctor, inundated with patients, said he couldn't see my husband until the next day, if then. We bundled up in our little tent, and Strong Hickory immediately went to sleep. His forehead touched the back of my neck, and I had never felt such a temperature. I told myself I could not fall asleep.

In the night, Strong Hickory said, as clearly as the ringing of a church bell, "I'll build our cabin on that hill across the river, in the oak grove. I'll start now."

But he did not move. I couldn't stay awake any longer, and I dreamed of a cornshuck pony my grandmother had made for me when I was a little girl.

When I awoke the next morning, Strong Hickory's forehead was cold against my neck. The Raven Mockers had followed us to Missouri, had trespassed into our tiny tent while I dreamed of a play-pretty and he dreamed of a house on a shady knoll beside the Oostanaula. Strong Hickory had loved me since we were children, had always wanted us to be married. I was glad I had become his wife and he had become my husband.

I never got used to the dying. For that I was grateful to God. Some did. They could step over a body and barely realize they had done it. The same assailants that had terrorized the Cherokees in the stockades—dysentery, pleurisy, bilious fever, measles, whooping cough and heartbreak—were joined on the trail by pneumonia, tuberculosis, fatigue and cold. I never stopped hating them.

A black slave died with her head in my lap. I washed a dying Cherokee brave's face while a shaman danced and chanted in vain. I burned the blankets of the dead. I followed the lone white doctor on his rounds, doing anything he asked—which included nursing him when he became ill. I knew what it was to be sprayed with vomit and worse and to deliver babies and to hold a person down while his arm was amputated. I borrowed a blowgun and killed and cooked a squirrel for a sick girl who said she would rather die than eat another bite of salt pork. She died anyway.

I had sex with a filthy white farmer in exchange for some eggs that I cooked and gave to a woman who said she, too, would rather die than eat another bite of salt pork. She, too, died anyway.

How many Cherokees died? No one knows for sure, but four thousand would become a widely accepted estimate. Half perished in the stockades, half on what would one day be called the Trail Where They Cried.

Our regiment was the first to complete the journey. We arrived on January 4, 1839—four days before my twenty-fourth birthday. We had left our homeland on October 4, embarking on what the leaders had estimated would be an eighty-day trip. I grieved for those still on the trail, for winter's winds were blowing increasingly colder. The last caravan would not arrive until March 25.

I did not look back. All I wanted was a cabin beside a sweet stream. And if I could walk from Georgia to okla-homma I could damn sure cut the trees.

EPILOGUE

A BIRTHDAY PARTY ENDS

The people are tired of playing games, and I am tired, period. I know the sooner I open the rest of the birthday presents the sooner they will go home, so I ask Poppy to stack the packages beside me on the couch.

The visitors station themselves before me in a semicircle, and it's almost as if one long grin stretches from flank to flank. I open the presents, and Poppy comments on each one. The givers are delighted to hear their selections are treasures that will enrich my life.

She saves hers until last. It is a book bound in brown leather. The title and the author's name—mine—are in gold. "For the greatest Cherokee novelist," Poppy declares, and everyone applauds.

It is the first of my nine novels. Poppy worked at the mercantile in town after school and on weekends to earn the money to order a copy from the publishers and then to have it bound in leather.

Inside she has written, in English: "To Amaw from Poppy on her 98th birthday." Then, the three strongest words in any language: "I love you."

I begin to cry. The guests are uneasy, and they talk in that loud, reassuring, patronizing tone that is reserved for children and old folks. They hug me and pat me on the back, say their goodbyes and vamoose. Good.

Finally there is only Poppy and me. She flops on the couch and whews and grins. Then there is the most loving look on her face, and she dips a pen, opens the book and says, "For some day."

I know what she means. Under the inscription that she has written to me I write, "To Poppy from Amaw. I love you." She means that some day I will die, and we both know that day can't really be far away, and when it arrives she wants there to be no misunderstanding. She wants the family to know this book is hers.

When she was eleven Poppy read a newspaper story that called me the greatest Cherokee novelist, and she asked me if it was true. I don't lie to Poppy, so I said yes, it was true. She vowed to tell all her schoolmates and teachers and everybody in the world. Fine, I said, but for goodness sake don't tell them I said it.

The experiences of my life, before, during, and after the death march to Oklahoma, have provided enough material for a hundred novels.

I even patterned the central character in one of my books after my fourth husband, Pepper Rodham. My fictional fellow was a low-key, can-do kind of man who took a younger wife.

Pepper and I were married in May of 1839, four months after we arrived in the Indians' promised land. I was twenty-four and he was forty-six. We were like thousands of other couples: he farmed, and I did the wife's work.

I also began to write fiction, more from personal satisfaction than from any hope of it ever being published. But I met a newspaperman from New York who was gathering material for stories on the transplanted Indians, and he was fascinated by a Cherokee farm wife who was penning a novel. He wrote a story about me, and a publicity-minded editor for a New York publishing house read it and contacted me. He liked my work, and I signed a contract. At thirty, I was a published author.

I can't say I married Pepper for love, but I can say I grew to love him. We had thirty-two good years together before he died. He gave me three children, two girls and a boy. I have outlived two of them. You aren't supposed to outlive your children.

Pepper knew I couldn't love anyone else as I had loved Charley Marley, and that didn't bother him. He even joked about it. He was a calm realist, and I was a dreamer who was too easily agitated. We got on well together. He never did squeeze the farm for all that was in it, and when I'd fuss he'd grin and say, "Oh, hush, Mrs. Bramlett."

My sweet Pepper was there for me at a time when I truly feared for my sanity.

Removal of the Cherokees to the West did not cancel the animosities that had existed in the East between John Ross's followers and members of the Treaty Party. Ross himself urged forbearance, but without his knowledge others held a secret meeting and read the law against the unsanctioned sale of Cherokee land. They "tried" Major Ridge, John Ridge and Elias Boudinot.

In the early morning of June 22, 1839, assassins entered the home of John Ridge on Honey Creek, dragged him from his bed into the yard, and with Sarah and their children watching, stabbed him twenty-five times, cut his throat, flung his body into the air, stomped it and rode away.

Major Ridge that morning was riding to Van Buren in Arkansas, where one of his slaves lay ill. Shots rang out from bushes alongside the road, and he fell from his saddle, his head and body pierced by five bullets.

Elias Boudinot was having a house built in Park Hill, and he was at the site that morning when four Cherokees arrived. One stabbed him in the back, another cleaved his head seven times with a tomahawk. His neighbor Samuel Worcester and his wife Delight reached the scene in seconds, but they saw only death in Elias's eyes, and the murderers had run away.

"Nancy Swimmer, I have signed my death warrant," Major Ridge told me as he left Elias' house on the night of December 29, 1835, the night he and the other Cherokees had written their names on the Treaty of New Echota. And his prophecy had come true.

I wasn't sure I wanted to live after that, but Pepper's patience and love helped me recover.

Murder after murder followed, Ross man knifing treaty man, treaty man shooting Ross man, but the Cherokees did enjoy a period of progress and prosperity. They opened schools and churches, and Tahlequah, the capital, and Park Hill became centers of culture and industry.

But then came the white man's Civil War. Most Cherokees sided with the Confederacy, but not all. We were divided among ourselves, and our land was ravaged, as was most of the defeated South.

Talk about irony: Stand Watie—the brother of my beloved Elias Boudinot—burned my house. Bowlegged Stand Watie went down in history as the last Confederate general to surrender.

Though more than two thousand Cherokees had fought for the Union, the United States developed a hostile posture toward the entire tribe after the war. Under terms of a treaty, the Cherokee Nation was required to surrender land and open its territory to railroads. That was bad. It was required to free its black slaves. That was good.

With the railroads came white interlopers, demanding the opening of Indian lands. Thousands of white squatters moved in, stealing stock and timber and robbing travelers. Federal troops ignored their responsibility to remove them. If that was familiar, so was another pattern that developed, that of portions of our land being sold under pressure from the U.S. government and U.S. citizens. We were severely weakened as a people when land that had been owned by the tribe was allotted to individual Cherokees. Whites used any methods they could think of, ranging from robbery of orphans to misuse of notary seals, to wrest millions of acres from the Cherokees.

The United States, fueled by a pioneer spirit, was rolling westward, now to the sound of such wonders as the train and the mechanical harvester. The whites had no patience with a style of life that left acreage unfarmed, forests uncut, minerals unmined. One had to be a naïve red man indeed to believe Manifest Destiny was going to halt for him.

It didn't. On November 16, 1907, President Theodore Roosevelt officially proclaimed Oklahoma the forty-sixth state. The Cherokees became citizens, and the Cherokee Nation ceased to exist as an independent political unit.

Poppy, my little Oklahoman, has run out of steam, as the trains seldom do, and with her head on my arm she is asleep.

But I get my second wind, and I smile when I remember that funny beaver hat that Charley Marley wore.

Cherokee Syllabary

D *a*	**R** *e*	**T** *i*	**Ꮄ** *o*	**O** *u*	**i** *v*
S *gu* **O** *ka*	**F** *ge*	**Y** *gi*	**A** *go*	**J** *gu*	**E** *gv*
Ꮚ *ha*	**P** *he*	**Ꮙ** *hi*	**F** *ho*	**Γ** *hu*	**Ꮵ** *hv*
W *lu*	**Ꮄ** *le*	**P** *li*	**G** *lo*	**M** *lu*	**Ꮑ** *lv*
Ꮧ *ma*	**Ꭴ** *me*	**H** *mi*	**Ꮓ** *mo*	**Y** *mu*	
Ꮎ *na* **Ꮤ** *hna* **G** *nah*	**Λ** *ne*	**Ꮒ** *ni*	**Z** *no*	**Ꮻ** *nu*	**O** *nv*
T *qua*	**Ꮗ** *que*	**Ꮝ** *qui*	**V** *quo*	**Ꮿ** *quu*	**E** *quv*
U *sa* **Ꮣ** *s*	**4** *se*	**Ь** *si*	**Ꮨ** *so*	**Ꮬ** *su*	**R** *sv*
L *da* **W** *ta*	**S** *de* **Ꮲ** *te*	**Ꮧ** *di* **Ꮣ** *ti*	**Λ** *do*	**S** *du*	**Ꮱ** *dv*
Ꮪ *dla* **Ꮬ** *tla*	**L** *tle*	**C** *tli*	**Ꮹ** *tlo*	**Ꮲ** *tlu*	**P** *tlv*
Ꮐ *tsa*	**V** *tse*	**Ꮯ** *tsi*	**K** *tso*	**J** *tsu*	**C** *tsv*
G *wa*	**Ꮗ** *we*	**O** *wi*	**Ꮼ** *wo*	**Ꮗ** *wu*	**6** *wv*
Ꮿ *ya*	**Ꭾ** *ye*	**Ꮵ** *yi*	**Ꮖ** *yo*	**G** *yu*	**B** *yv*

Sounds represented by Vowels.

a as a in *father*, or short as a in *rival*.
e as a in *hate*, or short as e in *met*.
i as i in *pique*, or short as i in *pit*.

o, as aw in *law*, or short as o in *not*.
u, as oo in *fool*, or short as u in *pull*.
v, as u in *but*, nasalized.

Consonant Sounds

g nearly as in English, but approaching to k. d nearly as in English but approaching to t. h.k.l.m.n.g.s.t.w.y. as in English. Syllables beginning with g except Ꮝ have sometimes the power of k.Ꭰ.Ꮝ.Ꮝ. are sometimes sounded to, tu, tv, and Syllables written with tl except Ꮣ sometimes vary to dl.